About the author

David Ahern grew up in a theatrical family in Ireland but ran away to Scotland to become a research psychologist and sensible person. He earned his doctorate but soon absconded to work in television. He became a writer, director and producer, creating international documentary series and winning numerous awards, none of which got him free into nightclubs.

David Ahern enjoys pretending that writing the Madam Tulip mysteries is actual work. He lives in the beautiful West of Ireland with his wife, two cats and a vegetable garden of which he is inordinately proud.

To find out more about Madam Tulip and David Ahern, visit
www.davidahern.info

Also by David Ahern
MADAM TULIP
MADAM TULIP AND THE KNAVE OF HEARTS

GW00470150

To Breda,
thanks so much for reading the draft!

Madam Tulip

and the

Bones of Chance

Love from
David Ahern

DAVID AHERN

MALIN PRESS
Ireland

MALIN PRESS

First published 2018

This paperback edition published 2018

ISBN 978-0-9935448-5-9

Malin Press, Ireland

Malin Press is an imprint of Malin Film and Television Ltd

Registered in Ireland 309163

Dedication

For Sheila, aka Beezie

Acknowledgements

My special thanks to the wonderful people who generously read and commented on the draft:
Ces Cassidy (editor-in-chief), Theresa Casey, Aisling Chambers, Sheila Flitton, Stephen Flitton, Anne Kent, Patricia Mahon, Breda McCormack, Iris Park, Wendy Smith.

Madam Tulip

and the

Bones of Chance

1

Many people doubt psychic powers exist, but the doubters do not include actors. Everyone in showbusiness knows that as soon as one actor learns of a casting, actors of all ages, ethnicities, creeds and genders are instantly aware of every detail. Einstein claimed that faster-than-light communication is impossible. Einstein was not an actor.

On a dreary morning in mid-October, three young actor friends sat in a coffee shop in Dublin city centre. All knew the calendar of upcoming shows was blank and would probably stay blank until beyond Christmas. They needed no psychic powers to guess that a call from their agents any time soon was as likely as a call from Santa.

After an hour of fruitless speculation, the friends lapsed into silence. Obeying the custom observed by out-of-work actors the world over, they pretended to drink their overpriced coffee and stared out the window at passing shoppers.

'Disgusting,' said Bella, her steel tooth glinting with disapproval as she eyed passersby flaunting vast bags emblazoned with the names of luxury brands and exclusive emporia. Bella was known to have few sympathies with ostentatious displays of wealth. As an actress her employment prospects in the Emerald Isle were even worse than the norm, given that she was black and 99.9% of all roles on offer were pink. 'Wouldn't you think they'd have some tact?' she continued, frowning at a shopper sporting a bag worth more than her own little car. 'If I had that kind of money, I'd tell nobody. What if I was asked where I got it?' Bella was from Belfast.

'But who says they're happy?' said Bruce. 'They've probably been married to the same person for thirty years. I mean, what's left but shopping?'

Derry O'Donnell smiled. *Life is short* was Bruce's motto, perhaps because before he turned actor he was a US Navy SEAL. Derry was American like Bruce, but she was still vague about what a SEAL actually was. She did know she should never say he was a soldier. 'SEALs are Navy, dammit,' Bruce would insist, but in a resigned way, accepting her ignorance as due to her being female, civilian and straight.

'The problem we actors have,' announced Derry, 'is that when an actor isn't performing, they're not developing. Like when they freeze people and send them into space—'

'Do they do that?' said Bruce.

'Well okay, not exactly, but if they did and the person, like, woke up five hundred years later on Mars, they'd be no better at being an astronaut than they were when they left home. Right?'

Bella and Bruce quit contemplating the passersby. Derry saw with some satisfaction that she had their full attention. In the five years since all three had left Trinity School of Dramatic Arts, they had spent shockingly more time not acting than acting.

'Say if you're a poet, you can keep on writing poetry—nobody can stop you,' continued Derry. 'Or a painter. As long as you can scrape up enough cash to buy oils and canvas, you can keep on working. But we need producers to invest, people willing to take a chance on a creative project.'

'Willing to lose other people's money,' said Bella. 'Fine by me, but you'd think someone would notice.'

'They don't *have* to lose money,' insisted Derry. 'Anyhow, that's theatre—theatre is *for* losing money. What we need are movies.' She sighed, knowing the industry was just plain hopeless.

Those who knew Derry would describe her, without hesitation, as both talented and professional—qualities that would all but guarantee a glittering future in any other line of work. Derry was also good-looking, though with perhaps more character than could be accommodated by the term beautiful. She had fair hair, green eyes and a figure that men seemed to find greatly interesting, though in her opinion fatally prone to a pound or two every time she took her eye off the scales.

Altogether, Derry was well qualified for a career in show business. But, as Derry's awesomely successful mother liked to point out, show business was no kind of business at all. Or if it *was* a business, the performers were the office furniture—like a coffee table. The bosses decide which table to buy and where to put it, and when the coffee stains get too obvious they throw it in a dumpster and get another.

'I worked for a producer in LA for a while, after the Navy. I was his driver,' said Bruce. 'He made calls all day. In one call, he'd say, "Sure we got the budget," then in the next call he'd say, "No, can't raise a cent." Then he'd say, "Such-and-such an actress is so talented, she's gonna be a great lead." Then he'd come off the phone and say, "What a boring cow, only place she acts is in the sack."'

'Are they *all* pigs or just the ones we work for?' said Bella.

'Then one day he disappeared,' continued Bruce. 'Left his cell phone behind—that's how I knew someone whacked him. That phone was his beating heart. Cops thought he'd run off 'cos he owed people money, but producers always owe people money. I don't like to speak ill, and all that, but he wasn't a nice man. No sir.'

'We don't have to like them,' observed Derry. 'Just so long as they fund the shows. Actors have enough to worry about just acting.'

They all agreed heartily with that. The world of business might be tough, but an opening night is tougher.

'At least you've got Madam Tulip,' sighed Bella. 'It's your show, nobody can take that away from you.'

Derry was touched by Bella's remark. Madam Tulip, society fortune-teller, had been Bella's creation as much as anybody's. They had sat drinking cheap wine in Derry's little apartment wondering how to make some money—any money. Derry was telling Bella's fortune by reading the cards, as she often did to entertain her friends, and the idea of Madam Tulip was born.

The plan was that Tulip would tell fortunes at society events and make some cash. She wouldn't even need to fake it—Derry was known to be genuinely psychic, at least a little bit. In Ireland, everyone knows that seventh sons of seventh sons have since time immemorial been gifted with extraordinary powers of perception. Lately, it seemed daughters were also included. This spirit of modernity was surprising, though broadly welcomed by the psychic community as showing that Ireland had changed for the better.

Though Derry had been forced to accept her gift as real, she insisted her powers had never been of the slightest practical use. Mostly they seemed to tell her things after the fact, along the lines of *aha, I told you so*. Or else they were utterly incomprehensible until the fact had actually happened and had done whatever it meant to do in the first place. And recently, Madam Tulip, gift or no gift, had gotten her into situations she would have much preferred to avoid.

'I love being Madam Tulip, really I do,' said Derry with a sigh. 'But what is it about rich people?'

Bella and Bruce made sympathetic faces. They knew that Derry, as Madam Tulip, had experienced some unpleasant events as a result of telling fortunes for wealthy and celebrity clients. Unpleasant, as in almost fatal.

'Secrets,' said Bella darkly. 'And money. Bound to be trouble.'

'I thought I was helping people, listening to their problems,' continued Derry. 'Like a psychiatrist, only cheaper. Maybe I should say, *hey let's make a deal—how about I do the talking?*'

'No way,' said Bella. 'They want their money's worth. Rich folk are like grab, grab, grab. Take the eye out of your head.' She grinned. 'So how do we get rich?'

Just as Derry and Bruce opened their mouths to say *not acting, anyway*, Derry's phone rang.

~

Caller ID is rightly viewed as a modern miracle, a boon for those wanting to think before taking a call. Unfortunately, Caller ID can also have the opposite effect. Instead of allowing the brain time to take precedence over the mouth, the sight of certain names can so excite a person that brain is skipped altogether.

'Pam!' said Derry. No sooner had she spoken than she realised she should absolutely not have uttered the name of her agent. What she should have done was retire discreetly to a more private spot, preferably outside and down the narrow alleyway with the designer chocolate shop. Under the remorseless gaze of her friends, Derry felt as a school of sardines might feel stalked by a pack of hungry dolphins.

Derry stood, hemmed in by Bella, Bruce and a waiter called as reinforcements. Derry could see the waiter's grip on reality faltering as Bruce insisted on perusing the menu—astonishing behaviour in a customer known to be an actor. At the same time, Bella was vigorously questioning whether the lettuce in the salad was in fact organic. But Derry knew her friends—while their mouths were faking conversation, their ears were remorselessly tracking every word.

The coffee shop was noisy with chatter and clattering cutlery. Derry pressed the handset tightly to her ear ignoring everything she'd read about cell phones and brain tumours. 'Could you say that again, Pam? Sorry, I didn't quite catch you.'

Pam repeated what she had said. So surprising was her message that Derry forgot to keep her poker face. She listened. She asked the obvious questions. Pam's answers left her feeling only dismay. 'No,' said Derry. 'I'm sorry. I couldn't. Thanks for calling.' She hung up.

Derry sat down. The waiter hovered, ignored by Bruce and Bella whose whole attention was focused on Derry like cats waiting for a mouse to come out and play. They didn't lick their lips and make soft growling noises but looked like they might at any moment.

'Could I have an Americano?' said Derry to the waiter.

'Make that two?' added Bella. 'Three,' said Bruce. The tab would be Derry's. Anyone who had taken an unsolicited call from their agent was morally bound to buy the coffee.

'What were we saying?' said Derry. 'Oh yes, we really need more producers. Maybe we should start our own theatre company. I mean, why not?'

Silence is sometimes described as stony. This silence bore no resemblance whatever to a rock. In spite of appearances, rocks are not great listeners. You might think they are hanging on your every word, but they are not; they are ignoring you. No, the silence in which Bella and Bruce sat was more the sort of silence in which a sponge sits. Think of a dry sponge, inexorably drawing towards it every wisp of vapour, every drop of precious, life-giving moisture.

'How come it's so busy in here at this time?' observed Derry, casting her eyes around the near-empty cafe. 'Okay, it's quiet; but for this time it's busy. Wouldn't you say?'

Many a detective, real and fictional, has observed that humans cannot abide silence. If you wait long enough they will start talking, and they will tell the truth. Bruce and Bella may or may not have heard this famous dictum, but they seemed to know instinctively that if only they resisted the temptation to speak, Derry's resolve would crack.

'Really, I don't see why we shouldn't start a theatre company. It can't be that hard.'

Two expressionless faces, topped by four quizzically upraised eyebrows and four eyes open a little wider than the norm, created an irresistible suction.

'Um, that was Pam.' Derry tried to make her statement casual, lighthearted in a *twas nothing,* kind of way. Her audience was having none of it.

Derry shrugged. If she were English she might have thought, *fair cop guv,* or *bang to rights,* but she was American so the word that sprang to mind was *busted*.

'Weird,' said Derry. 'Really strange.'

Bella and Bruce frowned. Of course it was weird. Unsolicited calls from one's agent were by definition weird. Derry's statement was not information, it was a truism and did not satisfy.

'She asked if I knew Torquil.'

'Oh,' said Bruce. His expression proved that at least one thing was more surprising than a call from one's agent.

'And *he* is?' asked Bella.

'Hard to explain,' said Derry.

'English guy,' said Bruce. 'Some kinda lord.'

'No he's not,' said Derry. 'He's engaged to Lady Charlotte, but even when he marries her he won't be a lord.'

'The question is,' Bella continued, 'who or what is this Torquil?

'Didn't he say he directed videos?' said Bruce.

'Sure,' said Derry. 'YouTube though, I think.'

'Meh,' said Bella. Directors of dramas playing only on YouTube were, in the eyes of the acting fraternity, no better than rank amateurs. Their lowly status would rise dramatically the moment they began to pay actors, but that day was likely to be far off.

'Seems he's involved in a movie and got the production company to call my agent,' continued Derry.

Eyebrows shot skywards. Rapt attention. The magic word had been uttered—*movie!*

'Did you say …?' said Bruce and Bella together.

Derry nodded.

'More!' said Bella. '*Now*, if you please!'

'The producer wanted to cast me. No audition.'

Some revelations take time to digest. This one was on a par with an announcement that humankind was not in fact descended from apes but from those seagulls that steal your lunch at the seaside. The concept of being cast *with no audition* was so incomprehensible that neither Bruce nor Bella could find it in themselves to interrogate further, or at least not in the English language. Bruce got closest.

'No …?' he said, but couldn't utter the actual word. Bruce's pathological fear of auditions was well known to his friends. Remarkably, a man who thought exiting a submerged submarine while carrying a full load of limpet mines a hoot, was terrified to the point of nervous collapse by the prospect of an audition. Now his face shone like that of a saint glimpsing the promised land. The very idea that auditionless casting existed somewhere in the universe promised to change life's whole complexion.

'Of course, I said no,' said Derry.

Silence.

'You know, for a minute there,' said Bella, 'I thought you said you'd turned them down.'

Bruce guffawed, making the occupants of three tables around turn and stare.

'I did,' said Derry.

'Can't we start this conversation from the beginning, just so I know I'm not losing my mind?' said Bella. Her face was a mask of the deepest concern. 'They offered you a role—'

'—with no audition,' whispered Bruce reverently.

'—and you turned them down *without even reading the script?*'

'I don't have to read the script,' said Derry. 'I know Torquil. He is …' she hesitated. Derry was not someone who spoke harshly about people if she could help it and never in gratuitous obscenities. But if she held back where Torquil was concerned, that was because nothing could ever be gratuitous or obscene enough. 'It's hard to explain,' she finished, lamely.

'I am sorry,' said Bella. 'You are a dear friend, but some things in this world need explaining or dire threats must be issued. Shall I start now?'

'Um, maybe I could, like, fill Bella in some?' said Bruce.

'Be my guest,' said Derry.

'Our little stay at that English stately home? With the Countess and all?'

Bella nodded. She had heard at least part of the story.

'Torquil tipped off the press that Derry—Madam Tulip that is—had identified a missing person. Dead in fact.'

'So what's wrong with a little PR?' asked Bella.

'But she hadn't identified anybody. Torquil was bound to know Derry would get into big trouble. And she did, didn't you honey?'

Derry nodded. She had been used mercilessly, and Torquil had known perfectly well what he was doing. He had betrayed Derry to solve a family problem while at the same time ingratiating himself with his media contacts.

'But what's he got to do with the production?' said Bella. 'I mean who cares as long as he's not the director. What is he anyway?'

'Pam didn't say. Not the director or producer though.'

'*Sooo* …' said Bella and Bruce in unison.

'There's another reason I can't do it,' said Derry. 'They want me to play Madam Tulip. In the movie.'

Bella and Bruce differed in gender, ethnicity and orientation, but their baffled faces said exactly the same thing in exactly the same way.

'It's another one of those time-travel stories,' continued Derry. 'Somebody goes through a portal and ends up somewhere in the past and gets to fight with swords and wear fancy costumes.'

'I like it,' said Bella.

'And they want Madam Tulip to be a fortune teller who predicts the future. They're shooting in Scotland.'

'Mmm, kilts,' said Bruce, wiggling his eyebrows lasciviously.

'First off, I am not having anything to do with Torquil and his friends,' insisted Derry. 'Second, I am not playing Madam Tulip.'

'Hey, hey, stop there,' said Bella. 'Forgive me if I'm being stupider than a stupid thing, but don't you always play Madam Tulip? You pretend to be Madam Tulip, right? Pretend equals play. Or am I missing something?'

'Piece of cake, right?' added Bruce. 'No audition. Makes sense.'

'No,' said Derry. 'Not doing it. That's all. Sorry.'

On the faces of Bella and Bruce, puzzlement was replaced by concern. Was Derry unwell? Was she losing that vital confidence every actor must have even if it's deeply buried under multiple layers of no confidence whatsoever?

'Maybe Torquil's trying to make up for what he did,' said Bruce. 'Maybe he's sorry.'

'It's not only Torquil,' said Derry. She wondered how she could explain, when she wasn't even sure why acting Madam Tulip in a movie was out of the question.

'When I'm Madam Tulip, I'm acting, right?'

Bruce and Bella graciously conceded the point.

'And she's Madam Tulip, but she's me too, right?'

More nods.

'So …' Derry realised she was stumped. What was bothering her so much? She started again. 'Madam Tulip is fun, okay? And I'm trying to make a few dollars, sure. But I do my best for my clients, I really do. I'm *acting* Madam Tulip, but she's *real* with her clients.'

This time the nods were a little more hesitant. Derry was uncomfortably aware she was straying into territory way more metaphysical than anyone should have to deal with sober and in daylight.

'So if I were acting Madam Tulip and my clients were actors too, Madam Tulip wouldn't be helping them at all. I mean, Madam Tulip would be, like, pretending to be Madam Tulip.'

'That,' said Bella. 'Is the biggest load of old bollox I ever heard in my life. You sure you're not losing your bottle?' Bella's accusing tone said she suspected Derry was in imminent danger of being Negative. Bella was, as all her friends knew, a sworn enemy of that damaging and dangerous attitude.

Derry thought about that. Maybe Bella was right. Sometimes an actor was tempted to turn down a peachy role out of fear they wouldn't be good enough. But a moment's thought told her that fear had nothing to do with it.

'No. Really,' said Derry. 'It's … it's like Madam Tulip is being hijacked. They'll put words into her mouth. Make her talk nonsense. Why don't they write their own fortune-teller?' She shrugged helplessly. 'Maybe I'm just being stupid.'

'So you'll do it. Great,' said Bella. 'You said Scotland? That's nice. When do they start shooting?'

'No,' said Derry. 'I mean it.'

'I get what Derry is saying,' said Bruce. 'It's like Madam Tulip is being used. Nobody likes that, right? Sweetheart, you follow your instincts. It's only money.'

'That,' said Bella, 'is my point. Did Pam mention a figure, by any chance?'

'Um,' said Derry.

'What was that?'

'Uh, normal rates.'

'Big normal or pathetic normal?'

'Pay no mind to Bella,' said Bruce. 'There'll be plenty more jobs, of course there—'

But Bruce never got to finish. Instead, he sat with his mouth open as if caught unawares in a photograph. Bella too stared, transfixed. Derry's phone, sitting in front of her on the table was ringing, its screen flashing urgently.

Some say this universe is only one of countless parallel worlds. If true, then a universe exists in which Derry O'Donnell reached for her phone, saw the caller was her agent Pam and rejected the call with a decisive swipe. This was not that universe.

'Pam?'

'They've been on again! I have to say it's all a bit unusual.'

'They?'

'The Scottish film. I told them you were busy. They put your friend Torquil Ormsby-whatsit onto me. He's Associate

Producer, whatever that means. Probably sleeps with the real producer—you know how it is.'

'He's not my—'

'They must really want you,' continued Pam, not bothering to hide her surprise. 'Now they say if you agree to Madam Tulip, they'll cast your friend Bruce Adams as well. Isn't he with Beryl?'

Derry agreed that, yes, Beryl was indeed Bruce's agent.

'I said to them they should contact Beryl, but they said it depended on you saying yes. And I was to tell you Lady Charlotte sends her love. I mean—*really*.'

Derry knew now what Pam meant by unusual. This was a strange way to run a casting.

'You said no auditions?' asked Derry. 'Like, for either?' she added, trying not to name names.

'That's what they said. Not even video. By the way, they've got Darian for the male lead. The singer? I know what you're going to say, X-Factor wannabee, but so what. He's got like a couple of hundred thousand Twitter followers, and that's good enough these days. Never heard of the female—Carla Francini. She seems to have done one or two things, but nothing much. Honestly, I wouldn't care if I were you. By the way, they're offering a thousand a day. Pounds. I *could* ask for more.'

Derry thought at first she had misheard, but she hadn't. The rate wasn't Hollywood, but it was the best she'd yet been paid acting, and twice as much as you could expect in a week working in the theatre.

'They think you'll be getting ten days anyway, though it could run on.'

Derry couldn't bear to think what that kind of money would mean. Bills sat on the table in her apartment unopened for weeks on the principle that if she didn't open the envelope the contents didn't exist. Bruce laughed at the way she did that. 'Schrödinger's cat,' he said. Something about a cat being both dead and alive until you opened its box and looked. Bruce liked weird physics.

Derry felt her resolve crumble. She felt indescribably guilty. Bruce hadn't had a decent role in months other than a bit part in some training videos. Now, she was refusing on his behalf a job that didn't even demand an audition. But something wasn't right. Even if Torquil was trying to do her a favour under pressure from Charlotte, why would they conjure another part for Bruce out of thin air?

'No,' said Derry. 'I don't like the role. That's all.'

'As your agent, I have to say I think you're making a mistake,' said Pam. Do me a favour, take the weekend and have a think.'

'Okay, I'll think about it. But I doubt I'll be changing my mind. I'm sorry, really I am. Thanks for calling back.'

Pam signed off.

'Well?' said Bella and Bruce together.

'They seem to really want me. But there's no way.'

'You were right to stick to your principles, honey. Don't let anyone say different,' said Bruce, giving Bella a look that made clear who he meant by *anyone*.

Derry felt bad before, but she felt awful now. She was sure even if Bruce knew Derry's stubbornness had cost him a job, he'd say the same thing.

'Lunatic,' said Bella, who was made of less idealistic material. Where she came from, ideals were things that got you shot unless you moved to another country and changed your name twice. 'It's a *part*! Who cares if the role is Madam Treetop—she's just a fortune teller.

'She wanted me to say I'd think about it,' said Derry.

Bella grinned. 'That's it then. Make 'em wait, that's what *I* say.'

'I'm not making them wait,' said Derry. 'I'm being polite.'

'Great! You'll enjoy having a few pounds in your pocket,' said Bella.

'I said I wasn't going to do it.'

'Sure,' said Bella. 'You're not going to do it. I heard you.'

Whatever Bella thought, Derry was sure she would not be changing her mind. Her reasons were complicated, but the more she thought about it, the more certain she was that her decision had little to do with Torquil. She was protecting Madam Tulip. Simple as that.

She hadn't known how much she cared.

2

The afternoon train to Galway was no more than half full, so Derry had a corner of the carriage to herself. She should have felt the pleasing sense of adventure she usually enjoyed when she left the capital. Instead she had the uncomfortable feeling she was on the run. She had texted her father to say she'd come for a visit if that were okay. Jacko had answered her text with the single word, *Party*!

Derry was jolted from her thoughts by the train conductor inspecting tickets. 'Not the end of the world Miss,' he said.

Derry smiled up at him.

The conductor was a portly man of middle age. He waved his arm vaguely at the scenery whizzing past. 'Sure there's nowhere like it,' he pronounced with satisfaction. 'God's own country.'

Derry agreed the Irish landscape was indeed enchanting, though at this point flat and a boggy shade of brown.

'You wouldn't be used to this kind of scenery, now,' added the conductor. He had detected Derry's transatlantic accent.

'Oh, I'm half Irish,' said Derry with some pride. Although her mother was American and Derry had grown up mostly in the States, her father Jacko was a native. 'I came here all the time as a kid. I've lived in Ireland for years now,' she added, anxious not to be mistaken for a mere tourist.

'I been to New York, of course,' continued the conductor. 'And LA, and Vegas. But they've nothing like what *we* have.' The implication was clear—the failure of the named cities to resemble Ireland was a tragedy, and their citizens were surely inconsolable.

'You'll enjoy the West,' said the conductor. 'Very scenic. How long is your holiday? Your *vacation*.'

Derry thought of reminding him that she was not in fact on vacation but gave up the idea as a lost cause. 'Do you get to visit the West much yourself—outside of stations that is?' she enquired, content to be civil.

'Oh no!' said the conductor, frankly surprised at the naivety of the question. 'Amn't I a Dub?'

Just then, Derry's phone rang, and she could excuse herself from what promised to be a lengthy dissertation on the mortal risk to a true Dubliner of recklessly breathing rural air. The conductor frowned at the interruption but had no option but to move on, calling 'Tickets, please.'

'Mom!'

'Darling!' said Vanessa. 'Just called for a little chat. I do hope I haven't caught you at a bad time?'

Derry was instantly on her guard. She loved her mother dearly, and the feeling was more than likely reciprocated. But Vanessa indulging in idle chat was like a leopard, loping along behind a gazelle, claiming to be jogging for the good of its health. Derry's mother was stupendously successful—an international art dealer, owner of fashionable galleries in New York, London and Dublin, and a high-powered agent representing the cream of the art world. Vanessa had not reached those dizzy heights by wasting time on *little chats*.

'No, not at all,' said Derry. 'I'm on the train—on my way to see Dad.'

'Oh, how fortunate! *Such* a coincidence.'

'Is it?' said Derry, certain it was not. Her mother laid no claim to psychic powers of any kind, unless it was guessing the size of a client's bank balance, but where her ex-husband was concerned she displayed a startling aptitude.

'I say *coincidence* because I want to ask you a little favour—'

'I'm fine, Mom,' said Derry. Somebody in the family, Derry reasoned, had to keep up standards. Just because both one's parents were egomaniacs was no reason to abandon the normal courtesies. 'And how are you?'

'Fine, I guess,' said Vanessa. 'What I really wanted—'

'Me too,' said Derry. 'I've one or two possible jobs coming up, so that's good.' There she was of course lying. Well, not really lying. Strictly, Pam's call did constitute a job—two jobs in fact—and was indeed an offer, even if Derry wasn't going to take it up.

'Wonderful, dear,' said Vanessa, briskly. 'Hopefully, you'll get paid as well. If the producers go broke, you know you can always call your mother.'

Derry wasn't at all sure she liked where this was headed. She had only recently evaded her mother's plans to take her on as her Personal Assistant, her PA, or was it PR? The danger was extreme, and with Vanessa, it would never do to relax one's vigilance. Life as Vanessa's P-anything would be like being trapped inside a hall of mirrors with a shopping list written in hieroglyphics.

'You mentioned Dad,' said Derry.

'I'm mounting a show to open the Edinburgh gallery. Did I mention I was opening in Scotland? The city is a big financial centre now. Lots of *hedge funds*.' As she pronounced the magic words, her voice dropped a reverential octave.

'Um … I don't think—'

'Would you mention it to your father, darling? Exhibition, New Year, Edinburgh. Add *big-ticket buyers* to that if you feel it necessary. Alright?'

Derry almost agreed. Vanessa had that effect on people. As if she knew about some button in your head, pressed it, and out of your mouth came an automatic *yes*. Derry caught herself just in time. Where the byzantine relationship between her parents was concerned, keeping a benign distance was the way to go.

Derry's parents had divorced many years before, with mutual and barely disguised sighs of relief. But Vanessa was still Jacko's agent, and as everyone knows, relations between artists and their agents make the average guerrilla war look the spirit of compromise.

'Sounds cool,' said Derry cautiously. 'A major show—terrific.'

'I've got a Scottish investor, something in politics, lots of *financial* connections. He wants to partner with me on the gallery. It's a wonderful opportunity.'

Derry suspected the opportunity would be all Vanessa's.

'He's a big fan of Jack's work,' continued Vanessa. 'He's positively insisting Jack has to be our first show.'

'That's great,' said Derry. 'Why not call Dad? Won't he be thrilled?'

'There's just one small thing,' said Vanessa. 'My investor is also a *huge* fan of Edgar Booth. He wants us to mount a joint exhibition. Thinks the press would gobble it up. He's right, of course.'

Derry's heart sank. Edgar Booth was a client of Vanessa's even more famous than Jacko and, unforgivably in Jacko's eyes, a far bigger earner. Already she could hear Jacko's voice when he learned the appalling news. The least offensive name he had ever called the hapless E. Booth was 'that pasty-faced gobshite.' The animosity was entirely mutual. On one famous occasion when the two artists inadvertently met at the opening of one of Vanessa's shows, only the intervention of a Chinese oligarch's bodyguards prevented the conflict escalating to an armed response by New York's finest. As it was, the caterers fled the building, leaving four trestle tables of complex organic nibbles upended and the designer chef sitting on the floor weeping piteously.

'The theme will be Celtic. Isn't New Year Celtic?'

'I don't think so,' said Derry. 'Doesn't everybody have New Year?'

'Edgar has Scottish roots. He's very proud of them. Promises to wear a kilt at the opening. Won't that be charming? And Jack is nearly Scottish, being Irish. Same thing. Do you think he might wear one? I think he'd look rather fine, don't you?'

'Mom, *no*. Edgar Booth! You know what Dad will say!'

'Darling, I'll be frank, I do have a little problem. Just between us, my investor has his heart set on the double exhibition.'

'I'm sorry Mom, I do *not* want to get involved.'

'Please, dear. Just for your mother? A special favour to me?'

'Oh, Mom!' Checkmate. Vanessa had played the *mother* card.

'Say you'll try?'

'Oh, alright, I'll mention it once. That's all. Whatever he says is whatever. Okay?'

'Thank you *so much* dear. I knew I could count on you. Why don't you come and stay in Edinburgh with me while I'm putting the show together. You'll love the city. So quaint. Lots of turrets and battlements. Fake, of course.'

'Sure, I'd like that,' said Derry, not wholly sincere. She was sure that an hour after she arrived she'd be put to work hanging pictures or sweeping the gallery floor, while graced with a grandiose title and no pay.

'Bye honey! Let me know when you've spoken to your father, won't you?'

Derry promised she would, unsure whether she was lying or not. She hung up, sat back in her seat, sighed and closed her eyes. Now she knew two things about other people that they didn't know and she wished *she* didn't know. Her father was innocently unaware of an impending duet with the detested Booth, and Bruce didn't know that Derry had cost him an auditionless job. If the train conductor had sat beside her and confided he was leaving his wife for a cute engine driver called Bill, Derry wouldn't have been in the least surprised.

3

The morning was sunny and the wind from the southwest unseasonably mild. Last night's party had done what parties are supposed to do, and Derry took her vague but undeniable hangover outside for some curative air. Jacko had yet to surface.

Jacko's home was a substantial two-storey farmhouse with a walled courtyard in front and a little harbour with a crumbling jetty behind. You would guess right away an artist lived there. A stone barn boasted skylights on its north-facing roof. Carefully chosen lumps of driftwood stood like alien sculptures around the yard. An old farm cart, painted brightly, pointed its shafts jauntily skywards. Wind chimes made a cooing noise, making Derry jump. She smiled—how could she be startled by something that had happened every time she came here since she was a kid?

Derry made her way down to the tiny harbour, passing a clinker-built wooden sailboat up on props, another of Jacko's half-finished projects. Beside it was a new addition, a tracked mini-digger that had once been yellow and was now orange with rust.

Last night she had barely had time to change her clothes and grab a coffee before Jacko had whisked her off to an artists' party in the old city centre. Derry had a vague memory of dancing with a grey-eyed, black-haired charmer who tried to persuade her that her father, being an artist and therefore liberal by definition, wouldn't mind at all if she took him back to the house. Derry politely declined, pointing out that no man deserved to be interrogated by Jacko the following morning. By then she had noticed that the charmer's attractive tan didn't extend to a thin band of telltale pale skin around his ring finger. Mischievously, she suggested they might go to his place, and awarded maximum points for creativity when he spun a yarn about a devastating flood and the builders practically living in the house.

'Urgh,' said Jacko, following up with a cough. Derry turned to see her father stretching and gazing out to sea as though somewhere amongst the islands of Galway Bay lived the answer to a forgotten question.

'How did we—?'

'Cab,' said Derry.

'Ah,' said Jacko. He sniffed the air doubtfully. Jacko had the dishevelled look of someone who had slept all night on a park bench. Derry wondered if he had undressed for bed. He was wearing the same clothes as last night, right down to his flowing green riding coat of indeterminate vintage, high leather boots and floppy, wide-brimmed, black felt hat.

'Did I insult anybody I shouldn't have?'

Derry smiled at the implication there were people who should in fact be insulted.

'No more than usual. You gave me a good idea though.'

'Did I, bedad?'

'About the movie.'

In the taxi home, Derry had told her father about the strange film offer from her agent. Jacko was sympathetic, calling the producers *a lazy crowd of no-good cheapskate parasites*. Madam Tulip was Derry's intellectual property, he insisted, and if the producers wanted her they should pay for more than a few days' acting. He didn't seem much concerned with her integrity, being far more interested in the price.

'You said I should ask for more money or tell them I'll do it if they change the name.'

'Ah, so I did. Did you?'

'I'm only just up!' The idea had seemed inspired last night but looked a lot less plausible in daytime with a hangover.

'Thought you said it was a good idea. Bluff. Called. How about now?'

'Now?'

Jacko shrugged and gazed out to sea. He took deep rhythmic breaths, of the profound sort he imagined taken by athletes at the peak of their powers.

Why not? thought Derry. Somehow nothing seemed as big a problem here as it did in Dublin. Derry took out her phone and dialled. Jacko tactfully wandered off to inspect a rock pool.

'Pam, can you ask them something for me?'

'Go on.'

'Ask if they can change the character. A fortune teller, okay, but not Madam Tulip.' Derry told herself to think like Vanessa. 'Mention lawyers. Tell them they'd avoid copyright claims, trademarks, whatever.'

'I thought you might find the fee creatively stimulating. Okay, I'm on it. I'll call you back if they say anything definite.'

Derry thanked her and ended the call. Jacko sauntered over.

'She'll get back to me,' said Derry. 'Amazing she didn't rule the idea right out.'

'That,' said Jacko, 'is because the plan is redolent with intellectual vigour and generally cuts to the core of the thing. Is one entitled, with all due humility, to point out that your mother isn't the only one with finely honed business skills?'

Derry smiled. She remembered Vanessa's call and her own promise to bring up the tricky matter of the Edinburgh exhibition. Maybe now was as good a time as any. On the other hand, Jacko's hangover was unlikely to help the case. Perhaps later. Much later.

Jacko turned to face the open sea, his hands clasped behind his back, his mane of silver hair shining in the autumn sunlight. He drew himself up to his full height, chin thrust out purposefully like the captain of a sailing ship, brass telescope under his arm, magnificent in a full gale.

'Want to see our castle?'

~

'So where *are* we going? ' said Derry as Jacko's battered pickup lurched off the smooth surface of the main road and raced inland through the narrow, potholed lanes of South Galway. Farmland bounded by hedgerows stretched into the distance. In her teens on vacation here, Derry had only rarely cycled out this way, finding the flatness good for cycling but the landscape unendurably monotonous.

'Did I ever tell you what this district was called?' roared Jacko over the din of the engine. 'Ballydonnell,' he announced triumphantly. 'What do ye think of that?'

Derry made a noise possibly indicating she was impressed but mostly leaving the matter open for future debate.

'*Bally*, as in *estate* or *place of*, and *O'Donnell*. Not on the map now, of course.' Jacko frowned, as though the carelessness of modern mapmakers was a failing someone should bring up with the national authorities. 'This,' he said, waving both arms to encompass the country in general and making the pickup weave perilously, 'is the land of our ancestors.'

Some weeks ago, Jacko had confessed to Derry he had bought an old ruin of a tower house. He claimed he meant to convert it into a studio, though Derry was sure the plan had more to do with secretly wanting his address to be Jack O'Donnell of Castle O'Donnell and, now she realised, Ballydonnell.

They swung around a bend, and there in a field to their right, on a low rocky outcrop, stood a high fortress tower. Easy to recognise the place as the ruin Jacko had shown her in photographs. The roofless castle, half covered in ivy, looked even more dilapidated than in the pictures. But Derry had to concede it was impressive. Not large by castle standards, more a fortified house, but a genuine stronghold. Strange that the place had belonged to her very own ancestors.

They left the pickup at the bottom of the field and trudged up a slight incline towards the looming grey mass. Picking their way over grassy humps concealing fallen rubble, skirting impassable tangles of hawthorn and briar, they climbed to stand with their backs against the castle's massive stone bulk. The ivy on the tower walls rustled as if suddenly coming alive. Great black birds circled high above, squawking.

The ridge gave a panoramic view of the land for miles around. Jacko surveyed the scene with a proprietorial air, adopting a masterful pose against the towering backdrop as though a portrait painter were already at work. 'What do ye think?' he said. 'Wasn't I right?'

Derry peered up at the grey bulwark above—romantic as only a castle without a roof can be. Not so romantic if you were planning on paying for the new roof. 'Isn't it going to cost a fortune to fix up? What does the architect say?'

'Ah, well to tell the truth now, I only spoke to Paddy this last week.'

'Paddy?'

'Architect.'

'You bought it without an architect looking at it first? Didn't you get a survey?'

'Sure there was no time for all that malarkey,' said Jacko. 'What if some internet billionaire came and snapped it up!'

Derry doubted that the barons of Silicon Valley, whose tastes she imagined ran more to superyachts and jetliners, would have stampeded their way to Galway for a crumbling ruin.

'So what did the architect say?'

Jacko sucked in his cheeks. He whistled through his teeth. He made a clucking noise as if to indicate that the opinions of architects could be taken or left as one saw fit.

'Dad, *what did he say?*'

'True enough, he pointed out one or two technical issues, but nothing that can't be put right.'

'Meaning?'

'Our little project may need a somewhat larger budget than foreseen and may take a biteen longer than anticipated.'

'Like a lifetime of penury! Dad, this kind of job costs millions.'

'I admit, we may encounter obstacles,' said Jacko, conceding a minor point, 'but for the time being we must put mere material considerations to one side.' He led Derry to the base of the tower. 'Enter!' he said, leading the way through the massive stone doorway.

Derry stepped into the gloom. Inside was like being in an enormous chimney, the only light filtering down from above. A stone stairway wound its way up to what would have been the upper stories if all the floors hadn't vanished. Open fireplaces gaped in mid-air. Collapsed stonework covered in moss and ferns littered the ground underfoot.

'Can't you feel it?' whispered Jacko. 'A thousand years of O'Donnells.'

High above, crows croaked what might have been a warning, and in a flurry of black wings soared and circled. A sudden gust of wind made a rustling whoosh in the ivy-draped stonework overhead, and Derry was sure she saw the top of the wall sway. She backed cautiously out the door.

'Dad, this place is a death trap.'

'Nonsense,' said Jacko following her outside. 'Sure aren't you my lucky charm? Tell me,' he said, moving closer and taking her arm as though about to confide a secret. 'Did you feel anything … special?'

Derry wondered how to confess that mostly what she felt was that her right foot was wet and she should have worn a hat, preferably a hard hat. 'I guess the place *is* spooky. Can't say I'd want to spend the night here.'

Jacko frowned. 'Surely you feel *something*? Our ancestors were the descendants of kings! Powerful!' His voice dropped to a conspiratorial whisper. 'Rich!' He paused, contemplating that blessed state. 'Until dispossessed by the dastardly foreigner, of course,' he added, matter-of-factly.

'You mean the English?' enquired Derry. Jacko's take on history could be idiosyncratic.

'If,' said Jacko, 'by *English* you mean Frenchmen of Danish descent, yes.' He shook his head mournfully. 'Tragically, they confiscated the lands of many great families and reduced the Irish nobles to penury.'

'I thought great-great-grandfather O'Donnell lost his land in a bet on a boat race?'

'*That* was later,' protested Jacko. He contemplated a raven landing on the battlements. 'I'm wondering if we might try a little experiment? Humour your old da?'

Jacko led Derry to the waist-high stones of the wall that had once surrounded the tower but was now only a fern-covered line of rubble. 'How about we take a little stroll,' he suggested, pacing ostentatiously as if measuring out the perimeter. Derry had no choice but to follow.

'Feel anything, by any chance? Any … presence, at all?'

'Dad, what are we doing?'

'I'd say if you relax, it should help. Stand quietly now. Free your mind. Feel the vibrations—'

'What vibrations? I don't feel anything. Why *should* I feel anything?'

Jacko took Derry by the hand and drew her onwards, stopping every ten yards to ask, 'Anything at all, at all?' Derry felt like she'd been drafted into some arcane druidical ceremony. Next he would be asking her to stand on one leg and point like a heron. Seemingly the ancient druids used to do that. What they meant to achieve nobody had ever explained. Perhaps it was some kind of mime. *Look I can do a heron! See!* And the peasantry would be impressed and ask them could they do, like, a hare or a broody hen.

'Dad! What am I *supposed* to feel, for goodness' sake?'

'Ah,' responded Jacko. 'I'm … not sure exactly. Say I was looking for something?'

'Like what?'

'Um, say I'd lost something a while ago and needed to find it?'

'Lost what? Dad … what did you lose?'

'Ah … not me as such,' said Jacko. 'But if we let our spirits flow free—'

'Dad, I have no intention of letting my spirit flow free. It's freezing. My feet are wet. What am I doing here?'

Jacko stopped his pacing. 'Say I had a little bet with someone—'

'Ah, no,' said Derry.

'Harmless,' insisted Jacko.

'Bet what? And *no!*'

Derry knew what was coming. Jacko was the seventh son of a seventh son. He had the modest allocation of second sight traditionally associated with that inheritance, but it never helped him when he gambled. His faith in Derry's ability, if she so chose, to circumvent whatever supernatural rule was interfering with his chances was touching, but Derry always refused. Surely the Other Realm, whatever that was, had its mind on higher things than tipping a horse at 40-1. Derry hoped so or the world's religions were in for a nasty shock.

'A favour to me?' Jacko gave Derry his most appealing look, a decent impersonation of a big cuddly bear. 'Why don't we chat as we walk?'

Derry gave a sigh. 'Bet about what?' she repeated. 'With who?'

'With Paddy. The architect. We were talking about the history of the old place, and I said, "I bet you I can find the lost grave of Thaddeus O'Donnell—"'

'And he is?'

'Was,' said Jacko. 'Head chopped off in the sixteenth century. Legend said he was buried secretly somewhere near the castle wall after the place fell to the enemy. I wagered Paddy I could find him.'

Derry stopped, making Jacko bump into her. 'You bet you could find a dead— Dad! That is … Why is that bothering me? Could it be because it's the crassest thing I ever heard in my life? And how much did you bet?'

'The best of motives, dear girl, I assure you!' protested Jacko. 'Thaddeus is one of our greatest ancestors. I merely mean to erect a memorial stone on the spot. With all due respect, of course.' He assumed a mildly offended expression.

'*So*, how much did you bet?'

'I didn't,' said Jacko, with the manic grin Derry associated with his wilder enthusiasms. 'He bet me his fee I couldn't find it! And you know what those fellas charge!' He rubbed his hands.

'And if you lose?'

'Nada,' said Jacko smugly. 'I pay him his exorbitant thousands, as normal. What do you think of that?'

'Dad, you are betting on a dead man. No, I correct myself, you are betting on a *dead relative*. This has to stop right here.'

'Right here?' said Jacko.

'Right here,' said Derry. 'I am absolutely having nothing to do with this.'

'Can't you consider it a debt repaid to one's ancestors? Restoring them to—'

'This is *not* a debt repaid! This is a bet!'

'What if he's trying to communicate with us? What if he's saying, "Please, please, O descendants give me a—" You don't feel you want to walk on a biteen more, to be sure?'

'No! Not another step. Whoever he is—and he was probably no better than he should be—he's dead. And he's best left that way. He should not be jumping around going *coo-ee here I am*, when he's supposed to be six foot under and oblivious like any decent dead person. When I'm dead I'm not talking to anybody. I have no intention—'

'Six foot you say?'

'Sure,' said Derry, puzzled. 'Isn't that what they do?'

'I knew it!' said Jacko, beaming. He took something from his pocket, looked around warily, bent down and stuck it in the ground. He stamped the spike in with his foot so only a few inches showed. 'I knew you wouldn't let me down! Six foot!'

Right then, before Derry could protest, her phone rang.

'Pam! Hi.'

'Thirty-five years in the business, and this is a first,' said Pam. 'Actually, several firsts. Yes, they'll call the character something else. Only thing is, they've pulled the shoot forward and they want you over next Thursday for scenes Friday. Short notice, I know, but is that alright with you?'

The news was so surprising Derry had to tell herself not to gabble. Even so, she forgot to pretend that she had to consult her packed diary. Then again, the one person you could never fool by pretending to consult your packed diary was your agent who knew well what blank looked like. She tried to concentrate. Thursday was shockingly soon. Then again, the less time to get nervous the better. 'I guess,' was all she could think of saying.

'Super. I'll send you the contract when I get it, ditto the location details, accommodation, and anything else I can find out. Bruce's agent will contact him direct. By the way, I checked on the Executive Producer. Based in the States, and it seems he's a whiz at getting amazing international distribution deals. He just piles up the territories. He's known to be pretty tight on the budgets, but who cares as long as you get your name out there.'

'What about a script? When can I see that?'

'No script yet. They're still tinkering with it, but they promise you'll get it soon. Your scenes are mostly improvisation anyway, they say. You're comfortable with that?'

Improvisation was always more nerve-racking than delivering scripted lines, but some directors liked to work that way. 'Sure,' said Derry. 'Not a problem. And ... thanks for everything. I know this as a bit ... unconventional.'

'Like I said, I've never seen anything like it. But who said this business wasn't barking mad. Remind me to be reincarnated as a rich divorcée.' She hung up.

Derry stared at her phone. A movie. Amazing. She hadn't even thought to ask who the director was so she could look him up. She could phone Pam on Monday about that. Meantime, who cared?

'Am I right in thinking that another O'Donnell victory has been won?' said Jacko. 'I take it they said, "yes, dear heart, come and be in our motion picture, name your price?"'

Derry laughed. 'Not *name my price* exactly. But yes, they'll call the character something else, and I've got the job. Shooting end of next week.'

'Delighted! I claim all due credit. The drink is on you.'

On the drive back to the house, Derry wondered should she call Bruce to tell him the news but decided against. This was between him and his agent. Anyhow, he shouldn't know that his job had been conditional on hers. Derry smiled as she thought of how happy Bruce was going to be. *No audition.*

Sometimes, good things do happen.

4

'Oh, the glamour!' said Bruce. 'Would you pass me the hubcap, honey? Thanks.'

Derry watched him finish fitting the spare wheel. She didn't bother to wipe the oily dirt off her freezing hands. No point, she thought. Playing mechanic's assistant seemed to be her required role for the day. Or night, strictly, considering they'd been driving for hours and the time was after eleven p.m.

Bruce's van was pulled in by the side of a dark Scottish road. A chilly drizzle was falling. In general, Derry disapproved of women blaming men when the car broke down but was preparing to make an exception for herself on the grounds of being stranded in the dark in the middle of nowhere.

As they resumed their journey, pressing on through the gloom, the fair part of Derry's brain pointed out that it wasn't Bruce's fault the ferry from Ireland had been delayed for hours. Or that the film production company didn't want to pay for flights and taxis, even though the location was a remote part of the Scottish west coast, almost a hundred and forty miles from Glasgow.

At least, thought Derry, the company had arranged accommodation in what was billed on the internet as a Country House Hotel. When she and Bruce did finally get there, if ever that blessed moment came, Derry meant to pamper herself without conscience. Room service. Bath. Bed. Not necessarily in that order.

'I am really freaked out about only getting the script three days ago,' said Bruce. 'How were we supposed to learn our lines? Aren't you freaked out?'

Derry sighed. When you travelled with actors, punctures did have one thing going for them—they put a temporary stop to the endless talk about jobs, agents, the iniquities of casting directors, the failings of other actors and the horror of nerves. Derry was as guilty as anyone of these occupational obsessions, but Bruce was the worst.

'Do you think I should tell the director I get nervous?' he continued. 'Sometimes I think it helps to be honest. Don't you think that can help?'

Derry feigned sleep. She was as fond of Bruce as of a brother, and there was nobody in the world she would rather have around if she were in trouble. But she was running out of ways to say *for goodness' sake stop worrying!* She knew she was being callous. Bruce's fears were genuine, and she really should be more sympathetic, but what was the point fretting?

'What if he's one of those directors who gets off on being horrible, like he's into the power, you know? You ever had one of those?'

Derry felt bad about what she was about to do, but sometimes you had to be cruel to be kind. She quit pretending to sleep. 'Bruce,' she said, expertly modulating her voice to convey deep anxiety. 'I am *so* worried about the improvisation. I don't think I've done that since college. Do you think I'll be able with the crew and all looking on? I mean—'

'Oh, there's the sea,' said Bruce brightly, pointing vaguely towards the pitch-black ocean.

'What if they ask me to—'

'Look, there's a big island out there! You can just make it out. Did I ever tell you about when I …' And he launched into a tale, unlikely but probably true, about spending a month in the Nevada desert eavesdropping on some guys drilling an oil well where the government might or might not have lost an atomic bomb. Or was it aliens?

Derry smiled to herself and closed her eyes. *Take a bow, Miss O'Donnell.*

Acting was the coolest profession.

~

They roared through a tiny village, no more than a dozen houses, a pub and a little shop. As they bounced over a bridge lit by a single street lamp, Derry saw the road ahead vanish into the blackness of moor and mountain. Bruce's newly acquired satnav was loudly insisting they had arrived at their destination when plainly they hadn't. If the satnav sounded anxious, Derry felt it had every reason to be. Scotland seemed to consist of countless miles of nothing at all. The way she felt now, settling down in a nice wet ditch would be preferable to driving endlessly into the darkness.

'Hey! We got it,' said Bruce. He swung the van right, powering up a narrow curving lane. In the beam of the headlights, Derry saw tall stone gateposts and an impressive sign— *Bunnapole Country House Hotel.* She gave silent thanks.

'Funny they call it a country house hotel,' said Bruce. 'I mean, it's in the country, right? Why bother? Ain't never heard of a *city* house hotel.'

'I think it means posh,' said Derry, her befuddled brain unwilling to deal with the niceties of branding at this late hour. 'Thank goodness our calls aren't early.' Both Derry and Bruce were scheduled to turn up for Wardrobe at a civilised noon the next day. The way film jobs usually went, that could have been six a.m.

As the van scrunched its way to the top of the gravelled driveway, in the darkness you could just make out lawns flanking either side. Ahead stood the hotel, a large Victorian house perhaps once a gentleman's residence. Steps led to a colonnaded porch. Bruce pulled up opposite and parked, headlights trained on the doorway.

'Hmm.' He switched off his lights, plunging the court-yard into blackness.

Derry paid no attention. She was busy imagining downy white beds floating vaguely in a room somewhere on the second floor. In her mind she had already forgotten to get undressed and had sunk between crisp white sheets (though a duvet would be perfectly acceptable). She had remembered to set her phone alarm for a civilised nine a.m. and had just emitted an anticipatory sigh of pleasure, when the meaning of Bruce's exclamation struck home. The hotel was dark. Not a light shone anywhere. Not even in the porch.

'You sure this is right?' said Derry, although she knew they had to be in the right place—the sign said they were.

'Sure,' said Bruce, turning on his headlights once more to illuminate the entrance. 'Hold on here. Let me do a recce.' He jumped out of the van.

Derry watched, her heart sinking, as Bruce climbed the steps, inspected the door and peered through the narrow windows flanking the doorway. He stood holding his finger on what Derry guessed was the bell. He must have doubted the chime worked, because now he put his ear to the door while he pushed the button. He stood back, shrugged and trotted down the steps to stride along the frontage of the house, peering up at the darkened windows. He turned to Derry and in the white of the headlights gave an exaggerated shrug like a mime artist in the spotlight.

Again Bruce set off, this time disappearing around the side of the building and into the shadows. A moment later he was back at the van.

'There's a light on in an upstairs room round the side. Must be the night guy goofin' off when he should be down at reception. Come on.'

Derry groaned a protest, struggled into her jacket and climbed out of the cab, buttoning up against a chill breeze. Bruce left his headlights switched on so they could see their way to where the path curved to skirt the right side of the house. A light shone from a single window on the third storey.

Bruce bent down and picked something up. He opened his hand to show a fistful of small stones. Derry had hardly grasped what he meant to do before he let fly at the glass. He was a good shot. *Clack* went the first stone on the windowpane. *Clack* went another.

'Bruce! What if you break the glass!'

'Aw, these itty bitty pebbles won't break nothing,' said Bruce, grinning.

Derry was appalled to see he was enjoying himself. Bruce's arm flew out once more. Clack! 'Go on. Your turn,' said Bruce as he collected more ammunition.

Was it Derry's lack of sleep? Some instinctive response to the tone of command in Bruce's voice? An unwillingness to be dismissed as a mere girl? Whichever it was, before Derry thought about it, she obeyed. She flung a stone skyward, trying for the impossible compromise of throwing gently to avoid breaking the window yet hard enough to hit the target. She missed by a mile. Bruce smirked, shaking his head, as if to say, *chicks*. Or perhaps *civilians*. Or maybe *straights*. Stung, Derry picked another missile, this one bigger. She reached back. She took careful aim. She let fly.

As any dedicated sports fan will tell you, timing is a funny thing. One shot, kick or throw fails dismally to hit its mark, caught by some random gust or an opponent's sudden move, while another, in all respects similar, hits the bull's-eye. This truth was now forcefully impressed on Derry. At the very moment the projectile left her hand and flew towards the window, the sash was thrown up and a head thrust belligerently out. Derry's stone thwacked impressively against the wood of the frame, inches above the head. The head ducked then reappeared wearing an expression of the deepest outrage.

'What do you think you're doing!' The voice was a strangled cross between a bellow and a hiss.

Derry hid her hands behind her back, trying unsuccessfully to persuade herself the man at the window couldn't possibly have seen in the shadows. She wondered if whistling nonchalantly would help, maybe accompanied by some idle inspection of her surroundings as any ordinary non-stone-throwing hotel guest might do. She rejected both ideas as implausible and downright overacting.

'We've reservations,' roared Bruce, not quite as loudly as he might have on a ship's deck in a gale.

'*Shhh!*'

Bruce lowered his voice to what he imagined a whisper. 'We got held up. The ferry was late. You the night guy?'

'Certainly not!' said the head. 'What do you think you're doing? It's one o'clock. We're closed! We close at midnight!'

This was too much for Derry. 'You can't be closed!'

'Come back tomorrow!'

'We booked!' insisted Derry.

Perhaps a British or Irish person would have slunk off into the dark, shamed into obedience and accepting that their status as a customer rendered them beneath contempt. But Derry was American, and the American in her knew that somebody was paying this man good money. But, angry as she was, as a trained actress Derry was keenly aware that starting high would be a mistake. The trick was to begin quietly, then take off. She spoke in the reasonable, academic tones of a quizmaster in a television gameshow.

'Have you ever heard that the customer is always right? Are you really saying we have to sleep tonight in the …' Derry almost said *van* before realising that the connection with itinerant performers, funfairs, and men selling fake designer bags at Saturday markets wouldn't help her case. '… in the vehicle. What kind of a hotel *is* this?'

'This is *not* a hotel!' said the head, who seemed to view the description as the lowest kind of slander.

The blatant effrontery of the statement almost threw Derry off her stride.

'This is a *Country House!*' the head proclaimed, as though the logic should be obvious to the meanest intelligence, even people who threw stones in the middle of the night.

'Sign!' shouted Derry at the top of her voice. The benefits of years of training in the art of voice projection and her assiduous study of intercostal diaphragmatic breathing came to her aid at once. '*At your gate!* It says H-O-T-E-L! Did someone sneak in at night and paint it while you were asleep?'

At moments like these, Derry knew she was her mother's daughter and didn't mind one bit. Sometimes what people needed when they got uppity was a piece of New York. Right in the neck.

'Now get down here and open that door!'

Bruce looked embarrassed. He seemed to think throwing stones at a hotel window was fine, but dishing it out verbally to a moron who didn't know he worked in a hotel was a step too far.

'Open up or I will have this dump plastered over every social media page on the planet before morning!' continued Derry, righteous indignation propelling her onwards. 'Wanna know what trolling looks like? What about your website? I know hackers! Hundreds of hackers!'

Derry wondered if she'd overdone it. She didn't know any hackers, except possibly Bruce who could fix anything to do with computers. And she didn't do social media much on the principle that fellow actors only friended you to take comfort in the fact that you were out of work too.

'Alright! Just be quiet! Please! Guests are asleep!'

The head disappeared. The window slammed shut. Bruce looked at Derry. Derry looked at Bruce. They both shrugged.

Derry dropped, she hoped inconspicuously, her remaining collection of stones and wiped her hands on her jeans.

'We could have used you in the Navy,' said Bruce.

'It said HOTEL,' insisted Derry. 'H-O—'

'Okay, okay!' conceded Bruce, grinning. 'I get ya.'

5

Only one other resident was in the hotel dining room when Derry came down to breakfast. By this time, ten o'clock, the rest of the cast and crew would have been on location for hours. Bruce had risen early, texting that he had breakfasted and gone off to explore.

'Welcome to *Stalag Luft*,' said the elderly, distinguished-looking man, putting aside his newspaper.

Derry smiled. 'Did we wake everybody last night?'

'Oh, nobody minds that,' said the man, 'as long as you annoyed the Laird.' He grinned. 'He's a pompous fool, and we hate him. Wife's nice, don't know how she puts up with it. He wears his kilt all the time. Thinks he's Bonny Prince Charlie. I'm Richard Adderley, by the way. Duke of Cumberland's Quartermaster.'

'Hi, I'm Derry O'Donnell,' said Derry. 'Um, Gypsy Fortune-teller.'

'Lovely,' said Richard. 'We've a scene together. I look forward to that.' His accent was faint but definitely Scottish. Nice he was being friendly.

'Me too, said Derry. 'What's a laird?'

'A minor Scottish title. About as low as you can get without being a mere *Mister* like the rest of us plebs. Means *landowner* really, although in this case I doubt he's got ten acres of bog. Doesn't stop him insisting on being styled *The Much Honoured* on his letterheads. 'Prat. I hope he didn't give you a hard time?'

'He moaned a bit,' said Derry. 'Came down in his bathrobe to let us in. But he was okay in the end. Showed us to our rooms complaining about makeup on the sheets and actors stealing breakfast rolls.'

'All true. I suggest you nab a few rolls yourself.'

'Surely the catering's not that bad?' said Derry. Usually the food on a film location was excellent, a compensation for long days hanging around in the cold.

'You haven't heard anything about this little show? I suppose you mightn't have. Let's say the food is the least of our complaints. But if it tells you anything, the director gets his lunch made specially, won't touch the muck we get.'

That didn't sound good. Still, thought Derry, at the rate she would be getting paid, a poor lunch was a minor inconvenience. 'Maybe I need to diet anyway,' she said, smiling.

'Certainly not,' said Richard, gallantly. 'You are quite perfect as you are, and don't let anyone tell you otherwise. Had your call sheet yet?'

All Derry knew was that she was to be in Wardrobe at twelve. 'They were a bit vague about the arrangements to pick me up and get me to the location. Is it far?'

'Depends on where they're shooting today—windswept bog, halfway up a mountain or possibly in some sea cave with the tide coming in. Wherever it is, it will be pouring rain and Wardrobe will be as far away as it can possibly be. What we suffer for our art. Though what genius thought it a good idea to shoot a movie in Scotland in October I can't imagine, except he should probably be in Parliament. Must go, dear. I may or may not be getting picked up in five minutes or ten or never.'

He stood, folded his newspaper under his arm and made to leave. He stopped at the door. For the first time, his expression was serious. 'You haven't heard we've had some mishaps?'

No, Derry hadn't heard.

'The locals say it's because we shot some scenes on a Sunday. I prefer to think it's an old-fashioned jinx. If you've got any gypsy lucky charms, bring them along. You could name your price.'

~

Derry's breakfast was served by a shy middle-aged woman who seemed flustered, as if she were always being reprimanded. She brightened when Derry told her it was her first visit to Scotland.

'I'm a McKenzie, myself,' the woman said proudly. 'Moira McKenzie, as was. Taggart now, of course.' Derry wondered if she were supposed to offer congratulations. Instead, she smiled to indicate she was happy to look positively on all things McKenzie. She was rewarded by a nonstop flow of information.

The hotel was full, with sixteen or so actors and crew staying, confided Moira. There were other hotels, all full too, but this was the nearest to the village. This was the third film the producers had made around these parts.

'All about highlanders and clans and so on?' enquired Derry politely.

'Of course,' said Moira. 'Very popular with Americans like yourself. We're hoping the tourists will come to see where the films are made. We depend a lot on visitors. The body helped a wee bit,' she added. 'It was in the news. Can I get you some more coffee?'

'Um, yes. Please. You said *body*? Did someone …?'

'Last year, it was. Caused a right stir, let me tell you. The JCB was up the moor digging a drain for the new windmills.' Moira dropped her voice to a whisper. 'Nobody wants them, but the estates do what they like. We have a petition, but they'll no tak' a blind bit o' notice.' She sniffed her disapproval.

'The body ...' said Derry. 'I don't want to be nosy ...' she left the sentence hanging, the way people do when they are in fact being shamelessly and obviously nosy. Moira didn't seem to mind.

'Och, such a stir!' she continued. 'A real hue and cry, wondering who the poor man could be and how could such a terrible thing happen. Some were making guesses it was ... well anyway it wasn't. For three days we were in a tizzy. The word was he'd been *strangled*.' She paused to let the full horror of the picture do its work. Derry felt a shiver run up her spine.

'He was cut almost in half, they say. Or at least his leg was. My husband was working on the site and he saw it all. Probably the digger did the damage, he thinks. He said the man was a strange sight, sort of squashed, and as I said, with a leg, or possibly twa legs, missing. Mayhap they'll turn up.'

Derry had been contemplating polishing off the rather tasty brown toast, done just the way she liked, although she had finished the homemade strawberry jam. Like the butter, the jam had been served in tiny bowls hardly big enough for two slices, never mind the half dozen on the rack. But now she wasn't sure she felt like toast. The picture of a man buried in a bog, deformed and missing a limb wouldn't leave her mind.

'And do they know who ...?'

'*I* maintain he was a McKenzie,' said Moira, with surprising *sang-froid*, as if confiding that although the dead man was a relative, he wasn't an especially close one, she'd never much liked him, and anyway these things happen. 'My husband says they didn't have second names then. Or if they did, we don't know what they were.'

'I'm sorry?' said Derry. 'They know who he is … was?'

'Not to say exactly, but in a way. It was on the radio. They call them …' she lowered her voice as though what she was about to say was indelicate '. . . *bog bodies! Thoosands o' years old!*'

'Oh,' said Derry, sufficiently relieved to reexamine the toast. 'They have those in Ireland. Um, Bronze Age. Or are they Iron Age? One of the Ages. Old.'

Moira didn't seem pleased that some other place might have produced comparable wonders, especially Ireland, a country all of thirty miles away by sea and therefore demonstrably and traditionally foreign.

'Be that as it may,' continued Moira, reserving her position, 'They say he was murdered as an offering to the gods.' She dropped her voice to a whisper. 'They might ha' been McKenzies, or they might not, but they were *awfy pagans.*' She nodded slowly, as though to say *and we know what they got up to.*

Moira finished clearing the next table and left with a friendly smile, seemingly satisfied with her efforts on behalf of the local tourism industry. Derry had turned once more to the toast, regretting she had forgotten to ask whether she mightn't have more jam, when the dining-room door opened. A woman stepped in, smiling apologetically. She wore a blue windcheater and jeans and carried a folder under her arm. Her dark hair was tied neatly back. Derry guessed she was in her late twenties.

'Derry O'Donnell?' the woman enquired, closing the door behind her. 'I'm Jessica Wade, Mr. Carson's PA.'

Derry had no clue who Mr. Carson might be.

'The executive producer,' explained Jessica.

'Ah,' said Derry. 'Sorry. Is there a change to the call sheet?' Usually the production manager or assistant director would deal with a film's cast and manage the arrangements. What an executive producer's personal assistant was doing handling things was a mystery. Executives were about the meetings and the money, not the messy business of making the movie.

'It's not that—mind if I sit?'

'Please,' said Derry. She was sure now that Jessica was American.

Jessica drew up a chair. She gave Derry an appraising look. 'You're … younger than I expected,' she said.

Derry didn't know what she was supposed to say to that. Was *younger* a bad thing or a good thing? No surprise Jessica worked for a film producer. In this business, actors were always too tall, too short, too fat, too thin or whatever else you happened to be and couldn't easily change.

'Mr. Carson wanted me to ask you a favour,' Jessica continued. She stopped as if unsure how to go on. 'You're a fortune-teller. I mean a real one.'

'I'm an actress,' said Derry, frowning.

'Yes, of course. But Torquil said you told fortunes.'

Torquil. Derry tried not to let her irritation show. 'You know Torquil?'

'The publicist? Yes.'

So much for Pam's belief that Torquil was an associate producer. Publicist made far more sense.

'That's how Mr. Carson knew about you,' continued Jessica. 'Would you come to the castle this evening after shooting? That's where we stay—it's not far. A small party. Not dinner, but there'll be a buffet.'

'I'd be delighted to meet Mr. Carson, of course,' said Derry, frantically wondering how she could politely refuse. She was, after all, here to do a demanding job that would need all her attention. 'I'll have scenes tomorrow. Maybe when I've done?'

Jessica frowned. 'Mr. Carson *asked*.'

'I'm sorry,' said Derry. 'I don't mean to be ungrateful—'

Jessica carried on. 'Mr. Carson's wife and daughter are here,' said Jessica, as though she hadn't heard. 'He'd like you to tell fortunes for them. Mrs. Carson especially.'

Derry was astonished. All she could think was: *Actress, Buy One—Get Fortune-teller Free!*

'Mr. Carson would really like you to say yes,' said Jessica.

Derry had to work hard to hide her annoyance. Jessica called this an invitation, but it was an order. How could you refuse the man who was funding your movie, who'd effectively given you your job?

Derry remembered an older actor she'd worked with when she was fresh out of college. He seemed to like her in an amused kind of way and gave her valuable tips about acting technique and about the business. One piece of advice stood out in her memory, maybe because it had annoyed her so much at the time. 'In showbiz, you leave your pride at the stage door,' he'd said. 'We're paid minstrels, that's all. Clowns and jugglers. Don't ever imagine it's any different.'

Alright, thought Derry. *Juggler, fortune-teller—whatever.* She'd do as she was asked. She'd be careful not to drink, and she'd leave early. But somewhere in the back of her mind a voice said, *One day, if she works hard enough, Derry O'Donnell will be a big enough name to say 'get lost.'* She smiled at the thought. 'I haven't brought my costume or crystal ball or anything. But I could improvise, I guess.'

'Good,' said Jessica, as though no other outcome had ever entered her mind. 'Mr. Carson will be grateful. Seven o'clock? I'll arrange for someone to pick you up.'

'Say thanks to Mr. Carson for the invite,' said Derry. 'I hope he'll understand I'll have to leave early?'

'Of course.' She gave Derry an appraising look. 'Your character is Bessie Green, a gypsy fortune teller?'

The abrupt change of subject took Derry by surprise. 'Yes. Lots of improvisation, I'm told.'

'I have a suggestion for you,' said Jessica.

'Sure,' said Derry, puzzled. 'Fire away.'

'The director, John Hamilton, he's ... how can I say this ... Don't let him get to you.'

6

The sky was clear with a few fluffy white clouds, nothing like a typical late October day. An island-studded sea sparkled, blue and other-worldly. The water was stunningly transparent, so clear you could see a dark band of weed stretch out under the swell for a hundred yards before the sea bottom dropped away and the colour changed to a deep azure. A heather-covered hillside, golden red, rose steeply inland. In the distance, mountains reared up, grey and forbidding. Scotland was wearing its best clothes and seemed more than happy to give its bedazzled visitors a twirl.

Derry was entranced as the car taking her and Bruce to the film's location swept along the narrow coast road. She made a valiant attempt at engaging their driver in conversation, praising the scenery and giving him the chance to claim the credit for himself as a local had every right to do. But the man seemed to believe conversation with actors was no part of his contract.

If the driver was unmoved by the stark beauty of the Highlands, or pretending to be, Bruce seemed to know everything about the place. 'Those mountains to our right go on for fifty miles west and north. Mostly moorland, a little forestry, a couple of rivers. There's a big lake up there, but you can't see from here. Should get snow on the higher ground any time from now on, right?' He addressed his last comment to the driver, who grunted grudging agreement. 'Not much doing up there, I guess, except some grouse shooting and deer hunting.'

'*Stalking,*' said the driver. He spoke reluctantly but obviously couldn't let such a serious error pass uncorrected. 'Here we call it by its *richt* name.'

'Gotcha,' said Bruce, cheerfully, '*Stalking*. And that beautiful stretch of sea—all those islands? Man, that is pretty. Oh, wouldn't I just love to get diving out there.'

Bruce turned to Derry. 'You think we'll get a day off Sunday? Wanna go diving?' He spoke to the driver. 'Can you hire scuba gear around here?'

'That ye can.' The driver spoke cheerfully. 'But nae on a Sunday.' If the back of someone's neck could smile smugly, that's what the back of this man's neck was doing now.

'Pity,' said Bruce. 'Like Amish, right?'

The driver shrugged, showing no inclination to venture into the tricky waters of comparative religion.

'Hey! Here we are,' said Bruce. Ahead, cars were parked haphazardly along the grass verges for a hundred yards. An open gate led to a fenced industrial site, obviously once a quarry. The enclosure was crammed with trailers and trucks. On the far side of the road, where a grassy field sloped down towards the sea, an avenue of white military-style tents looked like a circus until you noticed red-coated British soldiers cradling their muskets and lining up on parade. A watching crowd and bright lights said a scene was being filmed.

The driver slowed at the entrance to the quarry. The double gates were wide open. Two security men in padded jackets, walkie-talkies at their hips, stood chatting. They ignored the car as it nosed into the yard.

'Do you know where the office is?' said Derry to the driver, 'We'll need to find Wardrobe.'

If the driver knew, he wasn't saying. Without answering, he pulled up in front of the encampment. Derry and Bruce climbed out of the car. Derry bent down to the window to say thanks, but the driver was already pulling away as if to stay would risk catching some horrible disease.

≈

One of the most surprising and unlikely of all human achievements is the way the chaos of a shoot actually produces a film. All over the lot, people milled about, seemingly aimless, many in costume with coats or parkas on top. Most of the passing faces were decorated with carefully streaked makeup representing mud. Derry wondered whether people a couple of hundred years ago were as reluctant to wash as film directors seemed to believe.

A sign on a trailer announced it to be the production office. Derry and Bruce stepped inside. A woman in horn-rimmed glasses, obviously the production manager, frowned at Bruce.

'Are you the bagpiper?'

'Uh-uh,' answered Bruce. 'But I could learn,' he added, following the age-old actor's mantra—*never* say you can't do something. You can always take classes.

'Oh, no, I see! You're the Returned Canadian Patriot, Captain MacBride,' said the woman, peering at a printed sheet. 'We've no blasted internet today, can you believe it? Yesterday we had, today we haven't. How are we expected to run a shoot?'

Derry and Bruce made sympathetic faces.

'And you're the Gypsy Fortune-teller, right?'

Derry agreed she was.

'You'll both need to speak to Jeff, the AD, but he's on set. It's been crazy, we've had two falls off horses and a trampled foot already today. At least that was better than yesterday. Hold on.' She picked up a radio handset, shouting into it like she was in the middle of a crowded bar and needed to be heard. 'Jeff, I've got the Gypsy Fortune-teller and Captain MacBride here. I'll send them to Wardrobe, shall I? Over?'

Derry couldn't make out the answer crackling over the handset but guessed Jeff, the assistant director, had more on his mind than a fortune-teller and a captain however patriotic. The production manager led them to the door and pointed to a trailer across the far side of the lot, with instructions to report to Wardrobe and await further orders. 'And if there's nobody there, just wait. I think there was a costume emergency, but they may be back.'

As Derry and Bruce made their way across the yard, trying not to get their feet so muddy they committed the cardinal sin of tramping dirt into a wardrobe trailer, Bruce suddenly stopped. 'Derry, I can't do this.'

Derry knew the signs. And they hadn't even changed into costume.

'Bruce, you'll be fine! What's gotten into you? We rehearsed your lines a million times.' The day before they had travelled, Bruce had come to Derry's apartment. She had heard him his two dozen lines until she could recite them in her sleep.

'Captain MacBride! They never said!'

'You knew he was a captain—what difference does it make what he was called?'

'That's not it! They said *patriot*, I get that. They never said *Canadian*!'

'Oh, I wouldn't worry about—'

'Derry! Canadians are completely different! They talk different! I practiced my Scottish accent, I can do "Och, major I dinnae ken" and "Awa' wi' ye, Tom," but Canadian … I'm from Texas!' His despair was as deep as if he were from the dusty wastes of Mars and had been told he was to play a dolphin. 'They don't even speak English up there!'

'That's Quebec, Bruce. Most Canadians speak English. Okay, they say *aboot* when they mean *about*—' Hey! That's Scottish, right? Canadians say *aboot* like the Scots! From all those Scots who emigrated to Canada!'

'Oh,' said Bruce. He looked doubtful.

'Anyway, if he was a Canadian Scot in the eighteenth century, he wouldn't talk like a Canadian, would he? He'd talk like a Scot!'

Bruce's face lit up. 'Derry, what would I do without you? You are *smart*.'

He strode towards the wardrobe truck and knocked. 'Och Major, I dinnae ken,' he proclaimed at the top of his voice. A woman opened the trailer door. She recoiled frowning, until she noticed how good-looking Bruce was. 'Come in, come in,' she said, beaming.

Entering a wardrobe trailer is like walking into someone's closet and pulling the door closed behind you. A narrow corridor runs between racks of hanging costumes packed thickly on either side. At the top of the trailer is a space with full-length mirrors for fitting and a cramped worktable with a sewing machine.

Derry and Bruce perched on stools while the wardrobe mistress and her young male assistant explained how they had just repaired a British officer's tunic that had a split the back seam. 'It should be in actors' contracts—no steak pies or curries between casting and shoot,' said the wardrobe mistress. 'This one must have put on two stone since he sent in his measurements. And we're supposed to deal with that with a needle and thread? What *he* needs is a gastric bypass.'

Within half an hour, Derry had been transformed into Hollywood's idea of what a gypsy fortune-teller looks like— ankle-length voluminous skirt, wildly colourful blouse, bangles, huge earrings and a straggly black wig. Then it was Bruce's turn. Derry sat and watched as the wardrobe mistress and her assistant fussed until Bruce stood resplendent in a kilt fashioned from a plaid cloak, a fine linen shirt, a waistcoat, and a bonnet sporting a feather. No doubt about it, Bruce looked magnificent. He posed, admiring himself in the mirror. 'Cool,' he said. 'Can I keep it? What *this* would do for my Saturday nights.'

The wardrobe mistress and her assistant laughed indulgently, leaving little doubt that either would be happy to help Bruce pass any Saturday night he might care to suggest.

'You'll need to pop in next door to Makeup,' said the Wardrobe Mistress, 'then off to Ally in Props to get your sword, dagger and pistol. And–' she looked up her list and turned to Derry—'you'll need your bones.'

7

Derry stepped out of the props trailer, leaving Bruce, Ally the props man and Tony the armourer toying happily with a flintlock pistol. She was wondering where she was supposed to be next, when Jeff the Assistant Director appeared shouting into his walkie-talkie. Obviously harassed, his mind on some unfolding catastrophe, he absently thrust two pages of script at Derry, telling her the director would be ready in ten minutes. Her scene would be in one of the big tents in the field across from the quarry.

Derry sat on the steps of an unoccupied trailer. Experience told her that five minutes of quiet was a precious commodity—time in which she could read her script, collect her wits and calm her jangling nerves.

In her scene, Derry's Gypsy Fortune-teller was plying her trade, predicting the future for the English General and the Duke of Cumberland's Quartermaster. Her job was to predict overwhelming victory against the rebellious Highlanders. The good news was that she was to be seated at a table, so no walking around and no worries about hitting her marks. Her moves, according to the script directions, mostly consisted of 'Mystical Looks And Gestures.' 'Wide Eyes' figured more than once, along with 'Rhythmical Rocking Motions Back and Forth.' Strangely, bones got no mention at all.

'Sheep's knuckles,' Ally the pleasant young props master had called them, handing Derry a little leather pouch containing five small, knobbly bones—like dice but irregularly shaped, each about an inch long. Derry had expected a crystal

59

ball or some cards and hadn't got the remotest idea what you did with bits of a ruminant's skeleton.

'I dunno,' said Ally. 'Just throw them on the table and start talking, I guess. Make with some, like, mystical looks?' he added, hinting at a missed vocation as a scriptwriter.

Derry had heard they did something like this with chicken bones in the Ozark Mountains but had never seen it done. She guessed you threw the bones like dice, and they told the future by the way they fell. *How come five bones?* Derry wondered. Her knowledge of animal anatomy was sketchy, but she doubted sheep had knuckles at all. Or if they had, she was sure they didn't have five fingers. Only people had those. She shook off an unwelcome thought. These belonged to sheep, she reminded herself. You felt sorry for their former owners, but there was nothing at all creepy about them.

Of course not.

~

The gravel track leading down into the field was already churned into muddy ruts. Derry held the hem of her skirt with one hand and her script pages with the other. Below was the line of tents. By the biggest stood a battery of lights on tall stands, surrounded by reflectors and all the mysterious technology of a movie. Derry felt her heart beat faster.

What is about a movie set that gets the pulses racing? The intense concentration of the crew must have a lot to do with it. Like a well-drilled circus troupe they say little, but everyone—Camera, Sound, assistants, grips, gaffers, runners, continuity—all seem to know exactly what they are doing.

Dozens of onlookers stand and stare, huddled together trying anxiously not to get in the way and mostly failing. Extras and locals alike suffer being brusquely ordered about by anybody wearing a parka and carrying a radio.

Derry's arrival generated an instant buzz in the crowd. Was she famous? Should they recognise her from some TV show? Jeff, the assistant director, led her inside the largest tent in the row. The front of the canvas was pulled back, exposing the interior so the shot could be lit. Derry stepped into the charmed space near the camera, giving a warm smile to the crew who, as every actor knows, can be your best friends or your worst enemies. Richard, the actor she had met at breakfast, and the English General, whom she was meeting for the first time, greeted her in the friendliest way.

Any minute now, the director would arrive to take over, but meantime Jeff got the three actors in position. They took their places seated at a camp table, while the camera was focused. The soundman and his assistant squatted in the corner twiddling knobs.

Derry, Richard and the General quickly ran through how they might play the scene. Derry was confident in her lines, although the first time she tried casting the bones two rolled clean off the table. But her nerves were well under control, and to her surprise she was starting to enjoy herself.

The director pushed his way into the tent, seeming to fill the interior. John Hamilton was tall and broad-shouldered, jowly and overweight, like a football player gone to seed. Derry guessed he was around forty. He wore a heavily padded jacket, muddy hiking boots and a startling red baseball hat.

At first Hamilton seemed pleasant enough, and Derry wondered whether Jessica's warning hadn't been misplaced. Then she wasn't so sure.

'For goodness' sake!' said Hamilton, fixing Derry with an impatient glare after what had seemed to her to be a competent run-through, *'Do it like this!'*

'OOOh!' moaned Hamilton. 'WOOO!' he crooned. The sound man grimaced, pulling his headphones off his ears. Hamilton lowed and quavered. He rocked back and forth. 'Mwahaha!' he proclaimed, waving his arms about. Suddenly, he stopped. 'See?' he said. *'Be supernatural!'*

The camera assistant sniggered then buried his head, pretending he was adjusting something vital. Derry took a deep breath. Richard and the General gave her intense, supportive looks. The crew looked away tactfully as if unwilling to collaborate in her humiliation.

'Action!'

Derry tried, she really did. She cast the bones, making what she imagined were mystical gestures. She crowed and grimaced—enough to satisfy Hamilton, she hoped, but staying just the right side of demented. She delivered her lines well she thought, not fluffing anything despite her racing pulse.

'Cut! Cut! I thought you were a real bloody gypsy!' Hamilton was shouting, his face flushed, his finger jabbing at Derry.

Derry thought her heart would stop. Her mouth was dry. Sweat broke out on the palms of her hands. Shock, then a depressed gloom descended on the crew, actors and onlookers. Everybody knew that when a director lost his temper, nothing thereafter would go right.

'If I might make a small suggestion?' Richard, the Duke of Cumberland's Quartermaster, spoke calmly and with a friendly smile at Hamilton. Derry wondered had Richard saved her right there from crumpling, breaking down into tears and sobs. She could feel the choking in her throat that meant disaster was close.

'Why don't we try to pick up the scene a little earlier?' suggested Richard. 'Get into the spirit of the thing—if that's not a pun too far, my dears?'

Hamilton glared.

'Maybe I could just cast the bones a couple of times first?' suggested Derry, a catch in her voice she covered up by clearing her throat. 'And then I'll add … what you suggested and introduce the lines as we go?' Derry was amazed her words came out at all.

'Get on with it then,' barked Hamilton.

'Is that Action?' enquired the cameraman, innocently.

'Yes, bloody Action!'

Derry threw the bones. They scattered on the canvas that served as a table covering and sat mutely. What now? Hamilton was an obnoxious bully. His crew didn't respect him and didn't mind showing it. Alright, if he wanted garbage, he could have garbage. Mentally Derry apologised to whatever muse, patron saint or guiding spirit governed the dubious talents of actors.

She launched into a melodious alto, quavering syllables, mostly vowels chosen at random. Hamilton gave an enthusiastic thumbs-up, nodding furiously to signify she should carry on and the camera should keep rolling. The manic part delivered, she declaimed the first of her lines without missing a beat.

The crew beamed. Derry could feel the waves of support as the scene played on. In the corner, the soundman too was smiling. Then he stopped smiling. He looked around, puzzled. He pulled a headphone off an ear. Derry had to fight to keep her concentration and prevent her eyes flicking over to see what was happening. Now the soundman was looking up to the roof of the tent. Then they all heard it. The thump-thump-thump of an approaching helicopter.

'Cut! Cut!' screeched Hamilton, following up with a stream of obscenities. He elbowed his way out of the tent, forcing his way through the gaping crowd.

'Hey,' said the cameraman, addressing nobody in particular. 'It's only money. Why not waste some more.'

'Time to stretch our legs, dears, don't you think?' said Richard, as though nothing more unusual had happened than someone calling a tea-break. He turned to Derry. 'By the way, you handled that well,' he said, his voice low to her ear. 'He's not only a bully, he's a talentless bully. You're a pro, my girl. Always delighted to work with the real thing.' The General looked on, smiling benevolently.

Derry was dumbfounded. A compliment from an old-stager like Richard was something to be treasured. She wanted to say thanks, but the words wouldn't come out properly, and already everyone was pushing outside to see what was going on.

The helicopter's rotors stopped turning. Out of the bowels of the machine stepped three men. The first was a fit-looking man in a leather jacket who stood beside the helicopter, legs apart as if prepared to defend the chopper and its distinguished occupants from all comers. Emerging behind was a big, heavily built man in a green outdoor jacket, tartan trousers and a surprising Scots bonnet, the sort worn by marchers in a pipe band.

'Well if it's not our Mr. Carson,' said Richard. 'He *does* like an entrance.'

The third man was chisel jawed and slim. Perhaps in his mid-forties, over his business suit he wore a beautifully tailored cashmere coat. His smile as he greeted Hamilton was friendly. Something about the way he held himself, his air of command, said *this chopper is mine*.

A black SUV drove briskly across the field towards the helicopter and pulled up a safe distance away. The three strode towards the vehicle and climbed in. The driver, another fit, youngish man, held the doors open. Oddly, the SUV didn't drive off. A conference of some kind? In the absence of interesting developments, the crowd slowly dispersed, reverting to the normal business of hanging around customary on a film set.

Jeff, the assistant director, returned to the tent, talking into his walkie-talkie and signalling the crew should return to their stations. To the actors, he said, 'Mr. Hamilton says I should go through the scene with you guys. We'll go for a take, though, okay?' He turned to Derry. 'I liked the way you did it first time.'

It took a few minutes to get the actors and crew back in place and concentrating, a few more minutes for the three actors to gather their thoughts, and they were off. This time, the scene flowed. Derry's movements dealing the bones were natural and unforced, with no fumbling. She delivered her lines low-key, quietly drawing the other actors into a tense intimacy, before Richard's final words closed the scene.

'Cut!' said Jeff. 'Terrific. Just hold your positions please for the moment.'

While Jeff and the crew fussed with the usual technical checks, the actors breathed a sigh and could at last relax. Derry felt exhausted as though she'd run a marathon.

'Well I think we were bloody marvellous,' announced Richard. 'We must get you to throw those bones for us sometime when we're off-duty,' he said, turning to Derry. 'You are *so* convincing. What did he mean by saying you were a real gypsy? Are you? How exotic.'

Derry laughed. 'No, Irish-American. Not at all exotic.' She gathered up the bones, putting them back in their little bag. 'These *are* fun, though.' It occurred to her that the bones could be useful for Madam Tulip, something to offer besides the cards and the crystal ball. Either way, she could do with practicing some more, as she would need to cast the bones in two more scenes.

'That's a wrap for you boys and girls,' announced Jeff. 'All lovely.'

As Derry and Richard trudged together across the field and up the track to the road, they heard the helicopter's engine cough into life. The chopper lifted off, climbed and circled, gaining height as it followed the shoreline before roaring away north.

'Oh, the music of money,' said Richard with a sigh.

∾

Derry sat in the armchair in her room wondering what to do now. The place was comfortable, with a bed, a dressing table, a small table with its own chair by the window, and a vast mahogany wardrobe. The radiator worked, although the fireplace, pretty with its colourful tiled surround, hosted a cold grate, empty but for a couple of decorative peats. The TV might even have worked, though she didn't check.

She had at least a quarter of an hour to kill before someone was to pick her up and drive her to the castle as Jessica had promised. She checked her email on her phone but saw only a 'hiya' from Bella. She'd answer later, when she had something more positive to say than *got through today without complete meltdown—just.*

The most irritating thing about having to go to the castle was missing the chance to meet her fellow actors at dinner. Bruce hadn't been sympathetic. 'What is it with you and aristocrats?' he'd said, grinning in a way calculated to drive Derry to distraction. 'They just love ya. Hey, maybe you can bag a laird.'

'*One,* I have no intention of *bagging* anybody. *Two,* Carson is not an aristocrat. And *three,* I do not enjoy being summoned like a … a …'

'Stay cool, honey! We riffraff need to stick together.' Bruce was in an irrepressible mood after a good day on set, his scene for the day an outdoor skirmish shot by the second camera unit. No dialogue. All he'd had to do, he said, was act heroic. Or at least, act what civilians thought heroic looked like.

Bruce had taken his leave, and Derry was left to get ready. While making up, She tried to think clearly about how she was going to manage this strange situation.

She'd meet Carson and his family, and whoever else was there, say hello—then what? If she were going as Madame

Tulip she wouldn't worry. She'd have her costume and treat the occasion like a show. But telling fortunes as yourself was different. Still, there was no point fretting—far better to do something constructive. She took from the dressing table the little pouch of bones she had used in her scene.

Ally, the props man had suggested she take the bones away with her if she wanted to practice as he had a spare set—an unexpected offer but helpful if she were to get comfortable in her role. She sat at the table by the window, opened the drawstring of the pouch and poured out the bones. Playing her scene, she had thrown them as if she knew what she was doing, but she'd had no time to study them properly. Now she saw that when you rolled a bone it could fall on one of four sides, like a dice. She picked one up and inspected it closely. The faces were wobbly, but definite. One was more or less flat. Another was twisted. The third was hollow and a fourth bulged out. She examined all five bones, and yes, they all had the same arrangement of faces. Did the ancient diviners have names for the different sides? She guessed they did.

Derry threw the bones, watching them roll and tumble on the table. She swept them up and threw again, this time amusing herself by practicing gestures like those she had improvised in her scene that day. The business was dramatic, highly visual, and she could easily imagine Madam Tulip casting bones for her clients in a satisfying way. Again and again, she swept up the bones and threw, noticing they came to rest in different combinations every time, just as dice would do.

Then they didn't.

A most unlikely thing happened. All five bones sat on the same face, the twisted one. Derry squinted to make certain she was right. She had to look carefully to be sure, but yes—amazingly, all five had landed the same way. The odds against that were … what? Derry tried to remember how you worked it out, casting her mind back to high school and vague ideas about permutations. Or was it combinations?

She had just concluded that unlikely things were bound to happen sometimes, when she saw something had changed. She squeezed her eyes shut to make sure her vision wasn't playing tricks. But yes, now she saw it. The little bones had changed colour. They had been white. Now they were yellow. And there! They had darkened again. The alteration was almost imperceptible. The effect was like she had blinked and missed the change, then opened her eyes and the transformation had already taken place. But she hadn't blinked; she was sure of that. And as the bones changed colour, they seemed to become even more motionless than before—like there was a state called *still* but another called *absolutely dead still.* So static they made you want to stop breathing. Then they were black.

Each black spot began to tremble—not a slow vibration like they were being shaken, but a humming, high frequency, so their outlines blurred. And the sound, a strange buzzing—the pitch rising slowly, the hum growing louder in a crescendo of frantic energy.

Like ties had snapped, all five black vibrating objects leapt into the air at once. Instantly, like a swarm of insane and bloated bottleflies, they raced for Derry's head. She slapped wildly at her hair. She waved her arms, desperately trying to flap away the fat, buzzing creatures, frantically warding them from her nostrils and her eyes.

Did she scream? She couldn't tell. Had she blacked out? Probably not, but her heart was racing and her breath was coming in gasps. She opened her eyes, trying to gather her wits. The table was bare. But on the carpet lay the scattered bones. And they were white, normal. Just bones. She must have swept them off the table on to the floor.

Derry knelt, picking up the bones one by one. She had to fight to keep her hands from shaking. She reached under the table to find the last. Where was the bag? There, on the table where she had left it. She poured the bones back inside the leather pouch and pulled the drawstring twice.

She grabbed a bottle of still water she kept on the dressing table, drained it until it was empty, and slumped into the armchair. She hoped she hadn't shouted. Hopefully, at this time most people would be down at dinner. At least nobody was knocking on the door wondering was she alright and what was going on. Derry leaned back and closed her eyes, refusing to think. A blank mind was better.

Hardly a minute had passed when her phone rang, jolting her out of her trance. *Unknown number.*

'Hello, Derry here.' Her words came out hoarsely, so she had to repeat herself.

'Hi. Derry? I'm in the hall. Your carriage awaits.'

The man's voice was so real that when Derry said thanks she was really thanking him for being a human being, flesh and blood like her. She was thanking him for making a lame joke out of the simple offer of transport. For having a soft deep voice and speaking slowly. For not asking was she losing her mind.

8

'Robert Dalgleish,' he said. 'Call me Rab.'

He stood in the hotel hall, just inside the door, shaking Derry's hand formally. About thirty years old, with reddish hair and brown eyes, he had the weathered face of someone who spent his time outdoors. His clothes were country—tweed jacket and corduroys—and he sported a faint suggestion of beard, a nod to cosmopolitan fashion but no kind of statement. Derry said little as he led her outside and opened the door of his old green Land Rover for her to climb in. She was still shaken from her strange vision—hallucination, whatever it was—still unable to rid herself of the panic and disgust.

'Hope you weren't waiting too long,' said Rab as they left the hotel behind, passed through the village, and pressed on along a dark and narrow coast road. From behind Derry, two musty-smelling dogs pushed their snouts between the front seats to investigate. 'Dinnae mind them,' said Rab. 'They're just curious. You'll be getting a lot of that round here.'

At first Derry could barely make out the sea in the darkness, until the moon broke out from behind cloud, turning the surface to gleaming sheet metal. Islands loomed in the glow, mysterious silhouettes, the largest showing rows of glimmering lights, like a liner sailing majestically in the bay, headed who knew where.

'It's beautiful,' said Derry.

'It is, that,' said Rab. 'The phone system is rubbish, the hospital is hours away, it rains three-quarters of the year, but we love it. You're in the film?'

Derry told him she was, though playing only a modest part.

'I don't know how your nerves stand it,' said Rab. 'I run away if anyone tries to take a photo.'

Derry smiled. Usually people said how great it must be to be famous and hang out with all those stars, as though actors spent their time in one long party. At that point you were supposed to start dropping names. The temptation to make up outrageous stories about celebrities you had never met was sometimes irresistible, but for some reason she didn't feel like teasing this man.

'Have you been to Scotland before?' enquired Rab, politely.

'No, this is my first time. I nearly got a theatre tour here once, but it fell through.'

'You'll not have seen Castle Finn then.'

'No. I only arrived yesterday. Mr. Carson owns the place, is that right?'

'No, no. Mr. Dunbar from Edinburgh owns the estate. He bought it from Lord Talbot. His Lordship owns the estate to the North, about eight miles away. That's where I mostly work. Castle Finn is more for sport than farming. It's the sporting estates you showbusiness people like.' He smiled at Derry, as though to say it wouldn't be long now before she too would be in the market for a little grouse shooting and a couple of miles of nice salmon water.

'Part of the castle is private and the rest Mr. Dunbar rents out for weddings, shooting parties and the like,' continued Rab. 'His friend Mr. Carson from America takes the castle for a month or two every year, and sometimes he makes a film on the estate. All very exciting for us. And it's work for the locals—building sets and what have you. And the hotels of course.' He paused. 'How are you enjoying your stay at the Country House?'

Did Derry detect amusement in the question? 'I've not been there long enough to tell,' she answered, diplomatically.

'I suppose not,' said Rab. 'Let's say the laird has a reputation that we Scots absolutely do not deserve. The miserly Scot is a calumnious stereotype, but unfortunately the proprietor fits the bill to a T. I know I risk defaming the man, but on grounds of national pride I insist on getting my retaliation in first.'

Derry smiled. Rab was obviously not someone to curry favour with the gentry. And she had never before heard anybody say *calumnious*.

'Do you eat venison by any chance?' asked Rab.

'I guess,' said Derry. 'Isn't it supposed to be healthy and all that?'

'So they say. I predict it'll be on the laird's menu tomorrow night or possibly the night after.'

Derry was expected to ask how he knew, so she asked.

'Let's say I have psychic powers?'

Derry frowned. Was he teasing her? But Rab gave no sign he was making a clever remark at her expense. She glanced over at his face but couldn't make out his expression in the dark. She realised she was being oversensitive. Rab was unlikely ever to have heard of Madam Tulip.

She changed the subject. 'I saw Mr. Carson and two other men land at the location in a helicopter today.'

'Yes, that would be Mr. Dunbar's machine,' said Rab. He said *machine* as a Victorian might speak of his newfangled bicycle.

'Sounds like the way to travel in these parts,' said Derry, as they hit an especially vicious pothole that made the Land Rover rattle.

'if you owned an oil well or two,' observed Rab.

'And does Mr. Dunbar own an oil well?'

'I couldn't say,' said Rab. 'Although he *is* from Edinburgh,' he added, as if nobody from the West would be in the slightest surprised at what anyone from that notoriously uppity capital might own or do. 'I believe he's a banker of some kind.'

'I thought Scottish castles were owned by dukes and earls,' said Derry, not so much because she was interested in the important question of land ownership in Scotland, but because she wanted to hear him speak some more. Rab's accent was that soft musical lilt of the west coast and the Isles, with its impeccably precise pronunciation of English.

Rab laughed. 'Not a bit of it,' he said. 'We've all sorts. Inland we've got a pair of famous hairdressers, next along a hedge fund man from London. That island out there belongs to a pop star, and so does the one beyond it. Then there are the Arabs.'

'Don't you mind outsiders coming in and buying up everything?'

'True enough, outsiders own almost all the sporting estates. But the incomers bring cash and jobs to us and that's what we need here if we're to keep the place alive. Personally, I'd like to see a lot more smaller landholdings amongst the great estates, but nothing revolutionary. These things are easy to break but harder to fix.' He paused and in the reflected headlights Derry saw him turn and give her a shy smile. 'Sorry for the manifesto.'

'No need,' said Derry. 'Not at all.' She smiled. She was aware she was smiling. She was also aware that her smile was lasting longer than it had any right to last. The truth was she was happy to listen to Rab's voice for as long as he cared to talk. But she really should say something—if not to sound sentient at least to seem awake. 'You're connected with the estate?'

'Aye,' said Rab. 'But I work for Lord Talbot. I'm the factor, the estate manager. For ... various reasons, I'm looking after both estates just now. Luckily I've a good gamekeeper and lads to manage the sport. They're overstretched surely, and it looks like they'll have their work cut out over the next few days, with word of poachers about. But usually they manage well enough. The rest is upkeep really. Aye.'

Derry was sure what Rab had just said was interesting, possible very interesting. But somehow most of it had gone past her. All she could remember was the way he had said *Aye*. She should have been ashamed of herself, she knew, but she wanted to hear him say *Aye* again. The sensible and civilised part of Derry's brain insisted she had just proven herself to be an airhead and a bimbo. The other half spotted its chance.

'You must have so many repairs to worry about,' said Derry innocently.

'Aye,' said Rab.

Derry breathed out as quietly as she could. A small but distinct and unambiguous tingle had developed at the nape of her neck. Could she try one more time?

'Did you say an estate manager was called a factor here?'

'Aye,' answered Rab, gloriously.

～

Castle Finn was impressive, the floodlit walls blazing white. The place was like the fairy castles Derry remembered drawing as a little girl—way too tall, with rounded towers shooting up to pointy conical hats like so many stone rockets stacked in a clump. The place was more like an elaborate birthday cake than a stronghold to be held against murderous clansmen.

'Looks like a film set,' she said, as they drew up on the gravel forecourt.

Rab laughed. 'You're not far off there. Apart from Mr. Dunbar's private wing in the old tower, the rest is only a hundred and fifty years old—practically modern. I imagine the man who built it read too much Walter Scott,' he added, getting out and opening the door for Derry.

She jumped down. 'Thanks.'

'A pleasure, surely.' For the briefest moment, he looked as if he were going to add something but didn't. 'I'll show you to the door, then I'll be off.'

'Oh,' said Derry. 'Aren't you coming in?'

'No, no. I was just on my way by, and Jessica asked could I pick you up.'

'Oh,' said Derry. 'Ah.'

'Yes,' said Rab. 'Indeed.'

'Well,' said Derry.

'I'll just ring the bell,' said Rab.

'Thank you,' said Derry.

'I hope you—' The door opened before Rab could finish. A man stood silently, waiting for them to speak—whether a guest or a retainer of some kind Derry couldn't tell. He seemed neither friendly nor unfriendly, as though he had no particular expectations about what should happen next.

The man was perhaps in his late thirties, with a narrow face and high cheekbones. Something about the quick movements of his eyes suggested a coiled energy, reminding Derry of a whippet or lurcher, one of those poachers' dogs her father's more disreputable friends owned. He was neatly dressed, in a dark suit and impeccably polished black shoes. The only incongruous touch was a narrow bracelet of red and black beads on his right wrist, like something you'd get at a concert or a festival. Derry wondered was the display the man's nod towards unconformity, a discreet rebellion.

'Johnny,' said Rab, 'this is … um … Miss O'Donnell.'

'Derry,' said Derry. 'Derry O'Donnell.'

'I'll be off now. Enjoy your evening,' said Rab.

Before Derry could reply, he was striding back towards the Land Rover.

'Thanks,' Derry called out.

Rab turned and smiled, jumped into his vehicle, turned on his lights and pulled away.

'In you come, then,' said Johnny.

The hallway was grand and spacious, as you'd expect in a Scottish castle. More surprising was the decor. Instead of the circular shields and claymores of clansmen, hanging on the walls were the most extraordinary objects Derry had ever seen. A row of gleaming black facemasks with unseeing eyes, head-dresses sprouting fans of feathers, matted fibres hanging like a cloak beneath. African, for sure. But before Derry could think of a polite way of asking Johnny what they were doing here, Jessica strode into the hall, smiling.

'So glad you could come,' she said 'Thanks, Johnny, I'll show Miss O'Donnell in.'

Beyond a wide staircase ascending the height of the hall to galleries and floors above, a broad passage led deeper into the castle. Jessica led Derry down the corridor. Here the furnishings were much more the kind you expected—long wooden benches heavily carved, a suit of armour standing in an alcove, smoky portraits in heavy gilt frames. Derry wondered whose ancestors they were, those whiskered men in highland dress posing with their muskets. Dunbar's? Or were the pictures a kind of set dressing to go with the fake turrets and battlements? The impression she had stepped into a movie only grew when Carson himself emerged from a panelled doorway, dressed in a tartan kilt, tweed jacket and knee socks.

'Jim Carson,' he said, holding out his hand and smiling to show flawless American teeth. 'Delighted you could come. My wife especially wanted to meet you.'

Carson led her inside, Jessica following a couple of paces behind.

'You must forgive me for imposing on you like this,' said Carson, 'but I'm a slave to the women in my family.' He guffawed, as though nothing more amusing could be imagined than someone as important as he being a slave to anybody. 'Come in, come in. Just the girls here. A few more folks will be along soon.'

In the sitting room, an open fire of logs burned in a great fireplace surmounted by a marble mantelpiece. The furnishings were old-fashioned, informal and comfortable—Persian rugs, deep sofas and armchairs, yet more portraits, even a piano. The effect was grand but threadbare in a superior kind of way. From the wall above, a stag's head with enormous antlers stared down.

'Meet my girls,' said Carson proudly.

The contrast between the setting and the appearance of the two women couldn't have been greater. They sat at either end of a huge sofa like a pair of matching ornaments, their perfect hair and makeup looking as if they had stepped out of an LA beauty salon. Derry wondered how they managed, far from anything remotely resembling a boutique nail bar.

Carson introduced his wife, Sally. Derry guessed she was about forty. She had the tight-faced look hinting at the handiwork of some pricey LA surgeon, but she was a good-looking woman to start with, blonde and slim, though tall and strongly built. She sat primly, her dress a soft green woollen creation with an elegant matching cape over the shoulders.

Sally didn't stand. Her eyes gave nothing away as she held out a languid hand to be shaken. 'So pleased,' she said. She may or may not have been pleased—from her expression it was impossible to tell.

Carson turned to Derry. 'I'm trying to persuade Sally to take up golf, seeing as how we're in golfing paradise here in Scotland, but she won't have it. Says she can't abide the clothes. Anyhow, Sally is from Nevada. She prefers killing things. Only way I can get her to come here is to let her massacre the wildlife. Just don't get her mad, she can hit a stag at half a mile.'

Sally's smile didn't change. She neither went along with Carson's attempt at banter nor rejected it. Her eyes never left Derry's face, and Derry had the uncomfortable feeling she was being weighed up. Surely not as potential competition, though some women did look at you that way when they learned you were an actress—like actresses were somehow more likely to steal their husbands than other women.

'This is my daughter, Amelia,' said Carson.

Amelia sat curled up, her feet bare and her legs tucked beneath her. 'Hi,' she mouthed, before turning her attention back to her phone. She wore a pristine sweatshirt and leggings, as though any minute she meant to set off for an expensive gym.

'Amelia is having her gap year just now,' said Carson. 'She'll be travelling to Thailand soon, before college next year— UCLA. I tried to talk her into going East for the experience but she won't have it.'

'Come on Dad,' said Amelia, her voice weary. 'East, like Siberia. Like here.'

Carson leaned towards Derry as if confiding a secret. 'I try to get a little culture into my offspring but it's a lost cause. Only way I could get her to come here this time was to raise her allowance for her Thailand trip. The only surprise is she hasn't sent me an invoice.' He laughed loudly. Amelia ignored him.

Carson drew himself up at the mantelpiece, posing impressively like the nineteenth-century chief of some clan. 'My ancestor Samuel Carson left Scotland in eighteen hundred and fourteen. I feel those roots in my blood. Maybe women don't feel that thing.' Carson addressed Derry as though for the purposes of this conversation she was absolved from the sorry state of womanhood.

'We're just waiting for Alex, then we'll eat and have a drink,' continued Carson. 'Afterward, you can do your thing. Sally is looking forward to that, aren't you darling? Amelia might or might not, depending on what her phone tells her to think.'

Sally smiled vaguely. Amelia scowled. All the while, Jessica stood blending into the background. Derry had almost forgotten she was in the room. Was that a skill PAs perfected? Staying out of the limelight? Out of the way of their boss's ego?

The door opened to admit a man Derry instantly recognised. He had emerged from the helicopter that afternoon behaving as though the machine were his. Impeccably tailored city clothes; chiselled, handsome face; dark hair and dark eyes—the banker, Dunbar. Derry guessed he was in his mid-forties, though he was fit and might have been older. He stood at the door for a moment, politely waiting to be invited in, even though he owned the place.

'This is my old friend and partner, Alex,' said Carson. 'Alex Dunbar.' To Dunbar he said, 'Come on in Alex, we were just getting to know each other here. Come and meet Derry O'Donnell—I told you about her.'

Dunbar held out his hand to shake Derry's. He made no attempt to kiss her on the cheek. His greeting was more the way one might greet a business colleague—direct, confident, efficient. The preliminaries over, he stood quietly with his hands clasped behind his back. His air of polished competence reminded Derry of somebody in some unexpected way, but she couldn't think who or why.

'I believe you are acting in Jim's production,' said Dunbar politely. His Scottish accent was cosmopolitan and easily understood. Derry was sure he must have known she was at the castle to tell fortunes, but instead he emphasised her acting. Something about his quiet intelligence said he might well have made a deliberate choice.

'Yes,' said Derry. 'An interesting role. Hopefully I'll do it justice.'

Her answer was the stock response, but Dunbar didn't probe. 'I'm sure you will,' he said, smiling. 'I look forward to seeing the end result.' He turned to Carson. 'Release, in May, is that right?'

'If Hamilton gets his finger out of his ass, sure thing,' said Carson.

For the first time, Derry saw an expression flit across Sally's face, the merest hint of a frown. Her husband's crudity sat badly with her. Derry wondered at that—surely Sally would be accustomed to the ways of movie producers by now.

'I'm told Derry here is famous,' said Carson. 'She finds dead bodies—how about that?'

Only years of training as an actor enabled Derry to hide her annoyance. 'No,' she said. 'Really, I don't do that. Fortune telling, that's all. For fun,' she added, mentally adding *or for nothing in this case.* Fun she wasn't too sure about either.

'Well that's not what Torquil our publicist says,' said Carson. He spoke in a loud stage-whisper. 'I guess it's like the CIA, she has to deny everything.'

Sally spoke up. 'My husband likes to tease people. He thinks it reveals their character. I'm not sure it's *their* character that's revealed.'

Carson laughed. 'Touché, Sally. Okay, I promise I won't press Derry any more for her trade secrets. Anyhow, she's missed her chance round here.' He turned to Derry. 'You know we had a body? Caused quite a stir let me tell ya. Turned out to be Methuselah's grandpa.'

'I heard,' Derry answered, determined to stay polite. 'But like I said, it's not what I do. Although I'm sure the history of these parts is interesting,' she added, anxious to steer the conversation away from corpses.

'It certainly is,' said Dunbar. 'Wars between the clans, wars with the English. Like all wars, destructive for some, profitable for others.' He waved his arm to take in the opulence of the room. He smiled and his gaze rested on Derry as though he were evaluating her reaction. Perhaps bankers were like that with everyone, Derry thought. But she had to admit his coolness, that half-amused detachment, was attractive.

'We got our own wars too,' said Carson. 'Poachers. A rough lot.' He turned to Dunbar. 'Pity you don't have an M-60 on that bird of yours Alex. Not like the old days. Six hundred rounds a minute would give 'em something to think about, hey?' He grinned at some in-joke.

'We flew over an obvious poaching gang on the hills as we came over today,' explained Dunbar. 'Not much we could do about it other than make the reports.'

'One day they're gonna take a potshot at you in that bird, Alex my friend. Everybody says they're getting crazier every year.'

Dunbar addressed Derry, as if anxious she should understand. 'This is nothing like the old-fashioned local poacher out to make a few pounds with his gun. These are city gangs, well organised, well equipped. Venison is valuable, especially now Christmas is coming. The gangs can net thousands of pounds in a few hours. They care about nothing—leave wounded animals to die on the moors. Appalling.'

He brightened, dismissing the subject. 'When your work allows, Miss O'Donnell, you must let me give you a tour of the castle.' He smiled, and Derry saw his smile was the sort that though practiced was charming all the same. 'You don't have to, of course,' he added.

'Oh no,' said Derry, hurriedly. 'I'd be interested, really.'

'I advise caution,' said Dunbar. 'Admit you're interested in history at your own risk. You're in Scotland now.'

Carson guffawed. 'Maybe he'll show you his Howling Dungeon,' he said, glancing across at Dunbar with a grin that made Derry wonder how long the men had known each other. Something about that understanding said they were close.

Derry never got to ask what a Howling Dungeon was. At that moment, the door opened and a middle-aged woman in a domestic's uniform entered and nodded at Sally. 'Food is ready, folks,' said Sally. 'We can go in now.'

In single file, they trudged out of the sitting room. Jessica followed last, pulling the door closed behind her.

∽

All Derry had wanted was a quiet time in her hotel room reading a book—anything but talking to people. But as she entered the castle dining room, its table laden with food and drink, she could almost hear Bella say, 'Aw, isn't it a terrible life when you have to hobnob in castles and drink the best wine. Wouldn't you need counselling after the trauma.' She'd grin, leaving you no escape, and you'd have to laugh and admit to being ridiculous.

Another half-dozen guests had by now arrived—local worthies whose names Derry mostly failed to catch, but who seemed impressed when told she was acting in Carson's movie. They were even more impressed when told she was also a fortune-teller. At that, Derry could only smile and agree that fortune-telling was indeed fascinating. So she stood, forking a plate of chilli concarne but refusing wine, all the while pretending interest in the weather this year compared to last year and the year before. She noticed Carson saying, 'only one glass, now!' to Amelia, who rolled her eyes. All the while, Jessica stood quietly. She ate but Derry saw she too was drinking water.

That Derry managed easily enough was thanks to Dunbar, who politely asked where she was from and where she lived. Soon Derry found herself telling him about her New York origins and her move to Dublin to train as an actor. She was describing her mother's plans to open an art gallery in Edinburgh, when Carson approached.

'I see you guys are getting along just fine,' he said. 'What is it with bankers and actresses?' His leer invited Derry to smile back and be admitted to whatever club had conniving at stupid remarks as a joining fee. Derry declined, and Dunbar made a tiny gesture as if apologising for the vulgarity of his friend.

'Derry has been telling me her mother is opening an Edinburgh gallery,' said Dunbar. 'We should go through for the exhibition if you're this side of the pond for New Year.'

'Sure thing,' said Carson. 'That Edinburgh is some town. Jessica loves Edinburgh, don't you Jess?'

Jessica looked startled to be addressed and made no reply.

Carson turned to Derry, 'I think Jess has a fancy man in Edinburgh, and she ain't telling. But who knows, I might give her a day or two off in the next coupla weeks. I'm taking us back stateside when we finish shooting, and I wouldn't want to get in the way of the fond farewells.'

Jessica's face betrayed nothing, but Derry knew how she must feel as Carson teased her in public, flaunting his power as a boss. Dunbar too must have felt the discomfort. With practiced ease he turned the conversation to the art business, admitting he used to be a collector but had since sold everything, finding his collection too great a responsibility.

'Alright,' said Carson, as though the time allotted for pleasantries was over. 'You can do your thing in the library next door,' he said to Derry. 'It's private, so you can tell each other girly secrets without us boys knowin' what you gals are *really* like. Though we think we know already—that right Alex?' He laughed. 'Anything you need, Derry? I've fixed for some glasses and mineral water.'

'No,' answered Derry. 'Thanks.' She put down her plate. Obviously her temporary status as guest was up and, like Jessica, she was now an employee, for whom suggestions were orders.

Carson turned his attention to his wife who stood coolly watching, sipping from her glass. Having her fortune told might have been arranged by her husband as a treat, but she showed no sense of anticipation or excitement, no gratitude for his gesture. 'Sally, you wanna head on into the library?' Carson called.

Sally nodded, stepping over to Derry. 'Would you mind if Amelia had a reading too? I didn't think she'd be interested to be honest, she's more into juices and yoga, but she wanted to. I've asked the others, but nobody seems to want to try. It's a small village, I guess. Can't be too careful.'

Derry agreed that Amelia would of course be welcome, and anyone else who changed their minds.

'You should start a business. Make a few dollars,' said Carson.

Once more, Derry thanked the powers above for the poker face bequeathed her by the Trinity School of Dramatic Arts. There, she had learned to emote. She had also learned how *not* to emote. How to be enigmatic. She was enigmatic now, but her brain wanted to deliver a thoughtful and carefully calculated obscenity.

Carson waved his arm, pointing the way to the library. 'Come on ladies, roll up roll up! The future's come a'callin'. And it don't wait for nobody.'

9

'I want to know if someone is dead,' said Sally. 'Can you tell me that?'

Gone was the detached, cool observer. Sally wore the tense, ferociously alert expression of a competitor in a chess game. She drank from her wineglass, never taking her eyes from Derry's face.

They had taken their seats at an oversized library table, Derry at the head, Sally at her right elbow. Only a tall floor lamp and a small reading light lit the room, casting gloomy shadows. All around were bookshelves of dark wood, stacked high with leather-bound volumes that might or might not have been fake. In that small, overstuffed space the effect was claustrophobic and oppressive.

Derry had taken her cards from her bag and begun to shuffle the deck. She was about to embark on the explanation she often gave clients before a session—the cards weren't to be taken literally; they were a place to start. Sometimes they were hints, sometimes symbols or metaphors. She hadn't gotten past the first words before Sally had asked her astonishing question.

'I'm sorry?' said Derry.

'I know what you said, that you don't find dead people. But Torquil said you were for real. Why would he say that if you weren't?'

Where to begin? How do you explain to a client that no you aren't for real? Or, yes you are, but not *that* kind of real? And how do you tell them the question they've just asked is either weird, scary or sad, without implying that the questioner must also be weird, scary or sad?

Derry shuffled the deck once more, buying time to think. What to say? She reminded herself that although she wasn't in costume, this gig really belonged to Madam Tulip. Alright, so how would *she* react? The answer came easily. Tulip would never dismiss a client as mad or weird. If someone came to Tulip with an honest question, they would have her full attention. But that wasn't the same as an answer; only the cards could give that. In any case, Derry had long ago learned that the question a client asked was not necessarily what they most wanted to know.

'You're from Nevada, right?' said Derry.

'Yes,' said Sally, tearing her eyes away from the deck in Derry's hands.

'Vegas?'

'No. Not raised, anyway. Nye County.'

'A country girl.'

For the first time that evening, Sally smiled broadly. 'Sure am,' she said. 'Brought up on a ranch in a valley hotter'n hell.' She paused. 'Hey, aren't I the one supposed to be asking the questions?'

Derry contemplated the woman sitting in front of her. Intelligent, sure of herself up to a point. But she was wary, like someone who had been long ago taken advantage of or been hurt and had sworn never to allow that happen again.

'Mrs. Carson—'

'Sally.'

'Sally, I'm being straight with you. I don't do the kind of thing you seem to think I do, whatever Torquil says. I can tell your fortune, sure. Maybe that'll help with whatever might be … bothering you. But that's all.'

Sally sat back, chewing her lower lip gently. She seemed to reach a sudden decision.

'I brought something of … the person's.' She leaned down and picked up her bag from the floor beside her chair and put it on her knee. She opened the bag and reached inside.

'No!' said Derry. 'Really. I'm sorry. I mean it.'

Sally sat motionless her hand still in the bag. She contemplated Derry, then zipped the bag shut. 'Okay,' she said with a sigh. 'Just do whatever you always do.'

Derry again offered the deck to Sally to cut. All the while, Sally never took her eyes from her face. Derry took the deck back and dealt a nine-card spread. No point overcomplicating things—a simple Past, Present and Future should be enough to start. Derry worked to free her mind for that peculiar blend of concentrating and not concentrating she always tried to attain in a reading. It was more difficult than usual, but that wasn't surprising—Sally had asked an unsettling question, that was all. Without thinking, Derry turned over all nine cards. She had meant to turn only the first.

How can you be surprised at nothing? The cards lay face up. At once a pattern should have emerged—the movement of a life from past through present to whatever future fate held in its hands. But instead there was … a blank.

Never before had Derry seen anything like this. Of the infinite statements the cards can make about a life, the one thing you can be sure of seeing is motion. Lives change, take turns—some surprising, some predictable, but never doubling back on themselves, always seeking out the next moment, the next hour, the next day. But not Sally's life. The life in those cards had settled into a strange immobility, a kind of trance. The whole bustling world seemed to flow around this woman who all the while sat unmoving.

'Why don't we try again,' said Derry.

'You see it?' She was frightened.

'No, no,' said Derry. 'Honest. Sometimes the cards take a little time to ... warm up. I didn't see anything. Really.' She shuffled the pack. Sally cut, and again Derry laid out a spread. This time, a conventional picture—noncommittal, but normal.

Derry made the ritual pronouncements—she sketched the past, and Sally played along agreeing that the cards had sensed the truth of her story—how she had moved from rural isolation to the falsehood and corruption that was Vegas. How her looks and a shrewd business sense had helped her survive a city where everyone was single-mindedly devoted to relieving visitors of their money with promises that could never be fulfilled. Derry gave her an opportunity to explain what it was she did in Vegas, but Sally preferred to talk about how her handsome suitor from LA had swept her off her feet and how she had left Vegas behind to become the wife of a movie producer who seemed to know everybody.

'Why don't we skip all that crap about me,' said Sally. 'How about this—you deal the cards and say what they mean, but I don't ask any questions out loud. What I ask in my head is my business, okay? I'll know the answer to my question when I hear it.'

'Mrs. Carson—'

'Sally.'

'You can make anything you wish of the cards. But you'll be hearing what you want to hear. And if you already know the answer, why ask me?'

Sally sat silently. Her jaw was clenched tight, her mouth narrow, but her eyes were brimming with tears.

'Sally, why don't we leave the cards as they are for a little while, and you tell me what this is about. Who is the person you're worried about? Are they family? A friend? If you tell me, we can see if the cards can help. Maybe we need to ask a different question.'

Sally took out a handkerchief and dabbed her eyes. 'I'm such a damned fool.' She paused as if weighing Derry on some balance whose scale only she knew. 'Okay. His name is Hamish. *Was*. Hamish Maclean. He was the estate manager here. Factor, they call them. Like a ranch manager. He used to look after everything on the estate for Alex. He ... taught me to stalk deer.'

'So ... you got to be friends?'

Sally looked Derry in the eye as she answered. 'Sure. Friends. Then he disappeared.'

'And you think he's ... something happened to him?'

'He wouldn't just vanish. Why would he do that?'

'He'd been here a while?'

'A year before we first came. He was in the army before that. A lot of the estate managers come from the British Army. Officers. They like to run things, I guess.'

'So what happened?'

'They say he stole money then ran away. I don't believe it.'

'And who ...?'

'Alex. After Hamish disappeared, Alex went through the books and said he'd been siphoning off funds or something. But like I said, it can't be true.'

'Did they call the police?'

'Sure. But they couldn't find him.'

'Sally—how can I put this—what makes you think it's not true? Doesn't it make sense he'd run if he was … doing what they said?'

'Sure. Except he would never steal. I know … knew him. Something happened.'

'But that's … Are you sure you're not letting your imagination run away? Lots of people up and leave their jobs. Even if there's some kind of disagreement, that doesn't mean anything bad. Could something else have been bothering him?'

Sally hesitated. 'Strange things happened before he went. Somebody poisoned one of his dogs. Then one day someone took a shot at his jeep. They said poachers, but I don't think he believed that.'

'Sally, maybe that's all there was to it. Maybe he got worried and thought to play safe.'

'Not Hamish. He was a soldier. Poachers didn't scare him. He'd laugh at that.' She lapsed into silence, then seemed to to reach a decision. 'When I was a kid, a guy came to work on the ranch next to us, about five miles away. Everybody knew him. Then he just upped and disappeared. He left his stuff and his papers. Everything. We all knew what had happened. Even the sheriff knew what happened. The whole county knew. But the sheriff was the husband's cousin. The wife left soon after that, and nobody mentioned it again.'

So what if a ranch hand had absconded somewhere in the wilds of Nevada? Why would Sally think that had anything to do with Hamish Maclean? At first, Derry was baffled. Then it dawned on her. She could have kicked herself for being so stupid. Ranch hand. Disappears. Sheriff is related to the husband. Wife slips away some tactful time afterward. Was this Sally's way of admitting she was having an affair with Hamish, but without spelling it out? Of course it was.

Sally sat quietly, poised, as though waiting for Derry to catch up like a slow child. Okay, thought Derry. I've got it. *You were having an affair.* Then it hit. Derry felt like the breath had been knocked out of her body. Sally wasn't being coy about her affair. She was saying she believed her husband *had murdered her lover.* Derry felt the blood drain from her face.

'Sally, this is Britain. No offence to Nevada, but—'

'I know what you're going to say. Nevada is like the Wild West and all that bullshit. You're an Easterner. You guys think we spend all day shooting each other. We don't. Look—right here, in this castle, in Alex's private wing, there's a gun cabinet with more guns than in most ranches. I know, I've shot a bunch of 'em. There's shotguns, side-by-side and over-and-under. Okay, no pumps or semi-automatics, but there's deer-hunting rifles you could hit a dime with at a thousand yards. Scopes, tripods. Everything.'

Derry had no clue what an over-and-under was, and she was certain she couldn't hit an elephant at a dozen yards no matter what scopes she had. But Sally sounded like she knew what she was talking about.

'When they found that body buried in the bog, I was sure it was Hamish. Then it wasn't.' She had a catch in her voice at the memory.

'If you've got suspicions that … something bad happened, shouldn't you be talking to the police?'

Sally's look said she wondered whether she had made a mistake confiding. 'Don't you see? Can't you work it out?'

Derry shrugged.

'I'd have to tell them why!'

Of course she would. No body. No sign anything at all had happened except the guy ran off with cash from his employer. Sally would have to explain why she was searching.

'Have you … asked around? Did Hamish have family?'

'No family. And I couldn't really … you know.'

'I understand,' said Derry. Sally could hardly go round the district asking questions or people would soon put two and two together.

'I need to know. I need to know is he … has he just left …' Her voice tailed off, but Derry mentally completed the sentence—*me. Has he just left me?* Probably, thought Derry. Most likely that was exactly what he had done. With the cash.

'Can you help me or not?' said Sally.

Derry took a moment to think. On rare occasions clients did ask her to look in the cards and tell them about their own future death. She always refused on the grounds her answer could change what the person did with the life they had left. Sally's question hung in the air. Would the cards answer if Derry were to ask? She didn't know. But what if the cards decided to tell her anyway, even if she didn't ask?

'We should stop,' said Derry. 'I'm sorry.'

'Come on! You can't do that. You can't just say, like, *no.*'

'I'm sorry, Mrs. Carson. I can.'

Sally sat back. Derry expected her to say, *Hey, my husband employs you. Don't you get that? You're just a two-bit actress.* But she didn't.

'Wow,' said Sally. 'An honest fortune-teller.' She shook her head. 'You know, you could feed me any old bullshit and you'd be off the hook? You could say, *hell no he ain't dead, he's fine.* What would I know? That's what fortune-tellers would do in Vegas. After they told me finding people is extra, big time.'

'Sally,' said Derry quietly. 'You asked me because you believed I'd tell you the truth.' She contemplated Sally's crestfallen face. Gone was the sleek, exquisitely groomed look. Now she seemed older, her features sagging. Here was a woman who had lost something precious to her. Derry couldn't help thinking of the man she herself had just met. Like Sally's Hamish, Rab was an estate factor. She remembered his quiet, compelling charm. His confidence. The sense he had his feet firmly planted in a landscape he adored. Had Hamish been like Rab? If he were, then Sally had indeed lost something. Whether she had been wise or foolish in the first place wasn't for Derry to judge.

'Why don't we look to the future? Whatever happens, you'll have a life. Why don't we see what might be out there? Just something to think about.'

Sally nodded. 'Okay,' she said quietly. 'Where do we start?'

~

When Derry told fortunes, she was rarely surprised. Not because she didn't see surprising things—she often did—but because surprise is an emotion, a reaction; and in a good reading Derry felt somehow tranquilised. She'd feel calm, a little dreamy, not quite in a trance but not fully awake either. But now, sitting with Sally Carson in that gloomy library, Derry was indeed surprised.

Right there, in a nine-card spread, the picture was as clear as peering through the thinnest of glass. The missing Hamish nowhere intruded into the picture, and still Sally's future was happy. Derry had no way to tell whether that happiness was next month or twenty years away, and in the nine of spades was a sign that the near future was uncertain. But they knew that already.

'And that's all the cards have to confide. The rest is in your hands and the hands of fate,' concluded Derry, sweeping up the cards expertly. She shuffled the deck as though she were returning the future to where it belonged, in the random stack of possibilities from which life could deal whenever it chose.

'Sally, are you alright?'

She was motionless, staring at the deck in Derry's hands. She looked up. 'Sure. Thanks. I guess it's that … I don't know what to do now.'

'Try to think ahead,' said Derry, working to be positive. 'Maybe when you get back home you could start some kind of project? Take up something exciting?'

'Like shooting?' said Sally, with a smile. 'I do that already. I guess I could do some more. Thanks again. Really.' She paused, considering Derry. 'You know what? You wouldn't last a week in Vegas.'

≈

Amelia's session was another surprise. Derry expected a surly teen pretending she didn't care and was only having her cards read because it was less boring than all the other boring things. But Amelia settled down at the library table like she had her fortune told every week.

The cards came out nicely. Travel, adventure, love, though the possibility of conflict was always present. You had to expect disagreements if you were travelling with someone, Amelia observed. Derry saw in her determined jaw a reflection of Sally.

'Mom says you're cool,' said Amelia. She gave Derry a thoughtful look. She glanced around, leaned close, and in one unbroken stream out gushed an adoring description of a boy for whom she had fallen head over heels. She meant to meet up with him on her gap year so they could travel together. The problem was, she had led her parents to believe she would be going with a girlfriend rather than a boy who was a college dropout, a musician and black. Not that her Dad was racist, Amelia added hastily. Not at all. Only when it came to boyfriends.

On the question of the boyfriend's place in her future, the cards were notably vague, but Amelia didn't seem to mind. Surprisingly, she seemed especially pleased at Derry's picture of a successful professional future after much study and hard work. Perhaps Amelia was a more serious person than she herself knew.

'Hey, thanks,' she said, as Derry gathered up the cards.

'The seeker must remember the path revealed is but one of the infinite futures within their grasp,' said Derry in her best Madam Tulip voice. The phrase was a new mantra she was trying out, partly because it was true and partly because it seemed to equate neatly with a big notice saying *if you choose to build your whole life on what you hear in here, that's your lookout; but don't think you can sue me.* She had occasionally wondered whether she should get people to sign something but realised that was her mother talking.

~

To her surprise, Derry had enjoyed herself. Who cared that Jim Carson, the big shot producer, had basically strong-armed her into working for free. Sally and Amelia had felt more like friends than employers. Maybe that was the bonus you got when you weren't being paid. Derry wondered if she might be learning not to judge things before they happened.

She had put her cards back in her bag and was checking her makeup in her mirror, when the library door opened. Amelia stuck her head in. 'Jessie wants a go too,' she said. 'I knew she wanted to.' Amelia stood aside, ushering Jessica in and closing the door behind her.

'I don't mean to impose,' said Jessica. She stood, uncertain.

Derry smiled. 'Not at all. Take a seat.' She retrieved the cards from her bag and settled down.

Jessica seemed nervous, nothing like the efficient, capable PA Derry had seen up to now. But you never could tell. Some people jumped at the chance of peeking into their futures and into themselves, and joined in with enthusiasm. Others sidled in edgeways as if against their better judgement, pessimism struggling with an insatiable curiosity. Was Jessica one of those?

'Believe it or not,' Jessica said, pushing her hair back from her forehead, 'I've never actually done this. I don't know why I'm doing it now.'

'The important thing,' said Derry, 'is not to take anything too seriously or too literally. Sometimes you don't know what the cards are really saying until sometime afterward. Something in your life works out a certain way and you say, *aha!* Or maybe none of it makes sense. But there's nothing to be afraid of.'

The strength of Jessica's reaction was a surprise. 'I'm *not* afraid!' she insisted, as though she had been accused of something shameful. 'I don't believe in all this; I'll be honest with you. I thought maybe I could settle something in my mind. That's all.'

'You don't have to believe,' said Derry. 'The cards say whatever they say, and if they help you it doesn't much matter how.'

'I guess,' said Jessica with a shrug.

Derry shuffled, handed the deck to Jessica and indicated she should cut. A nine-card spread, plenty scope for ranging widely. She had the feeling this would be more a conversation than a fortune telling session. Sometimes what people needed to find were the questions not the answers.

'Is there anything special you'd like to ask?'

'I'm kind of really interested in work,' said Jessica.

Derry saw that was true. As soon as Jessica mentioned her career, she lost her nervousness. 'We all want to know will we succeed,' said Derry, smiling. 'How about we start there?'

Derry let her fingers run lightly over the backs of the downturned cards. She felt a flutter of excitement as she often did when the cards were dealt but had yet to be seen and under-stood. 'Success comes in many forms,' said Derry. 'What is your wish—money? Security? Fame?'

Jessica thought about that. 'No. None of those. Anyhow, those things go together, at least in my business.'

Derry wondered what she meant by *my business*. Who ever heard of a rich and famous PA?

'Respect,' said Jessica. 'All of us want that, right?'

Derry had to agree with her. Why else did actors struggle for a pittance, putting themselves on the line in a theatre night after night only to face unemployment after a month? Respect. Recognition. She guessed respect was the one thing Personal Assistants seldom got from their wealthy and suc-cessful employers.

'Why don't we take a look,' said Derry, turning the cards.

She saw nothing simple, nothing like a straightforward journey along some known career path. Instead, a series of sharp, jagged breaks; twists and turns; transformations. But yes, there it was—Jessica would indeed earn respect. Whether by the time that respect came she would still value it as she did now, the cards didn't say.

'Good,' said Jessica. 'Most people don't think they deserve respect at all. They'll take any crap and be grateful. I don't think they *should* be grateful.'

Derry made no comment. Instead, she gazed steadily at the cards now face up. She was puzzled by how disjointed the picture appeared, how little coherence was in the story. But sometimes the cards didn't cooperate. Or maybe life wasn't cooperating.

'I'm looking for change,' said Derry. 'It sounds to me like you see a change coming or you want a change.'

'Damn right!' said Jessica. She sat back in her seat. 'There's a big … decision coming for me.' She hesitated as if wondering how much to say. 'A couple of weeks ago, I realised the time had come.' She stopped there, as though she had explained already. 'To decide,' she added at last.

'This decision,' said Derry. 'Did you make it? Or is it still to be made?'

'It's not mine. Not my decision. Somebody else.'

'So you're waiting for them to decide?'

'Yes.'

'Do you want to say what they're deciding? You don't have to.'

'No. I can't say.'

'Business or personal, can you say that?'

Jessica hesitated. 'It's … you know. Like, a guy.'

Well, well, thought Derry. *Romance.* Not one card in the spread had so much as hinted at love. But hadn't Carson teased Jessica about going to Edinburgh to meet a boyfriend?

'You think the person will decide soon?' asked Derry.

'Yes. Soon.' Jessica's gaze was fixed on the cards. 'But what I need to know … what I have to *decide*, is whether to, like, just out and tell him what I want. That's it,' she added, as if she only now understood her dilemma. 'Will I make it worse or will I make it better? If I … I guess I'm saying … if I say *or else*. You know—if I tell him what I'll do if he doesn't.'

In her mind Derry finished Jessica's half-statement. '. . . if he doesn't *do what I want.*'

'Jessica,' said Derry. 'You said yourself you didn't believe in the cards, that you were trying to make up your own mind. Whatever the cards say, the decision is yours, you know that.'

'Sure,' said Jessica.

'Why don't we cut the cards again,' said Derry. 'A simple cut and let them say yes or no.'

'Sure. Okay.'

A thought occurred to Derry. She knew she was right. 'This is about respect too.'

Jessica's eyes met hers. She nodded, slowly, in absolute agreement, her face profoundly serious.

Derry shuffled the deck. Jessica cut. Derry turned the half deck to expose the last card.

Queen of Clubs. Respect. 'It's yours, if you earn it,' said Derry.

Jessica breathed a sigh. Relief? Perhaps the feeling that any decision is better than the agony of inaction.

'I'll do it,' said Jessica. 'I'm gonna do it.' She stared at the upturned card as though the Queen of Clubs, having shown herself, would now reveal everything.

'This ultimatum …' began Derry. She wasn't sure how to put the question.

'I know what you're gonna say,' said Jessica quickly. 'Do I mean it. If I'm gonna say *or else*, what if he calls my bluff? Well, it's not a bluff. I do mean it. I've thought that through.'

Something about the determined set of Jessica's mouth told Derry she had indeed thought it through, that she would do what she said. 'One more thing,' continued Jessica. 'I might need to go somewhere. I don't know whether before or after.'

She didn't say before or after what, but Derry guessed she meant before or after she delivered her ultimatum. Derry shuffled the pack. Once more, she handed the deck to Jessica to cut.

Ace of Clubs. 'Perhaps you have some legal business?' said Derry carefully, 'Could that be why you need to be somewhere? Maybe something official?'

Jessica nodded. 'Sort of. Yeah. I'd have to take time off. But I don't know; should I plan to go or not?'

Many times Derry had been asked the direct question—should I or shouldn't I. Will I do a thing or not to do it. Like the person was saying, *tell me, so it's not my responsibility.*

'We could leave it to chance,' said Derry. 'But the decision belongs to you, not the cards. The cards can't tell you what's right or wrong. They can only tell you how you feel.' She shuffled and cut. 'Think of what you mean to do. Imagine yourself doing it.'

Jessica closed her eyes and nodded.

'A black card means you want to do this thing. A red card means you don't.'

She offered the deck to Jessica who opened her eyes, hesitated and cut.

Queen of Hearts. Red. 'No!' said Jessica. ' I ...' She stopped. 'I want to go.'

'Then go,' said Derry.

For a moment, they sat in silence. Derry could see the relief take hold of Jessica, smoothing out the lines of her face. A decision had been made. Or perhaps a decision long since made had been recognised and accepted.

'Thanks,' said Jessica. 'I mean that.' She stood. 'Really, I'm grateful.' She held out her hand to be shaken as if she were ending a business meeting. So Derry shook it.

Jessica left, pulling the door closed behind her. Derry sat, the cards still on the table, the Queen of Hearts sitting redly mute. If the Queen knew she had just revealed to someone the truth of their own desires, she showed no sign.

Why Derry remained at the table she didn't know; she should have gotten up, picked up her bag and followed Jessica. But she didn't. She felt the peculiar exhaustion that sometimes overcame her after a session, like she had been drained of whatever substance made action possible. Instead, she found her gaze lingering on the Queen.

Ever since she was a little girl Derry had been intrigued by the face cards—the king, queen, and knave—the way the figures were doubled so they looked the same whichever way up you held the card. The most impressive cards seemed to join the two halves of the person in such an ingenious way that the trick seemed natural. The brain objected, but the eye stayed transfixed, unable to help itself.

Such was the effect on Derry now as she idly contemplated the double Queen in her robes of red, blue, gold and black, halves joined cleverly at the waist. Then, slowly, almost imperceptibly, right before Derry's eyes, that beguiling symmetry began to unravel.

The colours, once neatly confined by clever curves to the panels, sleeves and bodice of the Queen's rich robes, spread like a creeping stain. The halves of the image were still joined at the waist, but now they threatened to uncouple at any moment, tearing the woman in two.

As the vivid inks of the Queen's robes flowed outwards, disappearing past the square boundaries of the card, Derry wasn't in the least distressed. She was tired, that was all. Too much concentration. Too much awareness. But as she watched, she felt the first stirrings of alarm. The Queen's face was stretching and distorting, two tilted heads smearing themselves over the glossy surface as in a misshapen mirror. Now the figure was barely recognisable as a Queen, hardly as a woman. As the colours spread like oil on water, she seemed no longer even human.

10

'Lucky chance,' said Rab, gunning the Land Rover out of the castle drive and speeding through the village. 'Handy I was on my way back just at the right time.'

On some other occasion, Derry might have wondered whether that coincidence was a coincidence at all. But though grateful to Rab for the ride, her mind was still in that strange, distracted space in which she often found herself after telling fortunes. All she could think to say was, 'Yes. Lucky.'

'I suppose the good thing about filming this time of year is you can't start too early,' continued Rab. 'You'll be filming tomorrow though, I'd say. The forecast is good. Maybe rain on Sunday. Though maybe not.'

He was making conversation. Derry felt obliged to play her part and be polite. She almost responded by explaining how bad weather could be a blessing for actors, in fact a goldmine, since most people got paid by the day. But wouldn't that sound mercenary, even venal, reflecting badly on the inner nature of the acting fraternity? As Rab's charming accent and velvety voice drifted through Derry's consciousness, she found herself keen that her own inner nature should put on its most acceptable face. Why, neither her inner nature nor her conscious mind cared to enquire.

The Land Rover swung off the main road and motored up the drive to park in the darkness opposite the Country House Hotel. They stopped no more than fifteen yards from the entrance, but the distance might have been the length of a football field so reluctant did Derry feel to open her door and step out.

'Well, here we are,' said Rab. He cleared his throat as though about to say something else, but instead lapsed into silence.

Was Derry's breathing growing louder? Or were her ears suddenly more sensitive? She felt like every breath she took was plainly audible however hard she tried to be quiet. And still she didn't move.

Her gaze was fixed on the hotel, but in the corner of her vision she sensed Rab lean towards her. Was he going to reach across to open the passenger door? Or something else? If *something else,* Derry hadn't quite worked out whether she liked the idea or not. All the same, she held her breath.

Oho!' said Rab, following up with an expletive. Derry opened her eyes. She hadn't remembered closing them, but they were wide open now. Headlights bathed the interior of the Land Rover in white light. Rab was sitting bolt upright, his hands clenched on the steering wheel, his expression triumphant. Out from around the side of the hotel emerged a battered, white van. As it passed through the beam of their own headlights, Derry saw the driver was staring at them, frowning. Rab was staring back. He pointed a finger at the driver, like he was aiming a gun. *'I'll have him yet,'* he said through gritted teeth.

The van slid away down the drive. Rab sighed and shook his head. 'Duncan Crabbie, our local poacher. Harmless, but he never gives up. The things that go on around here you would not believe.'

'I guess,' agreed Derry. 'I'd better go in. Early night.'

'Oh. Yes. Of course. Sorry.'

Derry opened the door. 'Thanks so much. Nice seeing you again.'

'Yes. Nice. Thank you,' said Rab vaguely, as if it were Derry who had driven him home and not the other way round.

Derry walked to the hotel entrance, aware of her feet crunching on the gravel. The door was unlocked. She pushed the handle and stepped inside. She heard the Land Rover pull away, but she didn't turn and wave. By the time she reconsidered, Rab was gone.

The hotel was eerily quiet. Perhaps the other residents were at the pub in the village or had decided on an early night. Derry was thankful not to have to make small talk. Once in her room, she threw off her coat and dumped her bag on the bed. She put her phone on the dressing table and wondered about checking her email, but decided against. She could think of nothing else to do but fill the kettle.

Her thoughts turned to tomorrow. In a way, having to go to the castle and tell fortunes had been a useful distraction, giving her no time to worry about Hamilton and her next scene. Would there be more histrionics? If he wanted a fight he could have one; she wasn't going to take abuse from anybody. The thought of doing the unthinkable, walking away from a set, from a job, had an instant and unexpected effect. Derry's mood lightened, and she found herself smiling. Was that freedom?

But whatever happened tomorrow, she would have to acquit herself well. Hamilton would pounce on any sign of weakness. And he might want her to throw the bones again. The lightness Derry had felt since she had resolved to make her stand vanished in an instant. There, sitting on the table where she had left it was the squat leather bag. Inside were those bones. Derry felt her skin creep and her palms sweat.

'Fool,' she said out loud. She knew that calling herself names was bad, signifying a lack of self-esteem, and she should probably counter that by complimenting herself on some achievement she couldn't think of at the moment. On the other hand, perhaps she *was* a fool and should be congratulating herself on a commendable spirit of objectivity.

She knew what she had to do, and there was no way out of it. She had to take the bag, loosen the drawstring and pour the bones onto the table. Then she had to pick the bones up and throw them. Otherwise, tomorrow, when she needed all the courage she could get to deal with Hamilton, she might freeze. She might be incapable of opening the bag, terrified of what could happen when she set free those sinister little objects.

The kettle boiled noisily. Derry reached for the little plastic box in which she kept a few sachets of borage tea. She dropped a sachet into a cup and poured the hot water. She watched the clear liquid turn honey-yellow as she prodded it with a spoon. The aroma was pleasing, a little sour perhaps, a hint of cucumber. *Borage for Courage* the old saying went.

Derry sipped and wasn't at all surprised when she found herself smiling. She stepped to the table by the window and sat. She took up the bag, squeezing a little as though to make sure its contents hadn't somehow escaped to hide in ambush.

She told herself not to be ridiculous. All her life she had experienced strange happenings—whether visions or imagination, who could say? Sometimes they had meaning. Other times they signified nothing at all, or the message was so obscure she imagined the other realm, if that's what it was, telling itself jokes in extinct languages and snickering.

Derry loosened the string and upturned the pouch. Out tumbled the bones to lie on the table where they fell. They sat mutely, passive as the bones of dead creatures should be. Derry told herself to relax, and she did indeed feel relaxed. Perhaps it was the borage, or maybe the knowledge that never yet had her visions harmed her in any way. She took another sip of tea, swept up the bones and threw. They scattered, tumbled and came to rest.

Nothing.

Derry smiled. Sometimes, nothing was good. She gathered up the bones and threw once more. She waited. Again, nothing out of the ordinary. Just bones lying where they fell. She collected them up and dropped them one by one back in the bag. She cradled the pouch in her hand. That thing that had happened before—the buzzing, disgusting swarm that still made her shiver to remember—must have been the stress of her work. Every actor knows how performance nerves can have an unhinging effect.

Derry stood, meaning to leave the bag on the dressing table so she wouldn't forget to take it with her next morning. She had taken only two steps when she stopped, the leather pouch in her hand. She opened the wardrobe door, knowing what she was doing was foolish. She put the bag carefully inside, placing it on one of the little shelves meant for gloves or shoes. She closed the door with a clunk.

She turned the key.

11

One moment the camera drone hovered motionless over the battlefield, the next it swept down the lines of red-coated soldiers like a weird bird of prey quartering the field. Any moment you expected it to plunge down for the kill. Instead the little machine darted off, giving the uncomfortable impression it knew exactly what it was doing.

Derry was still in gypsy costume, wearing her coat against the chill air. Her second scene had been shot that morning and had gone well, as if the unpleasantness of the previous day had never happened. The bones hadn't been called for, though she was confident she'd have had no difficulty. Now she was basking in that peculiarly relaxed feeling every actor has when the next scene is too far away to worry about.

The knot of spectators included cast members, locals and costumed extras waiting to be called for their moment of fame. The morning's battle scene had attracted more than the usual compliment of hangers-on. Lunchtime was still twenty minutes away and, like on any movie set, time was a tedious void and any distraction welcome. Derry watched as the redcoats levelled their muskets at the line of sword-waving Highlanders and the drone swooped to capture their faces. 'That is so cool,' she said. 'First time I've seen a camera drone on location.'

'Saves a fortune,' said Jessica. 'No need for camera cars or helicopters. A lot safer too. Filming is dangerous enough.'

Derry was standing with Jessica and Carson in the lee of Carson's silver SUV, one of the few vehicles privileged to park in the field. Carson was being friendly, introducing Derry to the male and female leads, neither of whom Derry had met before. Darian was a Glasgow heavy-rock singer whose band was the unlikely winner of a TV talent show. Carla Francini was another Glaswegian—good-looking, with curling black hair and big brown eyes, who held her head poised like she was always on stage. This was, Derry knew, her first lead part, and she seemed acutely aware of the crowd.

On the battlefield, a ragged cheer broke out as the Highlanders charged the Redcoats, waving their swords and shields impressively. The spectators perked up, but only for a moment. Someone with a megaphone issued a tinny order that wafted towards the spectators on the breeze. The running men wavered and stopped, to stand awkwardly waiting to be told what to do next. A rehearsal. Derry could see Hamilton waving his arms and pointing. Even at that distance you could see he was blaming somebody for something.

Jessica looked at her watch. 'All he's doing is churning up the field. Is he going to get through this before dark?'

Carson shrugged. He turned to the actors, smiling. 'You guys think you've got a hard job? Try watching your money go up in smoke while auteurs take their shot at an Oscar. Jeez, all we ask for is a beginning, a middle and an end. How can it be that hard?'

Derry felt her phone vibrate in her skirt pocket. She had retrieved it after her scene but still tactfully kept it on silent. She checked the display. Unknown number. She stepped away from the group around Carson.

'Miss O'Donnell, Derry, it's Alex here. Alex Dunbar.'

'Hi,' said Derry. She walked away to stand out of earshot of the rest.

'I apologise for phoning you like this, but I didn't want to drive down and churn up the place more than it is already. I'm by the gateway, top of the field, you'll see me if you look. Black SUV.'

And yes, there by the gate, but inside the barrier rather than out on the road, was a black Range Rover. Its lights flashed rapidly, once, twice, three times.

Derry had that uncomfortable feeling you get when you answer your phone to see the caller standing the other side of the store waving and smiling, looking straight at you. You instinctively wave and smile back but somehow feel like you've been caught shoplifting.

'I was wondering if you'd like a tour of the castle. When you're free. Perhaps tomorrow afternoon if you're not filming?'

Derry hesitated. A call from Alex Dunbar was the last thing she'd expected. What were you supposed to feel when you were phoned by a castle-owning millionaire? Flattered? Harassed? These things were so much easier when all the male had was charm and a cool haircut.

But Alex Dunbar was undoubtedly good-looking in a smooth sort of way and was pleasant too, even charming. From somewhere in the back of Derry's brain a voice suggested that perhaps being stupendously rich and successful wasn't his fault. After all, accidents do happen.

Another thought occurred to her—Dunbar might have phoned rather than asking in person to make it easier for her to refuse. *Points for sensitivity.*

'Yes,' said Derry. 'Thank you, I'd like that. Sounds interesting.'

'Excellent,' said Dunbar. 'How about I send someone to the hotel to pick you up around two p.m. tomorrow?'

'Great, thanks.'

'If you'd like, and if the weather's good, we could take a trip in the chopper. The scenery is truly magnificent.'

'Well—'

'You don't have to decide now. See what you feel like.'

The call ended. Derry stood staring at her phone, uncomfortably aware of a tingle of excitement before remembering she was probably still being watched. She briefly considered whistling in an unconcerned kind of way, before dismissing the idea on the grounds that whistling wasn't made for long-range impact. A casual stroll back to Carson's SUV seemed the plainest show of indifference available on the spur of the moment. But with her back safely turned, she allowed herself the most discrete of smiles.

As Derry passed the knot of crew vehicles and onlookers by the boundary of the field, someone shouted her name. She turned automatically, before realising the name wasn't hers. Or it was and it wasn't.

'Madam Tulip! Hey, Tulip!'

~

Mostly, actors are in love with cameras. The merest glimpse of a two thousand dollar Nikon or a chunky TV lens loudly proclaiming *Media*, and actors instantly smile, tilt their heads and twinkle their eyes as though already on the red carpet at Cannes. They might follow up with one or two careless tosses of their perfectly arranged hair.

But Derry felt no urge to smile or flash her teeth. The camera was on the shoulder of a man pushing his way through the throng, closely followed by a hard-faced woman in a parka, holding a microphone. In their wake strode Torquil, his fedora at a jaunty angle, a yellow scarf thrown carelessly around his neck, incongruous over his green wax jacket.

'Madam Tulip!'

When someone hears their name called in a crowd they usually react with an enquiring smile. Or if not, at least raised eyebrows and a little pucker of puzzlement. Was that why Torquil had called out? A reaction for the camera? The woman thrust her microphone into Derry's face. The cameraman took a pace back but kept filming.

'Madam Tulip—'

'O'Donnell, Derry O'Donnell.'

'Are you denying you are Madam Tulip the psychic?'

'Well no, I—'

'I'm from Crime News—your exploits in London, finding a murdered man for the police, have led to accusations of fraud. Comment please?'

Derry knew the camera was rolling. She also knew the one thing guaranteed to make anyone look guilty is when their eyes flick from left to right and back again, and they lick their lips. But knowing didn't help. Derry licked her lips. Her eyes flicked left and right, only to reveal that the crowd now pressing around her had lost all interest in Highlanders and Redcoats.

'I put it to you again, *Madam Tulip*, the police are accused of allowing themselves be duped by a fraud. Are you a fraud? If you aren't a fraud, why are you hiding?'

'I'm not—'

'You and an associate were involved in a violent incident connected with Russian organised crime. A cynical publicity stunt putting lives at risk—do you deny that?'

Fraud. Cynical. Criminal—until now, only words read in a newspaper or heard on the TV. Never in her life had Derry experienced anything like the shock, the creeping nausea, the sickening numbness of hearing those words flung at her.

'No! This is crazy!'

Derry turned away, forcing a passage through the throng of onlookers, pursued by the reporter and cameraman as though being chased by snapping dogs. She almost broke into a run, but the discipline bred by years of acting saved her. Instead, she strode fast up the sloping field, her head held high and her face without expression. The crowd followed at a trot. Camera phones flashed, and Derry knew that within minutes her humiliation would be all over the internet—fake gypsy psychic in league with Russian gangsters, caught hiding on a film set in Scotland.

If she could reach the base camp, perhaps she could take shelter with the wardrobe people or Ally the props man, closing the door against the mob and that pursuing lens. Her eyes were swimming. She could hardly see where she was going. She knew she should turn around and face her pursuers, shout at them, demand to know why were they doing this. But she didn't.

'Madam Tulip! Comment, please!' The woman with the microphone was jogging beside her, out of breath but relentless.

And there, right in Derry's path, an SUV. Carson's. It had swung around the crowd and now stood broadside on,

passenger door open, Jessica in the driving seat waving frantically. 'Get in! In!'

Derry threw herself into the seat, slamming the door
shut.

'I guess *where to* don't much matter?' said Jessica, revving
the engine and nosing her way past the onlookers for a clear
run up the field. Derry couldn't speak. Her feeble effort to say
thanks fell apart, the words coming out as a disjointed string
of gasps.

'I'll try not to run anybody over,' said Jessica. 'I'd hate to
make that woman's career.'

Only then did Derry see that the cameraman was trotting
alongside, his lens only feet from her face. As Jessica built up
speed, swinging wide towards the field wall and an area clear
of people, he fell back. But Derry knew he had the shot he
wanted. *The accused flees. Guilty!*

As the SUV reached the gate to the roadway, Derry looked
back. Below, the crowd hadn't yet dispersed. Surrounded by
her audience, the reporter was interviewing someone. And
now Derry saw who. In front of the reporter and her outstretched microphone, his yellow scarf unmistakable, stood
Torquil.

~

Jessica pulled the SUV into the quarry base camp, nodding at the security men as they waved her in. She threaded
her way between the trailers to park in a reserved space in
sight of a marquee set up as a makeshift eatery. Derry tried to
master her racing heart, working to stop her ragged breathing

giving away how near she had come to tears. All she felt now was blind fury.

'You tell Carson, don't ever let Torquil into my sight again!' She worked to keep her tone measured, enunciating her words with precision. 'Will you tell him that? And while you're there, tell Mr. Carson he knows where he can shove his film.'

'You never had that stuff happen before?'

No, Derry had never experienced anything remotely like that appalling ambush, that vicious personal attack. Those lies.

'A shock, I guess,' said Jessica. 'Mr. Carson saw what was happening right away. He said to go get you. He said you didn't look like you were much enjoying the publicity. He said to say you've a lot to learn.' She shrugged. 'He means it nice.'

Derry was so surprised, she forgot to be angry.

'I thought—'

'No, not Mr. Carson's idea,' said Jessica. 'He doesn't care about local publicity; he leaves that to the production company.'

'And that's Torquil's job?'

'Sure. We fund the movies; other people make them. They get the local rights; we get the rest of the world. Mr. Carson scores mainly in Latin America and Asia. Hey, how about that? You're gonna be famous in Bogota; a star in Manila.' She smiled, and Derry couldn't help smiling back. Jessica was trying to cheer her up, helping her put things in perspective. Good to know Carson wasn't behind what happened.

'So Mr. Carson's business won't much suffer when I murder Torquil?'

Jessica laughed. 'Heck, no. Murder away.'

'Will they harass Bruce? My friend, Bruce Adams.'

'The hunky one?'

'Returned Canadian Patriot.'

'He looks like he can take care of himself. But I'll call Mr. Carson, if you like. I'll ask him to tell Torquil to lay off.'

'If you call, tell him I meant what I said. I'm supposed to do a scene this afternoon. I won't be doing it unless Torquil is out of my face. Sorry, but that's it.' Derry paused. She knew she might have ended her career right there. Walking out on a production, even threatening to walk out, was the ultimate professional crime. She sighed. 'Nothing makes any sense.'

'Derry,' said Jessica, her tone patient, as if she were explaining to a child. 'This is showbusiness. Nothing makes sense. Unless you ask the right questions.' She let her words sink in. 'I promise, I'll ask Mr. Carson to warn them off. Why don't you go sit for a few minutes until you feel better. It's nearly lunch, you could get in line before the rush. I'm sorry I have to go, I've stuff to do. But hey, you already know what.' She gave Derry a conspiratorial grin. '*Respect*, right?'

For a moment, Derry didn't know what Jessica meant. Then she remembered—Jessica had resolved to tell her boyfriend something. Give him an ultimatum. 'Good luck,' said Derry. But Jessica didn't look like she needed luck. She seemed more excited than nervous. Derry wondered if the boyfriend knew what he was getting into.

'Thanks,' said Jessica.

Derry stepped down from the SUV. She glanced around anxiously, but all she saw was a small group of men, tool belts hanging around their waists, crew gathering to be first in the lunch queue when the hatches opened on the serving trailer.

The idea of lunch was a good one. Derry pulled her phone out of her pocket and checked the time—a few minutes before twelve. She took a place at one of the vacant trestle tables under the marquee to wait, acknowledging friendly nods from the carpenters, old hands who knew not to bother cast members uninvited.

Derry had just sat down when her phone rang.

'Rab here. The factor chappie.'

'Hi, Rab.'

'First, I'd like to say I'm sorry about last night.' Rab sounded genuinely contrite, as though he had taken some terrible liberty. Unfortunately, Derry couldn't remember any.

'I was perhaps a little vulgar—what I said when I saw that Duncan Crabbie.'

'I'm sorry?'

'The fellow in the van. For a minute I forgot my language.'

Derry was startled and charmed all at once by this pretty confession. Rab was a thoroughgoing outdoorsy, manly man; and he was apologising like it was eighteen-ninety and he had shockingly referred to ankles in female company. 'Oh, don't you worry about that,' said Derry. 'I didn't blush for more than, like, two hours.'

Rab forged on. 'I wondered, seeing as how tomorrow is Sunday, if you might like to come up the hills and do a little sightseeing. It's spectacular I promise you. Would you be free in the afternoon at all?'

'Oh, I'm sorry, Rab. I'm supposed to be … I've been asked to tour the castle. I've said I would. I don't think I can—'

'Och, If you've made arrangements, of course. Perhaps some other time. When you're free.'

'Yes, thanks. I'd like that.'

'Fine. Good. Well. Bye now.'

He cut the call. Derry checked it was disconnected, as though the phone might eavesdrop on her thoughts. She put the handset on the table and stared at the treacherous instrument. What was the point of being the daughter of a seventh son of a seventh son if your phone could make a fool of you any time it chose? Half an hour ago she had been pleased to be invited by a handsome millionaire to tour his castle and didn't protest when helicopters were laid metaphorically at her feet. And now here she was, wondering if she weren't missing out on a handsome non-millionaire with a voice that gave her goose bumps. In her head she heard Bella's voice, proclaiming her a shamefully fickle hussy and laughing as she welcomed her to the club.

A gentle breeze wafted through the marquee, making the canvas ripple and bringing with it an appetising smell of cooking. Derry suddenly felt hungry. Between her and the kitchen trailer a knot of people were already gathering. Had they witnessed her humiliation down on the field? Derry realised with a burning sense of injustice that she felt ashamed when she had nothing to be ashamed about. She told herself to ignore the curious glances. But what if the obnoxious Torquil showed up, as well he might?

The answer came as if borne on a celestial shaft of light. Where from, who knew? Whatever the source of that blissful inspiration, the gist was clear. What Derry needed to hand in case Torquil came to gloat was a bowl, preferably a *large* bowl, of thick, greasy soup.

12

'In my knickers!' said Richard, waving his dinner menu. 'Through the main street of the village!' The cast and crew assembled for Saturday evening dinner in the Country House Hotel clucked their disapproval and shook their heads, as if to say that with this production what could anyone expect.

A scene was to be shot at the old bridge. Wardrobe had sent Costume B to the new location to save time, while Richard had been rushed by car to the rendezvous, having been relieved of Costume A. Unfortunately, the car was forced to wait for a marching pipe band to pass, and the half-dressed actor found himself surrounded by a crowd of gawping, grinning spectators, noses pressed against the car windows.

At least, Derry reflected, her own afternoon scene had gone smoothly. The action called for Darian, ambling along the seashore in a vaguely heroic way, to come by chance upon the Gypsy Fortune-Teller. She was crouched by a fire of driftwood, which to Hamilton's fury kept going out in the stiff breeze when it wasn't billowing smoke and mortifying the sound man by making him cough. Derry had acquitted herself well, staying relaxed as Hamilton ranted at a military jet. In the middle of a take, the plane skimmed the waves of the bay at shocking speeds before climbing at a dizzying angle and swooping away, as though the pilot's mission had been to ruin whatever shooting schedule the director had left.

'I really wanted to try haggis,' said Bruce, frowning over his menu. 'I mean, this is Scotland, right?'

'Only tourists eat haggis,' said Richard darkly. 'It's a joke once pulled on the English. Scottish cuisine shows much evidence of humour. On the other hand ...' He coughed loudly and waved his menu in the air, demanding the attention of the room. 'Is it only me who thinks the animal kingdom boasts species other than deer and salmon? Has a giant meteor collided with the planet wiping out chicken, pig and cow? Has even the humble lasagna tree been purged from the face of the earth, leaving the last of its kind scorched and burning on the lonely heath?'

'And it says *wild*,' said a bearded and beer-bellied electrician from England, normally a cheerful man. 'That salmon is no more wild than my missus.'

A murmur of discontent spread around the room. Actors and technicians, so often mutually uncomprehending, were for once united. A tattooed, muscular man whom Derry recognised as a Grip spoke out boldly. 'If I see another plate of venison, no matter how much they try to disguise it in bloody awful fruit sauce, I swear I'll tip it into that fool's sporran.'

Rebellion and the heady taste of revolution was in the air. Menus were waving like pitchforks. No burning brands or guillotines were yet to be seen, but Moira McKenzie, her serving napkin over her arm, beat a sprightly retreat to stand with her back against the wall, clasping her notebook to her bosom.

The Duke of Cumberland began the chant. 'Real food!' he intoned, banging the handle of his knife on the table. The chorus was taken up by one diner after another, in rhythm, slowly and at first restrained, but gathering force. 'Real food!'

Right then, Derry's phone rang.

'Miss O'Donnell—Derry. Alex here.'

'Oh, hi.'

'I'm so sorry to call this late. I've only just learned I've had to change my plans. I must be away tomorrow for a time. I won't be able to offer you that tour of the castle we arranged. I truly am sorry.'

'Can you hold a moment?' said Derry. She could hardly hear, so loud were the raised voices. She slipped by Moira McKenzie to stand in the hall outside, pulling the door shut behind her.

Under the stairs, at a little alcove at an old wooden counter, sat a middle-aged, competent-looking woman Derry didn't recognise. She had her phone to her ear and was throwing anxious glances at the dining-room door. Derry nodded apologetically and took refuge down the hall by the main entrance.

'Sorry, please go on.'

'Perhaps when I get back, we could make another arrangement,' continued Alex. 'I hope you'll forgive me.'

'Of course,' said Derry.

'I thought perhaps you might be interested in something else tomorrow afternoon. Sally means to do some target practice on the estate range; it's where we train shooting parties before they go stalking. I wonder if you might not enjoy having a go. Or perhaps your friend … Bruce, is it?'

'Yes,' said Derry. 'I'm not really … I've never done that kind of thing, but Bruce might like it. I'll ask him, shall I?'

'Do that. You'd enjoy it, I'm sure. Just firing at targets. Nothing too red-blooded. Sally says two thirty would suit. Is that alright with you? I can arrange transport if you'd like.'

'No, thank you. We'll be able to make our own way. I'll call Sally to confirm, shall I? Or Jessica? I have her number.'

'No need,' said Alex. 'Just turn up. Wear something comfortable. And I'm sorry about the change of plan.'

'No, not at all,' said Derry. 'Thanks for the offer.'

As she hung up, the Laird emerged from a stairway Derry guessed led down to the basement kitchen. The woman at the desk folded her arms and glared but said nothing. Derry waited while the Laird opened the dining-room door. Somebody inside was shouting, 'Nobody told us cheese was rationed in Scotland!' The Laird closed the door, muting the uproar.

'My husband,' said the woman at the desk.

'Ah,' said Derry, unsure what the protocol was when discussing husbands trying to put down riots among guests.

'He's an ass,' said the Laird's wife. 'Sorry, you're American, aren't you—I meant *donkey*, not, you know, *arse*. He's that too of course.' She smiled a friendly smile. 'I'm Jen, Come and have a little drink dear, until it's all over and the crows are circling the battlefield.'

$\sim$

Only Derry and Bruce remained in the dining room by the time dinner finally arrived under the close supervision of Jen herself. The others had decamped to the pub, while the Laird had retreated to the basement in a sulk.

Derry had the salmon, farmed in Norway as Jen candidly admitted. 'I keep taking *wild* off the menu and he keeps putting it back on. Really, he's not trying to mislead anybody—I think he's just nostalgic for when the rivers around here actually *had* salmon. About forty years ago, I think. George is such a romantic.' Through wide reading of the classics and real-life observation, Derry knew that when a wife called her husband romantic, the statement was normally accompanied by a faraway look and secret smile calculated to irritate the single. But Jen was not in the business of faraway looks. When she said *romantic*, she rolled her eyes as if to say *romantic* as in *moronic*.

Satisfied that her little confidences had been appreciated, Jen left them unsupervised with the cheese. She even offered a carafe of wine. Derry was already light-headed from the glass she had accepted in the little office behind the stairs, but Bruce, surprisingly, accepted.

'Just one,' he said. 'I know it's bad before the wrap, but you know what? I'm gonna. Did you ever feel you were just too … I don't know … too much the good sailor?'

Derry had to confess she had never felt that.

'Don't you ever want to … fly?' His face wore a dreamy look Derry hadn't seen before.

'Maybe it's just because we're near the end of the job,' suggested Derry. 'How many more scenes do you have?'

'Only four, I think. My next one is okay—that was supposed to be tomorrow, but they've put it off so they can spend more time with Darian and Carla.'

'I heard they're having problems,' said Derry. Both leads were known to be struggling with their roles.

'That's what they get for hiring amateurs,' said Bruce. 'They just walk in, and they've never even done a class.'

True, the business was filling up with untrained wannabees who thought celebrity was its own reward, a mistake no real actor would ever make. Little statuettes, yes. Cash, certainly. But celebrity for its own sake was downright vulgar. In fact, celebrity was no more than acting for free and as such to be roundly condemned.

'I'm not looking forward to the last scene,' said Bruce. 'Hamilton's given me these terrible lines. I don't know how I'm gonna be able to learn them in time.'

Derry thought it wisest to change the subject. The time was nearly nine o'clock, and the subject of lines, directors and scripts could rarely be dealt with in less than two hours. 'Do you like shooting? Rifles, that is.'

'Uh, it's not exactly—'

'Just recreational,' added Derry, quickly. Asking a onetime US Navy SEAL if he liked shooting wasn't just dumb, it risked being off-the-scale crass.

'Alex—Mr. Dunbar—said Sally was going shooting on the estate practice range tomorrow afternoon and would we like a go. I said I'd ask you.'

'Sally?'

'Mrs. Carson. She's from Nevada. I like her. Do you go hunting?'

Bruce hesitated. 'Uh … You mean like … animals?'

'Of course I meant—should I change the subject now?'

Bruce laughed. 'No, honest.' He thought for a moment. 'I … don't really like killing animals. Nothing against the folks that do. Just not for me.'

Derry wished now she'd never brought up the subject of shooting. Or killing. How unthinking could she be?

'It's cool, hon. Honest,' said Bruce, like he had read her mind.

Bruce sipped his wine, his attention seemingly taken by a painting on the wall—a magnificent deer with huge antlers, posing proudly against a lonely crag. As if the stag had given him the answer he was looking for, Bruce seemed to come to a decision.

'You do a job that needs doing,' he said. 'You look out for your shipmates; try to get everyone out in one piece. You accept that's not always gonna happen. But then you have to put the whole thing in a box and … close the lid. Know what I mean?'

He ended on a note that reminded Derry of a young child— Bruce as a six-year-old boy, asking for approval, unsure about what he'd done.

'I didn't mean to pry.'

Bruce spoke quietly. 'I gotta tell you, I was having some trouble keeping that lid closed. You open it up, leads to all kindsa trouble. But, you know, if you do close that box and turn the key, that's not too good either. You get so you don't feel anything for anybody.'

Derry was almost afraid to breathe in case she disturbed his train of thought. But Bruce had said all he was going to say.

'Acting,' said Derry. 'It's about empathy, right? Feeling.'

Bruce nodded.

'Acting, you can open the box. But then, after the show, you get to close it again.'

Bruce thought about that. Again, he nodded.

They sat in silence. Bruce refilled their glasses. They raised their drinks and clinked.

'To opening the box.'

≈

Derry knew it was a dream even while it was happening. She was asleep in her hotel room, so it had to be a dream. And as in so many dreams, it began with puzzling happenings she accepted without question as normal.

She was walking along a rough stony track hemmed in by mountains. In the darkening sky, clouds tumbled and a gusty fretful wind tugged at her clothes. In her dream she remarked to herself how strange it was that leaves blew around her feet, but no trees were to be seen anywhere on the bleak hillside.

Oddly, though she saw no trees, she did see birds circling high in the sky. In her dream she wondered about that, until she observed a tall grey rock face, unnaturally angular, scoured clean by the gusts slicing down the valley. Of course, that was where the birds must nest.

Hearing raucous cries, some kind of commotion overhead, Derry looked up. As she did, a startling thing happened. One of the birds, big and black, changed its circling course and plummeted through the air. Had it been shot? Derry had heard no sound. But as it fell it spread its wings and like a streamlined black dart spinning slowly on its axis plunged straight at her.

Instinctively she ducked. The bird missed, checked its fall and climbed away. In her dream, Derry laughed at the creature's foolishness. Was it playing a game, almost colliding with her like that?

Now the bird was a shrinking speck almost lost against the darkness of the clouds as it climbed before rolling in an acrobatic turn of breathtaking skill. Down it came again, and Derry saw the bird was no longer alone. Another, as sleek and agile as the first, was streaking down in formation, the two like a salvo of sentient and malevolent missiles racing for her head.

Panic-stricken, Derry ducked, crouching, her arms shielding her skull, aware of her hair loose and blowing in the wind, a glorious target for outstretched claws, anchors for the swinging beaks that would peck out her eyes. She waved and waved but to no avail as more and more birds joined the mob and in a whirling, rolling ball plunged from the sky. Now Derry was running, running, but escape from the raking claws was impossible. Blinded by a stream of blood pouring from her scalp, she stumbled, recovering her balance just as something solid, moving at colossal speed in absolute silence, slammed into the back of her skull.

13

The helicopter lifted off from somewhere behind the trees, roaring a curving course over their heads away to the south-east. *Dunbar on his urgent business*, thought Derry. She and Bruce were walking along the tree-lined path from the castle to the field where would-be deer stalkers could practice their shooting skills with least risk to humanity. *Crack* went a rifle, the sound echoing eerily off the hillside.

'Don't worry,' said Bruce cheerily. 'If you hear the shot, it's already missed you.'

'I'd rather you were doing this,' said Derry. Bruce had politely declined the offer of an afternoon's target shooting, explaining that the crew with the camera drones were going to let him have a go, and he couldn't resist.

But why had Derry agreed to shoot? She had never felt the slightest inclination to hold a weapon. On the other hand, she was an actress, aware she might at any time be called upon to play the part of an FBI detective pursuing a serial killer. Such roles were especially demanding, as she would be required not only to shoot convincingly but to keep her hair and makeup in impeccable order. The offer of learning to handle a weapon was an opportunity no true professional could refuse.

The first sign they were approaching the range was a red flag flying from a pole. The only building was a brown wooden hut with raised decking, open at the front. The firing range was a long grassy alleyway between pairs of timber palisades looking oddly like theatre scenery. At the far end you could just make out the target, the white silhouette of a deer with a bulls-eye pasted just below its shoulder.

As Derry and Bruce neared the hut, Derry saw that the figure standing on the decking, peering down the range through a telescope on a tall tripod, was Rab. Their approach must have caught his attention. He took his eye from the telescope and held up his hand, signalling they should stay where they were.

Only then did Derry notice Sally lying on the decking beside where Rab stood, a rolled out carpet beneath her. Her cheek was clamped to an impressive-looking rifle with a telescopic sight, and on her head she wore ear protectors like giant headphones.

Crack, and the rifle jerked against Sally's shoulder. Rab took his eye from the telescope and nodded, seeming satisfied. Sally worked the bolt, ejecting a cartridge case, which tumbled onto the deck beside her. She did something careful with the rifle, laid it aside and clambered to her feet, before stacking the rifle tenderly against the wall beside another equally competent-looking weapon.

'Hi! Great you could come. Pay no mind to my terrible shooting—they make targets bigger back home. Rab is gentleman enough to pretend I'm not that bad. I doubt he was so sweet to his squaddies … isn't that what you call them?'

'If half my men had shot as well as you, I'd have been more than happy,' said Rab, smiling.

Ah, thought Derry. *Another ex-military man.* An officer, for sure. Perhaps you needed that kind of authority if you were to be an estate factor.

'Mrs. Carson is as good a shot as any I've taken up the hills here,' added Rab.

Why had Derry not expected Rab to be here? She found herself blushing. Perhaps he'd think she had been lying about the castle tour as a way of refusing his invitation. To cover her confusion, she apologised for interrupting their shoot.

'No problem, said Sally. 'I could do with straightening up.' She took a seat on a low wooden bench and stretched her legs. 'Great you could both come over. I was hoping Amelia could come too, but she's busy arguing with her father.'

'You've never been stalking, Derry?' asked Rab.

Derry shook her head. She had nothing in principle against hunting—or imagined she shouldn't since she wasn't a vegetarian—but she was uncomfortably aware that most of her friends would be appalled at her even talking to people they reckoned murderers of innocent wildlife.

'Do you shoot, Mr. Adams?' asked Rab, politely.

'Um, some,' said Bruce. 'And thanks for the invite, but I can't stay. Got a flying lesson.' He smiled but didn't explain. 'Catch ya later.' He leapt lightly down from the decking and strode away, heading back to the castle and his van. The idea was that he'd return in a couple of hours or when Derry phoned, whichever was the sooner.

'If you don't mind, Derry, perhaps I should explain a little about stalking before we shoot,' said Rab. 'I'm standing in for Jamie the gamekeeper here, so I'm afraid my spiel won't be up to his standards. I was at … a loose end so I thought I'd come down and help out.' Did he give a slight smile when he said *loose end*?

'We stalk the deer mainly because the wolves are no longer around to do the job for us. The deer have no natural predators and breed like anything. If they're not to starve, we have to cull them. We don't go in for trophy hunting here, though other estates do.' As he spoke his eyes flicked to Derry, as if he expected her to protest. But she already knew the arguments or some of them, and anyway she had no intention of shooting anything.

'If you want to do some stalking, we can arrange someone to give you the proper lesson in how to do it safely, and humanely for the animals.' Again he looked at Derry.

'No, thanks. Not for me.'

'But you might like a shot all the same?'

'Um, I'll have a go. Sure.' She sounded more confident than she felt and wondered uneasily whether the recoil she had seen kick into Sally's shoulder hurt.

'Terrific,' said Rab. 'How about now?'

The first surprise was the shocking closeness of the target as Derry peered down the scope. Lying on her stomach on a rolled out mat, ear protectors clamped to her head, she was looking down the range at the paper outline of the deer, bulls-eye on its chest. Some wag had painted Bambi eyelashes around the eyes.

Derry held the unloaded weapon against her cheek. The stock felt cool and the rifle, its long barrel supported on a bipod, was surprisingly light. To help her get the correct grip, Rab knelt beside her, holding her hand in his, closing his fist over hers. Derry was acutely aware of the contact, but only for a moment. Putting all distractions aside, she concentrated, determined to get this right. Following Rab's patient instructions, she practiced aiming, squeezing the trigger, and working the bolt to eject the spent cartridge casing after each imagined shot.

A lot to think about. But as an actress, Derry was used to working hard to get something right. Rab was encouraging, explaining that women's hand-eye coordination was superior to that of men, so they could be far better shooters. He explained too how the gun was set up to compensate for the way a bullet fell as it travelled the distance to the target. A good shooter also took account of the wind.

'Alright,' said Rab. 'Let's try a shot shall we? Ready?' Derry indicated she was. Rab loaded three bullets into the rifle—one, two, three—each with a little click. He stood to peer through the telescope at the target.

Derry took a breath as she had been told, steadied herself, told herself to relax, and squeezed the trigger. *Crack.*

Even as Derry fired, she knew she had messed up. Anticipating the kick of the recoil into her shoulder had made her flinch.

'Eject,' said Rab.

Derry did as she was told, surprised as the cartridge leapt from the breech when she slid back the bolt. She heard the casing roll on the decking beside her.

'That's your next round loaded,' said Rab. 'Now try keeping both eyes open. Relax, sight, and when you're ready, squeeze.'

Derry fired round after round. She was sure she was getting better, apart from when she found herself imagining how the FBI detective chasing a serial killer would leave her male comrades awestruck at her shooting skills, and promptly missed the target. Embarrassingly, she then tried to shoot having forgotten to eject the last cartridge. But she recovered, and by the time she had fired maybe twenty rounds, she was feeling comfortable. No markswoman, but not bad she felt sure. She was feeling pleased with herself as Rab told her to stand and check the breech was empty and the gun safe.

'Well done. Now sling the rifle—over your shoulder, that's it—and we'll take a look at your target.'

What a strange feeling, thought Derry–strolling down the alleyway between the palisades, her gun at her shoulder, Rab chatting amiably. For the first time in her life, she understood the intoxicating feeling of power a weapon bestowed. Her walk took on a swagger in spite of herself. In her imagination, she was taller—for an actor, a useful insight.

She didn't feel the swagger was quite so justified when she stood with Rab in front of the paper deer to examine the target. The animal looked like it had been machine gunned. But Rab didn't laugh or criticise.

'Not bad at all,' he said. 'You're not ready for a stalk yet—for that you need to reliably get three shots within a four-inch radius of the target, neatly grouped, at a hundred yards. You wouldn't want to wound the animal and have it suffer.'

Not a pleasant thought. A wild animal left to bleed slowly to death on a hillside.

'We always follow up and humanely despatch a wounded deer, no matter how much effort it takes,' said Rab, as though he knew what she was thinking. 'That's the difference between the true sport and the poacher. All they care about is the money.' Rab's eyes were cold. Derry thought she wouldn't like to be in a poacher's shoes when Rab caught up with him.

'Mind if I join the party?' shouted Torquil.

'Hey,' said Sally. 'Come on in. Jessica, come over.'

Jessica was sitting quietly in the driver's seat of a black SUV pulled up just behind the hut, elbow propped in the open window. She waved and smiled, but made no move to get out. Torquil approached with a jaunty step, hands in his pockets. He was dressed for a country weekend—flat tweed cap and brown padded hunting jacket, narrow tweed tie and a finely checked shirt. His cords were the regulation brown, his boots the equally regulation green. Torquil, Derry saw, was every inch the gentleman, freshly engaged to an aristocrat and finding the role fit admirably.

Derry unslung the rifle from her shoulder and handed it carefully back to Rab.

'Phew,' said Torquil. 'Why do I suddenly feel safer?'

'You're too skinny for the pot,' said Sally, laughing.

'Like a shot or two?' asked Rab.

'Not today, Rab my agricultural friend,' answered Torquil. 'I heard Derry was here. Jessica wants us to kiss and make up. Wants me to offer myself for judicial execution.' He turned to Derry, smiling, impervious to her glare. 'I demand due process.'

Sally raised an eyebrow. Rab took to peering through his telescope at the target downrange.

'Torquil,' said Derry, 'I want a word with you. Take a little stroll?'

'Of course. Turn around the block. Do us good. Lead on, dear girl.'

Derry led Torquil in silence along the path. Once out of sight of the hut, she stopped, turning suddenly, forcing Torquil to step backwards. She had visualised this scene many times. The script ranged from immediate and unhesitating violence, to a calm and rational elucidation of the error of Torquil's ways and a sincere wish he'd reform. Immediately followed by violence.

'Apologise. *Now!*'

'What for?'

'For what you did to me out there. You and that woman! It was crap and you know it. Why tell lies about me?'

Torquil shrugged. 'I'm not the journalist, Derry. She asks her own questions.'

'Don't give me bullshit!'

Again Torquil shrugged, with a smile that said, *I'm just waiting for an irrational female to calm down.*

'I don't know why I'm talking to you,' said Derry, turning away. Anger had turned to disgust and to a weariness she couldn't explain.

'Yes you do know,' said Torquil. 'You want me to teach you your business.'

Derry turned back, astonished. 'You fed me to that reporter. Why? You *know* what really happened.'

'I don't mean to offend, Derry, but last thing I heard you were an actress. You are in a film. I am the publicist. *Actress plays fortune-teller* is hardly going to set the tabloids on fire, is it.' He frowned. 'Should I be explaining this?'

'Stop treating me like a fool! How can lies sell the movie?'

Torquil burst out laughing. 'Am I really talking to a grown-up human being of the twenty-first century? I don't know whether to be touched or appalled.

'You had an opportunity to get your brand out there. Madam Tulip playing herself in the movie was perfect. Yes, you had an interesting history, murder, gangsters and whatnot, all good material; we could have built up slowly then joined the dots coming up to the UK premiere. We could have had a breakfast-show slot. But no, Madam Tulip goes all coy. Hence Plan B—play up the scandal and claim you are hiding. Well you *are* hiding, aren't you? You have only yourself to blame.'

There it was. The answer to the puzzle of why the producers wanted her so badly. And Bruce too, *no audition required.*

'Derry, the masses will feed happily on the latest outrage. They will tut-tut and shake their heads in a storm of Tweets. And they'll feel better about themselves because they're not as bad as whoever. In this case *you.*

'They will come to see the film out of curiosity,' continued Torquil. 'Some will come to see a genuine psychic; some will want to see a fraud. Half the population believe in psychic powers and aliens; the other half don't. This way we get both halves. Derry, I've done you a massive favour, and you don't even see it. The UK premiere will be in London. I guarantee you'll want to be there.'

He smiled, cocked his head to one side, and turned to walk away. 'Must go and make somebody else famous. Hope they appreciate it. Toodle-oo.'

~

'That Torquil, he was born sorry. Pay no heed,' said Bruce as they drove back along the coast to the hotel. 'You'd better get used to it. What happens if you get famous? You'll be running from the paparazzi and worrying about your hair before you go to the supermarket. And they'll secretly film you rocking out with your borage tea and your Jane Austen. Oh man, the scandal!'

Derry was about to wonder out loud if she were just plain unsuited to the whole business. This observation would give Bruce the opportunity to tell her how well suited she actually was, as he was required to do. But right then, her phone pinged in her bag. A text. From Jacko. With a photo.

Explain later, said the text. *Paddy is architect. Coming to Scot soon. Maybe CU. Love XXX.*

The image was a selfie; though taken from a little distance, presumably with a timer so the two figures in the picture could be seen full length. Derry instantly appreciated why someone thought full length was important. Against the background of what Derry recognized to be Jacko's Castle O'Donnell, her father stood with his arm around the shoulder of a short, round, middle-aged man. Both were grinning inanely, like men showing off a newly caught fish. You could see they were grinning even though they both wore masks.

Derry should have been surprised at her father wearing a mask; he was proud of his leonine hair and his impressive eyebrows, and believed his artist's eyes held a fatal fascination for women with a certain advanced aesthetic. But in this case, Derry understood straight away that the mask was entirely necessary. Batman always wore a mask.

Why her father should be dressed in full Batman regalia of cape, mask and Lycra body suit, and why he was posing proudly with an architect called Paddy dressed as Robin, Derry couldn't imagine. Nor did she mean to try. A lifetime as an O'Donnell had taught her that some mysteries, especially those involving close relations, were just mysteries.

'Did you ever think life was totally bananas?' said Derry.

'Sure,' answered Bruce, as if surprised the question needed to be asked. 'You know, they say the whole universe could be some kinda giant hologram? I mean, what if you're an actor already? Is that twice?'

'My father thinks he's Batman.'

Bruce kept his eyes on the road, but Derry saw he was considering her statement carefully. 'That's bad,' he said.

'I mean, how worried should I be?'

'I'd say, pretty worried. Ain't no room in a family for more than one actor, and that's a fact.'

14

Derry and Bruce trudged up the field, their scenes for the day done, warmth and a coffee beckoning. From behind came a ragged cheer—the Highlanders charging yet again—and a lazy popping, as the Redcoats fired a volley of shots.

As they passed through the security barrier and onto the road, a voice hailed from a black SUV parked on the verge. 'Hi, you guys!' Jessica was leaning out the window, binoculars in her hand, watching the filming. 'Wanna go sightseeing? Mr. Carson asked me to get a message to Sally. They're stalking on the hill. No phone coverage. Good chance to take a trip. Coming?'

Derry gestured helplessly. Neither she nor Bruce was going anywhere dressed as clansman and gypsy fortune-teller.

'Go ahead and change. I'll wait,' said Jessica.

'Cool,' said Bruce. 'I mean, I'm a Returned Patriot and I don't even know what I'm supposed to be patriotic about. Let's call it *research*.'

Derry smiled. 'Jessica, sounds great. Thanks.'

And why not? thought Derry. When you're an unemployed actor, driving up mountains to admire scenery is not an option. You absolutely need to be at home phoning your agent or moaning to your actor friends; anything else is delusional. But when you are working, like now, you're perfectly free to drive anywhere you want and admire anything you like.

It was called *a little vacation*.

~

The SUV was pure luxury. Derry found herself enveloped in sumptuous new-smelling leather, hand-stitched and soft. This was a Range Rover like the Queen of England drove— staggeringly expensive.

'I'm liking this a lot,' announced Jessica. 'Mr. Carson, he likes big Fords, all macho muscle. Says it's patriotic. He had to drive to Glasgow yesterday, and Alex said I could use the Rangie. You know, one day I'm gonna have me one of these babies. Yes I am.'

Jessica was in high spirits, seeming to relish the ruts of a stony mountain track barely wide enough for the vehicle. The road climbed over a heather-covered ridge leading to the high moor where, Jessica explained, a hunting lodge had been built over a hundred years ago for the convenience of gentlemen stalkers. You could see why a lodge would be a good idea— out here was a vast wilderness of heather and rock, mountain towering behind mountain as far as the eye could see. Not a telegraph pole, not a house, not even a windmill or phone mast.

Derry sat in the back, insisting that Bruce's legs needed more room than hers, before realising she could stretch out comfortably. She could get used to this, she thought idly—*the celebrated actress chauffeured through the landscape, her identity coyly veiled by the smoked glass of the rear windows.*

As they rocked and wallowed over the ruts and stony out-crops, the sense of being cut off from the rest of humanity was intense. Inside the air-conditioned cocoon was like being in a moon rover creeping over an alien landscape. Below to their right lay a long narrow lake, its shore strewn with enormous boulders, its shimmering length snaking down the valley for many miles. As if to show that—despite the bleak, inhospitable look of the place—humans had once counted these hills their own, on a massive outcrop overlooking the lake stood a grey stone tower. Beyond the tower a lakeside track disappeared into a heavily wooded pass through the hills, while the road they drove led steeply upwards to the high moor and the old lodge.

'They call it the Doon,' said Jessica. 'Just means castle. I guess that means Alex has two castles.'

You could see why the tower sat where it did. Its back was defended by the water of the lake, while the fortress dominated both routes into the hills. But the strangest thing was how familiar the tower looked. The grey walls were the twin of the ruin Jacko had bought. Less of a wreck—no ivy on the battlements and no encircling perimeter wall, but built to more or less the same design. Derry couldn't help smiling as the thought came to her that perhaps in those days, like in the Irish countryside today, people passed around a book of plans to save on the cost of architects. Did Lady Warlord say to Sir Warlord, *I don't like the dormers on that one. And couldn't we have, like, decking?* And he'd worry about whether the garage was big enough for two—

The glass didn't shatter.

That was the first surprise. Instead, in an instant, faster than Derry's brain could follow and way faster than it could explain, a spider's web appeared like magic in the side window just in front of Jessica's head. At the same instant, a second web appeared beside Bruce's face. No complex calculations were needed to work out that the two neat holes surrounded by a lattice of bright cracks were one and the same incomprehensible event.

That the human brain will insist on making sense out of what it sees, is a fact well known to psychologists. The grey matter will confidently assert that two plus two equals five if the deduction promises to get its owner to quit asking awkward questions. That was the game Derry's brain was playing now.

Obviously, said Brain in the confident tones of an expert witness, *the SUV, recklessly piloted by Jessica down a steep track, caused a stone to be thrown violently up, which flew through the windshield. Nothing at all to be concerned about.*

How a small stone thrown up by the wheel of an SUV could break not one window but two, Derry's brain didn't choose to explain. All the while, she felt like a bystander, helplessly watching her own mental processes, but a bystander who wanted to shout out a single word. Derry knew what that word should be but couldn't make the sound. Bizarrely, she even found she could spell the word, but still couldn't say it. *B-U-L-L-E-T*. But that didn't matter because Bruce's hoarse roar was already filling the cab.

'Right! Sniper! Gas! Go! Go!'

Instead of accelerating, Jessica slammed on the brakes. Derry was thrown violently into the back of the driver's seat. Bruce grabbed the steering wheel and swung hard. The SUV slewed left, reared up its nose and plunged, tilting crazily partway into the deep roadside ditch.

'Out! Out! Out! roared Bruce.

Derry didn't move. Jessica didn't move. Bruce flung open his door, and with a fist that seemed enormous, far too big to be a real hand belonging to a real person, he grabbed Jessica's jacket collar and hauled her bodily, head first out of the SUV to disappear in a rolling tangle.

And still Derry sat.

'Out! Out!' Bruce's face appeared at the open door. But now Derry's brain found itself fascinated by how everything seemed to be happening in slow motion. She remembered having made this observation to herself before but couldn't remember when. On the other hand, that was twice so it must be true.

'Out!'

Like she had all the time in the world, Derry considered Bruce's demand. What exactly did *Out* mean?' The word seemed both familiar and unfamiliar. But before she could answer, she was spluttering in a squelching, seeping wetness, gasping in shock, wallowing in a water-filled ditch. A disgusting taste of sour mud filled her mouth. She was spitting and coughing. She could hear Jessica sobbing, whether from the shock of the cold water or from fear, she couldn't tell.

Derry felt her collar seized once more, and she was on her feet. Bruce was urging them on, calling 'heads down, keep moving,' as he dragged and pushed them through the foul black water, their feet sinking into the peaty bottom if they paused one moment in their stumbling motion.

Blindly, they followed Bruce's orders, the heathery banks hiding them from view as they dragged themselves forward by hauling on the thick mat of woody stalks.

Just ahead their ditch turned sharp left, creeping by the flank of a rising granite bluff where gigantic boulders sat stacked up the slope amongst the vegetation. Shelter of a sort—a kind of natural terrace, barely discernible amongst the rocky crevasses dense with heather and bracken, the hill rising behind.

147

Gasping for breath, Derry dragged herself up by the stalks of the vegetation. Pushed and cajoled by Bruce, she tumbled from the ditch, struggled to her knees and threw herself up and over the bank to roll behind the blessed shelter of the nearest boulders. Sodden, breathless, she waited for the shots.

∼

No shots came.

All three were lying flat on their bellies. Derry felt Bruce's hand pressing down hard on her back between her shoulder blades, insisting she didn't move.

'You will both do as I tell you,' Bruce was saying. 'You will stay down. You do not care what's out there. *Curiosity killed the cat.* Do you understand what I am saying?'

Jessica was sobbing, saying over and over again, 'What was it? What happened?'

'You're fine now,' said Bruce. 'You're safe as long as you *stay down.*' Bruce had his phone in his hand. His expression said there was no signal.

Derry's world had shrunk to mere sensation—the cloying, chill wetness of her clothes, the spiky wooden stems of heather beneath her body, the lichen-covered grey stone by her face, the heady smell of some herb she couldn't identify. And now it was starting to rain, large slow drops. Where was the shooter? Not once had Bruce looked out to see where the shot had come from. Maybe he was too concerned she and Jessica would do something stupid.

'Bruce, we're okay. We'll stay put. I promise.' Derry's words must have been what Bruce wanted to hear. He squeezed her shoulder and wriggled backwards, then rolled, creeping to his right, searching for a vantage from which he could look back along the line they had come. Derry saw him stop at what must have been a gap between boulders and carefully part the stems of the heather.

'What's going on?' Jessica was shaking now. 'We have to get help.'

'Bruce will take care of it,' said Derry. Did she believe that? She thought she did, but believing didn't mean things would work out that way.

Bruce wriggled back, propelling himself by his elbows. 'A Land Rover coming down the track. Looks like they don't know what's happened.'

'What *has* happened?' Jessica's voice had an edge of hysteria.

Bruce ignored her question. 'Jessica, you know the vehicles round here. Come with me, stay down. When we're in position, I'll tell you, and you can take a look. Not until then. Okay?' Jessica nodded. She seemed relieved to have been ordered to do something. They crawled, Bruce first, Jessica dragging herself after.

'It's Rab!' You could hear the relief in Jessica's voice. 'He's coming down the hill. He sees the truck!'

Now it was Derry's turn to crawl. Lying on her belly, she took her turn peering out between the boulders.

Rab's green Land Rover was creeping down the steep track below. He pulled up just short of the abandoned Range Rover, threw open his door almost before he had skidded to a halt, and was running to investigate. His passenger followed—a woman Derry recognised at once as Sally. They bustled around the SUV, and Derry could almost read their thoughts as they stood scanning the landscape. Where were the occupants? What extraordinary thing had happened? Rab climbed onto the topsy-turvy vehicle and pulled open the driver's door. Surely by now he had seen the holes in the windows?

'Stay here you guys, okay?' said Rab.

Derry nodded. She knew what Bruce was going to do. Rab and Sally had found them, but who said the shooter was gone? Surely it was a stray shot, an accident. But what if it wasn't? Maybe Rab or Sally would drop before their eyes. Then again, as far as Derry could tell, they had only been shot at once. Wouldn't they have heard a second shot? Or did rifles have silencers that meant you would hear nothing until the bullet struck your flesh and tore through your bones. This time, her shivers had nothing to do with the cold.

Bruce left them, moving discreetly through the heather, always screened by boulders, careful not to betray where he had come from, sometimes disappearing in crevices or small gullies. Derry knew he would take no chances. Bruce disapproved of heroics.

Thirty yards away, Bruce stood on the edge of the rocky rise, waving both arms. He called out, jumping up and down, signaling like he was directing an airplane on a runway. If he had flown a ten-foot-high banner saying, *if you're there, shoot me!* he could hardly have done more to attract attention. *So much for no heroics*, thought Derry. But no shot came. The figures by the Land Rover pointed and gestured. Bruce waved to Derry and Jessica, signalling they should come down.

Jessica went first, crouched and stumbling but moving fast through the boulders and the peaty depressions, along some sort of animal track. Derry was a few yards behind trying to avoid the worst of the sharp stems and snagging vegetation. Jessica pushed ahead as if all she were thinking was to get to the safety of the Land Rover and leave behind the madness of creeping and hiding.

A cry of surprise, and Jessica disappeared. Like in slow motion, she slid down an incline on her back to be swallowed by a thick stand of bracken masking a narrow gully. Derry ignored the need to stay low. Breaking cover, she dashed to the spot, readying herself to slide feet first down the slope after Jessica and into the dense mass of vegetation.

She was crouching, thinking only of Jessica somewhere below, when it happened. An explosion of black flapping wings erupted in her face. The clamour was deafening—furious screeches, wild and raucous squawks, beating wings thumping the air like hammer blows. In the heart-stopping commotion, Derry reeled back, tripping and falling to lie in the heather as the birds shot skywards. She must have cried out, her shouts joining Jessica's, but the great black creatures were now wheeling high overhead shrieking their anger and frustration.

Derry fought for breath, her heart pumping. She hauled herself forward on her knees, meaning to peer cautiously down into the gully, when Jessica erupted from below as though pursued by demons.

'Ugh, ugh! Disgusting! Ugh!' Jessica was pedalling wildly with her feet, scrambling desperately through the bracken, frantic as though racing to escape some horror. She was beating her own head, waving her hands in front of her face, striking at her hair.

Flies. Coal black and glistening pearlescent blue. Buzzing. Implausibly fat. Horribly familiar.

Jessica looked like she wanted to get sick. She was tight lipped as though afraid to open her mouth. She kept brushing her hands furiously through her hair. 'Dead animal. Horrible. Let's go!'

Whatever the dead thing was, they left it behind. Derry's creeping flesh told her that however much she wanted to know, she didn't want to look. Not now. Later, she would ask—when they were out of here. When they were away from disgusting dead things.

And people who shot out the windows of their car.

15

Derry felt a strange sense of dislocation, like the events of the afternoon had happened to someone else. Being dressed in another's clothes only added to the weirdness. She guessed she must look like she had rummaged through a recycling bin and thrown on the first garments she found. If she had, the bin was somewhere in Beverly Hills. Amazingly, her phone seemed still to be working.

Sally had looked after everything. Back at the castle, she'd given Derry and Bruce bathrobes and slippers, collected their soaked and reeking clothes, made them dry their feet so they wouldn't wreck the carpets, and led them to showers. Jessica had gone to her own room to shower and change. Bruce ended up wearing a pair of Carson's tartan golf trousers, a loud plaid shirt and a quilted waistcoat. Derry wore a pair of Jessica's designer jeans, and an expensive cashmere sweater of Sally's. Amelia's clothes might have fitted better, but after coming to see what the commotion was about she had turned and stalked off, refusing to help. 'Teenagers are nuts,' was all Sally said, but she looked thoughtful.

In the castle sitting-room, Derry, Bruce and Jessica sat in armchairs by a roaring fire sipping coffee and nibbling cookies. Sally, Rab and a uniformed policeman were ranged around them, the policeman sitting with a notebook open on his knee and his hat on the floor beside him. Rab introduced him as Sergeant Sillars.

Sillars was a middle-aged man, portly with a florid complexion and bright blue eyes that flicked around the room when he first came in, as if taking in every painting and item of furniture. He seemed to know all about Sally and her husband renting this part of the castle from Alex Dunbar. Perhaps everyone in this sparsely populated part of the Highlands knew. Or perhaps Rab had filled him in on the background. Derry noticed the way Sillars treated Rab with special deference, a sign of the factor's respected place in the scheme of things. A factor wasn't a landowner, but in terms of status and local power, he was the next-best thing.

'Alright,' said Sillars. 'Tell me from the beginning how it happened.'

'I was just driving,' said Jessica in a soft voice. She lapsed into silence as though that simple fact explained everything.

Bruce spoke up. 'Uh, maybe I could help a little here.'

'Please,' said the policeman.

Bruce described all that had happened—the bullet passing through both windows, their escape into the ditch and their movement into the cover of the rocks. His description was matter of fact. Professional. So devoid of drama was his telling that Derry felt she was hearing a fictional story told by the fireside rather than anything real.

'I'm sorry for interrupting,' said Rab. 'I have a question for Mr. Adams. I should have asked before.'

'Of course,' said Sillars. He gestured for Rab to go ahead.

Rab gave Bruce a considering look. 'I hope you don't mind me asking—I'm guessing you have a military background?'

'Sure,' said Bruce. 'Navy.'

'Oh,' said Rab. 'I see.' He frowned, as though the answer wasn't the one he expected. 'But you knew what to do, that's the main thing.'

'Sure,' said Bruce. 'Get in the water. With us sailors, it's like … um … an instinct, you know?'

Derry was glad she wasn't sipping her coffee or she might have spluttered all over the mantelpiece. Instead she coughed like she was clearing her throat and pretended to find the pattern on the carpet fascinating. Bruce wore a guileless expression, his face innocent of the smallest trace of irony.

'Doesn't do to take chances,' said Rab, surprising Derry. He didn't call the way Bruce had handled things overreacting or imply he and Derry were hysterical, over-imaginative actors. Instead, he said, 'These people have to be stopped.' He shook his head, revealing what seemed to Derry to be a long-standing, deeply felt helplessness.

'You guys had this before?' asked Bruce.

Rab hesitated. He seemed to be wondering how much to say. 'We've had some nasty incidents. Poachers. Nobody hurt, but you have to wonder how far these people will go.' Derry remembered Sally's story about the last factor being warned off, his jeep shot at.

'One day they're going to kill somebody,' added Sillars. 'Though I doubt what happened today was deliberate, they're still a menace. Half these fellows don't know one end of a rifle from the other.'

'You checked the tower?' Bruce spoke casually.

'The Doon?'

'Shot came from somewhere that way. Worth a look, maybe.' Derry recognised Bruce's take-it-or-leave-it suggestion as the tone he used when he had considered a thing very carefully indeed.

'We'll maybe check that later, if we see the need,' said Sillars. He sniffed, as if to say no lessons were needed from sailors, Americans or actors.

Rab turned to Jessica. 'You said you stumbled on a dead animal?'

Jessica nodded. 'I didn't know what it was at first. A disgusting mess, but then I saw … a head. A deer. Other parts.'

'A stag or a hind?' asked the policeman. Rab looked equally interested.

'How would I …?'

'Antlers, said Rab. Did the head have antlers?'

'I don't … I think so, yes. It was horrible.'

Rab and the policeman looked at each other and nodded. 'Poachers,' said Rab. 'We're out of season for the stags. What you found was gralloched. They cut out the internal organs and take off the head and lower legs. Makes it easier to transport the meat.'

'A disgrace,' said Sillars.

'They come through from Glasgow,' added Rab, as though originating in that famous metropolis could explain any human wickedness.

'Still,' said Sillars, addressing the room in general. 'They've probably scared themselves as much as they did you. They won't want so much attention. That's not their way.'

'Helluva way of not gettin' noticed,' said Bruce.

Rab and Sillars looked at him, like he had spoken up in church, contradicting the minister.

'They're not always the brightest,' said Sillars, shaking his head. 'No accountin' for city folk.'

Word travels fast in the Highlands. Rab had driven Derry and Bruce back to the hotel. They had hardly reached the front door when it was flung open. Jen ushered them in, clucking and trying to manoever them into her private sitting room at the back. Pleading exhaustion and, thanking Jen profusely, Derry and Bruce pressed on up the stairs.

They had changed and rendezvoused to sit in Derry's room as arranged, when a knock came on the door—Jen, carrying a tray and two glasses of whiskey.

'You'll have a dram, and don't say you won't. And a little water to open it out.'

Derry and Bruce mumbled their thanks, but Jen had no intention of leaving without payment in the only currency that mattered. 'I don't know what the place is coming to,' she said. 'Rumours and shooting and upset. They say you were in Mr. Dunbar's motor. He'll have tae be careful now.'

Derry had meant to thank Jen firmly and hustle her out, but the reference to Dunbar was intriguing. 'They said poachers. An accident. Why should Mr. Dunbar be worried?'

'Mebbe it's poachers and maybe it isn't,' said Jen. 'There's more goes on here than poaching. There's a lot the tourist doesn't see.'

What did she mean? Derry remembered Moira McKenzie's comment about windmills and petitions. 'Is there trouble with the estates? I heard something about a windfarm.'

'There's that. And there's more besides. Outsiders come in with their money; they buy ten or twenty thousand acres and a big house, and they think they've bought us with it. They soon find out different.'

'They like to change things, is that it?'

'They think they're improving the estates with their forestry and their adventure centres and what have you, but they just walk over the tenants.'

'Tenants? What, like farmers?'

'Crofters we call them here—but yes, the crofters with their smallholdings. And others as well, you'll find one estate or the other owns half of every village if not the lot. And they bring in their own workers. Even their own cooks.' She seemed particularly offended at the implied slight on the local cuisine.

'Bad blood, right?' said Bruce, frowning.

'A couple of hundred years o' it. Some even say the old landlords, the real gentry, were better than the crowd we have now with their helicopters and their yachts.'

'Are you saying somebody could have shot at Mr. Dunbar's car deliberately? Thinking it was him?' asked Derry.

'Who can say? People have been known to send a little message. I wouldn't like to condone such things, but there's good reason for folks to be angry.'

Amazing. You looked around and saw a piece of heaven on Earth, an idyll of mountains and sea. Then you heard about shootings. Other things too. Derry remembered Sally's story. 'Somebody mentioned to me that someone had been shot at before. A factor. Wasn't that about poaching?'

Jen shook her head slowly. 'They said poachers from Glasgow, but you can be sure they were local. Nobody from the city could do the other things that were done.'

'They poisoned one of his dogs, I heard.'

Jen's eyebrows arched in surprise. 'You're verra well informed.' She regarded Derry with a new interest.

'So you think that was local poachers, not men from the city?'

'Local mebbe, but not a poacher. Not one of our own.' She seemed unshakably certain of the point.

'Why? You said outsiders wouldn't be able to do what was done.'

'We have a man or two round here known for poaching all their lives. Aye, and they'll have little time for a factor. Might even have a grudge, depending. But they'd never shoot at a man, not even a factor. And they'd never, *ever* poison a dog.'

Derry thought about that as she cautiously sipped her whiskey. She noticed Bruce was barely tasting his.

'Did you say the police had an idea who was behind your own fright?' asked Jen, innocently. Derry had said no such thing, and she was now expected to confirm or deny, both potential nuggets. But Jen's luck had run out—her phone rang. A kitchen crisis. Reluctantly, she tore herself away.

'You buy that about Dunbar?' asked Bruce after a moment's silence. 'Some folks unhappy about windmills? And what was that about poisoned dogs?'

Derry struggled to think clearly. Her thoughts were tangled, her brain fuzzy. Hardly the whiskey; she hadn't even half-finished her glass. 'Just something I heard. Some sort of campaign against a factor.' She kept it vague. Though the events were public knowledge, the source was Sally. Derry took seriously her duty of confidentiality as a fortune-teller—that Sally harboured wild suspicions about her husband could never be mentioned, not even to Bruce.

'What, someone took a shot at Rab?'

'No. Another factor. He upped and left. Didn't say where he was going.' She paused as Bruce's remark sank in. 'What do you mean *buy it* about Dunbar? Shouldn't I? Poachers, right? Or some local dispute with tenants, people who don't like an outsider landlord.'

'Maybe,' said Bruce. 'Whichever, poachers or locals, that shot was no accident.'

Derry felt the warmth drain from her body, so fast it was like she had stepped outside into freezing wind.

'I'd bet my bottom dollar that was an aimed shot,' said Bruce. His eyes took on a faraway look as though he were transporting himself back to the steep rocky track on that exposed mountainside. 'Big black SUV crawling along at six or seven miles an hour. Visibility is good. Open ground left, right and in front. High ground behind. Say there's a nice fat deer on the hillside beyond. Say there's a poacher with his rifle. He sees the deer, he looks through his scope and he pulls the trigger just as that same big SUV gets between him and the target?' He shrugged. 'I can't see it.'

No, it didn't seem likely. They had been as obvious in their black Range Rover as if they had turned up waving banners.

'An aimed shot, for sure,' added Bruce. 'Big question is, did he mean to miss.'

What could you say? Which was better, that someone had tried to kill someone and had missed, or that someone was willing to put a bullet through a window within inches of another human's head just to get their attention?

'Lots of reasons a guy could miss,' continued Bruce. 'He doesn't get the wind deflection right. Maybe he's just a lousy shot. But maybe he meant to miss.'

Derry tried to grasp what he was saying. 'Could it be us? I mean the movie?' The idea was horrifying. 'Remember what the cab driver said about filming on Sundays?'

'Can't see folks disapproving of Sunday filming being all that okay with shooting folk. Anyhow, much easier to sabotage the set or the equipment trucks.' Bruce shrugged. 'Maybe the cop was right. Crazy poachers from Glasgow.'

An overwhelming tiredness swept over Derry like a powerful drug she couldn't hope to fight. She couldn't think at all, couldn't remember what she was about to say or what had been said only a moment before.

'It's just a reaction, hon,' said Bruce. 'You get yourself into your bunk. Sleep it off.' He rose to go, squeezing her forearm. 'You gonna be okay?'

Derry nodded. 'Sure. Thanks. Like you say, tired.'

'What time's your call tomorrow?'

'Not 'till eleven.'

'Cool. Sleep tight.'

But Derry didn't climb into her bed right away. She sat in the armchair, seeing over and over again the bullet smacking through the glass beside Jessica's face. It was like Nature was saying, *It's important. You need to remember.* At the same time, some other part of Derry's brain plaintively protested—*Why? Why remember?*

Surely it was better to forget.

16

Derry slept badly and woke late. Getting up seemed an impossible task. Instead, she lay staring blankly at the stucco molding on the ceiling.

A brisk knock, and Jen's cheerful 'Morning!' was like a switch had been flipped. 'I'll leave your clothes here,' called Jen through the closed door. 'Your breakfast will be ready in ten minutes.' The last was unmistakably an order.

Derry checked her phone. A text from Bruce two hours old said, *Gone to fight the English. See ya later XX.* Outside her room, Derry found her clothes washed, dried, ironed and carefully folded in a basket. Even her sneakers had been somehow revived, though they'd never be the same again. Ten minutes later, she was sitting alone in the dining room contemplating that culinary phenomenon known as a *Full Scottish Breakfast.*

The Full Scottish Breakfast is indistinguishable from the Full Irish Breakfast and the Full English Breakfast. That is, if you ignore the technical terms. In Scotland, potato cakes are *tattie scones*, and sausages can be *Lorne* or not; but all three national editions of the Full Breakfast feature eggs, bacon, beans, toast, sausages, possibly black pudding, and a complete disregard for decades of government warnings about cholesterol.

As it happened, Derry had never in her life spent a single moment worrying about cholesterol. Cholesterol was invisible and quite possibly a theoretical construct existing only in the minds of scientists. Pounds, on the other hand, were all too visible and possessed of a fiendish intelligence allowing them creep up on you unawares. But cholesterol or not, Derry was finding the Full Scottish Breakfast extraordinarily effective at banishing anxiety and laying to rest troubling memories. Given recent events, Derry felt entitled to consider this particular Full Scottish Breakfast as therapy.

Did Derry's wholehearted enjoyment of her fourth sausage, crispy brown the way she liked them, mean she was a frivolous and non-serious person? Derry conceded to herself that perhaps it did. But she didn't care. She had a scene to film today with Darian, and that was all she meant to think about. She was vaguely contemplating a request for more coffee, when her phone rang.

'Rab here. I hope I'm not disturbing you.'

'No, not at all. Hi.'

'I just wanted to see how you were this morning. I'm sure you're alright, but in case you wanted to … talk over anything? Sometimes the reaction only sets in later.'

'It's good of you to call. But I'm fine. Really.'

'As long as you're sure,' said Rab.

'Sure. Eating sausages, in fact. Proves it.'

Rab laughed. 'In that case, nothing to worry about. Just wanted to be certain. I'll not bother you more.' He hesitated, and Derry was keenly aware this was precisely the point at which an invitation to coffee or a drink might emerge blinking into the light. If, that is, the other party was sufficiently motivated and had the quantum of initiative you liked to see in a man.

'Alright, so. All the best now. Bye,' said Rab.

'Bye. And thanks.'

He hung up. Derry sighed.

What could she do but reach for another slice of toast?

∽

Darian had fallen from his horse.

The yellow air ambulance took off with a roar of blades, swooping overhead as Derry, along with almost everyone else in the trailer park, trooped across the road and down to the far end of the field. Security were herding onlookers the opposite way, ushering them back up the hill.

At the spot where the scene had been shooting, a small knot of actors and a gaggle of extras stood aimlessly, leaving a space around the director Hamilton, the cameraman, Jeff the AD, Torquil and the lesser crew. All stood in silence watching the helicopter vanish into the distance.

Carson's silver SUV pulled up behind the tents. Derry was surprised to see Jessica in the driving seat. She wondered if she herself would be so quick to drive after what had happened yesterday. But Jessica seemed her normal self. No sign of a pale face or haggard eyes. She jumped down to follow Carson who strode into the circle of assembled crew.

'He said he could ride!' wailed Hamilton. Carson put his arm around the director's shoulder and walked him up and down like a coach calming a rattled athlete. The others followed at a safe distance—courtiers wary of an enraged king. Every half dozen paces, Hamilton stopped, burst into a stream of obscenities and demanded to know if anybody had bothered to check whether Darian knew one end of a horse from the other. He vowed to sue Darian's agent, and the horse, or at least the fraud who rented the creature. Carson led Hamilton into the biggest tent, followed by Jessica, Jeff, Torquil and the cameraman. Outside, people stood huddled around the tents and vehicles, crew talking among themselves, actors further away, like two chemicals had separated out.

'What happened?' Derry asked Richard, who stood beside her in the knot of actors, a parka over his redcoat uniform.

'Wasn't really the boy's fault. Those damned jets again. Streaked over the field like they knew we were here. Makes one wonder if the air force thinks bad films are a mortal threat to national security. Perhaps they are.'

'And how's Darian? Was he hurt badly?'

'Nobody knows. He's twisted an ankle—maybe broken it—and hurt his back, sprained a wrist and goodness knows what else. Might be serious, or maybe they'll patch him up and he'll be fine. Whichever it is, Hamilton will have to make some decisions. Reschedule everyone's scenes, I imagine, until they can get our man back.'

Although Derry had worked on movies before and was used to the constant reordering of scenes to take account of weather and delays, she had never seen a dramatic upheaval like this. Two of her remaining scenes were with Darian. Even those that weren't were likely to be rescheduled along with everything else.

'Not the luckiest production ever, is it?' Richard gave Derry a speculative look.

'Um, no. I guess not.'

'You … coping alright? From what I heard, you had a nasty experience.'

'I'm fine,' said Derry. 'Thanks.'

Jeff approached their little group. 'Okay cast, gather round please. Extras—I'll talk to you in a moment. We'll carry on with the battle scenes as planned, so reenactors stand by. Everyone else—we'll let you know when we've reworked things and when we know about Darian, okay? So stand down for now. We'll call a proper meeting as soon as we have a better picture. Look out for text messages. Thank you all.'

The assembled cast mumbled their assent. As Derry scanned their anxious faces she knew that all had the same thought—what if their scenes were cut or the film was abandoned? While delays caused by weather were always good, meaning extra pay and idle days, delays caused by misfortune were always, always bad.

Actors are a superstitious lot.

At the promised production meeting, the new schedules were handed around. Some of Bruce's scenes were brought forward, but Derry's next was put off until the following Monday, and even that was provisional. Worse still, her daily allowance, the *per diems* treasured by all actors, would cease as of the next morning. The production manager's answer to all questions was *talk to your agent.*

Sitting in her hotel room, Derry had reluctantly concluded she had better do exactly as the production manager had said. She knew that when an actor is put on standby to return at some later date, the biggest of arguments come down to the smallest of small print. Actor, agent and production company scour the actor's contract, lips pursed and brows furrowed, in search of the magic paragraph that wins the day. Surely Pam, with her decades of experience, would find that saving clause?

'Derry O'Donnell here, Pam. Sorry to bother you. I'm in Scotland. The production people said we should call our agents.' Derry took a deep breath and described her situation.

'Give me a second,' said Pam. The clicking of a keyboard said she was looking up Derry's details. 'This is where these non-union jobs get tricky, I'm afraid. Let me see.'

Agents know that lawyers are human, with all the fallibility that sorry state implies. As a result, many contracts are like a DIY garden shed, hastily knocked together from scavenged junk as the quickest way to turn cut-and-paste into a jaw-dropping invoice. And therein may lie the loophole, the discovery of which elicits from the keen-eyed agent a loud and triumphant 'Aha!'

But not in this case. Instead, Pam said, 'hmm.' She followed up with a comment on the parentage of the film's producers, its vulgarity relieved only by the adjective *clever*.

Derry did not want to hear that the producers were clever anythings. Neither did she want to hear they had rightly stitched anybody up, especially her. But the upshot was that she would get a minuscule weekly payment while on call, but no expenses, and couldn't refuse to come back and finish her scenes.

'What if I do refuse?'

'Um, they sue you for wrecking the film. Millions, I expect.'

'I don't have millions!'

'Doesn't matter. The lawyers get paid for suing, not for winning. More to the point, you'd never work again outside a burger joint, and even they might have second thoughts.'

That Derry didn't immediately accuse her agent of incompetence might seem surprising. But she didn't. In showbusiness, tradition is everything. The agent does the negotiating, issues the empty threats, and looks after the bluffs and halfhearted ultimata. The actor's role is to nurture their talent and protect their sensitivity in the safe space afforded by their heroic agent. Derry understood this long-standing convention. Basically, she could expect no say in anything whatsoever.

'Think of it as a rest,' said Pam brightly. 'Recharge your batteries. Take in the scenery.' She spoke as though Derry had just stepped off a cruise liner and was now faced with the delightful task of choosing her tour for the day.

Derry thanked Pam and ended the call. The thought occurred to her that she had arrived in Scotland as an actor playing a wandering gypsy fortune-teller. Overnight, she had become a wandering fortune-teller pretending to be an actor.

17

Dinner at the hotel was a miserable affair. Actors and crew sat in silence or muttered conspiratorially. The lively banter and raucous humour of previous days had vanished. So dampened were the spirits of all concerned that nobody complained when venison was served yet again.

Derry and Bruce sat together but spoke little. So heavy was the silence that every word uttered sounded like a speech, so you tried not to say anything. Only in Derry's room after dinner did she and Bruce get a chance to talk.

'Pam says I've got to show up when they say or they'll sue me,' said Derry. 'It's in the contract.'

Bruce made a sympathetic face. 'Take a vacation? Check out the Highlands?'

'That's what Pam said. If I could afford a vacation I'd be going someplace where the sun shines more than once a week. Anyhow, everything here is a hundred miles from everything else.'

'Isn't your mom in Edinburgh?'

Why hadn't she thought of that? She had toyed vaguely with the idea of going to Edinburgh at some point. Why not now? Derry had always wanted to see Scotland's most beautiful city, and Vanessa always took a spacious apartment wherever she went. Derry could get there by train easily enough. Then she remembered Jacko. She'd clean forgotten her promise to Vanessa to break the news about his exhibition with the reviled Edgar Booth. She wondered how to have a conversation with her mother while avoiding having one with her father. Or vice versa.

Derry's phone rang. The screen lit up, and if she hadn't been distracted by the demands of O'Donnell family diplomacy she might have checked the Caller ID. But she didn't check.

'One hesitates to ask if you saw it coming?' said Torquil. 'Teasing, honestly. I've got an idea I want to put to you. Shall I keep talking or do you want to hang up now? Won't be offended, I promise.'

Derry knew she should cut the call, but hesitated. The promise of information was too strong.

'Our little mishap with Darian?' continued Torquil. 'We've got rather a problem, and you might want to help us.'

'I'm sorry, I don't see how.'

Torquil gave a frustrated sigh. 'You can't have a leading man who falls off horses! This is not our intrepid lead getting bitten by an alligator in the jungle. This is *idiot rock singer from a talent show tries to play he-man and makes a fool of himself.*'

'So what's that to do with me?'

'Somebody took a shot at you guys on the mountain. Crazy poachers, right? Or religious fanatics that hate the movies and won't pull a sheep out of a ditch on a Sunday.'

'Torquil, what are you saying?'

'Everything's a trade, Derry. That's life. We give the press a cracking story about an actress being shot at by poachers, fanatics, organised crime—whatever, and they agree not to write about Darian's little embarrassment. Just one interview, ten minutes.'

At first Derry couldn't speak. 'Are you crazy? What organised crime?'

'There *could* be a connection, right? Russians? I don't know. Who's to say?'

'Are you trying to …' Derry stopped right there. What he meant was obvious. He was hinting *she* was the one being shot at. *Organised crime. Russians.* The TV reporter—that contrived ridiculous story.

'Torquil, you know what you can do with—'

'Derry, they'll make it up anyhow.'

'*You're* the one making it up!'

'We need you to do this. You can tell them whatever you like. Tell them it's poachers if you want. Don't take this so personally. It's nothing to do with reality. You should know that.'

Derry hung up.

She sat in silence, breathing heavily. Bruce sat watching her. 'You okay, honey?'

Derry nodded. She could feel the blood pounding in her veins. 'Torquil. More garbage.' She sighed. 'Edinburgh sounds good.'

18

The train carriage was almost empty as Derry settled into her seat by a window, plonking her bag beside her and rooting inside for her phone and her bottle of water. Both she placed neatly on the white formica-topped table that separated her seat from the one facing. Through the window she saw Bruce standing on the platform waving. Derry smiled and waved back. The scene was like some tearful leave-taking in a war movie, except no tears were shed and the sailor was the one staying behind.

Derry was still waving when Bruce turned away, distracted by something. A woman was rushing onto the platform, ticket in one hand and overnight bag in the other. She smiled and waved to Bruce but didn't hesitate or slacken her pace. Only then did Derry realise the woman was Jessica.

She appeared at the end of Derry's carriage, approaching along the aisle, her bag held in front of her. Derry gave the kind of long-distance smile you make when you recognise someone who hasn't yet recognised you. For a second, Jessica was blank-faced, hesitating before smiling in recognition.

'Mind if I join you? You know you've chosen the side for the best view? You going to Glasgow?'

'No, to Edinburgh,' said Derry. 'See my Mom. Kill the few days 'till my next scene. You for Edinburgh too?'

'Um, yeah.' Jessica didn't seem inclined to say more. Only then did it occur to Derry that she was leaving in the middle of what was, after all, a production crisis. Strange. Maybe she was being sent on some mission?

Jessica took an iPad and earbuds from her bag and placed them on the table. She kept glancing out the window as if waiting for someone to show up on the platform. But only Bruce stood there, giving Derry a little wave every time he caught her eye.

The carriage gave a lurch as the train crept forward, prompting a blown kiss from Bruce. Jessica watched, expressionless, until the station disappeared from view. She gave a sigh and sat back in her seat.

As the train picked up speed, the wheels going clickety clack in the soothing way trains are supposed to sound, Jessica seemed to relax. 'Your first time on this train?' she said.

Derry agreed it was.

'You're in for a treat. Prettiest rail journey in the world, they say.'

Already, Derry was finding that easy to believe. The line followed the shore and Derry saw that although the day was bright, the sea looked rough. Was there a storm somewhere beyond those fairytale islands?

'I shouldn't be going anywhere,' announced Jessica.

Derry made an interested face, polite but noncommittal.

'I have to be in Edinburgh. Just for … probably tomorrow.' She hesitated. 'I … told you about that.'

Ah. The boyfriend. The ultimatum.

'They have things pretty well under control,' added Jessica. 'Or as near as this movie ever gets.'

Derry realized she was talking about the production. She seized her chance for fresh intelligence. 'And how is Darian? Is he gonna be alright?'

'Nobody knows yet. With luck we'll be okay. Anyhow, whatever happens, the Carsons will be going back to the States, maybe the week after next. Not much time.'

Derry was wondering how to ask *not much time for what?* when her phone rang.

'Mom! Can you hold on a second?' She muttered an apology to Jessica, got up and made her way down the carriage to the little end-compartment by the doors. She leaned against the swaying carriage wall. 'Mom, hi!'

'I've got a gallery assistant, but she insists she's strictly nine-to-five,' announced Vanessa. 'She threatened an employment tribunal!'

'I'm looking forward to seeing you,' said Derry, forging on with a fluency born of long practice. Satisfying dialogue is, everyone knows, made up of two complimentary halves. But with Vanessa this was a wholly unrealistic ideal. As a lifelong veteran of conversations with her mother, Derry's policy was to take responsibility for her own half only, on the principle that to attempt anything else would to be to risk psychological collapse.

'Looks like we'll get in at four,' continued Derry, sticking to the plan.

'I need to brief you for the meeting, darling. You *are* my Personal Assistant.'

'No I'm n—'

'Of course you are. Didn't we have an arrangement? I'm sure we had. Anyway, it's just for a couple of days.'

'Mom, you said—'

'Oh that little thing! No publicity is bad publicity—isn't that what they say?' Vanessa had more or less banned Derry from her London gallery. Gangsters and the art business didn't mix she had insisted, in the face of all known facts. 'The important thing is I need a little backup for this meeting. The size of the delegation matters—ask any ambassador. Say you will?'

Derry hesitated. But what choice did she have? 'Sure, okay. Who are we meeting?'

'My investor. Well, potential investor. Gordon Anderson—a politician. Up and coming, I'm told. Wants to partner and thinks he can get us an arts grant for the gallery.'

'I guess grants are good,' agreed Derry, aware she was stating the very, very obvious, but keen to show business acumen. Grants were, by definition good—everyone in the arts knew that.

'By the way, I won't be at the gallery, as I'd hoped,' continued Vanessa. 'You'll need to come to the apartment. I'll text you the address. Entryphone number five. If I can't be in, I'll arrange for someone else to be there.'

Derry was touched. Vanessa's more usual approach to meeting her daughter was to arrange a time and place, change her plans after a call from a client, dispense incomprehensible instructions to an assistant, then blame them when she found she had mislaid a daughter.

'And you can help with publicity, darling. *Celtic Contemporaries*, remember?'

'Um, Mom, I didn't get to tell you—you asked me to mention the exhibition to Dad?'

'Oh that,' said Vanessa, airily. 'I'm sure we can work something out. Your father is coming to Edinburgh this week.'

'You told him? About Booth?'

'Oh no! ' said Vanessa cheerfully. 'Really darling, you need to start thinking!' She spoke as if Derry had spent her twenty-seven years on planet Earth in a largely vegetative state. 'Psychology, dear! I've told your father if he comes down from whatever cloud he's inhabiting, he can see the new gallery space—advise on the layout. Artists do so like to be consulted, makes them feel they matter. They do of course,' she added without much conviction.

What would happen when her father learned of Vanessa's plan, Derry didn't care to think. But neither did she mean to enquire. Hopefully, she could contrive not to be around when the nuclear button was pressed.

'You can tell me all about your glamorous film,' said Vanessa. 'Who knows, perhaps you might have a future.' Derry wondered was Vanessa experimenting with maternal encouragement. She decided to give her the benefit of the doubt. Best say nothing about lead actors falling off horses, or the high probability that anything Director Hamilton touched would have *turkey* written all over it in lights.

'And darling,' added Vanessa, '*Please* tell me you brought something to wear.'

～

'This is where they shot the Hogwarts Express for Harry Potter,' announced Jessica. The train was sweeping around a curving viaduct thrown casually across a broad heather-covered valley of breathtaking beauty.

'You like working with movies?'

'Sure,' said Jessica, as though surprised the question needed to be asked. 'Who doesn't?'

Derry wondered if Jessica secretly wanted a more creative role than PA to the producer but hadn't the confidence. Derry always tried to encourage people to give creativity a chance and go after their dreams if they could. 'Ever thought of writing?'

Jessica laughed. 'Thought of? Sure. I meant to be a writer. Then I saw what they do to scripts in this business. Morons like Hamilton.' She looked Derry in the eye. 'You know what I'm talking about.'

Derry kept her thoughts hidden. She had learned long ago not to reveal her opinion about a director or fellow actor to anyone except the closest and most trusted friends.

'It's the producers who call the shots,' said Jessica. '*You* know that. What they're good at is selling. They sell the idea to backers, directors, to distributors, to banks. They own the game.'

'So you want to produce?' asked Derry.

'Not want,' said Jessica. '*Do*. That's what I'm going to do.'

～

The journey to Glasgow was stunning, so much so that Derry played no more than a couple of hands of Patience. The rest of the time she was staring out the widow, bewitched by mountain stacked behind mountain, valleys with rivers rushing peaty over granite, more viaducts, and tiny stations you could hardly believe ever saw a passenger. Then the great Firth of Clyde, the broad and turbid waterway that had sustained the industrial metropolis of Glasgow for generations.

Civilisation, in the shape of Glasgow's busy Queen Street Station was a shock. After only a few days in the Highlands,

Derry had forgotten the din and the frantic motion of city life. Now she tagged along passively, hoping Jessica knew where she was going. But Jessica was unerring, confidently homing in on the right platform and the right train for the last leg of their journey to Edinburgh.

'Less than an hour,' said Jessica as they again took seats facing each other over a table, and the train began to move. From her tone, Derry knew she wasn't talking about how long it would take to reach their destination. She was thinking of something else. Less than an hour until some bad thing? Or until something long desired?

The carriage was half full, too early yet for commuters returning to the capital. Derry and Jessica had the table to themselves. Jessica took to her iPad. Derry gazed idly out the window at the flat, tedious landscape of central Scotland—a workaday place much like anywhere else. Farmland dotted with industrial estates and giant spoil heaps from defunct coal mines looking like ancient burial mounds. Derry shivered as the thought struck her that a coal mine could be just that.

Her phone, on the table in front of her, flashed urgently and rang. Jessica glanced up from her iPad. Derry stood, muttering an excuse, trying not to show her surprise at the caller. *Alex Dunbar.* As she made her way down the swaying carriage, she accepted the call.

'Just called to see how are you feeling, Derry. No ill effects, I hope?'

It took a moment for Derry to realise he was talking about the incident on the mountainside. 'Um, fine. Sure. Thanks.'

'I'm glad. I want you to know how deeply sorry I am. You're sure, no ill effects?'

'Yes. Fine. It's good of you to ask.'

'I take the safety of my guests personally, I assure you. And I promise, most sincerely, the men who did this *will* be caught.' He paused to let his words sink in. 'And Jessica—I hope you don't mind me asking, but is she ... how is she coping? She might imagine she has to keep up appearances, so I'm asking you to be frank. Does she seem ... upset?'

'She seems fine. But why not ask her—she's here on the train. We're sitting together. Not now, I'm in the corridor; but I can pass you over?'

'Oh,' said Alex. 'Ah. Train ... train to where?'

'Edinburgh. I've no more scenes for the week, so I'm visiting my Mom.'

'I see. No need to bother Jessica. I'll call her at a better time. I just wanted to make sure you were both alright.' He hesitated. 'You'll be in Edinburgh. So am I. If you're staying over, why don't you have lunch with me? Tomorrow?'

'Oh,' said Derry. 'That would be nice. I don't know yet what my schedule is going to be. Can I confirm later, after I've spoken to my mother? I'll be staying with her, and I don't know what she has planned.'

'Alright, I'll expect to hear from you later. Just text if you like, and leave me the address of where you're staying so I can send a car. One o'clock?'

'Sure. Thanks.'

'Have a good journey. Have you far to go?'

'No, We've just left Glasgow. Jessica says less than an hour.'

'Not so bad. You'll enjoy Edinburgh. I look forward to our lunch.'

'Um, me too. Thanks.'

Alex hung up. Derry found herself lingering at the end of the carriage, gazing idly out the window.

It was important to stop smiling.

∾

'I just had a call from Alex Dunbar. He was asking how we were. After what happened.'

Jessica looked up sharply.

'He seemed to want us to know they'd catch whoever did it,' explained Derry. 'He means well, I guess.'

Jessica swore. 'Awkward.'

How Dunbar asking after their welfare could be awkward, Derry couldn't understand.

'Mr. Carson will know where I am,' explained Jessica. She shrugged. 'Okay—so what.'

'He doesn't know you've gone?'

'He drove to Glasgow to talk to Darian's doctors before the insurance company meeting. I was uh, holding the fort.'

Some fort-holding. Derry had the feeling Jessica's employment prospects were even worse than her own. She hoped the boyfriend was worth it.

Jessica put in her earbuds to listen to music. Derry dealt herself another hand of Patience. Usually she found the game soothing—the rhythmic motions, the concentration, and above all the silence. But whatever calming power the game once had seemed to have evaporated. She felt an unaccountable depression, not the way anyone should feel travelling to a new city. Where was the excitement? With Alex Dunbar, she even had a date of a sort, yet the only feeling was an all-pervading sense of gloom.

She picked up her phone to text Bruce. Funny, she didn't even know what she wanted to say. Probably she wanted to say *miss you*, but that was silly. Or maybe it wasn't silly. Bruce always made her feel safe. Only then, as she thought of Bruce, did understanding come. Just below the surface of her mind lay a gnawing fear. She was frightened. But not about the future—her fears were for the past, for what might have happened; like her emotions were running to catch a bus she had just missed. She finished her text to Bruce. The message was a single word—*Thanks*.

Derry sat back in her seat, her anxiety ebbing away. Outside the window the scenery rolled past, just as bland as before, but now she felt interested. The farms, the spoil heaps too, were made over centuries by people toiling to make a living, just trying to get by. And here she was being whirled through the landscape at what to them would have been unimaginable speed, sending messages to her friends by magic. She had no earthly right to feel depressed. No right to feel anxious. And no need either.

Her phone pinged. Bruce. *Ur welcome. No fun without ya. XX.*

~

Linlithgow, said the name on the station board. The train stopped for only a few minutes, but long enough for Derry to take in the view—the spire of a medieval-looking church with a strange metal framework on top looking like someone had tried to make a tepee out of shiny aluminium and had given up half way. She was idly watching an anxious-looking man on the platform struggle to manoeuvre an enormous double bass through the ticket barrier, when Jessica's phone rang. She looked briefly at the screen but didn't answer. The phone carried on ringing. She lowered the ringtone volume but didn't reject the call. Minutes later, as the train pulled out of the station, her phone rang again, quietly this time. Again she neither took the call nor rejected it, instead she stared at the phone, blank-faced, until it stopped ringing. She offered no explanation.

The caller had to be Carson. Derry wondered was he demanding to know where Jessica was. Had Alex called him and said, *do you know your PA is on her way to Edinburgh?* Maybe Carson did know and was phoning to fire her. Not hard to work out that Jessica didn't mean to be fired, or at least not on the phone.

Almost at the instant Jessica's phone lapsed into silence, Derry's own phone rang. She stood, grimacing her excuses.

'Dad! Hold on a moment.'

Derry made her way between the seats to the end of the now crowded carriage. She stood again in the little compartment at the end.

'Dad, hi! Where are you?'

'Sure aren't I in Scotland? Alas, I find myself on the far side of Ben Something, preventing me rushing *tout suite* to my favourite daughter and demanding she buy me a drink.'

'*Only* daughter. But I guess I must owe you one for something.'

'You must accept your fate—a parent is a permanent creditor. But tell me, are the bright lights still shining and the creative juices flowing nicely at an agreed daily rate?'

Derry laughed. 'I guess the creative part is okay. Not sure about the agreed rate, but that's another story. I may have a … gap before I do my next scenes. I'm going through to Edinburgh to see Mom, take in the sights. I'm on the train now.'

'A magnificent city, to be sure. I remember a certain bar where the cream of Irish traditional musicians were wont to gather, carousing until the agents of law and order inevitably crashed the party. You will find that amongst the constabulary of Edinburgh, Calvin is not dead. Now Glasgow—'

'Where are you, exactly? What are you doing in Scotland? Mom says you're coming to Edinburgh this week.'

'Pretending to shoot grouse! Invitation I couldn't refuse, seeing as how it came from Himself.' Derry knew *Himself* was the senior royal personage who seemed to have taken Jacko to his bosom as representing the free spirit of creativity. 'We're only a couple of hours from Edinburgh, and your mother wants to confer. I agreed out of a spirit of scientific curiosity and on the basis she pays for my hotel.'

Derry wondered if scientific curiosity knew what it was letting itself in for. 'Speaking of Mom, uh … did she mention her plans for an exhibition? She says there's lots of money sloshing about Edinburgh these days. Hedge funds and so on.' Derry tried to sound confident. The idea was to suggest boundless opportunity, though if pressed she might have to admit she hadn't the foggiest idea what a hedge fund actually was.

'She did mention Celtic Something-or-other, or some such baloney. My Scottish friends tell me Edinburgh is as Celtic as Wolverhampton.'

'And did she … mention any details, like plans?'

'She did not. She said she meant to give me a major Scottish exhibition and wanted to talk about marketing. I shall ignore the outrageous phrase *give me an exhibition* as the condescension artists have come to expect from agents and their ilk. But if one's agent doesn't already know about marketing what, pray, is the reason for their outrageous commission?'

'Perhaps she just wants to consult, take on board—'

'*Take on board* my—'

'Dad!'

'I'm only saying there's more. I can feel it in me bones.' Jacko spoke with the absolute assurance of one married and unmarried to Vanessa for half a lifetime. 'All the same, in a spirit of cooperation, I have agreed to inspect the premises and make some suggestions. As it happens, I may need a little more by way of cashflow soon, so an exhibition may be timely.'

Derry smiled. 'The Castle O'Donnell studio gallery and ancestral party house?'

'Not … exactly,' said Jacko. He sucked in his teeth and made clucking noises the way he did when he was wondering whether to confess details of some unlikely scheme. To Derry's relief, he decided against. 'The main thing is to nip your mother's wilder flights of venality in the bud. By meeting face to face, I can be sure I'm talking to one person and not your mother, two lawyers and an accountant.'

'I'm sure you'll sort something out,' said Derry, much as one might remark *I'm sure the pilot knows what they're doing* in an airplane lurching wildly three miles above the Atlantic. 'Let me know when you're coming, okay? We could meet for a coffee.'

'Excellent. You can regale me with stories of your success so I can bore my peers in retaliation for their remorseless paternal bragging. Feel free to improvise and embroider—these days we must bolster our image daily to fuel the discontent of our Facebook friends.' Jacko cackled happily.

'Dad! You don't *do* Facebook. Behave.'

'Sure how can I behave, amn't I your father?'

Derry laughed, said her goodbyes and hung up. She leaned back against the swaying carriage wall and watched the countryside flashing past. She checked the time. Only twenty minutes to Edinburgh.

The door to the next carriage opened. A man entered. Odd—instead of sliding open the connecting door and stepping on through into Derry's carriage, he stood peering through the glass.

Time to return to her seat. 'Excuse me,' said Derry politely, meaning the man to stand aside and let her past. He turned from the window. 'Sorry,' he muttered absently. Then, 'Oh, hello.'

At first Derry couldn't place him. His face was familiar but not familiar.

'Forgot something,' he said. And he was gone, the door to the adjoining carriage sliding closed behind him.

Johnny. Wasn't that his name? The man from the castle, some kind of assistant to Dunbar. Not a particularly friendly guy, but maybe he wasn't sure where he had met her. No reason why he should. Then Derry remembered—Dunbar was in Edinburgh. This man worked for him, so presumably he had come through to Edinburgh with his boss. Maybe he lived in Linlithgow?

Derry took her seat opposite Jessica. 'Small world,' she said.

'Oh?' said Jessica. She seemed distracted. Was she playing in her mind the possible scenarios that might await her in Edinburgh? Derry sympathised. Would it be *happy ever after* or would she get a *see ya 'round*?

'Johnny. That guy who works for Alex Dunbar?' said Derry. She had a vague idea that taking Jessica's mind off her dilemma might help. 'He opened the door for me that time I came to the castle? I just bumped into him.'

'Johnny? You sure?'

'Yeah. He said hello when he realised he couldn't *not* say hello. Not too friendly.'

'They're all like that, Alex's men,' said Jessica. 'All his old veterans put on that cool look.'

'What, like Dunbar is military?'

'Was. That's how he knew Mr. Carson.'

Derry remembered thinking Dunbar reminded her of someone. Bruce, of course. That composed confidence, the relaxed but alert stance. Alex had military written all over him. But Jim Carson had none of that.

'Mr. Carson worked for the State Department. Doing trade deals or something. They got friendly when they were both stationed in Africa someplace. In the nineties. Sierra Leone, I think.'

Derry remembered the incongruous collection of African ceremonial masks and weapons in the castle hall. *Souvenirs.* She remembered too the easy closeness between Dunbar and Carson.

'You're sure it was Johnny?' Jessica asked once more.

'Like I said, he remembered me.'

Jessica hesitated, like she was sizing Derry up, wondering whether to trust her. 'Can I ask you a favour?'

'Sure. I guess.'

'I ... better explain something.'

Derry made an interested face. Sympathetic.

'I told you about ... Edinburgh?'

Derry nodded. *The boyfriend.*

'Something you need to know about Mr. Carson ...'

Almost before Jessica spoke, a voice inside Derry's head was saying, *'Oh no, don't let it be that she's having an affair with her boss. Car crash!'*

'No. Not that,' said Jessica quickly, as though she had read Derry's thoughts. 'Nothing like that. But he can be ... how can I say it ... he can be spiteful. If he thinks you're disloyal or you haven't kept your part of the deal, he takes it personal. And, okay, yeah—he has hit on me. He doesn't push it, just drops hints. But it's uncomfortable.'

'But doesn't he know about Edinburgh? Didn't he say something about you and ... somebody when I was at the castle?'

'Sure, he knows. That's the problem—if he thinks I'm gonna leave he won't like it.'

'But it's just a job, right? He can't stop you leaving.'

'Well, he sort of can. Whenever we travel he keeps the passports. Puts them in Alex's safe. He always does that.'

'So you think he might give you problems if you want to leave?' Derry could see the situation now. If Jessica decided to give up everything, stay with her boyfriend in Edinburgh and dump the job, she'd need a passport.

'Can't you get another from the embassy?'

'That's where I'm going right now. The consulate's in Edinburgh. I'm gonna tell them I lost it. I need to be able to go back home if things don't work out in the next couple of days and I get fired. I have to know I can get on a plane.

'I'd prefer if Mr. Carson didn't know about the consulate— about me getting a new passport. If he thinks I mean to leave the job, he might decide to push me before I jump. If I do leave, I want to do it my way. So, I'm asking a favour.'

'If I can …' Derry hoped her shrug said *sure I'll help you, but it's not a blank cheque.*

'Would you come with me to the consulate? You don't have to wait, just come with me in a cab. Then, if I'm asked, I can say it was you doing something there and I just tagged along.'

Derry checked the time. 'Don't embassies close at five?'

'I have an appointment. I'll just make it. If I get the application in, I can come back tomorrow and do the rest. I don't want to waste any time.'

Derry took a deep breath. Every instinct in her body shouted *Stay out of it! Boyfriends, bosses, lies—trouble!*

But how do you say no, I won't share a cab?

∼

The taxi was red tartan all over, inside and out. The driver quickly established his passengers were American, the cue to launch into a well-practiced monologue. He began with a lamentation.

'It's a pity ye didn't come in the summer. Dinnae get me wrong, Edinburgh is always nice, but you've chosen mebbe not the best day. Or week.'

As the cab emerged up the ramp from the covered station into the open, Derry saw what he meant. A vicious wind drove the sleeting rain horizontally, rocking the cab as it stood waiting to make a right. Even so, the cabbie seemed intent on his patriotic duty, encouraging his passengers to crane their necks backwards to admire the vast looming bulk of Edinburgh castle on its crag, or as much as could be made out through the rain-spattered windows.

'Regent Terrace, you said? Is it the consulate you're looking for?' The cabbie delivered his line as he seemed to imagine a TV detective might, impressing acolytes with his powers of deduction. 'I can go some of the way up,' added the cabbie. 'But the road is blocked—security, ye ken. You'll have to walk the last part. Sorry aboot that.'

Regent Terrace was a raised row of elegant Georgian town houses running above and parallel to the main road. You could tell the consulate from the flagpole flying a bedraggled stars and stripes. 'Ye see I cannae get past the bollards,' explained the cabbie, pointing to the concrete obstructions barring access to the central part of the street. 'I'm sorry.'

Just as Jessica was about to open the door and step outside, her phone rang loudly. She looked at the screen, seeming uncertain what to do. The cab rocked in a sudden gust. Derry turned tactfully away pretending to inspect the rainswept street. 'Tak yer time,' said the cabbie, as though his meter wasn't running.

'Hi,' said Jessica. The voice Derry heard through the tinny speaker was probably male, but she could make out nothing the caller was saying.

'Yeah, I am,' said Jessica. 'Sure, yeah. Can you hold on, I'm just getting out of a cab.' She made a face at Derry, signalling she was about to leave. Still holding the phone to her ear, she reached into the overnight bag lying at her feet. She was obviously fumbling for her purse. Derry waved her away. Jessica mouthed a token protest before smiling her thanks.

As Jessica opened the cab door, a wild gust almost snatched it from her hand. She stepped out into the downpour, dragging her bag after herself and slamming the door closed. Derry watched as, braced against the wind and rain, Jessica struggled towards the consulate.

'Dundas Street,' said the cabbie, pulling a U-turn. As they swept around, Derry peered through the rain-streaked glass. Jessica was standing in a doorway two houses from the embassy, the phone pressed intently to her ear, her back turned to the wind.

19

As she changed and brushed up in Vanessa's elegant apartment, Derry congratulated herself on being entirely presentable. She had brought her fifties floral tea dress with the high neck and shaped waist—maybe a little summery for Edinburgh in late October, but versatile, that was the point. Combined with Victorian-style button-up ankle boots, the effect was, Derry thought, highly satisfactory. She was keenly aware that going anywhere with a mother who could afford to collect Dior posed a special challenge.

As Derry and Vanessa taxied from Vanessa's apartment to a restaurant across town, Derry had to admit that Edinburgh was pretty. Even in the dark and rain of an October evening, she could make out battlements, turrets and quaintly pointed roofs. Surprisingly, these defences belonged not to castles and fortresses but to hospitals, banks, schools and apartment blocks. In the eighteen hundreds, the cabbie explained, Edinburgh architects had hallucinated themselves into the fifteenth century by reading too many novels. Imagine, he wondered, what the city would look like if they'd had television.

The restaurant was surprising. Not least because Mikayel, the owner, appeared in full Armenian national costume, wore moustaches of heroic proportions and seemed besotted by Vanessa. So extravagant was his devotion that before showing Derry and her mother to their table, he dropped to one knee proposing that he and Vanessa should ride off into the mountains together. Vanessa smiled indulgently, an artfully raised eyebrow suggesting she might consider the proposition, if her suitor tried *much* harder.

Derry looked the other way, pretending to inspect the venue. On the walls hung ancient framed portraits of bearded Armenian generals in furry hats and bandoliers. Dusty Victorian volumes filled battered bookcases. An old iron bicycle hung from the ceiling. A collection of vintage glass bottles confirmed Derry's suspicion the place had been furnished from the back room of a bric-a-brac shop.

Vanessa patronising such an unlikely establishment was a puzzle. She was known to choose restaurants solely on the grounds of decor and clientele—a strategy laden with culinary risk, but consistent. Derry wondered, could her mother have been charmed out of her insistence on taste at all costs?

'Please, I show you and your friend to your table,' said Mikayel, his voice husky, his eyes blazing.

'Thank you, Mikayel,' said Vanessa, bestowing on him a gracious smile. The misunderstanding about *friend* she let go uncorrected.

Only as they were ushered down the length of the busy dining room and on to an annex did Derry grasp why they had come to this particular restaurant. There, hung haphazardly on bare granite walls, frames almost touching, were a dozen or more startlingly modern paintings. Derry saw right away they included three of her father's works as well as others she recognised as artists also commanding serious prices. She wondered did the regular clientele have any clue what these walls were worth.

Their table was for four, the seats hard church pews that their host assiduously buffed with his cloth for the sake of Vanessa's costume before disappearing to fetch the menus.

'Gordon suggested we meet here,' said Vanessa. 'He's an old friend of Mikayel's.

'Gordon?'

'My investor! *The politician.* He should be here any minute. A quick briefing, darling—as I told you, I need a little backup for this meeting …'

'A meeting? *Now?*' Derry had fondly imagined that Vanessa's invitation to dinner was an affectionate gesture towards the daughter not seen for several weeks; something about a fatted calf sprang to mind. Instead, she was to be filed under Necessary Business Expenses.

'Gordon wants to partner the gallery. He'll invest—strictly behind the scenes, of course,' continued Vanessa. 'Nothing … public, although he will—how can I put it—champion the gallery in the corridors of power?' She leaned forward, her voice a conspiratorial whisper. 'Gordon helped get the premises and the planning permission. He's managing the conversion for me, hiring the tradesmen and so on.'

'Ah,' said Derry, in a way she hoped conveyed she had some grasp of the agenda. 'So is that his business?'

Vanessa sniffed impatiently. 'Business isn't everything, darling. Gordon has a wide portfolio of interests, I believe, but he also has a highly developed sense of social responsibility. That's why he's a politician. Creating jobs, promoting equality and so forth. As I told you, he thinks he can get the gallery a large grant as a groundbreaking cultural institution. We'll have to show some works by the locals now and again, of course—children, convicts and so on—but a small price to pay for cashflow.'

'He's promised that?'

'He's confident.'

'But aren't there lots of galleries in Edinburgh? I mean, why—?'

'That's why Gordon wants to talk about publicity,' said Vanessa. 'He says to get public money these days, you have to promote equality etcetera, while being edgy and provocative. But at no time unacceptable, of course.'

'Acceptably edgy?'

'The problem is that *edgy* has been done to death. Once you've preserved your unmade bed in formaldehyde, where is there to go? I need your help, dear. You're supposed to be creative. Why don't you think about it overnight. Think headlines—well maybe not headlines. Page two. *Gallery Caravaggio-something-something shock*? Perhaps not *shock*—surprise?'

Derry would be the first to admit she was no expert in marketing, but she suspected that *surprise* lacked punch, even by the standards of page two. Vanessa's expensive coiffure did little to hide the anxious crease on her brow. Derry wondered should she feel concerned, but it soon dawned that Vanessa was suffering from no more than the greed assailing any functioning business person faced with the possibility of free money courtesy of the taxpayer.

'I'm counting on you for some fresh thinking,' continued Vanessa. 'Remember—*edgy*. Gordon insists on that. And *equality*, that part's important. Nothing *elitist*. He's coming tomorrow at noon to see how the building work is coming on. You can take notes. Make him feel important.'

'Oh,' said Derry. 'I'm supposed to be somewhere. Um, lunch.'

'Darling, this is *business*.'

'I *could* let him know I can't come,' said Derry, regretting her words at once.

'*Him?*' observed Vanessa. 'And might I ask …?'

'Just somebody I met.'

'Handsome?'

'Mom!'

'Please say *not an actor*, darling.'

Derry sighed. 'No, not an actor. Just a … someone I met. It's only lunch Mom!'

'A conquest is a conquest, dear,' said Vanessa, smiling broadly. 'Lunch where?'

'I don't know where! He said he'd send a car.'

Vanessa beamed. 'You should have said!' In Vanessa's world, *sending a car* as distinct from *sending a cab* was a phrase laden with meaning. If the date did happen to be an actor, an actor who can send a car most likely has his Oscar safely tucked up at home. 'I guess I can do without my Personal Assistant for a few hours. No need to come back early.'

How many times can you insist to your mother that your date is only a lunch? Not an afternoon assignation. Not a *cinq à sept*. Not the start of some great anything. Worst of all, when Derry did come back from lunch she knew Vanessa would give her a speculative look, followed by an infuriating smirk.

'When's Dad coming?' asked Derry. It was a low trick. Many options were available for a change of subject, and she felt a teensy bit guilty at picking the one most likely to irritate her mother the most. She said it anyway. On cue, Vanessa frowned.

'He hasn't said, but probably the weekend. Your father likes weekends.'

'How will you ever get him to agree to a shared exhibition? He hates Edgar Booth. He'll go crazy.'

'Oh, no,' said Vanessa, airily. 'All that's sorted out. This exhibition is *happening*. It is happening whether Jack likes it or not. In time, he may learn that Edgar is also exhibiting.'

'You're not going to tell him?'

'Of course he'll have to know. He'll see the publicity and so on. The point is not *if* he finds out but *when*. At that time, we'll have a mature discussion in which I tell him what I mean to do. Meanwhile, I expect you to respect confidentiality.'

'You mean not tell—'

'Darling, dealing with artists is like dealing with children. Sometimes you have to tell little white lies. For their own good, of course.'

Derry wasn't at all convinced that little white lies, however justified, could fairly be delegated. Especially not delegated to her. She was about to make the point, when Vanessa looked up sharply and whispered, '*Gordon!*'

The man who entered the restaurant and approached Mikayel at the counter was small, podgy and pasty-faced, with thinning grey hair and wire-rimmed glasses. His front teeth were prominent—just enough to make a political cartoonist's life easy, but not so hideous as to make the man unelectable. He smiled a practiced smile at Mikayel and slapped him on the shoulder. Mikayel returned the compliment with the open-hearted affection owners of restaurants bestow on people with healthy expense accounts and a lively social life, both qualities known to attach to politicians the world over.

'Vanessa!' said the man. His effusive cheek-kissing suggested that if he and Vanessa were not siblings tragically separated at birth, they were soulmates prevented from communicating for many sad and tearful years.

'My personal assistant, and daughter, Derry,' announced Vanessa.

'Gordon,' said Gordon. 'Gordon Anderson,' he added, in case Derry had mistaken him for other, lesser Gordons. He held Derry's hand a moment longer than strictly necessary before taking his seat and reaching for the menu.

'This is, of course, on the gallery,' said Vanessa. 'That is, if you are allowed eat without declaring it to an ethics committee or finding yourself pilloried on Twitter.' Vanessa smiled the smile she reserved for especially worldly-wise jokes.

'If you don't tell, I won't' said Gordon. His laugh was a curious monotone like a child's recitation, every syllable pitched the same as the one before.

Pleasantries over, almost at once the conversation turned to the latest artistic controversies—the amazing ability of the Tate and the Turner Prizes to win column inches, tweets and likes, and how Gordon, Vanessa and Derry were right now sitting in an Edinburgh restaurant talking about those very prizes. 'Is that proof, or is that proof?' declared Gordon.

Vanessa nodded and looked thoughtful. Derry tried to look equally thoughtful but hadn't the faintest clue what she was supposed to be thoughtful about. She adopted the attentive yet neutral pose she imagined PAs adopt when their betters were talking strategy. Blending into the background seemed to be expected. She did some blending.

'Which brings me to our little project—can I say that? I mean, *our*?' said Gordon.

Vanessa smiled a charming smile that said, of *course, how nice.* Lawyers would be mentioned all in good time.

'Free money,' continued Gordon with satisfaction, taking a healthy swig of his wine. 'But we do have a little problem.'

'Oh?' said Vanessa.

'Elitism,' said Gordon darkly. He shook his head as if to announce the outbreak of an especially virulent pestilence. 'Not that I believe there's anything elitist about great art. But there are those in my party, and more to the point *on the grants committee*, who see things differently.'

Vanessa's face assumed an expression of deep sadness. Her look implied that any such imputation was wholly unjust. 'Making the arts accessible has always been one of my most cherished ideals,' she said. 'Isn't that so, Derry, darling? How many times have I said, Art Is For The People?'

Derry had no memory whatever of Vanessa mentioning the People's stake in art. Vanessa's interests tended more towards the collections of billionaires, banks and multinational oil companies. Uncomfortably aware of her designated role as backup, Derry did her best to signal agreement without actually agreeing.

'You can see my problem,' continued Gordon. 'Some say that by awarding taxpayers' money to modern art we are subsidising the cultural pretensions of the leisured classes at the expense of the ordinary working person. The voter takes a dim view of artists in ivory towers turning up their noses at plain folk and talking hoity-toity. At least your artists aren't English or we'd be rightly scunnered.' He frowned. 'You see our dilemma.'

Vanessa adopted a pose calculated to project sympathy and shared concern while signalling confidence in the organisation's ability to meet challenges going forward. Derry took her cue, radiating what she hoped was team spirit and the ability to think out of the box while at the same time respecting boundaries.

'I think I have the answer,' said Gordon.

'Oh?' said Vanessa.

But Derry didn't hear how Gordon meant to counter the grievous charge of elitism. Her phone rang. She fished the handset from her bag. *Alex Dunbar*.

'I'm sorry, would you excuse me for a minute? I need to take this.' Derry got up and made her way between the tables to the door. She stepped into a kind of vestibule, the walls plastered with garish posters from last summer's theatre festival.

'Hi.'

'Alex here. I'm afraid tomorrow is … difficult for me. I have to return to the castle urgently. I am so sorry. You must think badly of me.' He paused. This was obviously where Derry was supposed to say, *No problem, these things happen. I have so many things I need to do anyway.* But Derry had no intention of making life that easy. What was it with men?

'Not at all,' said Derry brightly. 'These things happen! There are so many things I need to do. Edinburgh is so wonderful.' She even smiled, not strictly necessary on the phone.

'I'm truly sorry. I hope we do get a chance to—'

'Sure,' said Derry, even more brightly than before. 'You bet. Look, I'm sort of busy right now. Thanks for calling.'

'Oh,' said Alex. 'Yes. Of course. Goodbye.'

He hung up. Derry leaned back against the wall, noting sourly that a play poster opposite said—*A Coup de Theatre!* and *You'll Never See it Coming!*

She scowled. Why did she feel more angry with herself than with Dunbar? All she'd done was take a couple—no *four*—phone calls. Two saying *how about X* and the other two saying *sorry about X*. It wasn't like she had invited the calls in the first place. But like a sly detective interrogating a suspect, a little voice in her head whispered knowingly. *Was it the castle? The helicopter? For a little while you felt special. So now how do you feel?*

Sturdy shoes are in many ways a blessing. Derry's ankle boots were a different kind of blessing now. Below the posters, the wall in front of her boasted convenient wooden panelling. Derry administered a sharp, though cautious, kick. The panelling was resilient but produced a gratifying thump.

Instantly, Derry felt better. She administered a second kick, if anything even more satisfying, having gained from the first a useful understanding of the relevant physics and the materials involved. She might even have emitted a moderately cathartic 'Ha!'

At that very moment, two customers entered from the street, a man and a woman shaking out their sodden umbrellas. They stopped, staring in alarm at the maniac assaulting the wall.

Derry sighed as though resigned to a tedious but necessary routine. She kicked the panelling once more, this time a delicate tap. 'Damned prosthetic,' she said, smiling heroically.

Without a word, the couple retreated into the street.

~

When Derry returned to her table, she found Vanessa and Gordon had been joined by two men, one jowly and pompous who turned out to be a lawyer, the other sharp-faced and fidgety. Both were politician friends of Gordon. Inevitably, the conversation turned to politics, a development warmly welcomed by Mikayel who wore the smile every restaurateur wears when male egos compete and the wine list is freely consulted.

Remarkably, Vanessa showed no signs of boredom, instead projecting an amused and cosmopolitan interest. Derry did her best to mimic Vanessa's *sang-froid*. She smiled dutifully at the men as their stories got sillier and their voices louder. She regretted no female politician was at the table whom she could observe by way of research. Who knew but Derry might one day have to play a thrusting, ambitious, yet warm-hearted and caring woman courageously climbing the greasy pole to smash the glass ceiling and reach the dizzy heights of power. But no female politician was present, possibly because they were at home putting male politicians' children to bed and reading them gender-neutral stories.

Vanessa mimed a delicate yawn and glanced at her watch. Instantly, the jowly man announced they should all go to a club. 'Too late tae stap noo,' he said.

Vanessa laughed indulgently, instantly summoning Mikayel to tell him she would gladly accept the bill for the meal—the wine would be separate. The three politicians' glanced anxiously at each other, but from Vanessa's end run there was no coming back. Three credit cards duly emerged from reluctant wallets.

'Can ye get us a taxi,' said the sharp-faced one to Mikayel. 'Make that two,' said the jowls. 'Three, Mikayel thank ye,' added Gordon. That the destination for all three was the same didn't seem to surprise their host. Expense allowances had to be preserved no matter what the inconvenience. Vanessa requested a fourth cab to take her and Derry home.

'By the way,' said Derry, as they sat in the taxi swishing through the sodden Edinburgh streets, 'My lunch tomorrow has been … um, changed. I can be at the gallery.'

Vanessa gave Derry a sympathetic look, like she had read her thoughts. Vanessa had always dismissed the paranormal on the grounds that if telepathy existed capitalism would instantly collapse, but her infuriating smile said she knew—Derry had been stood up. 'Never mind dear,' she said. 'What *you* need is a career!'

20

Vanessa's apartment was uncannily familiar. The paintings on the walls had come from her London home. The ceramics, the exotic and exquisite throw over the couch, the flowers—all announced Vanessa's impeccable taste and ample means. A contract with a local florist would have been arranged within minutes of Vanessa taking possession, as would a cleaner and a cook.

'Goodnight dear!' said Vanessa as soon as they had entered. Derry marvelled that her mother showed no ill-effects from dining and drinking all evening but was as fresh and poised as if she were about to step out the door. A peck on the cheek and Vanessa retired to her bedroom.

Derry hung up her jacket and put the kettle on. She rummaged in her bag for a sachet of borage tea. Tea made, she sipped, content that she really was, in a way, on vacation—she had a job to go back to, a feeling actors rarely knew. She would return to the movie refreshed and confident. And when she got home she would have a night out with her friends, and they'd share horror stories about directors and laugh.

Derry finished her tea, undressed and climbed into bed. The sheets were of the highest quality—Egyptian cotton, Derry guessed. *Sometimes*, she thought, smiling as she drifted off to sleep, *having a wildly successful mother isn't all bad.*

The surprise was that she was casting the bones. Or that was the first surprise. The second was that she was capable of being surprised at all in a dream.

She was sitting at a table as she would to tell a person's fortune. She was Madam Tulip—Derry knew that because of the heavy beaded necklace she wore and the way the bangles on her wrist jangled as she cast the bones onto a green baize table. The bones rolled and skittered for far longer than they should have. In her dream, Derry imagined casting bones on the moon might be like that—a slow-motion tumbling that went on and on.

Now they came to rest. Five bones—there were certainly five. Derry counted them, while at the same time laughing at how she was being obsessive. She stared hard to discern the bones' meaning—the client so much wanted to know. But who *was* the client? And how could Tulip understand what the client wanted without looking into her eyes? But Derry found she didn't want to look into her eyes. She didn't want to see the client's face when the woman learned what the bones were saying.

On the smooth baize table, the bones were no longer still. They were moving—at first barely perceptibly but in motion all the same, rolling and tumbling in a lazy, circular dance. Slowly they gathered momentum, swirling in a tightening spiral like stars in a galaxy spinning ever closer to the black hole at its heart. Beneath the bones, the green baize of the tabletop turned darker than the blackest night, and now the spinning stars were a necklace of gleaming, whirling suns.

Some instinct made Derry finger the beads she wore round Madam Tulip's neck. The string was heavy, falling in loose and generous loops, but now it seemed the loops were tightening in bizarre imitation of the spinning stars from which she couldn't tear her gaze. She wrapped her fingers round the string and pulled—who cared if the necklace broke? But it wouldn't break. And now her desperately clawing fingers could barely fit inside the constricting rope of beads. As her strangled gasps for breath were choked into fading gurgles, and the spinning stars whirled faster and faster, panic overwhelmed her. Even the chance to scream was gone.

Across the baize table the client sat watching, seemingly unmoved, uncaring, hardly a person at all. And Derry's last, dying thought was the worst anyone could have. The words came slow but distinct.

It's all my fault.

21

The cab lurched to a halt, then took off, abandoning Derry and Vanessa the way a stagecoach in old movies dumps its mailbag and thunders on before anybody can take a shot.

'This is it!' announced Vanessa proudly. 'Isn't it *too* charming?'

Derry guessed that *charming* was a term rarely applied to Leith and its docklands—a mind-boggling jumble of Victorian tenements, industrial parks, warehouse apartments and abandoned backstreets, all looking like they had been dumped from a passing spaceship to lie where they fell.

Down a narrow cobbled alley, a pair of massive gateposts led to an old stone building set in a courtyard rank with weeds. Two battered white builders' vans sat, seemingly abandoned. Beyond, high-rise blocks loomed—the sort local authorities sooner or later dynamite in that gracefully choreographed way that gets millions of views on YouTube.

'The place was a dairy,' explained Vanessa as they picked their way across the yard. 'Perfect for an installation. Edgar has a fully working gas station fitted out for colonoscopy and symbolising our perverse appetite for hydrocarbons. The press will *love* it.'

'Vanessa! Derry!' Gordon Anderson emerged from the old building beaming as though their arrival was a notable achievement. He had stepped out through enormous wooden double doors blackened by charring. 'They get pretty creative round here,' said Gordon grinning at Vanessa's anxious look. 'But nobody will want to steal paintings, I can promise you that.'

As they entered the gallery, stepping over piles of rubble to view what Gordon assured them would soon be a beautiful exhibition space, Vanessa looked anxious. The place echoed with whining electric drills, thundering kango hammers and shouted swearing—but no signs the work would be finished anytime soon. Vanessa shouted questions over the din, but Gordon's answers all seemed to involve jobs that couldn't be done until much bigger jobs were finished. As instructed, Derry took notes in a little pad, fulfilling her designated function as Personal Assistant for the day.

'Why don't we go for a cup of tea,' said Gordon hastily. 'We can have a chat, then come back when they've stopped for lunch. Get a bit o' peace and quiet.'

As Gordon led them past the rubble and out the front door, Derry dutifully scribbled in her notebook—*Cup of tea. Get a bit o' peace and quiet.*

Vanessa stopped, holding out her hand for the notes. She took the pad and read. For a second it looked as if she were about to comment, but she didn't. Instead she slowly shook her head, as though wondering how she could have produced a child so dense. Or perhaps she was contemplating the comforting possibility that twenty-seven years ago there may have been a lucky hospital mix-up.

∼

They stood at the door of one of those small, austere cafes patronised by delivery men, builders and truck drivers. 'Best bacon roll in Scotland!' announced Gordon, beaming as he ushered them inside.

The floor was covered in faded brown vinyl, the tables graced by red plastic cloths on which sat encrusted sauce bottles and bowls of crumbling sugarlumps. On one wall hung a lopsided tourist poster of Edinburgh castle. At a corner table sat three truckers, all staring at Vanessa like their familiar and comforting haunt had been invaded by a prima ballerina in a tutu or a yeti stamping its feet and brushing snow off its fur.

'*Gordon!*' hissed Vanessa, visibly alarmed. She clutched her Burberry parka tightly around herself. Mesmerised, she followed Gordon to a table, like they were taking their first steps onto an alien planet.

Derry's phone rang. *Bruce.* She signalled for the others to carry on without her, while she stepped back outside.

'Bruce! Hi! How's the war?'

'You want a job done right, send an American. Man, those redcoats didn't stand a chance.'

'You're supposed to be Canadian.'

'Gee—guess you're right.' He hesitated. 'Um, can you talk?'

'Sure. You okay?'

'Fine, yeah. Just that they've, uh, pulled the movie. Thought you'd need to know, soon as.'

'What do you mean *pulled*? Postponed or what?'

'They called a meeting, 'bout a half hour ago. Carson, Hamilton, everybody. Short and sweet. Darian won't be well enough to carry on. He'll be okay, but doctors say he can't work right now, and the insurance won't let him anyway. Carson made noises about trying to pick up again later, but nobody believes a word. They'll pay for the hotel tonight, then that's it. We're on the streets, honey.'

Derry's head should have been buzzing with questions but wasn't, like she had always known this movie would never make it to the end.

'I just hope it's not my fault,' said Bruce.

Derry snapped out of her reverie. 'Your fault? How could it be your fault?'

'I had all my scenes done except two—then yesterday they came up with all this new script. I was going crazy trying to learn it, but you weren't around to rehearse me and I didn't want to ask anyone else—you know how it is.'

'Bruce, you said it could all be your fault. How?'

'I feel like I've dodged a bullet here. I mean, could I have been sort of wishing for it, and then, you know, it happens?'

'Bruce, Darian fell off his horse. Did you push him?'

'No, of course I didn't push him.'

'Well then! The movie wasn't cancelled because of you! If you were that good at mind control, you could wish everything back again, right?'

'I guess,' said Bruce. He sounded doubtful.

Derry sighed. The film gets cancelled. Dozens and dozens of people are out of work, and all Bruce can think about is a narrow escape from doing a couple of scenes that worry him. Were all actors that self-centred?

A thought intruded. 'Did they say we'll get paid?'

'Guess what—they said *talk to your agents, everything will be fine.*

'So what do we do?'

'Home sweet home, honey, I guess. Back to the Emerald Isle, right?'

'I guess I could fly back from here.'

'Cost a fortune. Say, why don't I meet you in Glasgow? I can leave tomorrow morning. You can do the same. Jump a train, I meet you at the station and we see if we can get a place on a ferry. Shouldn't be a problem. Low season.'

'You sure about that? It's kinda awkward for you.'

'Sure I'm sure. We got cell phones. We got a van. What more do we need?' He paused. 'Jobs I guess.'

~

The woman behind the counter was fat and jolly as befitted one whose occupation in life was dispensing calories to the hungry.

'And what can I get ye, hen?'

Derry had never been called *hen* before, but guessed it was a quaint Scottish-ism. She liked it. *Hen* sounded sympathetic, and she deserved a little sympathy.

She had meant to settle for a coffee, but a tantalising smell of bacon wafted from the griddle on the stove behind. 'Um, maybe I could have a ...' She realised she didn't know what anything was called.

'Bacon roll? With an egg?' enquired the woman in the helpful tones one might use to address a lost traveller from a distant land.

Derry passed on the egg. The bitter blow of a cancelled movie certainly justified a large bread roll stuffed with butter and bacon, but to go to the extreme of egg might invite further disaster in cosmic retribution.

'Bacon roll it is, hen. You jest tak' yer seat, and I'll bring it to ye. Here's yer coffee.' The coffee was instant, the powder ladled from an enormous tin retrieved from below the counter.

Derry did as she was instructed, gingerly bearing her cracked mug of doubtful coffee back to the table at which Gordon and Vanessa sat.

'I've been explaining to Gordon the wonderful relationship you have with your father,' said Vanessa, smiling her fondest smile. She had put her own coffee, untouched, to one side.

'Terrific,' said Gordon, his face almost obscured by the roll he was munching. 'Can't beat family, eh?'

'Gordon was wondering—we were both wondering—if you could help a little.' Vanessa paused, cocking her head to one side as though listening for distant birdsong.

'You might know I have a wee television company?' said Gordon.

Derry made interested noises. All actors instinctively welcome fresh intelligence about television shows. Actors recently abandoned by movies in which they were supposed to play a modest but useful part could be expected to show even more attentiveness than usual.

'We make all kinds of shows,' continued Gordon. The usual stuff—Hitler, aeroplanes, ghosts. But we have a game show too. Diversification,' he added. *'Mair Money than Sense.'*

Derry tried to look like she had some notion of what he was talking about.

'Gordon was telling me about an idea he has,' said Vanessa. 'It's to do with your father.'

'What I was thinking—' continued Gordon. He stopped, eyes on the door.

Everyone knows that thinking about a person can make them appear at that very instant. Naming them guarantees they'll walk right in. That's what happened now.

Jacko was probably not the first person to enter these particular premises wearing a green riding cloak, calf-high top boots, a broad leather belt and a floppy, wide-brimmed hat. The building was, after all, a couple of hundred years old. But he may have been the first patron so dressed not to be hanged soon afterwards.

The table of truckers inspected the arrival. Being blessed with an ancient and picturesque dockside, Leith had sprouted luxury apartments with a river view and security gates. These bastions were linked by well-known pathways down which the incomers felt it safe to travel, like the runs made by small furry creatures scuttling from burrow to burrow. None led down here.

'Jack!' said Vanessa, attempting her most charming smile but finding it came out in installments, like a self-assembly coffee table whose instructions had been lost. 'So nice! How did you find us?'

Jacko strode to the table and kissed her cheek. 'Beautiful and elegant as ever,' he announced, ensuring the whole cafe could hear and agree. Vanessa frowned, hauling herself back from the brink of being charmed.

'Derry, me darlin',' said Jacko. He kissed her, and Derry was pleased to see he looked in the pink, overflowing with that vital energy any fond daughter would be delighted to observe in her beloved dad. On the other hand, she thought, you could have a little too much vitality, especially if those impetuous spirits were about to collide with news of an impending duet with the detested Edgar Booth.

'Didn't I get a surprise lift down from the Highlands—I won't say with whom,' explained Jacko, tapping his nose conspiratorially. 'I proceeded forthwith to the gallery and enquired of a man with a kango. So here I am.' He grabbed a chair and sat.

'This is Gordon,' announced Vanessa. 'He is helping us with the gallery. Gordon is a politician. He might be Prime Minister of Scotland some day, so be nice.'

'First,' interjected Gordon, simpering. 'In Scotland we say *First* Minister.'

'Do ye now?' said Jacko. The glint in his eye made Derry cringe inwardly. 'In Ireland we say First *Gobshite*. We find it fits no matter which party is gouging the people at the time.' His manic grin said, *do ye have a sense of humour? Because if you don't, never mind—we could always arm wrestle.*

Gordon sat, his face frozen like it had shifted into Park while his brain worked out how to respond.

'Before I risk an order,' said Jacko, 'can I confirm I am the client and hence *guest* of Carravagio Galleries in my capacity as star performing seal. If, that is, seals eat sausage.' He loudly ordered a sausage roll with bacon and egg, while calling the proprietress *Dear lady*, and getting a coquettish 'You can call me May!' in return.

Vanessa beamed graciously, 'Jack darling, you know we try to take care of our starving artists. Why, we have been known to send emergency bottles of Guinness to their garrets to save them from death by thirst. How selfless are we agents, when a dead artist can be so much more profitable than a live one.' She smiled at Gordon, including him in the joke as a fellow sophisticate in the realities of the art business.

'Your mother jests,' said Jacko, fixing his grin on Derry, 'but not a word of a lie, we artists are like the spouse around whose neck hangs a hefty life insurance—wondering about the bitter taste in the coffee and the repeated invitations to *take a little stroll by the cliff edge*. When your work becomes an *oeuvre*, you're ripe for the chop. Speaking of *oeuvres*,' he added, turning his attention to Vanessa, 'tell me you won't hire a grocery van to send my pictures up from London but will for once procure the services of a reputable transport firm that knows the difference between a work of art and a bag of rocks.'

'Jack darling, you paint the pictures; I'll take care of the difficult part.' Vanessa smiled triumphantly.

Jacko frowned. Vanessa sniffed. Gordon pretended to study his phone.

Derry felt rising alarm. Edgar Booth had yet to be mentioned, and already battle lines were drawn. Time to display some initiative. 'I'm sure the exhibition is going to be a wow,' she said brightly.

If Jacko and Vanessa had differences of opinion, which more often than not they had, they were of one mind now. At the same instant, each turned to Derry and frowned. Their expressions said precisely the same thing—teenagers shouldn't get involved, this was parents' business; and if they chose to enjoy it that was their business too.

That Derry hadn't been a teenager for many years made no difference. She instantly felt fourteen. She was involved, present, aware of most aspects of the program, yet had no vote. *Ridiculous*, she thought. I am a grown woman in the company of persons who happen to be my parents. Fortified by the thought, she forged ahead. 'We had a nice meal last night, Dad. The restaurant owner said he remembered you. He's Armenian.'

'Not Mikayel?' said Jacko, beaming and prepared to be gratified.

'He called you the finest artist in Europe and said you were the only man not from Armenia who could make cabbage soup as good as himself.' True, Mikayel had spoken of Jacko like they were comrades who had come through several wars together. 'He's got three of your pictures hanging in the restaurant,' added Derry.

'Mikayel is a man of taste,' pronounced Jacko. 'A *collector*, not a mere dealer.' He gazed idly at the fluorescent strips on the ceiling, in a way that said *not looking at any particular art dealer in the room*. 'And at least he has a wall to hang them on,' he added.

Vanessa scowled. Gordon's fascination with his phone showed no sign of diminishing.

'We were talking about publicity just now,' continued Derry, ploughing on. She turned to Vanessa. 'What was it you were talking about before Dad came in? Didn't Gordon say he had an idea?'

Derry sat back in her chair. She felt moderately pleased with herself. She wondered was it her training in the arts that made her sensitive to the slightest nuances of human communication. Such a finely tuned intervention was well beyond anything you'd expect from a mere Personal Assistant. Rather more in the executive mould, when you thought about it.

'Oh, look at the time,' said Gordon. He was on his feet and shaking Vanessa's hand. 'I have to be in town. I'll call you later—sorry to rush.'

'Surely, you don't have to hurry,' said Vanessa, wiggling her eyebrows and making the grimaces adults make when exchanging tactical messages in front of very young children.

'Sorry, I'll call,' said Gordon. 'Let me know how you get on.' He gave a vague wave at Derry and Jacko, and was gone.

'Ninety-nine percent of all statements are either lies, exaggerations or diversions,' announced Jacko loudly. 'A hundred percent for politicians.' The truckers at the table in the corner gave Jacko a thumbs-up. He might dress in a way that made you suspect he was mentally unstable, or perhaps English, but the man talked sense.

'So what was Gordon's idea?' said Derry, filling the silence like a barrow of gravel being dumped down a chute.

'The main thing is the space,' insisted Jacko, ignoring Derry's intervention. 'How pray, can one have an exhibition at New Year—*this* New Year— if you haven't got a gallery you can tell from a hole in the ground? I may add that I am as much interested in the success of this exhibition as my agent might be.'

'Delighted to hear that,' said Vanessa sourly. 'If we agree to meet on planet Earth, we should be able to achieve something.'

'Might I remind my agent that I have delivered on my part of the bargain—pictures are painted, pictures of the highest calibre. Agent's task is to assemble persons of discernment.'

'Buyers, darling. That's what we call them,' said Vanessa.

'Buyers *of discernment*,' insisted Jacko.

Once more Derry felt inspired to intervene with a constructive way forward. She wondered if she wasn't rather good at this. 'Mom and Gordon were talking about how to get publicity. Publicity means sales, right?'

'As I said, I wish this venture to succeed,' agreed Jacko. 'And I appreciate your point that in the modern world publicity is the oxygen of success. I shall, therefore, play my part, never fear. But I do not intend to be paraded around like a tame bear. I may contemplate a written Q and A with a carefully selected critic who understands something about art, though the odds against finding one are as great as the chance of discovering the crown jewels in May's microwave.' He gestured loftily towards the named appliance, eliciting from May an instant enquiry as to whether he wanted another cup of tea. 'Thank you May, and an excellent brew it is, to be sure,' responded Jacko. May beamed her approval.

'As I was saying, if you assemble a list of suitable interviewers with their *curricula vitae*, I'll be happy to consider them.'

'Jack,' said Vanessa. She spoke quietly, her expression penitent. 'There's something I need to tell you.'

'Oh,' said Jacko. He gave a little cough of the sort that said *I am listening, seeing as how I recognise that tone of voice due to having been married and unmarried to you for aeons.*

'If you really want to make this a success … You said you *do* want a success?'

Jacko shrugged in a take-it-or-leave-it kind of way that didn't fool Derry for a minute.

'We need to attract significant interest to get the gallery off the ground. Gordon …'

At the name, Jacko frowned.

'. . .Gordon thinks he can get the gallery a grant.'

Jacko's frown vanished. Jacko was, after all, an artist, for whom the word *grant* held its full quota of magic.

'Gordon felt that including some other, *less interesting*, works would help achieve the main objective. Which is of course to sell more of *your* pictures. *Capisci?* Her tone was conspiratorial, even flirtatious, holding out the promise of financial delights to come.

'A few pictures by Edgar, minor works, nothing especially impressive, and perhaps a couple of others to … fill things out?'

Jacko was silent. Was an explosion coming? Wasn't it rash of Vanessa to grasp the issue head-on in this way? Derry braced herself. Time to check her phone for messages and to see how the battery was doing.

'Minor you say?' mused Jacko.

'Marginally interesting,' said Vanessa.

'It would help, you think?'

'Definitely,' said Vanessa.

Jacko sucked in his teeth. 'I get the front space?'

Vanessa hesitated, then smiled. 'Of course. Although we might have to be a little … flexible?'

'Naturally,' agreed Jacko, the mature diplomat who knew what was what.

Awesome. Derry wondered if her mother might not be wasting her talents. Ambassador to the UN? Secretary of State? Humbled in the face of brilliance, she wondered if she shouldn't demote herself back to PA. Clearly, the road to the executive table would be long and the learning curve steep.

'Why don't we head back to the gallery,' suggested Vanessa. 'We can do the detail there. Alright with you?'

'You're the boss,' said Jacko.

The shock was profound. The words Derry had just heard were the stuff of hallucination. She felt dizzy, like she was tumbling freely in space. As Vanessa paid the bill, and they left May's cafe to its loyal clientele, Derry wondered at the fickleness of the universe and its way of snickering when you thought you knew anything whatsoever.

22

As a city of culture, Edinburgh is justly famous. Galleries, theatres and concert halls are as common as bookmakers and shopping malls in other less high-minded conurbations. So cultured is Edinburgh that the unwary, looking for a public convenience, an ATM or an egg mayo sandwich with parsley and chives, can easily find themselves trapped in the Ring Cycle, with Valkyries barring the exits and no hope of rescue until the final curtain seventeen hours later. Worse fates are possible. You can clamber into what you think is a cab only to find inside a performance of Hamlet, complete with massacre in the final scene. Bad enough, until you find the cab is on its way to Glasgow, as one of the cast has to be at his brother's stag party or he'll never be forgiven.

But in the weeks after the Edinburgh Festival ends with fireworks, parades and tearful leave-takings, the city lapses into a coma. The wind blows harder and colder down the near-deserted streets, the theatres are dark, and nobody can be bothered playing music as their hands are frozen and anyway nobody's listening. It's as though the town had put on a comedy mask, jumped around making pirouettes, had too much fun, then woken with a hangover and the horrible feeling it had made an ass of itself.

Encouraged by Vanessa to play the tourist for the afternoon while her parents talked business, Derry had found a small piece of Heaven. The paradise in question was an emporium famed far and wide for its vintage clothing and accessories. The shop hid between a bar hosting afternoon strip shows and an antique bookstore, but when it came to vintage clothes Derry had a hunting instinct the equal of any bloodhound.

Now she was sitting in the lounge of a nearby hotel sipping latte and watching windblown passersby through an enormous plate-glass window. By the side of her chair, in a huge paper carrier-bag, were a beaded swing dress from the 1940s—a triumphant discovery by anyone's standards—the cutest imaginable clamshell purse and a little silver art deco brooch with fake pearls. Derry was fully aware that as a newly unemployed actress, such indulgences could be seen as reckless. On the other hand, which was worse—a temporary financial inconvenience or a fatal collapse in morale?

In a vain effort to stop smiling and prove she was a responsible adult, Derry took up her phone to check the train times to Glasgow for the following morning. Right then, a text pinged—Jacko. *Refuse to sit in bar. Telling woes to strangers what point? Volunteer? XXX.*

Derry frowned. Beneath the mangled syntax, Jacko was clearly upset about something. The word *woe* rarely figures in texts about what's for dinner or forgotten house keys. The menu on the table bore the name and street address of the hotel. She inserted it into her reply along with a simple message—*I'll wait.*

She ordered another coffee and sat wondering. Should she be worried? Her parents had just had a business meeting. When you thought about it, *woe* was likely an understatement.

≈

When her father entered the hotel, Derry saw at once he was distressed. The lobby boasted several large modern oil paintings, but Jacko ignored the chance to condemn their creators for tourist art. He sat down heavily, passively accepting Derry's offer of a coffee. He even failed to produce an unlit cigar and wave it about, foregoing the chance to create panic and complaints to the management.

'Ye don't know what freedom means 'til ye're about to lose it,' pronounced Jacko in a hollow voice. He slumped in his chair and stared blankly into space.

This was not the Jacko Derry liked to see.

'And to think I was only doing me bit to save our national heritage.'

'Dad, can we start at the beginning? You're not happy, right?'

'Happy, is it?' said Jacko. 'Oh, I'm happy right enough. What man still breathing has the right to say he's unhappy. I'll be long enough buried under a sod—'

'Dad! Stop it!' If Derry had been wholly American, rather than semi-Irish, she would perhaps have been more sympathetic. She might have felt her father was facing a crisis of meaning in his life. She might even have suggested he see a therapist to confront the issues fatally undermining his self-esteem and preventing him approving of himself in the way insisted upon by all the best authorities. But, being half Irish, Derry knew that when someone laments the fact they would soon be buried under the sod, the statement was to be filed under the general heading of *weella, weella, wallya* or, alternatively, *ochone, ochone, ochone*. Such lamentations were mostly about the tune, not the words.

'So what happened? Did Mom say something?'

Jacko sighed. 'I don't blame your mother.'

Unprecedented. Refusing to blame an ex-spouse and current agent was unheard of. Lesser men than Jacko would never fall at that particular hurdle.

Jacko took off his hat, placing it carefully on an empty seat, like a judge retiring from the bench by putting aside his wig. 'Television,' said Jacko, his voice hollow. 'Who'd have thought it could happen to me?'

'What's this got to do with television?'

'That politician.'

'Gordon?'

'He owns a television company making drivel.'

Derry shrugged. Television was known to employ actors. A hasty condemnation would be rash. One man's drivel, etc.

'I'm supposed to go on a … show.' Jacko closed his eyes to shut out the horror.

'Oh come on Dad, some sort of arts program? You'll be a hit.'

Jacko shook his head.

'Then what?'

'A … game show.' He gasped out the words.

Derry stared. Jacko's view of television was that by simultaneously consuming with millions of others, you joined a giant group mind. This appalling mental intimacy he likened to being trapped in one of those long snaking dances Greeks do at weddings.

'You have to guess how much a modern painting was sold for without knowing the artist. The contestant who guesses the price wins points. Then a dealer comes on and he gives the real price. But some pictures are by schoolkids. *Ho-ho-ho.*'

Derry winced. Not dignified, she had to agree.

'There's more,' moaned Jacko. 'The loser has to let themselves be body-painted. All over. In the High Street, then sign photos and auction them for charity.'

Derry couldn't help it. She burst out laughing. The image of Jacko standing in the street being body-painted on television was too glorious. 'Wow, and it's October! Maybe November when they get around to it. December, even!' She hooted, making patrons at a nearby table stare. 'In Scotland! I hope they've got an ambulance standing by!' She struggled to regain her composure, putting on her most serious expression, 'I can see a problem there. Will they let you choose the colours? I mean, for an artist, that's a big deal, right?'

Jacko didn't laugh. 'That's what I said. Prison.'

'No you didn't.'

'Sure I did.'

'Dad, they can't send you to prison because you don't want to join a silly game show.'

'That fella Gordon says he can't get your mother a grant for her gallery if I won't agree.'

'But you still said no, right? If she doesn't get her grant, she doesn't. What's it all about anyhow? How is a TV show going to help the grant or sell paintings?'

'I'll be proving I'm not elitist.'

'You'd look like a moron.'

'Albeit a man of the people.'

'So refuse. What can Mom do? She could give the exhibition to Booth, but hey—you win some you lose some.'

'Can't,' said Jacko. His face sagged. His shock of greying hair, his crowning glory as an artist of distinction, sagged lanky and depressed. 'I'm in a little eeny bit of a jam.'

'Ah,' said Derry. 'You need the money.'

Jacko nodded sadly. 'I had a small piece of bad luck, don't ye know. Sure wasn't I only trying to do the right thing for Thaddeus.'

'Thaddeus?'

'Your ancestor! Thaddeus O'Donnell. Anyway, I brought up the digger.' Jacko sighed and lapsed into silence, as though psychic powers should be sufficient to spare him a narrative too painful to relate. Perhaps it worked; Derry had a sudden memory.

'That rusty old yellow thing you had out back?' Derry remembered a small tracked digger seemingly abandoned by the shore at Jacko's house.

'The same. Sure didn't you show me where to dig?'

'I didn't show you anything!'

'Ah, but you did! So I got the digger on the trailer and brought it up one night.'

'You were using a JCB to dig up a relative? In the dark? Dad!'

Jacko sniffed. 'Ancestors and relatives are not at all the same thing.'

'Was he there?'

'Not … exactly.' Jacko paused. 'It depends on what you mean by *there*.'

'Dad, he was either there or he wasn't.'

'I thought I'd found him. Four foot down, the bucket on the digger scraped on this great big article like a headstone.

Only it wasn't a headstone. I scraped it clean, and there was the O'Donnell coat of arms and a date.'

'And was he under it?'

'Nothing was under it. And no bag neither. So much for local legend.' He sighed.

'But that's cool. You said you wanted to put up a memorial, right? Now you don't even need to get a memorial made. You can just reinstate the stone. Bag, what bag?'

'Um, well, not that relevant ...'

'Dad, what bag?'

'An old story mentioned he might have been buried with a bag. Sure you wouldn't believe these things.'

'A bag of what? Not potato chips, I'm guessing. Money? Gold, even?'

'No ... Not gold. A few old emeralds, maybe. Rubies. But sure 'twas only a rumour.'

Derry stared. 'You had me walk around looking for some crazy ancestor when all you were thinking about was money!'

'I needed the cash to restore the castle! You said yourself it would cost millions. All I wanted was for the owner—the previous owner—to pay his fair whack.'

Derry took a deep breath. What was the point arguing? 'Okay, you didn't get lucky. So you're no worse off than before. And what's this about jail? Nobody gets sent to jail because they can't restore an old ruin.'

'Ah, well didn't I have a wee bit of trouble with the digger. There's two levers, d'ye see.'

'Dad, tell me nobody got hurt.'

'Only meself—a few bruises, nothing to whinge about. I was just reversing to turn around.'

'And?'

'And she ... wouldn't stop. And then she did stop. And wouldn't you think they'd have built them walls better than that?'

'You knocked down some wall?'

Jacko nodded.

'How much wall?'

'A fair old bit, I'd say now, if you were being fussy about it.'

'The whole thing?'

'Not exactly. Maybe half the height of one wall. And just as well the old digger had a good roof, with the stones bouncing off it. And then the digger toppled over, and all I could hear after were the bloody birds croaking and squawking and going mad.'

'You could have been killed!'

'Maybe better if I was,' said Jacko mournfully. 'Sure wouldn't it solve the problem?'

'Don't say things like that. Anyhow, what problem? Just leave the place alone. Maybe Thaddeus was telling you to mind your own business.'

'I can't! Paddy says he has to get paid for what he's done because now he'll have to start all over again.

'Paddy who?'

'Paddy the architect. He did the plans for the restoration and the new studio, and we had a wee arrangement ...'

'You had a bet.'

'He wants fifteen thousand and he wants it now. I don't have fifteen thousand! Didn't I spend every cent on the wretched heap of stones.'

'Can't you tell him to wait?'

'I did, until after the New Year exhibition.'

'Ah,' said Derry. 'The TV show. No show, no exhibition?'

Jacko nodded dolefully. 'I can't do it. I'll go to jail and be done with it. Promise you'll visit.'

'Dad, he can't send you to jail for fifteen grand. Come on!'

'He says he'll report me for damaging a historic monument. If I pay up he'll say nothing, and nobody will notice anyway.'

'How much jail?'

'Five years. Or they can fine me a million.'

'A million! Can't you sell the castle? What about your royal friends?'

'Haven't they got pucks of castles already? Anyway, the English owned it before. It would be like buying your old car back.'

'Put it on eBay?'

'And who but me would be such an eejit as to buy it?'

Derry was stunned. In all her life, the one unchanging rock of stability was Jacko's unswerving faith in his own judgement in blatant disregard of the evidence. To see her father defeated was heartbreaking.

'You need the exhibition, okay? So you have to do the TV, that's all. Why don't I give you some acting tips—you treat the whole thing like a role, a part in a play. Like, *I'm not here on a dumb game show; the real me is having a quiet pint in Galway?*'

Jacko spoke solemnly, like a man facing the gallows resolved to hold his head high. 'Dear girl, I thank you, but it's no use.

If Jack O'Donnell must choose between his principles and his freedom, Jack will choose his principles.'

'Dad, you're not choosing principles, you're choosing jail. Come on, it's only TV. You can't go to prison just because the alternative is embarrassing.'

'The world may sell its soul for filthy lucre,' continued Jacko, warming to his theme, 'but a true artist must spurn the call of Mammon. *Let them do what they will!*'

As his voice rose, the patrons at nearby tables stared. Obviously the man was famous, but they couldn't put their finger on who exactly he might be. A woman stood, camera at the ready, but far from being deterred by the attention, Jacko seemed to find new depths of resolve. His back grew straight. He thrust out his chin. His hair miraculously sprang back to life, its leonine waves of silver shining with a halo's radiance. He replaced his broad-brimmed hat on his head with a flourish and stood, magnificent, strong, a man calmly accepting his fate.

'If they throw me in jail,' he proclaimed, arms outstretched, 'sure I won't be the first artist to endure persecution in the cause of creativity. If they evict me from my little home, I won't be the first poet to tramp the roads of Ireland begging the rich to throw me a morsel that I might keep body and soul together. They may take from me my substance, but they will never take my Art and my Integrity!'

The applause was instant and resounding. Cameras flashed. A man, American from his accent, cheered. 'My kinda guy! Stick it to the Man, buddy! Yeah!'

Jacko acknowledged the acclamations with a bow. He gave a soulful smile tinged with regret—regret not for the fate he was bravely striding to meet, but for the sorry state of humanity and its wilful blindness in the face of Truth.

'I think I should buy you a drink,' said Derry.

~

Like many ancient buildings in Edinburgh, the pub to which Jacko led Derry had on its outside wall a plaque enthusiastically commemorating one of the city's more colourful historic atrocities. Whether the event was a witch burning, religious massacre, bodysnatching or hanging, Derry didn't linger to check, being intent on escaping a sudden freezing downpour.

Inside, the pub walls were dark with mahogany panelling but enlivened by dozens of framed photos of musicians performing in days gone by. But now, at three in the afternoon on a Thursday, no banjos plinked, no dirges filled the air with regret for times past, no wannabe bodhran player was being summarily ejected. Instead, a handful of tourists sat sipping half-pints of cider and wondering when the culture would start.

Derry had just delivered Jacko's pint and a glass of wine for herself, when her phone rang.

'Derry!' The voice seemed familiar. 'Jim here.'

Derry struggled to know who *Jim* might be. Then it clicked. Carson.

Derry signalled to her father and headed for a small empty annexe at the end of the bar.

'Sorry, Mr. Carson—hello.'

'Thought you might be interested in doing something for me.'

Bizarre. No mention of the cancelled film. Carson's voice was upbeat, as if he wasn't the producer of a disintegrating movie. 'A little job,' he added.

Derry recognized in herself the faintest stirrings of excitement. What actor, however modest about their talents, doesn't secretly dream of being spotted by a producer and offered the break for which they had been waiting? Derry dismissed the idea. Her scenes so far had been competent, even good. But nothing she had done in this movie should single her out for special attention. The brutal reality was that any good actor could do the job she had done—some a little better, some a little worse.

'It's for my wife,' said Carson. 'Sally. I'm planning on having a party at the weekend. Get a few of the neighbours along. Saturday is Halloween. We like to have a Halloween party even if we're in the States—but hey, we're in Scotland. Alex is game, says it'll help the atmosphere round here. We'll be heading back to the States after that. Chance to say thanks an' all. Would you do your, uh, Madam Tulip? That's what you call her, isn't that right?'

Whatever Derry had expected, it wasn't this.

'Sally truly enjoyed what you did when you came over. I'm told you can do the whole number—crystal ball, costume, all that. What do you say?'

'I don't know, Mr. Carson. I'm grateful for the offer. I just need to think it through.' A host of practical problems raised their heads at once—what about her Madam Tulip costume and props? And how would she get back to Ireland after? But even as part of Derry's brain was thinking through the logistics, she felt an unmistakable gloom settle over her.

'I'll pay of course,' continued Carson. 'Say a thousand. Plus expenses?'

Derry knew she should refuse. A half-finished acting job. Sally and her obsessions. And Alex, whom she really didn't want to meet. Maybe she should follow her father and stand on principle whatever the cost? But this wasn't about principle, was it? This was about work. Back home she could be waiting weeks or months for another role. And if she couldn't pay her bills, what then? Spend the next years in a call-centre being shouted at? Work for Vanessa?

'Pounds?' The question came before Derry knew the decision had been made. Pounds were worth more than dollars.

Carson hesitated. 'Um … sure. Pounds.'

'Expenses? I'll need to make new travel arrangements.'

'I guess. Within reason.'

'That sounds fine. Thanks.' Derry wondered how she was going to get her costume by the weekend. Maybe Bella could go to her apartment and courier a bag to Scotland by Saturday.

'Great,' said Carson. 'I appreciate it. Call me if you have any problems, okay? You have my number now. Not many actors can say that.' He laughed.

'Thanks,' said Derry. 'I appreciate it.'

'By the way, Jessica says to say hi.'

23

Sitting on the train, Derry wondered at the way things sometimes seemed planned by fate. Here she was, returning to the Highlands not as Derry O'Donnell, actress, but as Madam Tulip, fortune-teller. So smoothly had the elements clicked into place, she felt like she was sliding downhill on a toboggan.

Bella had agreed to race to Derry's flat, let herself in by arrangement with a neighbor and assemble Madam Tulip's costume, accessories and props, including the essential crystal ball. She'd pack all into a hard suitcase and arrange a courier.

But while Bella was enthusiastic, when Derry had called Bruce to tell him the plan, he seemed doubtful.

'You sure coming back is a good idea? Mixing up different jobs?'

Derry explained she didn't think that would be a problem at all. The film was finished. This was another show.

'You don't mind working with folks that mightn't even pay us for the work we've done? Aren't you afraid you might tell Carson what you think of him and his movie?'

No, Derry didn't think she would pick a fight with Carson. Surely Bruce knew her better than to think she'd be so amateurish. She felt a small twinge of disappointment. Usually Bruce supported her in anything she wanted to do.

'Uh, okay,' said Bruce. The change was instant. He spoke lightly, as though he had never doubted her decision. 'Tell you what, I'll stick around. Keep you company.'

'Thanks, but honest, no need,' said Derry. 'You shouldn't change your plans for me. I can get home okay.'

But Bruce insisted, claiming he had nothing to do in Dublin that couldn't wait a couple of days. He guessed the hotel would be happy to have them stay on now the actors and crew were leaving or had already gone. He'd check the train time right away and pick her up at the station. 'Hey, I can be Madam T's assistant,' he added. 'As long as y'all don't want to saw me in half.'

'Ho ho,' said Derry. Since this was only the thousandth lame Madam Tulip joke inflicted on her since the character was created, she reserved the right not to be amused. But her mood instantly lightened. With Bruce in the picture, everything seemed simpler than before. Not only because he'd drive them both to the ferry and home, but because he was there, helping her keep things in proportion.

Derry smiled. She had a job to do, and work always made her happy. Playing Madam Tulip was fun. It was, after all, acting. Except with Madam Tulip, she was the producer, the director and the star.

∾

'Strange to be back like this,' said Derry. Strange how her hotel room felt somehow different now the magic of making a movie had vanished.

'I brought your stuff,' said Bruce, pointing to Derry's travel bag sitting on her bed. While she was in Edinburgh, her belongings had stayed in Bruce's room.

Bruce took a chair and sat. He stretched his long legs, clasped his hands behind his head and contemplated Derry.

'Say, hope your Madam Tulip stuff gets here tomorrow.'

'Looks okay. Tracking says it's already in Glasgow.'

'So what's the routine?'

'It's all a bit vague. I'll need to get set up before the party. Maybe Jessica will know. From something Carson said, I guess she's back.'

'She was on the train to Edinburgh with you, right? Did you guys talk? Did she say anything about us getting paid?'

'Uh-uh. Maybe she thought Darian would be okay. Maybe not though—she was going to Edinburgh to sort a passport problem. It's kinda weird.'

'Weird like what?'

'She got back here yesterday. But to do that, she'd have had to leave on the early-morning train. She must have given up on the passport.'

'Maybe Carson said, get yo' ass back here or else. Crisis. All that.'

'Could be,' said Derry. 'Strange, that's all. Why go all that way for nothing?'

～

Derry had just showered, changed and was about to go downstairs for dinner when her phone rang.

'Derry? I got your text.'

'Jessica, hi.'

'We have a schedule for tomorrow; can I go through that with you now?'

No preamble, no *how did you get along in Edinburgh?* No recognition of the confidences shared on the train. Just business.

'The party will start at eight p.m. with drinks. Then a buffet, then maybe some Halloween party games. That's when you'll be telling fortunes. Then a barbecue if the weather is okay, then fireworks. You'll have your costume?'

'Tracking says it'll get here in the morning.'

'Fine. We can give you a room to use for dressing if you don't want to come over in costume.'

Good news. Socialising in costume was a no-no; that was a rule of the theatre—no audience should ever see you offstage in character. 'That would be great,' said Derry. I could change and join the party later, if that's okay with Mr. Carson?'

Derry wondered at how Jessica sounded so confident, so businesslike, when she must surely be in Carson's bad books for disappearing in a crisis. It was like the Edinburgh episode had never happened.

'Sounds good,' said Jessica. 'Sally says she's looking forward to Madam Tulip. Me too. I might have a little test for you. See how good you really are.' Jessica's tone was teasing, but just beneath the surface, Derry was sure she heard excitement—repressed, buried, but it was there.

'By the way, the weather forecast for tomorrow is good. And since we're leaving for the States next week, Sally wants us to have a picnic in the hills. At the old tower. Early afternoon. She said to ask you along.'

'Oh.' Derry didn't know what to say. Mixing socialising with Madam Tulip was uncomfortable, but refusing might seem bad manners. 'Sure, thanks. Bruce is staying to keep me company and get me home; is it okay if he comes along, if he wants?'

'No problem,' said Jessica. 'I checked already.'

Did Jessica check everything? How did she know Bruce had decided to stay? But nothing about Jessica any longer surprised Derry. Maybe she was one of those women bound to end up running a corporation. Efficient. Tough. Ambitious. All the things Derry knew she herself wasn't.

'Come to the castle at noon, okay? Jim wants to talk to you about something. We can take it from there.'

Even as Derry said thanks, Jessica cut the call. Only then did something in the back of Derry's brain register a striking fact. Jessica had gone to Edinburgh without permission, leaving her post in a crisis. She had risked the anger of a boss who had already made uncomfortable advances.

But now he was *Jim*.

~

At dinner, Jen had served Derry and Bruce herself. Moira McKenzie was nowhere to be seen. Had she been let go or had her shifts cut now the hotel was almost deserted? The only other person in the dining room was a middle-aged man in a thick woollen sweater, the multicoloured sort Scandinavians wore and mothers bought sons for Christmas. A salesman? He finished his meal and left with a polite good evening.

'It was good of you to stay. You didn't need to,' said Derry.

Bruce shrugged. 'Scotland's cool; I like it.'

'Want to come to a picnic tomorrow? In the hills?'

'Sure. I'll bring the bug repellent.'

'Jessica mentioned a tower. I wonder is it the same one.'

Derry knew she didn't have to explain what she meant by *the same one*. Ever since Jessica had announced the picnic, the question had lurked in the back of Derry's mind.

'I sure hope it's the same. Wouldn't mind a look,' said Bruce.

'Look? Why?'

Bruce picked up his phone and tapped the screen before laying it on the table in front of Derry. 'See that?' He turned the phone around so Derry was seeing it the right way up. Google satellite view. A brown, featureless landscape. Or nearly featureless—a mountainside, a lake, and on the lakeshore a building. 'Screen's too small, let me draw it.' Bruce took a pen from his jacket pocket and filched a paper napkin from the next table. He scribbled a rough outline. 'See the lake? And two roads—one going up the hill, the other branching down to the tower and swinging round by the lakeside. We were here.' He drew a cute little SUV just past the intersection.

As Derry took in the scene, it was as though the hastily drawn sketch, so like a child's drawing, melted away to reveal that bleak hillside. As the memory tried to creep back under her skin, she fought to suppress the images. *It's just a map.*

'I'm a hundred percent sure the shot came from the tower,' continued Bruce. 'Probably the top.'

Derry hesitated. She could understand Bruce's fascination. But she wished he'd taken a minute to think about whether she wanted to revisit that terrible day.

'Thing is,' said Bruce. 'If you draw a line from the tower to where our truck got hit, you can see it's an easy shot. 'About six hundred metres.' He drew the line. 'This is definitely where we were—right beside that kink in the track. The shot went through the two side windows, straight through, almost no angle. If the shot had come from any other direction, the bullet wouldn't have passed through both. So you draw the line and there's the tower. The slope down looks about forty feet. That would put a shooter on the top of the tower almost dead level with the SUV. Okay, it's not certain—lots of guesswork here—but I'd lay a bet. Just thought you'd like to know.'

Bruce's eyes were guileless, his tone casual. He shrugged as if to say, *hey, just an interesting thing. No big deal.*

～

That night, Derry dreamed of a theatre. The show was about to start. The packed audience waited in their seats, but her Madam Tulip costume couldn't be found. The wardrobe people had gone missing, and Derry was left frantically rifling through hundreds of costumes hanging on racks. But she could find no Madam Tulip dress, no wig, no beautiful feather headdress, gloves or necklace. The stage manager, the producers, the director and her fellow actors shouted desperately for her to go onstage regardless. *Nobody cares about the costume*, they screamed. *This is the theatre, they'll have to use their imaginations!*

Reluctantly, Derry walked out onto the vast stage. The house lights were up, and she could clearly see the audience's faces. They stared in silence, and Derry understood she was expected to tell their fortunes. She knew because now she was wearing a Halloween costume—a man's suit, black like an undertaker's, and a top hat. She was looking out through a white plastic facemask of the sort kids wear for trick-or-treat—a skull, a death's head.

Now she realised what she was there to do. She was to predict that everyone in the audience would die. She knew they would be angry. The words would leave her lips, and instantly, howling with rage, they'd storm the stage and tear her to pieces.

24

By the time Derry had woken, dressed, showered and gone downstairs for breakfast, her horrible dream was a fading memory. And, despite her premonition, her Madam Tulip costume had arrived.

The suitcase was strapped tight with tape, like an Egyptian mummy. Derry lugged the case upstairs to her room and threw it onto her bed. Opening it, she saw that Bella had done a beautiful job. Madam Tulip's dress was carefully folded and wrapped in tissue paper. The wig too was wrapped; the box in which it usually lived must have been too big for the case. The feather headdress with its three small blue feathers and two bigger yellow ones nestled safely in tissue paper. A padded corset—essential to Madam Tulip as a mature woman of middle years—was present and correct as was her full complement of accessories. So too were her crystal ball, wrapped in a richly embroidered velvet tablecloth, and her antique ten-minute timer, like an egg timer only bigger. Finally, tucked into the corner of the case was a little stack of business cards, each boasting a red tulip, a crystal ball and the legend, 'Madam Tulip—Fortune-teller.'

As she closed the case, Derry felt tears come to her eyes. Silly, but there they were. She reached for her phone to text Bella her thanks. She ended, *Owe U XXX*.

A minute later, she got the response—*Ask Tulip predict score 2nite.*

Derry smiled. She texted back—*Tulip Giants fan. Future uncertain.* But she doubted Bella meant a football game.

~

Derry pulled the bell, but heard no answering peal. The castle's heavy, iron-studded door stayed shut in her face. At least the morning was mild and dry, and the breeze pleasant. She was idly imagining the kilted retainer in buckled shoes and powdered wig who would have greeted guests in ancient times, and was wondering whether to tug the bell-pull again, when the door swung open.

'Can't go on meeting like this,' said Johnny. Instead of stepping aside to usher her in, he stood blocking the entrance, smirking. Derry said nothing. Was this his idea of flirting? She stood calmly and waited. At last he stood aside.

For the second time, Derry stepped into the hall. As before, the grimacing African masks, all wild hair and striped ebony cheeks, glowered down from the walls. Strangely, this time they didn't seem out of place. How did the weird become normal so quickly?

Johnny pointed down the corridor to where Jessica stood waiting.

'Derry, thanks for coming,' she said. 'Jim so wanted to do something special for tonight.' She was smiling, but Derry could see her smile was that of a bank teller or an airline steward, not a smile that said *ask me personal questions, like why did I come back so soon*. So she didn't ask. Instead she said, 'Please thank Mr. Carson for me.'

'Sure,' said Jessica. 'But you can thank him yourself. Like I said, Jim wants you to drop in to him before we head off for our picnic. He'd like a word.'

There it was again—*Jim*. And a word about what?

Jessica led Derry into the dining-room, familiar from her last visit but this time festooned with Halloween decorations—spiders' webs made of string, plastic skulls grinning whitely from alcoves, masks of witches and ghouls hanging from the walls. At the grand mantelpiece, Sally was arranging seasonal decorations of pine cones, acorns, and little turnips painted with spiders' webs and bat faces. She turned around as Derry and Jessica entered.

'Derry! How nice to see you! I'm so glad you could come tonight. And to our little picnic.' She put the finishing touches to her creation, before stepping over to meet Derry, greeting her with a kiss on the cheek like they were old and dear friends. How different from the cool and reserved Sally that Derry had first met. Derry again marvelled at how Madam Tulip could sometimes create an unexpected but pleasing bond between very different people.

'I've gotta rush,' said Sally. 'You have no idea how much I have to do.' She smiled at Derry and left.

'We're not ready yet, but we're nearly there,' said Jessica. 'It'll be a fun party.' She gave Derry a knowing look. 'Lots of surprises, I can promise.' She paused. 'Let me show you your fortune-teller's booth. Isn't that what you call it?'

Jessica led Derry into the library, opening the door with a flourish. She flicked on the light.

Derry was astonished. Cascading from ceiling to floor, masking the bookshelves, hung folds of African fabric. She stared, mesmerised. Blazing reds, browns like freshly turned clay, repeated patterns fooling the eye into imagining them symmetrical until you realised they were nothing of the kind. Concentric circles of overlapping orange and blue. The effect was spectacular. And the table—the whole centre section had been taken out shrinking the whole and making the library seem way more spacious. What looked like a full cowhide covered the table surface, and on it sat a small lamp adapted from an old oil lantern. In the corners of the room drums squatted—tall wooden cylinders topped with hide and fat little cord-bound gourds. Two, sitting side by side, had abstract human faces carved on their sides. Their eyes were closed as though seeing some kind of vision.

'Different, huh?' Jessica was smiling.

'Did you do this?'

'Sure. Johnny gave me a hand. Alex has rooms full of this stuff. You like it?'

Like was probably not the word. But impressed, certainly. The effect was as far from the clichéd frilly drapes of the fortune-teller's caravan as you could get. Derry wondered would it change the way Madam Tulip worked, maybe even influence what she saw in the cards or the crystal. 'Oh, I nearly forgot,' she said. She reached into her bag and took out the little pouch of sheep bones. 'Ally in Props said I could use these for practice. Maybe you could give them back to whoever?'

Jessica shrugged. 'Everyone's gone. I guess we could post them to London, but what's the point? Hey, why not use them tonight? I hear you were a wow on set. Bones would go great with the theme—Halloween, two worlds collide, the dead and the living, all that. I wrote a script once set at Halloween. Maybe it'll get made now, who knows?'

Derry returned the bones to her bag. It felt a little like stealing, but Jessica was surely speaking for Carson. And maybe they'd be a good addition. Casting the bones in a setting like this could be mesmerising for the client. Every showbiz instinct in Derry nodded approval. Point a lamp to shine on the cow-hide-covered table to where the bones would tumble. Leave the rest of the room in near darkness, just a glow from the dazzling wall hangings. *Lovely.*

'You mentioned there'd be someplace I could change,' said Derry.

'In there's a storeroom,' said Jessica, pointing to a door between the bookcases. 'Past that there's a service passage from Alex's part of the castle—you could use that and avoid coming through the party. I'll check with Alex, but I don't see a problem. Come and take a look. We can get to Jim's office this way anyhow.'

'Great. I appreciate what you've done. It looks amazing.'

Jessica smiled, the first spontaneous smile Derry had seen from her so far that day. 'Showbiz, right?' she said. 'Production values—can't beat 'em.'

'By the way,' said Derry, responding to Jessica's friendly tone, 'did things work out okay for you in Edinburgh? You didn't wait for your passport in the end?' She expected Jessica to say, *sure, I gave up on the passport idea, thought I'd better come back to help Carson with the movie.* But she didn't.

'It worked out fine,' she said, with a satisfied smile. 'I came back with Alex. In the chopper.'

Some things are so surprising, you don't even know how to ask the million questions exploding in your mind. Derry didn't know where to start or even if she were entitled to ask any questions at all. But Jessica had already moved on. 'This should be okay for changing,' she said, leading Derry into the storeroom. 'I'll sort you out a mirror and a chair. There's some shelf space I can clear. Is that alright?'

Derry forced herself to put everything out of her mind but the job in hand. She surveyed the room. Shelving, packed with cardboard boxes, files and binders, covered most of the walls; other shelves held cleaning materials—detergents, dusters, brass polish. A couple of filing cabinets stood in the corner. The place looked rarely visited, a repository for a million things that might or might not be useful someday, but it would do fine as a changing room. Derry had seen worse on tour.

'Jim's office is this way,' said Jessica, opening a heavy, black-painted door in the far wall. As Derry stepped through into a narrow corridor, she knew at once she was in the oldest part of the castle. The passage was of roughly hewn stone, the walls whitewashed. The floor was of bare flags worn smooth by centuries of feet. Derry wondered how she would react if she chanced to meet Dunbar here. *Cool*, that was the way. *Polite.* Friendly but amused, like she had other games to play with men equally rich and handsome. In fact, richer and handsomer.

'Oh!' said Amelia. She was carrying a mannequin, an almost full-sized female figure in a long black dress, and as Jessica had turned a sharp corner, she had almost bumped into her.

'Hey, is that the witch?' asked Jessica.

'Will be,' said Amelia, almost hidden by the figure cradled in her arms like an oversized child. 'I've found her a cloak. And a floppy hat. Still looking for a broom.'

'Good luck,' said Jessica. 'See you later.' She manoeuvred past Amelia and her witch, and strode on, leaving Derry and the girl momentarily face to face. Derry smiled a greeting.

Amelia shot out a hand, seized Derry's wrist and squeezed hard.

'Hey!' exclaimed Derry. She tried to pull her arm away, but Amelia's grip was strong. Her fingernails dug into Derry's flesh.

'*You bitch,*' she said. She spoke quietly, savagely, following up with a stream of carefully enunciated expletives. A final, hate-filled stare, and she released Derry's wrist and stalked away, mannequin under her arm.

Derry stood, speechless, her heart beating hard in her chest, unable to think or to imagine what had just happened.

25

Jessica knocked on an ancient door. 'Derry's here, Mr. Carson,' she called. They waited a moment until Carson answered they should come in. Jessica ushered Derry inside and left.

Carson was sitting behind a desk piled with papers. Against the wall was another desk, on which Derry immediately recognised a small video edit suite used for roughly stitching together newly shot footage to check scenes. Two screens sat side by side flanked by professional-looking speakers on stands. Filing cabinets filled what little was left of the floor space. Carson closed the lid of a laptop and stood, beaming.

'Thanks for coming. Please sit down.' He gestured to an office chair. 'I appreciate it.'

Derry struggled to put out of her mind her extraordinary encounter with Amelia. This was business. She needed to concentrate.

Carson's tan was fresh and smooth. His eyes twinkled and his pearly teeth glistened as he smiled. He looked nothing like a film producer facing the loss of millions. No haunted expression. No dark circles under his eyes.

'I sure am looking forward to this party,' he said. 'I always loved Halloween, ever since I was a kid. Must be the Celt in me. You do pumpkins when you were young? You got kids?'

Derry shook her head. She was sure Carson had no interest whatever in her answer.

'All that stuff about zombies and witches? He went on. 'All crap. Fun, but crap. You know what Halloween is?'

Derry allowed her face to express polite enquiry. For now at least, Carson was her employer.

'At Halloween,' continued Carson, 'all the dead get to wander around for the night. But you don't want to be bothered by other people's ancestors, they might have some kinda grudge, so you go round with your face blacked or wearing a mask so the ghosts don't know you. But back home, you put out a table with food and drink on it. You leave the door unlocked, so your own ancestors can come in and sit by the fire.' He paused. 'Cool, huh? I wouldn't mind meeting my ancestors. They were some bunch, by all accounts. You like the setup? Jessica's done a great job.'

'Terrific,' said Derry. 'I love the ... what is it, African stuff? Really nice.'

'Alex's souvenirs. The good old days. We were young bucks then. Full of it.' His gaze lingered on Derry until she felt uncomfortable. She remembered what Jessica had said about his unwanted advances. *Please,* she thought, *don't let this be a proposition.*

'Something I wanted to mention to you. You don't mind?' Carson continued.

Derry gave a cautious shrug.

'Sally and me have been married for nearly twenty years. She's a wonderful woman.' He paused. 'Sally ... she's not been well lately. Not for some time. She ... how do I say this ... when people are ill, like depressed, they get some strange notions. They can get ideas in their head that don't make sense to anybody else. But they believe them. Know what I mean?'

Derry nodded.

'My wife … I'm embarrassed talking about this, but I feel I can trust you. She gets … enthusiasms. Obsessions. She got a fixation—I guess you'd call it that—on a guy who worked here a couple of years back. He managed the estate. I'm not saying there was anything between them—no sir, nothing like that. But she was kinda taken by him. Maybe you'd call it a crush. And when he upped and left, she got it into her head something bad had happened to him. And she won't let go. Truth is, he left because he was caught with his finger in the till. You understand what I'm saying?'

Derry nodded like she did understand. But she didn't. Why was Carson telling her this? What had this to do with her?

'It's not good for Sally that she believes this kind of stuff. Not good for her health. She's not a strong person.'

Strange how two people could have such different ideas about somebody. The last thing Derry would have said about Sally was that she wasn't a strong person. But then, she hadn't been married to Sally for twenty years.

'Mr. Carson, I don't see what this has to do with me.'

'I feel you could maybe say something to her. Like … I'm not asking you to do anything unethical, but you could do some counseling? Maybe when you're telling her fortune you could say she has nothing to worry about. That somebody— someone she might be concerned about—is just fine? Put her mind at rest.'

'Mr. Carson—'

'Jim.'

'Jim, I can't say what I will or—'

'Tell you what, fifteen hundred. You don't have to say yes or no. I'm gonna give you that anyway. And, uh, I've got some nice projects coming up. Fine actress like you, I could easily find you something good.'

'No,' said Derry. 'I'm sorry.'

Carson frowned, his expression like he had stepped in something unpleasant. Perhaps the experience of being refused was new to him. *Out of work actress turns down free money. Man bites dog.*

'Okay, look, you don't have to say anything. You've agreed to the show, you'll do that, right?'

Derry nodded. She had indeed agreed to do the gig. And she couldn't blame Carson for being concerned about his wife.

'Please understand what this means to me,' said Carson. His voice was pleading, his eyes soft. 'Derry, I love my wife.'

Silence hung between them like they were both standing on a tightrope, afraid to breathe, a dizzying plunge below.

This is appalling, thought Derry. *The man is begging me to save his marriage or his wife's sanity or both.* 'Mr. Carson, I can't say what I will or won't tell a client in a session. I don't do that. If you accept that and understand where I'm coming from, I'll be happy to do the job. No promises on either side. At our original price.'

Carson fixed her with a steady gaze—an appraising look— not cold, not hostile, but unreadable. 'Sure. I appreciate your integrity. Not much of that in our bad old world. Thank you, Miss O'Donnell.'

He stood abruptly, as if a piece of business had been satisfactorily concluded and he saw no further reason to charm.

26

The vehicles gathering on the smooth gravel of the castle forecourt said an expedition was planned. Bruce and Derry sat in the van, parked off to one side, watching. They still had ten minutes to go before the time arranged for setting out. The idea was they would ride with the others, as the van had no chance of making it up the hillside.

Over at the castle door, Johnny loitered by Dunbar's black SUV, leaning on the hood, smoking. The vehicle's windows had been repaired. Behind it, Carson's SUV sat empty. As Derry and Bruce watched, an old Volvo station wagon pulled up. Jen from the hotel got out, stepped up to the castle door and was let in, by whom Derry couldn't see. Next came a green Land Rover—Rab. He sprang out, opened the tailgate and released his dogs to race aimlessly around the yard. He waved to Derry and Bruce before ambling across to chat with Johnny.

'You think they paint this place every year?' said Bruce.

Derry was startled at the question, until she remembered Bruce had been a sailor of sorts. Didn't sailors paint everything? 'I guess,' she said. 'That's why you have to be a millionaire to own one.'

'I'm sure looking forward to getting a look-see inside. Must get me some pics, show folks back home.'

'If you do, you'll only confuse everybody,' said Derry, smiling. 'The place is more like a … like an African museum. All weird masks and spears and witch-doctor type stuff.'

'Hey!' said Bruce. 'Cool. Weird, but cool.'

'Seems years ago Dunbar and Carson were in …' Derry tried to remember where exactly Jessica had said they had been. 'Sierra Leone? Dunbar was in the British Army.'

'You don't say,' said Bruce. 'I been there.'

'Bruce, is there *anywhere* you haven't been?'

Bruce grinned. 'That Sierra Leone was one messed-up place. The worst thing any country can have is diamonds. Like a curse. They had guys there with their own armies—I mean like *real* armies. Killing. Stealin'. And the people so nice an' all, I don't know how they didn't go crazy it got so bad. Maybe they did.'

'How come you were there? I didn't know we were—'

'No, we didn't get into the war. Left that to the Brits. We were training locals to fight pirates. Saw a lot of the place, though. Man it got weird. Everybody afraid of spells and curses an' all. Ever heard of a witch gun?'

Derry shook her head.

'Just about everybody there believes in the witch gun. They believe it so hard, if they think they been shot with one they up and die.'

'What, the witches have guns?'

'Naw. Not real guns. The witch gun is secret magic. You get a grudge against somebody, so you get a witch doctor to use his witch gun. Sometimes it's just a grain of rice, but he fires off that thing, and sure enough the person gets sick and soon he dies. Or he gets shot with a real bullet when nobody else around him is shot. Sounds weird, but the place was so insane with all the killing and craziness, even our guys started to believe that stuff—everybody started wearing little charm bracelets or carrying magic stones, supposed to protect 'em.'

'What, you too?'

'Too right! What if you say *no that's garbage*, and it's not garbage? A little believin' don't cost nothing. Anyhow, all sailors are superstitious. Soldiers too, though they don't admit it.'

Amazing. Not for a second had Derry imagined Bruce would believe in witchcraft or charms. She was about to ask him if that meant he believed in fortune-telling, when Jessica emerged from the castle doorway, followed by Sally and Jen. She stood by Carson's SUV and beckoned for Derry and Bruce to join them.

The idea was that Derry would travel in Rab's Land Rover, a two-seater when the back was taken up with the trestle table. Bruce would go with Sally, Jessica and Jen in Carson's SUV. Carson and Dunbar would follow later. As Derry and Bruce headed across the courtyard to join the rest, Bruce spoke quietly. 'Maybe you could check with Rab about the tower? Ask him if there were signs anyone was up top?'

'I guess,' said Derry. 'I don't know will he be keen on outsiders sticking their noses in. Why should he tell me anything?'

Bruce gave her a look bordering dangerously on a smirk. 'Hey, maybe he just likes you?' Derry gave him a scowl meaning she couldn't retaliate right now, but his card was marked.

'Maybe you could do some of that mind-reading,' continued Bruce, seeming determined to live dangerously. 'Like you fortune-tellers do? Pick up a few hints?'

'Bruce, I-DO-NOT-READ-MINDS!'

'Okay, whatever!' Bruce's grin was infuriating. 'Let's say vibes, okay? You check his vibes.'

For the millionth time in her life, Derry wondered if she were carrying around a brain belonging to someone else. She meant to ask Rab a question any sane person would rate a nine on the scale of serious questions—*Did the guy who nearly killed us shoot from the tower?* Instead, her brain noticed his voice still gave her little goose bumps, and she wanted him to keep talking. The only conclusion any intelligent person could reach was that she was an irredeemable airhead who shouldn't be allowed stray out of the beauty parlour in case she walked under a bus.

'I'm glad you came back to us,' Rab was saying, as they motored towards the village and the hills beyond. 'Shame about the film.'

Derry agreed it was indeed a shame.

'A lot of people are owed money, I imagine. I hope the producers will be decent.'

Startling. The idea that a film company and its backers could have decency as any part of their business was an original idea. But that Rab thought being decent mattered was sweet.

'Did someone say you were performing something at the party tonight?' continued Rab.

'Sure. I do a kind of fortune-teller. For fun. I used to do it just for friends, but people ask me to do it at events now. Like a show.'

'Maybe you could tell my fortune,' said Rab, smiling. 'Or maybe best not. I'm not sure I want to know.'

'Oh, are you going along?' Derry found her throat strangely dry.

'Surely. Quite a few of us from the estate are going.'

The thought of holding Rab's hand for a palm-reading while dressed as a fifty-something, full-bosomed psychic in a wig was horrifying. Derry fervently hoped he meant what he said about not wanting his fortune told. Best change the subject. 'Do a lot of people have picnics up there, at the tower?'

'At the Doon? Not many. But visitors like it. Mr. Carson and Mr. Dunbar sometimes bring guests. Romance of the Scottish Glen, I suppose. But it is beautiful. Even if you live here, the magic never really wears off.'

Now they were turning up the mountain track, following Sally's SUV twenty yards ahead. Behind Derry's seat, the dogs shuffled restlessly. Perhaps the smells brought memories of chasing hare and grouse. As the winding track ahead grew more and more familiar, Derry's stomach tightened, as if saying *Warning! Bad things happen here!*

'Quiet boys,' said Rab, sharply. The dogs obeyed, settling down but panting in anticipation.

'I'm surprised Jessica doesn't mind coming back this way,' said Derry. It occurred to her she was probably not talking about Jessica but about herself.

Rab gave her a sideways glance. He spoke gently. 'You must all have gotten a terrible shock. I did wonder if it wasn't thoughtless to bring everyone back here. But it seems Mrs. Carson wanted to see the place once more before the family left for the States.' Rab's expression was bland. He kept his eyes on the track, but in his voice was a hint of disapproval.

For the next ten minutes they lurched up the trail in silence. Then, as though no time had passed, Rab suddenly spoke. 'Talking of Mrs. Carson ... You might find this a bit strange.' He hesitated. 'Mrs. Carson is ... I think she wouldn't mind me saying this ... she's a sensitive woman.'

Derry forced herself to stare straight ahead. Earlier, Carson too had called Sally *sensitive*.

'I don't know how to say this without being indiscreet,' continued Rab. 'But I feel I can trust you.'

Derry made the most noncommittal shrug she could manage.

'I told you Mr. Dunbar had his own estate factor, before I took over?' Derry nodded. 'He … left suddenly. Under something of a cloud. Mrs. Carson had a lot of … respect for Hamish. She didn't like to see his name in the mud when she was sure he had done nothing. When he disappeared, Mrs. Carson worried that something had happened to him. We had, as you know, some incidents. One of his dogs was poisoned. That's his other dog, Charlie in the back there.'

Derry looked around. Charlie's ears pricked up, like he was pleased at the introduction.

'I honestly don't know how to say this,' continued Rab. 'I happen to believe … I *know*, that Hamish is okay. I am sure he didn't do what they said he did. Perhaps there were … disagreements.'

Sure, Derry thought. *There were disagreements alright. Disagreements about a wife.* Was it fair to let Rab carry on like this, tying himself in knots trying not to say Sally and the factor were having an affair? But that wasn't certain, was it? Perhaps their relationship was, as Carson had said, a crush of some kind.

'Rab, what has this got to do with me?'

'You're going to be telling fortunes tonight at the party.'

Often in her life, maybe more frequently of late, Derry had the disturbing sensation that time and space had somehow drifted apart. A recent event would suddenly morph into something that hadn't happened yet or might happen or could happen to somebody else. Perhaps it was her modest gift, or maybe just human intuition, but she knew exactly what Rab was going to say next. She waited.

'I thought perhaps you could … give Mrs. Carson a hint? You could tell her not to worry? Tell her that Hamish … had to go away?'

Derry pretended to think. She had to pretend, because actual thinking was impossible. Nothing would compute. None of this even began to make sense. Every instinct in her body said, *Stay away. Leave it alone. He has no right to ask.*

'I appreciate your concern, but I can't do that.' She tried to keep her voice level, to let none of her anger show. 'I'm sure you mean well.'

'I apologise, I—'

'I understand. Really. Can we change the subject?'

'Yes. I'm sorry. Truly I am.'

Derry kept her gaze settled on the landscape ahead. She knew she should have been feeling nervous now, as they climbed ever closer to the terrible place seared into her memory.

But all she felt was disappointment.

27

Rab swung the Land Rover to the right, down a trail even rougher than the main track. A few hundred yards further on and a little below stood the Doon.

Perched on its rocky pedestal by the lakeside, the tower was plain and angular, the walls stark and brutal—naked grey granite pierced by high, narrow windows. Derry saw at once that the steeply pitched roof was girdled by a plain stone parapet—the perfect vantage for a shooter.

'Rab?' said Derry. His surprised look said he hadn't expected to be spoken to again, or at least not civilly. 'Bruce and I were talking. He thinks the shot came from the tower. From the top. Did anyone check there? Could someone have gotten inside?'

Rab frowned as he negotiated a deeply rutted section of track. He chose his words carefully. 'I did take a look the day after. The door was locked. Nobody had tried to force it, so far as I could see. But they didn't need to climb up on the tower; they could have shot from anywhere around here. There's plenty of cover.'

'But how would they get away? Wouldn't we have seen a jeep?'

'Maybe not a jeep. A quad would get someone away quick enough. You'd be hard pressed to spot it.'

'Quad?'

'ATVs, you call them.'

Derry could see he was right. An ATV racing away from behind the tower on the lakeside track would scarcely be visible from the road above. A short sprint, hidden by rocks and heather, and it would vanish into the dense birchwoods flanking the hillside.

Ahead, Derry saw Sally's SUV swing around a rocky outcrop to pull up on a rough forecourt, an expanse of flat ground directly beneath the looming bulk of the tower. Rab followed, parking the Land Rover. He killed the engine but didn't move to get out. Instead, they sat in silence, watching as Sally, Bruce, Jessica and Jen climbed out and took in the scene, gazing across the sparkling waters of the lake as though mesmerised.

Bruce was the first to stir. He opened the tailgate of the SUV, reached in and pulled out a fat wicker hamper, then a second. Jessica frowned at the sky in case it dared look like rain, but the sun was shining and the clouds looked innocent. As Derry watched, shadows crept across the mountainside, sliding up its flanks like living things, making her think of fish for some reason—a skate or a stingray, gliding frictionless over the surface, smothering the light.

'Your father's a painter,' said Rab. 'Famous, I hear.'

Derry nodded. Right away she noticed something strange, something missing. No tingling at the base of her neck. No flutter in her ribcage.

'We get lots of painters coming here,' Rab continued. 'It's the light. They come to see the way it changes every minute of the day. But the mountain always beats them. They try and try. Then they get frustrated, and every night they're in the bar drinking whisky, certain they're a failure and should quit.'

'And do they?'

'Seems not—they come back again and again. Could be the whisky, of course.'

By the tower, Sally was still standing motionless, gazing out over the lake below. 'Rab, about Sally,' said Derry, quietly. 'Why don't you tell her yourself?'

Rab shrugged helplessly. 'I cannae,' he said.

'Why not? Just tell her you happen to know her friend is okay. Anyway, how do you know that?'

Rab cleared his throat and sighed. 'Hamish and I were friends of a sort. Both army men, and so on. He must have known I'd look after Charlie here. But he'd still worry about his dog. He had to be sure. So he sent me an email. I don't know where from.'

Derry felt her head spin. An email. About his dog. She took a breath, not wanting to ask the question. 'Did he … ask about Sally?'

Rab shook his head. 'That's why I cannae tell her. I'd have to make something up.' He sounded helpless. 'It wouldn't be right.'

~

Derry stood watching as Rab opened the tailgate of the Land Rover, letting the dogs rush out to race around gambolling at everyone's feet. Charlie jumped up at Sally and licked her hand like they were old friends. *Of course.* Charlie was Hamish the factor's dog. As Sally smiled, ruffling Charlie's ears, Derry wondered about Rab's strange request. Why should he care?

A crazy idea came unbidden, playing out in Derry's head like the scenario for a movie—Hamish has an affair with the besotted wife of a rich man. But his friend Rab is keen on her too. Hamish runs off, and second fiddle wants Sally to forget him and fall into his arms. Derry almost laughed out loud, the idea was so crazy. All the same, she stole a surreptitious glance at Sally and wondered.

Rab dragged the first of two trestle tables from the back of the jeep, helped by Derry and Bruce.

'Can you put them there?' said Sally, pointing to a spot to one side of the tower, a flat stony patch with a thin grassy covering, affording a panoramic view of the lake valley and the flanking mountains. 'Isn't that magnificent? They sure knew how to pick their spot.'

Derry saw Bruce cover up a smile at the idea the warlike men of this mountain chose to site their defences where the view was prettiest. But it *was* gorgeous. No matter where you looked, you could see no trace of human habitation. Not a house, not a wisp of smoke from a fireplace, not an electricity pylon or telephone pole. High above their heads, two black birds circled on an updraft, observing the intruders below. Only the brute presence of the tower, and the primitive roads over which it stood sentry, showed humans had ever been here.

Jessica's phone pinged loudly, prompting her to check for a text. 'Alex has been delayed; he'll try to come later,' she called out. 'Jim is on his way now.'

Bruce frowned. 'Say, you got a phone signal?'

'Sure,' said Jessica. 'It's weird, but only down here. Go twenty yards any direction and nothing. We're kinda used to it.' Bruce looked thoughtful but didn't comment.

As Rab and Bruce set up the tables, and Jen fussed over the hampers, Derry found herself redundant. With Sally's blessing, she took the chance to examine the tower.

The entrance was plain and square, formed from massive granite uprights and a heavy lintel. Entry was blocked by a stout door clad in steel sheeting and secured by a sturdy bolt and padlock. Derry stepped back, peering up the sheer face of the structure to the parapet high above. She turned to look at the hillside. Would a vehicle travelling on the track above be visible from ground level? Maybe not, though it was hard to tell with no traffic to judge by. From the top of the tower? *Definitely.*

Derry walked around the base of the tower to stand over-looking the lake. From here the lakeshore track was obvious. The trail led steeply down to disappear behind a miniature cliff, before threading its way between outcrops and vanishing up the hillside into the trees and scrub. Could someone have escaped that way without being observed from the road? *Yes.*

Derry tried to bring to mind the map Bruce had drawn. Where did the lakeside track go? The trail seemed to vanish into the wilderness, but it must go somewhere.

'Sure is a fine view.' Bruce appeared from behind the tower. He stood beside Derry, gazing vaguely out over the lake. 'You know, I really might come back here. Next summer, maybe. Do some diving. Some climbing.' He paused. 'Sally seems sad to leave. Can't say I blame her.'

Derry kept her face expressionless. Bruce could have no idea just how much Sally would indeed miss Scotland.

'Bruce, remember you drew me a map? Where did that track down there go?'

At that moment a cloud obscured the sun, darkening the sky and causing a sudden chill. Bruce thought for a moment, before answering as though he were seeing the map in front of his eyes.

'After the woods? The trail goes on up into a high valley—joins the main track at the hunting lodge. Why?'

'How far is the lodge that way?'

'Uh, a couple of miles?'

'And how far by the other way, the track we were on?'

'A bit shorter, say a mile and a half.'

'You thought the shot came from the top of the tower.'

'Sure. Well, maybe. Can't be a hundred percent.'

'I asked Rab did they look to see had anybody been in the tower. He said he came here next day and checked the door. No break-in.'

Bruce shrugged. 'So maybe they didn't shoot from up there. It's sure a great hide though. Great exfil too.'

'Ex … ?'

'Bugging out.'

'Say the shooter had an ATV or a jeep, how long would it take to go, say, three and a half miles?'

'On a good ATV? Fifteen minutes? In a Land Rover, a little slower. He fell silent. 'Derry, what are you saying?' He stopped, shaking his head. 'Come on, that's crazy.'

Maybe it *was* crazy. So crazy she could hardly put the idea into words. But Rab's strange request about Sally had started a train of thought she couldn't stop. The whole tale had been so clumsy. And so unlikely. Concern for his boss's friend's wife? Why?

'Bruce, say there's something going on between Rab and Sally. Just let's say, okay?' Bruce gave a reluctant shrug. 'Rab lets himself and Sally into the tower. He's bound to have a key. Okay, either he or Sally shoots at us. They see us escape, so they jump on an ATV and race along the lakeshore, up the wooded slopes and on to the lodge in the valley. They pick up Rab's Land Rover and drive back down the main track. And big surprise, there's our truck in the ditch, and everybody starts talking about poachers.'

'Let's take a little stroll down here,' said Bruce. He led Derry down the stony track almost to the lakeshore, until they reached the foot of the rocky platform on which the tower stood. Nobody could approach unseen.

'Derry, just 'cos they could doesn't mean they did. Why? Why would they shoot at us?'

Derry shrugged. 'What if they were having an affair?'

'Even if they were, so what? If Sally's husband was in the SUV with us when we got shot at, maybe that would make sense. But he wasn't. It wasn't even his truck.' He fell silent. 'What about Jessica? What if she and Carson were an item and Sally found out?'

Derry remembered Jessica telling her that Carson had propositioned her and claiming she had rejected him. Was that true? *Had* she rejected him?'

'But if Sally was the shooter,' said Derry, 'why would Rab help her, unless they were lovers? But then why would her lover help shoot her husband's mistress?' Derry's head hurt just thinking about it.

Bruce sighed. 'Derry, we have to let go of this. It makes no sense. Sure it's right to be worried; someone took a pop. But I think you've got the wrong people. What do they call it— Occam's razor? The simplest explanation is always the best.'

'And?'

'Poachers. Or people who don't like the estate or don't like movie folk. Maybe they meant to hit, maybe they meant to miss. Maybe they didn't shoot from the tower. One thing is sure, they exfiltrated that-away. He nodded up the track. That's all we know.'

And that *was* all they knew. Derry felt her body relax. Her imagination had put two and two together and got five. Could she see Sally taking a shot at her husband? Yes, she could. At Jessica? Maybe. But not helped by Rab, that idea was way too far-fetched. 'It's this place,' she said. 'The Highlands. Everything about it is … mixed up. Like you can't tell what's real and what's for show.'

'Hey,' said, Bruce, craning his neck to gaze up at the tower. 'Imagine what it was like when they needed to build this thing just so they could sleep at night. Pretty real, I'd say.'

~

Sally and Rab had set up the trestle tables, covered them with a spotless linen tablecloth and arranged fold-up chairs all round. Jen had unpacked the hampers and set out plates and cutlery—real plates, Derry saw, not paper. Jessica had placed a bottle of champagne in an ice bucket, and Sally was handing out fluted glasses. Everything seemed so normal, a picnic with friends. Derry had to remind herself she had just imagined two of these people as would-be killers.

'Hey, like a tailgate party without the ball game,' said Bruce.

'Here, we have tables,' said Jen sternly. 'And why would you need a game when you have the finest views in all the world? T'would only be a distraction.'

Bruce laughed. 'I guess you're right at that, Ma'am.'

'Here they come,' said Sally. A black SUV was making its way down the track towards them, occasionally disappearing amongst the humps and outcrops.

'I'll uncover the food now, shall I?' asked Jen.

'Please,' said Sally. 'I'm sure we're all starving. I might even take a picture—show Amelia what she's missing.'

'That would be cruel, Mrs. Carson,' said Jen, smiling.

'She said she'd had enough scenery to last 'till she's old, like forty. Well, that's her loss. She'll learn.' Sally sounded artificially gay, like someone making themselves have a good time. Derry wondered was that because her husband was arriving.

With a crunching of tyres, Dunbar's SUV swung into view, pulling up on the far side of the forecourt as if meaning to turn around and leave right away. Carson stepped out, beaming like he was President of the USA expecting applause and a band to strike up. Johnny stayed in the driver's seat, checking his phone, engine still running.

'That Alex is a demon for work,' announced Carson loudly, addressing the company at large while striding across the empty ground towards them. 'I said to him, "Alex you gotta have some R'n'R."' He'll be coming to the party tonight though.'

Carson was dressed as though for an English shooting party—tweed trousers and wax jacket, green gumboots and a deerstalker hat. At the table, he greedily examined the spread of foods—game pie, cheeses, bread rolls and chicken legs. 'Jen, that looks mighty fine!' he said. He signalled Johnny to come over. 'Johnny!' he called. 'Come and get some. Take it with ya.'

Johnny opened the driver's door and jumped down. He strolled towards them, grinning.

Derry smiled at the contrast with Carson. No country clothes for Johnny. No careful aping of the British sporting gentleman. Instead, he was dressed in black jeans and sneakers with a padded black sleeveless jacket over a dark sweatshirt. He looked like he was heading for a nightclub rather than a Highland mountainside in the stalking season.

'I can wrap whatever you like,' Jen called out. 'The chicken is good, I spiced it myself.' She gathered up some paper napkins. 'I can even give you a box to put it in.'

Johnny's grin vanished. His pace faltered, as though some instinct, some unconscious sense, had alerted him to a hidden danger. He looked back towards the SUV, saw nothing amiss, then tilted his head sharply to scan the sky.

Too late. In a blur almost too fast for the eye to comprehend, a wild flurry of wheeling black objects seemed to fall from the air to dive, screeching at Johnny's head. His arms flew up, shielding his face against the violence as balls of fury, wings beating, talons outstretched, threw themselves into the assault. Insane in their single-minded determination to tear at scalp and flesh, the birds dropped out of the sky like they were dead, before springing to life inches from Johnny's waving arms to beat and claw before climbing away once more.

Instinctively, all at the picnic table crouched low, shielding their heads, hardly daring to look up as the attackers swooped terrifyingly close before wheeling up and away to regroup. But Johnny was getting the worst of it. He frantically ducked and weaved, bent double, arms over his head, as he was harried relentlessly. Now one of Rab's dogs joined in the melee, barking furiously, growling and snapping, chasing Johnny, making sharp dives at his legs.

Rab was first to recover his wits. 'Here! Charlie! Charlie! Get back here! Get back!' He raced to retrieve his dog, grabbing the protesting animal by the collar and hauling him back, while waving an arm above his head to deflect the birds.

The SUV's door slammed shut as Johnny threw himself inside. Even then, the birds never let up, striking glancing blows on the roof, black bodies thudding off the metal. The SUV made a frantic three-point turn. With engine screaming it accelerated up the hill and away.

The dog let loose a final salvo of barks and fell silent. The birds wheeled higher, quieter now, milling together in a lazy, loosely synchronised ball. Derry watched, stunned into immobility. The flock wheeled around the pinnacle of the tower, as though the Doon itself had hatched them, sent them out and was now calling its children home.

Carson stood upright, roared with laughter and slapped his thighs. Jen had her arms spread wide as though to protect her picnic from demons. Rab was admonishing his dog. Sally, Jessica and Derry were looking at each other, speechless.

'Oh man,' said Carson, grinning. 'You can't fall on your ass in this world without somebody shooting a video, and just when you need one …!' He shook his head. 'Wouldn't Alex just love to have seen that. Johnny departs the battlefield, white flag a-waving. That has made my day! Alfred Hitchcock right here for real!'

'It was the food upset them,' said Jen. 'I'm told they've verra good eyesight.' She was obviously shaken. 'I heard of such a thing but I never in my life saw it.'

'A drink is what I need,' said Sally, failing to disguise the trembling in her voice. 'That was crazy. Will they come back?

Should we go?' She knelt, ruffling Charlie's neck. Rab too was petting the dogs, reassuring them.

'Black,' said Rab. 'He was wearing black clothes. It's well known that crows and ravens will mob anything dark.'

'Jessica,' said Sally. 'Would you pour us all drinks, please?' Jessica did as she was asked, filling each glass to the brim. They all stood around the table, glasses in hand, trying to act as if nothing unusual had happened. But every few moments Derry found herself casting a wary eye skywards.

In the end, they stayed barely an hour, just enough time to eat Jen's picnic, though Sally insisted on opening a second bottle of champagne. Derry drank only a single glass, acutely aware she was to appear as Madam Tulip that evening, and a premature hangover would do little to help her predictions.

Conversation around the table was disjointed. Everyone was making an effort to pretend nothing alarming had happened, as though being attacked by the wildlife was only to be expected in the Highlands of Scotland. Carson insisted on reciting the history of the Doon and the chieftains who had owned it. Bruce and Jen talked recipes for game pie. Rab was subdued, and Derry occasionally saw him glancing in her direction like he wanted to say something, but she felt no inclination to help him out. Of them all, Jessica was by far the most animated, her good humour irrepressible. She reminded Derry of a kid on the afternoon of a longed-for party. Perhaps it was the effect of adrenalin, the release from tension.

'I guess it's goodbye,' said Carson, waving his glass expansively to take in the tower, the lake and the rearing mountains beyond. 'We've had some nice times here.' He glanced at Sally. 'Some nicer than others. But you know what? *Nothing lasts forever.*'

28

To anyone not an actor, the way Derry was checking and rechecking was plain obsessive. Her Madam Tulip dress, wig and accessories, cards, crystal ball and timer were inspected, laid out on the bed then carefully repacked into Bella's case. 'Gah!' she said, slamming the lid.

Bruce was sitting in the armchair, relaxed and, as always, punctual. 'Hey! What's got into you? We're going to a party. You tell a few tall tales about how folks are gonna meet a handsome stranger. They lap it up. Everyone happy.'

'Why do people complicate everything?' The words burst out of her. Derry slumped onto the bed beside her case.

'It sure is a puzzle.' Bruce spoke like he had long since accepted that particular aspect of human nature.

Derry realised she'd forgotten the bones. She got up, retrieved her bag from the dressing table and took out the little pouch. She flipped open the lid of the case. Just as she was about to tuck the bag in the corner and close the case once more, she stopped. The habit was too strong. *Check! Always check!* She pulled open the drawstring of the bag and emptied the contents onto the bed.

The bones scattered on the white hills of the bedcover, settling in a hollow. They fell in no particular pattern. *Five.* That was the important thing—all five bones were present. Derry gathered them into her cupped palm, idly rubbing the last between her fingers. As she did so, she thought of the party. Was she being too fussy, insisting she couldn't be seen as Madam Tulip outside her fortune telling booth? This was a

Halloween party. Maybe everyone else would be in costume too—Jessica hadn't said. Then again, where could anyone hire fancy-dress costume in such a small village? There probably wasn't a costume rental for a hundred miles. At least the party wouldn't have six people turning up all dressed as Batman.

Derry saw the effect before she felt anything. Her hand, the hand in which she cradled the bones, was trembling, shaking as though with a mind of its own, without cause or reason. And that hollow ache in her stomach—*fear*. Why?

She opened her palm half-expecting the bones to have disappeared or multiplied or behaved in some unaccountable way. But they sat inert, waiting peaceably for her to drop them back into their pouch and pull the cord. Forcing her hands to obey, she returned the bones to their little bag, opening the lid of the case and dropping the pouch inside.

She turned and slowly sat on the bed—slowly because she was unsure of her balance, uncertain of her ability to remain upright.

She took her phone from the nightstand. She didn't know why she was phoning or even whom it was she meant to call. Her brain was telling her to act, to do what she was told, but not to think. Because thinking would be bad.

'Dad? Hi.'

'My treasure! You find me about to shoot a grouse, if the grouse can be persuaded to walk rather than fly.' Someone guffawed heartily in the background.

'Dad I haven't much time. I need to ask you something. I'll explain later. Remember you and your architect, Paddy?'

'That blackmailing son of a—'

'Him. You sent me a picture. You were both in fancy-dress costume. Why?'

'Oh,' said Jacko, derailed by the question. 'Paddy wanted to show me the stonework up on the rampart, so we had to take precautions.'

'Precautions—what precautions?'

'The crows and ravens and what have you! Devils! They hate you going near their nests. You have to hide your face, disguise yourself.'

'You're saying they can recognise a person? A face?'

'Those birds can tell a man from his own brother. And if they catch someone climbing up to their nest, they'll hate him forever. And heaven help you when they gang up to drive you off. They'll take the head off you.'

Derry heard her own breathing. Sweat broke out on her hands. But her brain still wouldn't tell her why.

'Thanks, Dad. I'll call you tomorrow, okay? I've got to go now. Take care.'

'Are you sure everything—?'

'Sure. Fine. Thanks. Talk tomorrow.'

Derry hung up. She sat in silence. Now Bruce wasn't studying his phone anymore. He was watching her carefully, his expression mildly questioning.

'Johnny,' said Derry. 'It was Johnny.'

Bruce listened but said nothing. He only nodded as Derry spelled it out. Johnny could easily have had access to the tower. And he had been a soldier, so Jessica said. Trained to shoot.

But the birds had attacked him, perhaps even ruined his aim. And they never forgot a face.

'Bruce, when I was in Edinburgh—when I told you I needed to come back here—at first you weren't happy. Then you were all, "Hey, Scotland's cool. Sure I'll stay." Why?'

Bruce pursed his lips. He gazed up at the paint-encrusted cornice on the ceiling and shrugged. 'No big deal. I wasn't too comfortable, that's all. Folks shooting at folks. Ain't the kinda neighbourhood you want to hang around.'

Derry felt a sudden rush of warmth for this man of contradictions. He had stayed to keep an eye on her. *Just like him*, thought Derry. *Casual, but not casual. Relaxed but always aware.*

'Why don't I think you're being straight with me?'

Bruce sniffed. He followed up with a clucking noise, like a hen wondering whether to go left or right and taking her time about it. 'Uh, remember your shooting lesson with your friend Rab?'

Derry let the 'friend' part pass. 'Sure. What?'

'You looked through your scope at the target.'

'Yeah.'

'Imagine you're high up, the target is straight across from you, maybe six hundred yards. You're on the tower, solid stone. You lean the rifle on it, or maybe you've got a tripod.'

'Okay.'

'So picture it—what do you see through that big old scope?'

'An SUV driving up a mountain track?'

'Remember the target on the range?'

Derry remembered. Through the scope, the paper deer had looked huge. A bullseye had been painted round its heart, filling the lens. But why did she not want to think the next part, the next obvious, logical part? The part that said the head was big too? So big you could see its eyes clearly—black ovals on which somebody as a joke had painted eyelashes. *Bambi.*

Bruce waited.

'He couldn't have mistaken Jessica for anybody.'

Bruce nodded.

'He couldn't have mistaken her for Dunbar. Or Carson.'

Silence.

'Johnny … meant to kill Jessica.'

$\approx$

The human brain is a mysterious organ. When it becomes aware of a mildly troubling fact, it will torment its owner with anxiety, keeping her awake all night. But if some truly terrifying insight comes along, the brain will ignore the whole thing. *It won't happen*, reasons the brain. *It couldn't possibly happen. And if it does happen, it will happen to someone else.* And at once, showing an impressive turn of creative flair, the brain will suggest something quite different to worry about.

'Shoes!' exclaimed Derry. 'I never thought about the shoes! I can't believe this!'

'Derry,' said Bruce, gently, 'you're wearing shoes.'

'The right shoes! Madam Tulip's shoes! She's a middle-aged woman! She wears twenties dresses! She won't wear button-up ankle-boots!'

'Don't see why not. Anyhow, unless you plan on dancing on the table, who's gonna notice?'

'It's a disaster!' Derry's wail was the furious lamentation actors reserve for auditions where they won't let you read the script, insist on you standing rather than sitting, change your lines, or otherwise cause an unfair requirement for lateral thinking.

'And now I'm going to be late! Eight-thirty; I'm supposed to be there at eight-thirty!'

If Derry didn't complete the scene by stamping her foot and throwing things, that was because she knew with absolute clarity she was temporarily insane. This was like worrying about burning the toast when the house was on fire. And she knew it.

All the while, Bruce was fooling with the kettle, and now it boiled noisily. 'This your tea?' he asked. Beside the kettle was Derry's little box of borage. Bruce popped a sachet into the cup, poured and handed it to her. 'Careful, hon. It's hot.'

Derry nodded. She sat on the bed. The cucumber smell of the tea was calming. 'What do we do?'

'I guess we think.'

'I can't think.' Derry sipped the borage. She felt her breathing grow steady. 'We have to tell somebody. Tell the police.'

'Uh, don't yell at me, right?'

'I don't yell.'

'I didn't mean—'

'I am not the yelling type. I may debate—'

'Sure, okay—'

'Yelling is uncouth. It is *not* my style.'

'Sure, I get ya. I can say whatever I like and you won't yell.'

'That's what I said.'

'Okay.' Bruce paused. He took a breath. "Excuse me officer—" what was his name? The cop at the castle?'

'Sillars.'

'"Excuse me officer Sillars, but a bunch of birds got mad at us while we were having a picnic and especially mad at this guy Johnny, and I just know he shot at our SUV. And he was trying to kill the driver, 'cos—we don't know why, but I'm sure y'all can find that out being police and everything."'

Derry didn't shout. She didn't feel one little bit like shouting. 'But it's true.'

Bruce shrugged. 'Maybe.' He paused. 'Okay, let's say it was Johnny. Maybe they were having a little affair and she—'

'No,' said Derry. 'Not Jessica and Johnny.'

'Why?'

'I've seen them together; there's nothing there. He acts like he hardly knows her. Anyhow, he's an employee. A driver, whatever. Jessica would want more—a writer maybe, a director, some industry big wheel. She's ambitious.'

'What if he wanted her and she rejected him?' said Bruce. 'It happens.'

'Maybe. She does have a boyfriend in Edinburgh. Unless she was—' Derry stopped. She was oddly aware her mouth was open, but she couldn't finish whatever it was she was going to say, couldn't even remember. How had she not seen this before? What had she been thinking that she'd been so dense?

'*Dunbar!* He has a place near Edinburgh. She said she was going to see her boyfriend. That's who she meant. Dunbar. She told me she came back in the chopper.' Even as she spoke, Derry knew she was right.

'Why would she go to Edinburgh to see Dunbar? She could see him right here. Anyhow, I thought she was going to get a passport? Isn't that what she said?'

'She could still have done that, then flown back with Dunbar.'

The memories tumbled around in Derry's head like clothes in a dryer. On the way to Edinburgh, Dunbar calling to arrange lunch. Derry telling him Jessica was on the train. Then who turns up but Johnny just before they reach Edinburgh. The image returned of Jessica outside the consulate standing in a doorway sheltering from the rain, taking a call.

'Everything fits,' said Derry. But even as she said the words, she knew everything didn't fit. Maybe Jessica and Dunbar were having an affair—hardly a reason for Johnny to shoot her. And if Dunbar was seeing Jessica, why did he try to date Derry? Why invite her to the castle? Why ask her to lunch in Edinburgh? Then Derry remembered—Dunbar had called off that lunch for some urgent business. *Jessica business?*

'Did she seem worried to you?' asked Bruce.

On the contrary, at the castle this morning and on the picnic, Jessica had seemed more than happy, especially excited about the party. What had she said about having her fortune told? *A little test for Tulip?*

'There's maybe something you could do,' suggested Bruce, his voice casual. 'Think Jessica will want her fortune told?'

'Sure. She said as much.'

'Maybe you could say, like, "Hey, I see in my crystal ball something-something-something, best be a little …" I don't know … "cautious?" Fortune tellers know how to do that stuff, right?'

Now Derry *was* shouting. 'What is this! First off, Madam Tulip does *not* pretend to see things so as to scare the living daylights out of people! Second, what am I supposed to say? I gaze into my crystal ball and say, "Oops, better not walk under any ladders for a while? Better still, why not stay in bed for a month? Just make sure the fire alarm is tested? Oh and by the way, I'm telling you this 'cos I read in the cards that your boyfriend's driver tried to blow your head off!"'

'Woah! You promised no shouting. You said we had to do something. So what do we do?'

'Okay. Okay. Sorry. But Madam Tulip is not some sort of messenger for every crazy agenda. Alright?'

Bruce looked puzzled. He couldn't know he was the third person that day to suggest Madam Tulip should manipulate a client, feed them a story. 'We could go home right now.'

'What are you saying?'

'If we can't tell Jessica she's got a problem and we can't tell the cops anything they can use, and if we really think someone tried to murder someone, what are we doing here? Van's outside. We pay the bill and go.'

Was he serious? Derry wondered if she really knew this man at all. He was brave, she knew that. Decisive too. 'Bruce, how can you say we just run away?'

'The story is either true or it's not true,' said Bruce. If it's *not* true, you risk scaring the heck out of people and acting like a crazy woman for no reason.'

'And if it is true?'

'Then we're walking into something we don't understand, maybe stirring the pot by just being here—making things worse not better. If you're even half right and someone is trying to kill someone, and you go round telling folks about it, what do you think might happen to you?'

Derry felt her heart stop. She had been thinking of Jessica. Not for one second had the thought entered her mind that she herself might end up a target. But Bruce was right. She might as well walk around with a big sign saying *I know stuff you don't want me to know—shoot me.*

'So we should run away?'

Bruce didn't reply.

'How about we say it right out at the party? Like, tell everybody. Then no one could do anything bad. Not to Jessica, not to us.'

'So what would you say?'

'I wait 'till everyone is together, then I stand up and I say … "Excuse me ladies and gentlemen … I have something to tell you …"'

'And?'

'Somebody tried to shoot … somebody.' She stopped. 'Can I say who?'

'Your call.'

'What if Johnny is in the room?'

'He'll laugh. It's Halloween. Crazy fortune teller pulls a stunt. Most likely, everybody will laugh.'

'I could tell them about the birds.'

'Sure you could.'

'It doesn't matter if they laugh at me! I don't care. Nothing bad could happen after—that's all we want!'

Bruce shrugged. 'You could do it. We could have our stuff ready packed in the van. Bill paid. You say your piece, then we leave. Head for the ferry.'

'Should I say the shooter was aiming at Jessica?'

'Sure you could. And they'd stop laughing right before they threw us out.'

'But Jessica would be safe.'

'You sure about that? Say she has an accident sometime next week before they head back to the States. So somebody tells the cops, *hey this crazy fortune-teller said someone tried to shoot her a while back.* And the cops ask some questions, and everybody says it was poachers. Coincidence.' He paused. 'Derry, your story's not gonna convince anybody, and it's not gonna help anybody.'

'We can't just walk away!'

'Well, like I said, tell Jessica to be careful. Then it's up to her.'

Bruce was right. Jessica was a grown woman. She could believe what she was told or not. Act on it or not. And the warning had to be private. That way whoever was threatening her would be none the wiser. And *private* meant Madam Tulip would have to deliver the news. The *bad* news.

'I'll tell her,' said Derry. 'Not that I saw it in the cards. I'll just out and tell her.'

'Then we leave the party? Get paid, get back here. Hightail it out first thing in the morning. No looking back, okay?'

Derry nodded.

Bruce stood. 'Want to give me your case?' He took the Madam Tulip case while Derry checked her hair, threw on her jacket and picked up her bag.

'Shame they took back my kilt,' said Bruce. 'I thought I looked kinda cool.'

He was doing his best. Derry tried to smile.

29

The castle forecourt was blazing with light, its white frontage looking like the set of a grand opera. In an open grassy area just beyond the perimeter wall, a tall pyramid of branches and old packing crates stood ready for the traditional Halloween bonfire. A small party, Carson had said, but at least twenty cars filled the forecourt. Bruce was forced to park the van away to one side against a high wall separating the public frontage of the castle from the yard and outbuildings at the back.

'Oh I do like a party!' he exclaimed, insisting on carrying Derry's case. Derry marvelled at the extraordinary ability of this man to change gear at will—to be cheerful if cheerful was what he wanted to be, to be deadly serious when serious was the game. Outside of anything to do with acting, it was like he owned his emotions rather than his emotions owning him. Derry wished she were like that. But her growing nervousness told her she was not.

As they approached the castle door, Derry felt Bruce's arm clasping her around the shoulders, like he was her boyfriend. He gave a comforting squeeze, strong and confident. Derry felt her fears ebb away. She took deep breaths, steadying herself, and gave him a grateful smile.

Bruce pulled the bell. Only then did Derry realise what she had feared. Johnny. Both times she had come to the castle, he had answered the doorbell. But not this time. The face that greeted them with a broad smile of recognition belonged to Moira McKenzie.

'How nice to see you,' she said. 'And you'll be glad to hear all the guests are alive.'

∼

Derry's vocabulary deserted her. Bruce registered frank astonishment.

'No ghosties or ghoulies until after midnight, they say,' continued Moira. 'Though after that, anyone foolish enough to be about is fair game.' She laughed, delighted with her joke, and ushered them into the hall.

The entrance had been transformed. Spotlights picked out the African masks and headdresses on the walls above, making them dance and hover in the air like disembodied spirits. Somehow, they seemed even less out of place than before. Maybe fear, suspicion and the unexplained were the same everywhere.

'Derry! Bruce! Honeys!' Sally appeared, a glass in her hand, smiling the practiced greeting of the seasoned hostess. She wore a fringed rodeo jacket, a cowboy hat, blue jeans and fancy Justin boots. She seemed fresh and lively. A surprise—at the picnic that afternoon she had been drinking almost ostentatiously, as if to say to her husband, *I'm doing what I like; I don't care what anyone thinks.*

'Bruce, I'll show Derry her changing room,' she said. 'Why don't you head on in and grab a drink. You'll meet some nice people, don't be shy.'

Derry took her suitcase from Bruce. Sally signalled she should follow down the panelled corridor from where the sound of a piano and laughter said *party.* But instead of entering the public rooms, they turned right to halt by a door that looked more primitive than the rest, heavy and almost black with age. On it, someone had taped a notice saying *Private, No Entry.*

'This is Alex's wing,' said Sally, pushing open the door and ushering Derry through. 'It's the oldest part of the castle.'

The ancient passageway looked just like the rough corridor leading to Carson's office that Derry had seen before. A sharp turn to the left, and Sally pushed open a familiar door, flicked on the light and ushered Derry into the storeroom Jessica had already shown her. Opposite was the door to the library.

'I put a chair in here for you, and a mirror,' said Sally. 'Is that okay? I couldn't fix a table, there's no room, but I cleared this shelf for you to put your stuff on.'

'Great,' said Derry. 'Thanks.'

'I'm just so happy you could do this,' continued Sally, making no attempt to hide her excitement. Derry wondered how a woman so tough and worldly could at times seem so innocent, almost girlish. 'It'll be such fun. And I'm grateful for how you helped me when we … spoke last time.'

'I don't know that I did help,' said Derry.

'You did. You were honest. I needed to remember that honest people do exist. I have to tell you, when Jim suggested we get you for this party, I wasn't sure. Or at least, I wasn't sure I'd want to have you read for me again. But there's something I'd like to ask you about this time. Not the same thing. Or not exactly.'

'I'll do my best,' said Derry. She hesitated. 'The thing about Madam Tulip … what I'm trying to say is … the cards are about finding out what a person really wants. Mostly we don't know what we want. Or we think we do, but we don't.'

'I guess,' said Sally. 'But I haven't quit. Don't think I have.'

～

Derry laid her suitcase carefully on the floor. She hated leaving her costume unguarded, but that's what she was expected to do. Sally led her through the connecting door into the library, smiling at Derry's compliments on its exotic decor, before opening the door to the dining room. The yard-thick walls and heavy oak panelling must have done a good job deadening the sound, because suddenly Derry's senses were assailed by the babble of massed human voices fuelled by alcohol.

The room was thronged. Anyone wandering in might think they had stepped into a street carnival. A man in a skeleton body suit turned and smiled. His companions, two zombies in carefully disarranged bandages, raised their glasses in greeting. A Frankenstein monster was in deep conversation with a medieval lady in a conical hat trailing a scarf. The only familiar faces were those of Jen and her husband the Laird. He stood stiffly against the wall in kilt, tweed jacket and tie, glass in hand, frowning as Jen made a face signalling he was failing to do something he was supposed to do or was doing something he shouldn't.

In the corner was the mannequin Amelia had been carrying this morning—was it only this morning? The witch sat on a wooden kitchen chair, broom propped over her shoulder, glaring balefully at the revellers.

Of Johnny, Derry saw no sign. Nor of Jessica. As Derry thought of Jessica, she felt her belief in the story she meant to tell fading away. She glanced around the room, trying to remind herself of what she had come to do, but the idea seemed more ludicrous with every passing moment. She cast about for Bruce but could see him nowhere.

'This is Derry O'Donnell, the actress and *fabulous* fortune-teller,' announced Sally, taking Derry by the arm for the introductions. 'This is Rebecca, Lord Talbot's head gardener, and her partner Derek. This is Jamie Bradshaw—most famous hairdresser in London—and Charles his husband, who's decided he likes Scotland after all.' Derry smiled politely, and tried to think of complimentary things to say about their costumes.

'Come and see who else we have,' said Sally. She hauled Derry to the drinks table, refilled her own whisky glass, and led the way to the drawing room. Here it wasn't as crowded, and Derry spotted Bruce deep in conversation with a strikingly good-looking man dressed as Robin Hood, with green hose and Errol Flynn moustache. In the corner someone played traditional Scottish airs on a piano.

The introductions kept coming. Amongst them the Polish doctor—a tall blonde woman wearing a surgical cap, mask and a gown streaked with exuberant splashes of red; and an artist who had come as an artist, but insisted he was a dead artist, so that was appropriate. 'I'll leave you to chat,' said Sally, waving her glass.

'Sorry, Sally, when do I start?' asked Derry. She was feeling that nervous restlessness every performer experiences when forced to hang around before a show.

'Oh, give it another half hour, said Sally, airily. 'Jim is going to make a speech shortly, though he won't tell anybody what about. He likes his little secrets.' Derry wondered at Sally of all people accusing anyone else of having secrets, but kept her expression bland. 'You could start after Jim finishes. A couple of hours should be enough? We'll have the bonfire and fireworks then. You can come out and enjoy the party. Have a few drinks.' She waved her glass around amiably. 'Oh, here's Jim.'

Carson was decked out in the Highland gear Derry had seen him wearing before—kilt, sporran and waistcoat. He was leading Jessica by the hand and smiling broadly as he positioned himself by the great mantelpiece.

'Alex! Where's Alex? Come on over!'

Dunbar entered, making his way across the room to stand a little to one side of Carson. Following, taking station by the door, came Johnny. He was dressed casually—sweater and bomber jacket, jeans—and stood, legs apart, hands folded in front in the pose favoured by bodyguards everywhere. Another casually dressed man took position alongside him. He whispered in Johnny's ear. Johnny nodded. Derry felt her stomach lurch.

Derry now had a clear view of Dunbar. Instead of fancy-dress he sported an impeccably cut dark suit, perhaps Italian, and a muted tie that might or might not have signified past membership of some British Army regiment or a private school.

'Welcome everybody,' announced Carson. 'We're so happy you could come and celebrate with us this great Scottish festival. We'd also like to welcome, in traditional style, the ghosts of our ancestors—they'll join us later.' The room laughed dutifully.

'Meanwhile, I have an announcement to make.' He signalled Jessica should stand close beside him. 'For three years now Jessica has been my able assistant throughout the trials and tribulations of our crazy business. She's done a great job, let me tell you. And although most of you know we've had our troubles with this movie, the business goes on. Jessica has shown she knows what she's doing, and she has movie projects she wants to make. And we're gonna help her do that. We're gonna raise the cash she needs for not just one but a slate of movies. And for that we have to thank my old friend Alex. Alex is always happy to lose money, ha ha!' At Carson's joke, Dunbar smiled and shook his head, as if to say, *these creative types, what can a simple banker do?*

Standing in the crowd, Derry was glad all attention was focused on Carson and Jessica. If anyone had been watching her own face, they would have seen frank astonishment. She knew now why Carson had suddenly become *Jim*, why Jessica had remarked that she might get her film scripts made, and why she had been bursting with excitement since she had returned from Edinburgh.

Carson was speaking again. 'I'd like you all to put your hands together and congratulate Jessica on joining the unfortunate ranks of movie producers.' He turned to Jessica. 'Jess, you wanted it, now you got it. Be careful what you wish for.' Jessica beamed. The room guffawed at Carson's joke, every person imagining they knew what being a film producer was about—the stress, the heart pills, the fast talking, but also the yachts and the helicopters. 'So raise your glasses, please.'

Carson again turned to Jessica, handing her a glass and filling it to overflowing with champagne. 'Jess, we believe in you. Well done.'

Derry raised her glass dutifully with everyone else and smiled as she was expected to do. Carson and Alex too toasted Jessica. Then, to Derry's astonishment she saw Dunbar turn slightly to catch her eye. He raised his glass a little higher, as though he were drinking, not to Jessica, but to her.

30

'I want to apologise.'

Derry turned around sharply—Rab, dressed for the party in kilt, cotton shirt and tweed tie. Derry realised he had been the one in the corner playing the piano.

He approached hesitantly, but with the air of someone who had made up his mind. 'On the hill. I made a stupid suggestion. I'm sorry. I shouldn't have interfered.'

He was right—he shouldn't have interfered. Then again, he was only trying to help, hardly a hanging offence. And his reluctance to tell Sally what he knew was, if anything, caring. Not for the first time since she had taken on the role of Madam Tulip, Derry felt the burden of other people's secrets. How infinitely depressing to think how many were deceived, and how many deceived themselves.

Rab was taller than she remembered. His dark eyes were sincere. 'Don't worry about it,' said Derry. 'You were trying to help.' She looked around, wanting to change the subject. 'It looks like everybody knows everybody else here. Do they?'

Rab smiled. Derry saw he was relieved. Perhaps it had taken more courage to approach her than she realised. She had never thought of herself as intimidating, but perhaps she was—a foreigner, an actress; and she had been cold towards him, she knew that.

'It's a small world here,' he said. 'We all know each other, maybe too well. It's a long winter. Plenty time to gossip.'

'Halloween is about winter, isn't that right?'

'It is,' said Rab. '*Samhain* in Gaelic. In the old days, you'd bring the cattle down from the high pastures and haul the boats up from the shore. The peats would be in for the fires. It was even the end of the fighting season, not that some didn't break the rules. A different way of life. And for a short time, at Samhain, the dead are close. But they're not all unfriendly.'

Derry smiled. 'In the States our Halloween has been taken over by zombies. Do you have zombies?'

Rab laughed. 'No zombies. The dead get a night to cavort around and pay some house calls, then it's back to wherever. Strict rule. No exceptions.'

'Cool,' said Derry. 'Kinda civilized.'

Rab hesitated as if he were about to say something but couldn't find the words. 'I'd like to say … what I mean is … I don't know if you're going to be around later, after you've done your work? This party—it's rather formal. Likely it'll be finished by midnight or soon after, but in town there's going to be a ceilidh. It'll be much livelier, I can promise. And more … authentic I suppose, in that it's what we really do here. It's why I'm not dressed as a zombie.'

What to say? A thousand thoughts raced through Derry's head. Here was the promise of listening to that melodious voice, that deep caressing tone that made the back of her neck tingle, for as long as she wanted to listen. In any world but this one, the only possible answer was yes. But in *this* world she had promised herself she would do something important, something that, whatever her doubts, she had to follow through. And she had agreed with Bruce they'd leave for home right after, drive straight to a ferry.

'I'd like that,' she said.

Instantly, a voice in her head insisted she was crazy. She was about to tell a woman that someone in this castle had tried to kill her, and instead she was imagining being swept off her feet by a highlander in a kilt. Ridiculous. But, another voice said, so what? Do what you came to do, then get some normal life. Why not?

Rab's phone rang, the ringtone a surprisingly trendy band. Derry smiled at herself. What had she expected—*Scotland the Brave? Over the Sea to Skye? Auld Lang Syne?*

'Excuse me a moment?' He retreated, his back to the wall, while Derry stood waiting.

'Hey, thought for a minute you might be lonely.' Bruce grinned impishly. 'Uh, when you've finished your thing, I suggest we leave right away. Mission accomplished, back to the hotel. You can offer me some of your porridge tea. I might even have a beer.'

Derry was about to explain that maybe she might go to a ceilidh, when Rab reappeared at her side. He gave Bruce a friendly nod before turning to Derry. 'I'm desperately sorry. I have to go,' he said. 'Something important has come up. Work. I hope you understand. If I get away, can I call you? I have your number.'

Derry was about to mumble *sure, whatever* and trying not to add *and you can stuff your work and your ceilidh and I never liked men in skirts anyway,* when Carson's voice boomed out from across the room.

'Ladies and gentlemen! Like I said, later we're going to have a bonfire and some fireworks. Meantime, you can enjoy the amazing talents of our star fortune-teller, the famous Madam Tulip!'

'I'll call you. I'm sorry,' said Rab. And he was gone.

'Let me tell you about Madam Tulip,' continued Carson. 'She's a gypsy, she's a witch, she can talk to the spirits—yessiree! She even finds dead bodies for the police down in wicked old London! Tonight, she's gonna read your cards and gaze into her magic crystal ball and tell you all about that tall stranger you know you wanna meet!'

The audience laughed. Every face in the room was turned to Derry. She felt like a spotlight had suddenly blazed out, pinning her to the wall, freezing her body to ice.

Carson held his arms wide, like a Victorian showman introducing the bearded lady. 'Roll up, roll up! Madam Tulip will be in the library from fifteen minutes' time. Form an orderly queue, *if* you please.'

Only Derry's long training as an actor saved her, preventing her for protesting out loud, telling her host he was wrong, embarrassing the whole room. The consternation that flitted across her face was instantly replaced by a bland half-smile, a gracious nod of the head in acknowledgement. But inside she felt blazing anger.

Bruce was whispering in her ear. 'When you're done, we bail out. But right away, okay?'

Derry understood. No socialising, no small talk, no waiting around. Just melt away.

That idea suited fine.

31

'Oh, my!' Sally stood inside the library doorway, her hand over her open mouth. Derry should by now have been used to such reactions. But even in this strange and troubling situation, she couldn't help feel the intense satisfaction any actor feels when their costume and makeup wows an audience.

Derry knew exactly what Sally must have seen as she stepped into the library. The hanging African fabrics were picked out in pools of vibrant, almost hallucinogenic colour. On the floor, the drums with their disturbing faces seemed to sit waiting for the right moment to do—what? The table draped in cowhide was softened by a richly embroidered cloth on which sat the crystal ball, two decks of cards, a mysterious little pouch of brown leather and an antique glass timer.

But Sally's eyes didn't linger for long on the table and its arcane array of objects, Derry saw her gaze was drawn at once to Madam Tulip's unnaturally pale face, softly illuminated by the lamp at her elbow.

Tulip's hair was black and full, rendered exotic by pale grey streaks and her delicate headdress of blue and yellow feathers. She wore glasses framed in mother-of-pearl, emphasising her soft and compelling eyes. Around her neck hung strings of heavy beads. Her dress was pale blue with a high collar and a low ruff at the throat. Madam Tulip's bosom was ample and her waist thick, natural in the middle-aged woman she appeared to be. She wore long black velvet gloves, fingers exposed so she could easily handle the cards.

'You seek the wisdom of Madam Tulip,' said Derry in a low voice, comforting yet somehow detached.

'Oh my, just let me get my breath!' exclaimed Sally. 'I never imagined this—really.'

'If you come seeking knowledge,' said Madam Tulip, with an enigmatic smile, 'you are welcome. Please, take a seat.'

Getting dressed and made up in the storeroom without help in no more than fifteen minutes had been nerve-racking, but Derry congratulated herself on managing well. She had even put from her mind the prospect of seeing Jessica and saying what had to be said. Madam Tulip had a job to do, and she must put all else aside.

'Shall we begin?' asked Tulip. 'The cards or the crystal?'

'Oh, cards. Please. Not the Tarot—Halloween is spooky enough. Though I don't know what I'm asking to be honest. It's more that I wanted to tell *you* something.'

Sally put her elbows on the table and laced her fingers together under her chin. Her gaze was steady, and although Derry could smell the whisky on her breath, she didn't seem drunk.

Derry passed her the deck to shuffle and cut, while trying not to show surprise at Sally's words. The shuffle was rushed, as though Sally was so anxious to move on she hardly cared about what the cards would say. She cut without looking, her gaze fixed on Madam Tulip's face.

Derry dealt a three card spread. Best keep it simple and see where the cards might lead.

'What does the petitioner wish to learn?'

'Am I doing the right thing? Am I *going* to do the right thing?' Sally gave no hint what she meant by *the right thing*.

Derry turned the first card. *The past—Four of Clubs*. She worked to keep her face impassive and her breathing even. Usually the opening spread in a session was halfhearted, indistinct like the future was unsure of itself. The first minutes of a reading were like looking across a shimmering desert landscape in which the heat made distant mountains appear an illusion and mirages seem real.

But not this time. This time, reading was like looking down through a pool of such crystal clarity Derry could see and count every pebble on its floor. *Four of Clubs*. The meaning was as obvious as if the cards had stood and shouted. *Lies! Treachery! Betrayal!* But whose lies? Whose betrayal?

'The past is in shadow,' said Tulip. 'I see darkness. Lies create illusions within an illusion. An impossible life.' Where did the words come from? They emerged like Madam Tulip had a mind of her own, thoughts of her own, knowledge Derry didn't have, couldn't have. While Derry herself would have hesitated to name the crime, to use that most dreadful of all accusations—*liar*, Madam Tulip spoke what she saw.

Shock passed across Sally's face. She took a sharp intake of breath and blinked. 'Well,' she said. 'You sure don't make nice, do you. But I guess you've called it like it is—was.'

Derry flipped the second card. Even as she did so, she realised that although Sally had all but admitted her betrayal, she too had been deceived.

The present—King of Diamonds. 'A man. A man of influence. Of secrets.'

'Maybe you think what I've done is wrong ...' Sally paused as though waiting for Derry to contradict her, to say *no, not you*. When Derry said nothing, she continued. 'Before we met, Jim worked in Africa—he was in the trade section in the Embassy. Even now I don't know what he really did out there. He's like that about everything. You expect men like him to bring their work home? Not Jim. I thought that was a good thing. But I'm not so sure.'

Third card. *Two of Spades—Change.* Derry didn't doubt that card for one moment. She felt its truth. Soon Sally would experience a dramatic upheaval from which there could be no going back.

'I see a turning away,' said Madam Tulip. 'The decision is made.' She paused. '*Is* it made?'

Sally nodded. Her face was sombre but determined. Derry waited. 'I'm going to divorce him,' said Sally. 'I know it's not fair.' She hesitated. 'Remember what I told you? About my friend?'

Derry nodded.

'I still need to know what happened to him—nothing has changed. But I never wanted to be a liar. I never wanted to be a cheat. I need to forget what happened or I need to find out once and for all. Either way, I can't do it as Mrs. Jim Carson. It wouldn't be right. I've made up my mind.'

Derry remembered what Rab had told her about Hamish and his callous email. *Ghosted.* Wasn't that what it was called? When a man ups and disappears? No goodbye. No reason. Hamish the Factor runs away from the complications of an affair with his boss's friend's wife. And the husband arranges to cook up a story he was a thief to make sure he won't come back. Did Sally believe Carson had killed her lover because she needed to hate her husband in order to justify her affair?

'We used to meet at the Doon,' said Sally. 'Such a beautiful spot. Ever tried getting privacy in a Highland village? You have to go halfway up a mountain.' She smiled at the memory. 'So tell me. Am I doing the right thing?'

Derry swept up the cards. She handed the deck to Sally to shuffle and cut. She dealt and turned the first card face up. *Ten of Hearts.*

'Peace,' said Madam Tulip. 'Calm after the storm.' And the card did say *peace.*

Sally sat impassive, her eyes fixed on Derry, soft and guileless like a young girl's. Gone was the hard shell, the sophisticated veneer; even the tough Nevadan was gone. Sally was looking into Madam Tulip's eyes, but she was really looking deep into herself. 'No more lies,' she said abruptly.

She lifted her glass in a toast, raised it to her lips and drank. She wiped her mouth with the back of her hand. 'You helped me. Madam Tulip helped me. Shame we didn't get to know each other a little better. Amelia told me I should stay away from you. She wouldn't say why. Maybe she thought you were telling me what to do.'

Sally finished her drink. 'Let's stop there. I'm not sure I want to know any more. You say it'll be okay, I'll stick with that. And I won't be alone; I'll have Amelia. The rest, who knows.' She gave Derry a long look. 'I feel like I've been let out of jail.'

Sally stood and walked around to Derry's side of the table. She took Derry's shoulders in her hands and kissed her cheek. 'Thanks,' she said.

Each time the door opened, Derry's heart raced. And each time, she breathed a sigh as the person entering turned out not to be Jessica. The Head Gardner, Rebecca, came and went, happy with a Tarot reading saying she would wed within the year but unperturbed by the suggestion it might not be to her current partner. Lady Clifden, a delicate, elderly, bird-like woman with piercing eyes, proved keenly interested in the subject of secret admirers. A zombie, whose name Derry didn't catch, wanted Madam Tulip to put a spell on a girl who had been horrible to her all the way through school and now worked in the same office. Tulip politely declined, explaining that spells, especially curses, were not part of the service, not even for extra. When the crystal ball showed a change of job and a promotion, the zombie's thoughts of revenge seemed to fade. Possibly, Derry thought, Madam Tulip had averted a nasty workplace incident.

And so the clients came, at first in a trickle, then a stream, each one returning to the party to sing the praises of Madam Tulip. But still no Jessica. As the flow of enquirers dried up, signalling the bonfire and barbecue were starting outside, Derry relaxed. She was just wondering could she venture into the dining room unobserved to snatch a sausage roll from the table, and had just decided against, when the door opened.

'I brought you a drink,' said Jessica. She was carrying two glasses of wine. 'Red, wasn't it?'

'Thanks,' said Derry. Normally she would never drink while giving a performance. But maybe the wine would make it easier to say what she had to say.

'The rain has held off,' said Jessica. 'The barbecue is going ahead. You should come and join in.'

Derry smiled, wryly indicating her costume.

Jessica grinned. 'Not outdoor wear, I guess.' She took her seat without being asked. 'Jim sure gave you an introduction. Sorry about that.'

Derry shrugged, but she was surprised. Carson's speech hadn't been Jessica's fault. Why should she apologise? And there it was again, *Jim*. Derry imagined she already saw a difference in Jessica in the way she held herself. No longer was she fading into the background. She seemed to sit more upright, shoulders back, more aware of the impression she was making.

'I was going to test you,' said Jessica. 'I thought I'd be seeing you before Jim announced anything, but he jumped the gun. I was going to see could you tell I got my deal. Now I don't know what to ask.'

'There must be something more you want?' said Derry. 'Surely life doesn't stop when you get to make your movie.'

'*Movies*, plural,' said Jessica with satisfaction. 'I'm so happy I haven't even thought past which story I'm going to work on first. There's a lot to do before anything gets off the ground— deals to make, script to sort out. It's one thing writing scripts on spec. but another when you know everything's for real.'

Jessica seemed to overflow with energy. 'I have you to thank,' she said. 'You told me I should go ahead, take the risk, go for what I wanted. I was scared, let me tell you. But I did it. Last minute, but they gave in.'

A thousand questions took shape in Derry's mind, but she wasn't here to question. She reminded herself of what she had come to do. She needed to put aside Madam Tulip and tell Jessica what she believed. But somehow she didn't.

'And what does the seeker wish,' said Madam Tulip, 'the cards or the crystal?'

'No, no. The bones,' said Jessica. 'I told you. I saw what you did—your scenes were great. Don't you think cards are kind of boring? Go on, for fun, okay?'

Derry took up the little pouch of bones. Her hands moved slowly, reluctantly. She undid the drawstring and pulled open the bag. She took the pouch in her open palm and upended it on the table. Out tumbled the bones, *one, two three four*—and after the slightest hesitation—*five.*

Why hadn't she poured the bones into the cup of her hand as she had meant to do? She had always practiced that way, allowing some elegance of gesture as she cast. Instead, she had unceremoniously dumped the bag's contents without a thought, her mind on the warning she must somehow deliver and the certain knowledge she was stalling.

The bones seemed to roll for an inordinately long time, a slow-motion tumble, each bouncing leap a little higher than it had any right to be, like gravity was failing to pay attention. And even as the bones tumbled, Derry knew how they would fall. All five landed with their twisted faces uppermost.

Jessica watched, relaxed, seemingly aware only of bones tumbling naturally from their bag. Derry swept up the bones, cupped them in her hand, and once more tossed them onto the table. The bones rolled, collided and stopped. Five flat faces.

Before Jessica could protest or question her actions, Derry again gathered up the bones and cast. Tumble. Roll. Rest. All five faces the same. Every one showing its concave side.

'What's happening?' asked Jessica. She was smiling, but her voice had an edge of nervousness. Perhaps she wondered whether Derry was throwing and throwing again because she had seen something bad in her future. But what Derry had seen had nothing to do with Jessica. Three times Derry had cast the bones. Three times all five bones had fallen the same way. Derry was no mathematician, but what she saw was so unlikely as to be near impossible.

The message of the bones wasn't for Jessica. Derry knew that now. The message was for her. As clearly as if the bones had rolled, tumbled then vanished into air, they were saying, *No. We have nothing more to say. We refuse to let you hide. Tell her.*

Derry's hands went to the clips at the back of her hair. She would remove her wig and feather headdress, ceasing right then to be Madam Tulip, fortune-teller. She would become herself—Derry O'Donnell, unemployed actress, teller of frightening and unlikely stories. Fantasist. Probably crazy. Certainly the most unwelcome of unwelcome guests.

Derry fumbled, biting her lip. Instead of finding the pins easy to hand, they seemed to be hiding from her probing fingers.

'Costume emergency?' said Jessica, smiling.

'No, I'm fine. Just something sharp.' Derry's hands were shaking. All she could think was the first line of what she meant to say, something like—*Jessica, I have to tell you something serious. I want you to listen to me. Not Madam Tulip. Me. Somebody tried—*

Jessica's phone rang. Strange she hadn't turned it off as most did when they came for a reading. But film people hardly ever turned their phones off. At least, Derry thought, the interruption would give her time to order her thoughts.

'Hi, Jim.'

Derry heard the faint rasping of the handset but could make out nothing of what was said. But whatever Carson wanted seemed to surprise Jessica. 'Sure,' she said. 'No, it can wait. Okay. Thanks.' She glanced at her phone to make sure the call was cut. 'I have to go. Something has come up. Something good, I think. Jim and Alex want to see me.' She stepped to the door leading to Derry's little changing room and on to Dunbar's wing.

'Jessica, there's something—'

'Honestly Derry, I've gotta go. Right away. A call has come in from LA. I'm *part* of everything now. This is the real deal. Catch you later, okay? By the way, Sally said you could quit now. Get changed, get a bite to eat. Catch the fireworks.' She was breathless, her eyes sparkling. The door closed behind her.

Derry gave up fumbling with her wig. She stared down at the five little bones lying immobile, inanimate, innocent. She should have been so much more decisive. Instead of going through the motions of the session, as soon as Jessica had walked in the door she should have removed her wig and said what she had meant to say. But she hadn't. She had acted like a schoolgirl praying for a blizzard to avoid sitting an exam. What had she been waiting for? The known facts to magically rearrange themselves? History to change its mind? Or for courage to jump out from some secret store, like a surprise present on a birthday.

By Derry's elbow, the crystal ball reflected a distorted image of the door through which Jessica had blithely vanished, full of hope.

All Derry felt was shame.

303

32

Derry hardly recognised her reflection. The mirror propped up on the storeroom shelf showed a strained face still bearing the traces of stage makeup. She sat staring at the glass as though her reflection held the answer to some question she didn't know how to ask.

Her sluggish brain tried to force itself to think. A voice inside said, *Leave it—you tried.* In that comforting thought was a way out, an excuse to say, *Let's go, let's get out of this mess. I'm not up to it anyway. Who did I think I was?*

She stared, as if by peering into those blank and lustreless eyes she would see inside this stranger. And it seemed she did see. The person she saw was weak, selfish and a fool. And she thought of Bruce, waiting, wondering how she had gotten on, ready to bail out as they had agreed.

And still Derry stared, and the self she saw was older, sadder, harder like brittle glass that would shatter into a million pieces at the smallest tremor.

She closed her eyes. The woman in the glass vanished.

Derry felt the cool air on her skin. She grew aware of her breathing, each and every inhalation. The hard stool on which she sat was real. The castle was real. Jessica was real. Jessica—like an excited child stumbling happily into the unknown. Unwilling to see what she needed to see. Unwilling to be afraid.

Where had Jessica said she was going? Dunbar's apartments? She'd surely not be long. Carson would want to preside over the fireworks like the showman he was, and as always Jessica would be close. Derry could leave her costume here, go find Bruce and they'd wait until Jessica reappeared. Derry would say what she had to say, and if she had to warn Jessica in front of Carson, so what?

Derry opened her eyes. The eyes in the mirror stared back but no longer held any fascination. She frowned, took up a baby wipe and rubbed away the smear of makeup on her face. As she did so, in the mirror, in the periphery of the reflected image, the door behind swung open.

'You'll need your toys,' said Johnny.

Derry turned slowly, as though by taking time the image in her mirror would magically transform itself into something else. The man would cease to be Johnny, would become someone different, someone friendly come to enquire if she needed anything. The object in his hand would morph instantly into some other device, something harmless, not the gun it so plainly was.

'Here,' said Johnny. 'In the bag.' Derry saw that in his left hand he held a large holdall he now tossed onto the floor at her feet.

And still she stared, unable to comprehend. She understood *bag*—and there indeed at her feet was a bag. But what she was supposed to do with that object was beyond her imagination. How doing anything whatever would revert the world to its expected, everyday rules, she couldn't grasp.

'What are you waiting for? The crap, your junk, crystal, all of it, in the bag!'

Now Derry understood. Her props. Her crystal ball. Her cards. All sat on the shelf ready to be packed away. She picked up the bag from the floor, all the while staring at Johnny and the thing in his hand, unable to tear her gaze away, prompting an irritated wave of the gun. Derry tried to force her trembling hands to do as she asked. The heavy crystal—into the bag. The antique timer. The embroidered cloth. The tarot. The little bag of bones.

'Phone,' said Johnny, pointing to the bag. Derry understood. Into the bag went her precious phone.

'Zip it. Give it here,' said Johnny, holding out his hand.

In Derry's imagination she said the obvious things—*what are you doing? What are you going to do?* The words formed in her head—*you can't shoot me. You'd be tried for murder. Dozens of people are outside.* But however many times Derry's brain said *he's bluffing,* her body refused to believe it. And on the end of Johnny's pistol the neat little tube of a silencer offered its own, unanswerable reason for saying nothing.

She threw the bag. Straight at Johnny's head. His hands instinctively rose to block the impact, but already Derry had turned and thrown herself at the library door.

The handle rattled. With both hands, Derry grasped and twisted, pulling, trying to wrench open the heavy panelled oak. But the door was as solid and immovable as the stone walls of the ancient castle. *Locked.*

'Help! Help me!' She was screaming now, though her voice seemed to belong to some other person. But no answer came. Instead, silence—like the dozens of people Derry knew to be beyond those thick stone walls had vanished into another dimension. Derry's voice dried in her throat.

'I can use this if you want,' said Johnny. In his left hand he held the pistol. In his right, a short, wicked-looking club. 'Yes or no?'

Derry shook her head.

Johnny pocketed his gun and retrieved the bag from the floor. 'This way,' he said. He stood aside, nodding for Derry to walk ahead of him through the door by which he had entered. She obeyed. And as she stepped into the ancient passageway, it seemed to her she was walking back in time, away from everything familiar, away from anyone who cared, leaving behind sense, logic and reason.

Derry stumbled along the narrow whitewashed corridor, Johnny's club prodding between her shoulder blades. The passage was familiar, yet unfamiliar. Here was the corner where Amelia had passed carrying her mannequin, where she had called Derry names. At the door to Carson's office, Johnny ordered her to halt.

'Open,' he said. Derry obeyed, turning the forged iron ring that served as a handle, pushing open the door, almost falling as she was shoved roughly from behind.

Carson was seated on a swivel chair, wearing headphones, seeming intent on the screens and speakers on his desk. He slowly removed the headphones and turned to Derry.

'I should thank you,' he said. His smile was cold and artificial, his body rigid as if he were working to control a powerful emotion. 'Sit, please.'

A rough hand on Derry's shoulder forced her onto a chair. The hand stayed on her collarbone, a warning.

Carson leaned forward and tapped his keyboard. From the speakers came a voice—Derry's voice. *I see a turning away. The decision is made. Is it made?*

Then Sally—*I'm going to divorce him. I know it's not fair. Remember what I told you? About my friend?*

Carson hit a key. The recording stopped. His face was expressionless, a mask. A pulse beat heavily in his throat. 'Like I said, I should thank you.'

Derry felt like she had been punched in the face. He had heard everything—Sally's near confession of an affair. Her decision to divorce. A microphone hidden somewhere in the library shelves had relayed every word. Carson must have sat here in this office, raging as he listened, helpless, struggling to contain his fury.

Carson looked at his watch. 'We don't have much time. I need to be outside for the fireworks.' He forced a smile. 'Can't have the host missing the last act of the show.'

33

Once more, Derry was prodded and shoved. Again she was forced to stumble along the ancient passageway, this time with both Johnny and Carson on her heels. All the while, a voice in her head said, *Think! Think!*

Everything depended on her not crying, not panicking. She tried to take deep breaths but could hardly manage so fast was she forced to walk. She glanced left and right, counting doors as she passed—*one, two three*. Ahead was a narrow spiral staircase, twisting clockwise, the walls bare granite blocks. Up, up she went, tripping on the concave worn treads, falling to her knees only to be roughly hauled to her feet and pushed on higher.

At the topmost step, a door, dark and scarred with age. Johnny pushed past Derry's shoulder to rap sharply. The door was hauled open.

Derry could only see part way into the room, but instead of the bare cell she expected she saw Persian carpets covering a beautifully polished oak floor. On a wall hung swords and shields, spears and daggers, a stag's head with massive antlers. A couch was draped in throws of bright colours and striking patterns. And in a high-backed oak chair, looking relaxed as a host might on the entrance of an expected guest, sat Alex Dunbar.

Dunbar stood, but not to greet Derry. 'Did you get everything?'

'Sure,' said Johnny. Dunbar seemed satisfied. A second man, one Derry recognised from the party as another of

Dunbar's retainers, stepped forward and relieved Johnny of his holdall.

'I need to get back down to the party pronto,' said Carson.

Derry was shoved roughly forward, and now she could see the whole room, a spacious chamber the full width of the ancient tower. A massive stone fireplace glowed with burning peats. On the walls were more of those African masks and feathered capes. And off to one side, sitting rigid on an oak seat like a throne, the mirror of the one on which Dunbar himself sat, was Jessica.

She stared mutely, her arms bound behind the back of her chair. Around her throat was a leather band, a kind of noose wound around the seat back. The band can't have been tight, as Jessica showed no sign of distress, but the threat was plain. The sight made Derry's fingers reach for her own throat in sympathy—a reflex, an echo of a memory.

Derry didn't know who grasped her arms from behind, Johnny or his companion. Nor did she know which man clamped the back of her neck in a vice-like grip, steering her irresistibly to sit in a plain wooden chair placed in front of Dunbar. Someone forced her wrists behind her seat and taped them tightly together. She didn't protest. The strap around Jessica's throat was warning enough.

'Before we go further, I'd like to apologise.' Dunbar was speaking, but Derry could barely take in his words. She heard the sounds. She saw his lips move, but she could discern no meaning. She felt as an animal might, watching bemused as humans moved their mouths and made their strange noises to some purpose impossible to guess.

'You're a charming girl,' Dunbar was saying. 'Interesting. Attractive.'

What was he talking about? Next he would say *good sense of humour*, like some internet dating profile.

'You couldn't have known what you were getting into,' Dunbar continued. 'A shame. But in fairness, neither Jim nor myself brought this regrettable situation about. Betrayal is a terrible thing. We are the victims here, just as much as you are, I assure you.'

All the while, Carson stood, watching but saying nothing. Now he took a seat on the couch, carefully arranging the folds of his kilt. 'You should know who to blame,' he said. 'It's only fair.'

Even as she worked to control her thumping heart and ignore the tightness in her chest, Derry realised something was wrong. This was about Sally—Carson had said as much— her affair, her threat of divorce, her accusations. How could Dunbar be any kind of victim? And what did Jessica have to do with this? Or she herself? Hope blossomed—this was a Halloween prank, a bad joke, a crazy frat-boy escapade at the expense of women, like always. Derry felt the anger rise. This one she would not let go. Somebody would pay. *Not funny* didn't nearly cover it.

'Thing is,' continued Carson, 'Jessica here was way out of her league. Ambitious, but stupid. She threatened us. Can you believe that?' He looked genuinely puzzled, as though the idea was so far out of line he could barely grasp the fact.

'You need to understand that Alex and I go back a long way,' said Dunbar. His tone was serious, measured like he was in a business meeting clarifying a vital point. He got up and strode across the room to a wall hung with framed photographs. He took one down before returning to stand in front of Derry, gazing at the picture. He held it to her face. 'Recognise anyone?'

The photo showed men in jungle fatigues posing in two lines, the front rank kneeling. All were heavily armed with rifles and machine guns, their faces streaked with green camouflage paint. In the centre, the leader was instantly recognisable as Dunbar. Standing beside him, carrying an assault rifle, but in civilian tropical clothes, his face unpainted, was a much younger Carson. Dunbar replaced the picture on the wall and returned to his seat.

'Twenty-five years we've been in business together,' said Carson. 'Think we haven't seen wannabees and shysters, people who thought they could muscle in? And now who tries it on but a star-struck, half-assed assistant who thinks she can be a hotshot producer when she's never raised a cent.' He turned to Jessica, leaning forward like a bulldog on a leash. 'We *love* paying taxes, stupid! Don't you get that?'

Jessica sat rigid, her mouth open, her eyes wide. Derry doubted she could speak even if she wanted to.

'She pesters Alex in Edinburgh. Pretends to me she went to see a boyfriend. "I can do a better job than Carson," she says.' His voice was a whining imitation. '"Make me a partner." Alex fobs her off—keeps her sweet. Then *you* come along.'

Derry felt like she had been jolted awake from a dream. Carson was talking about *her*. A blatant cliché went round and round in Derry's head, something you couldn't possibly say in real life. But she found herself saying it anyway. 'There must be some mistake.'

Carson shook his head, as though despairing of the human race. 'I only wanted to hear what my mad bitch of a wife was plotting. Who knew Jessica would spill her guts? You women are crazy, you know that? Sit in front of some fraud with a crystal ball and you'll tell her everything. We didn't believe Jessica was serious. Then she tells you, right out. "It's not a bluff," she says. I didn't know what she meant, until next day Alex tells me she came to see him, making threats.'

'All successful partnerships are based on trust,' added Dunbar. 'How can you trust a blackmailer?' He contemplated Jessica, who stared at the floor, refusing to meet his eye.

'She threatened us with the tax man,' continued Carson. 'Can you believe that? She puts two and two together and gets five. Thinks we're a tax dodge squirreling away a pathetic coupla million a year. "You have to make me a partner 'cos I know enough to sink you guys," she says. You'd laugh except, like she told you, she wasn't bluffing.'

Derry was engulfed by nausea. Her surroundings blurred and grew faint. All capacity for movement, sensation, feeling had left her body. She knew now she would spend the rest of eternity bound and seated in this chair. Fixed. Unchanging. A stone with no inscription. A memorial to an event no one would ever recall. Amazingly, the words came out. 'You tried to shoot her,' she said.

'No comment,' said Dunbar, smiling. 'Poachers. We saw them from the chopper the day before that unfortunate incident. They couldn't win a teddy at a funfair.' He glanced slyly at Johnny, who grinned sheepishly.

Carson spoke again. 'I guess she couldn't believe anything really bad would happen over a tax rap.'

'And thanks to you,' added Dunbar, 'we learned of her little trip to the consulate in Edinburgh, no doubt to arrange an insurance policy—a sealed note perhaps? To be opened in case of mishap? And a passport, of course.'

'If she'd been as smart as she thinks she is,' said Carson, 'she'd have grabbed her passport and caught a plane right then.'

Dunbar spoke quietly. 'Instead, a simple phone call from me, some promises and a ride in a helicopter, and she believes she has won the day.'

Jessica raised her head. 'What was it?' she said, her voice hoarse. 'If it isn't tax, what?'

Carson shrugged. 'Jeez, you're dumb.'

Dunbar cocked his head to one side as though considering whether his audience was of sufficient value for him to take the trouble. 'Alright,' he said, fixing his attention on Jessica, 'Let me give you a hint—how much is a movie worth? I'll answer that. *Whatever someone says it's worth.*'

'That's right,' added Carson. 'You make a turkey for sixpence, get some idiot Brits or Irish to make it. They think it's their big break, they're gonna get an Oscar and calls from Hollywood. Spend three, four million dollars—pennies—the movie's awful, nobody knows what they're doing, but who cares? The money comes from a nice discreet investment company in the Caymans or someplace. That's Alex's game.' He grinned across at his partner.

Dunbar took up the thread. 'The investment company now owns the rights to the movie and sells them around the world. And in Brazil or Chile, a distribution company, also owned by an offshore fund, buys the Latin American rights for way too much. And in South-East Asia, a Thai company does the same. And in India, in Europe, wherever.'

'And what do you know,' added Carson. 'Our investors get their money back all clean and shiny and legal—dividends from their stake in our hugely successful movie business. Now multiply that by, what—?' He turned to Dunbar—'twenty-five movies? Thirty?'

Derry watched Jessica's reaction. Her expression of fascinated horror said she had suspected none of what she was hearing. She had been like a child thinking itself clever, playing with knives in the kitchen drawer.

Carson contemplated Jessica. 'I almost wanted to say—Jessica, how smart is it to get in the way of oh, a couple of hundred million dollars? How smart is it to invite tax authorities to inspect … what shall I call it … the tip of our iceberg?'

Dunbar continued. 'Understand that our investors are not friendly people. We have politicians, generals, people who will run their countries someday—people who run their countries now. Their wealth is, let's say, *unofficial*. We perform a valuable service. We've been doing that for a long time. As I said, business is about trust. *We* are trusted.'

Carson smiled. 'And like I told you, we *love* paying tax.'

'The problem,' said Dunbar, his tone matter-of-fact, 'is that with blackmailers you have only three options. You can pay them and keep paying; you can report them to the authorities—not always desirable—or … you can eliminate the threat.'

The word hung in the air, taking shape, seeming to become a solid object, sharp as the gleaming daggers on the wall.

Eliminate. Derry's carefully constructed calm threatened to dissolve. At any moment, her self-control, so brittle, so hard-won, could shatter into a million pieces, and she would beg. She could hear herself, as if she were pleading now, *Let me go! It's all Jessica's fault! Nothing to do with me!*

But she didn't beg. Why, she could never have explained. Something about these arrogant, remorseless men, so confident in themselves. Something about their power and their money. And something else.

Think! Derry told herself to imagine she was on a stage. What did they know of her thoughts, of the person behind the face of Derry O'Donnell? Nothing. No more than someone sitting in the darkened auditorium knows of the person behind the character in a play. She was bound and helpless, but the one thing they could not make her do was show her true self. Whatever she felt, that's what they mustn't see. Play the opposite. Play against the emotion. *Buy time!*

'There's no need for this,' said Derry, working to keep her voice relaxed. *This is no big deal, said her tone, nothing to sweat about. Later we can all laugh it off.* 'I don't know anything. Jessica didn't know what she was getting mixed up with, but she has no proof. Nobody would believe us anyway. This a Halloween prank, right? It stinks, but we just forget it. Jessica goes home. I go home.'

'You've got one thing right,' said Carson, as though considering Derry's argument. For a moment she felt hope, until his smirk and a darted glance at Dunbar showed Carson was laughing at her. 'Our little business venture sure is a far-fetched story. But how about this for a script?'

Carson stood, pacing the floor as a screenwriter might pitching a movie idea to a studio executive. 'Miss Derry

O'Donnell—a.k.a. Madam Tulip, fortune teller and fraud—has a *bad reputation*. In London she was mixed up with some nasty characters. Russians. *Organised crime.* She comes to Scotland to play a bit-part in a movie, but while she's here she preys on vulnerable women. One of those women …' he waved towards Jessica, '… is a movie business hanger-on. A party-girl. Another is a pampered ex-casino hostess from Vegas. A gun-nut. A drunk. At Halloween, the women, gullible and intoxicated, are fiendishly manipulated by the evil Madam Tulip and are drawn into the occult, into drugs, into *witchcraft*.'

Derry strove to keep her voice even, as though she were debating a point of philosophy at a dinner party. 'It's not witchcraft,' she said. 'You know that.'

'Who cares what *I* believe?' said Carson, pausing in his stride. 'What matters is what the public will believe—what the police will believe.' He grinned. 'You know, I'm gonna leave the end of the story for you to guess. Our movie can't be too predictable now, can it?'

'This is a joke, right?' said Derry with a shrug.

Dunbar shook his head slowly. 'Please understand, Jessica has left us no choice. Why should we spend the rest of our lives in a prison cell because her greed and ambition know no limits? Why should we risk the displeasure of clients who trusted us and would never forgive us for failure.' He let his words sink in.

'I'm sure you can appreciate that eliminating someone without getting caught is remarkably difficult. A husband will always be suspected when a wife meets with a fatal mishap. Business associates will automatically fall under suspicion if one of them dies in unexplained circumstances. But when three people meet a tragic end, what motive could there possibly be? And sadly, just when one of the … participants has been promoted by her admiring colleagues and feted in public.'

'We do have a small logistical problem,' said Carson. 'We need your full and absolute cooperation. But I believe we will get that.'

'Know what that is?' asked Carson. Johnny stepped out from behind Derry's chair. In his hand was an unfamiliar object. The handle was orange plastic. A foot-long black rod projected from the end. The tip was forked and, like the handle, it too was vivid orange. You could easily imagine the thing Johnny brandished was an oversized electric whisk like you'd use to mix a cake. But few cooks would hold their eggbeater like a pistol.

'Do you girls know what this is?' repeated Carson. 'No? What is it with you city slickers? This, dear ladies, is a cattle prod. One touch of this neat little fork at the end, by the magic of electricity, can persuade a two-ton bull to do what it's told and not argue. On a human with delicate girly skin … you can imagine. Would you like a demonstration or will you take my word on trust?' He nodded at Johnny who walked up to Jessica, grinning, waving the prod like some kind of magic wand, inching it closer to her cheek. Jessica cringed back in her seat, her eyes wide, her body shaking uncontrollably.

'Okay,' said Carson. 'You get the message. Behave?' Jessica nodded vigorously. She began to snivel, but with her hands tied behind her and the strap around her neck she couldn't wipe her tear-streaked face.

Dunbar stood, walking to a tall oak cabinet standing against the wall. He took a key from his pocket and opened the door. Inside was a stacked array of rifles. He took one out, using his handkerchief to hold it by the stock. He rummaged in a drawer at the base of the cabinet and extracted a small cardboard box. Cartridges. He lay the rifle and box carefully on a side table.

'My wife's favourite toy,' said Carson. He wasn't smiling.

'Where's Sally?' Derry was stalling, buying time, no more. What had Dunbar said, *three people meet a tragic end*. Derry tried desperately to concentrate on only part of that appalling statement. Better to worry about *three* than about *end*.

'This is where old friends truly are best,' said Carson. 'Alex was good enough to indulge me.'

Dunbar smiled modestly. A joke shared. A compliment acknowledged.

'May I?' said Carson.

'Be my guest,' said Dunbar.

Carson walked to the wall opposite Derry. At waist level a sturdy hatch of heavy dark wood hung on iron hinges. He released a catch and swung the little door open. Inside, Derry saw the rough stone of a cavity within the wall. A larder? A safe? Carson turned, grinned at Derry and put a finger to his lips. He waited a moment, put his face close to the opening and called out, 'Hello!'

A human voice, hollow, answered from far below like an echo from deep within a cave. Then a high-pitched wail. A woman's cry. Derry could make out no words, but words weren't needed.

'My Howling Dungeon,' said Dunbar. 'You like it? I thought you might appreciate its theatrical qualities. While the chieftain and his guests dine, they can hear their enemies pleading for mercy. In the old days, their cries would be … let's say professionally encouraged. But, let me assure you, *we* would not stoop so low.'

Carson guffawed. 'Those guys sure knew how to make an entertainment! No movies back then. No internet. Gotta make your own fun.' His smile vanished. 'And while you're at it show your dinner guests what will happen if they stab you in the back, make a fool of you … *betray* you.'

Derry stared at the hole in the wall. Somewhere in a dungeon far below, Sally was alone in the darkness, petrified, her cries melding into an endless heart-rending wail of pure despair.

'Time to go,' said Carson. 'Like I say, wouldn't want to miss the fireworks.'

34

It sounded like a battle. Rockets and Roman candles cracked and popped. Flashes sliced through the night sky. Derry sat huddled in the back of Carson's SUV, wrists taped behind her. She was squashed between Jessica and Sally, fighting claustrophobia and rising panic. From the front passenger seat Johnny menaced the captives with his electric prod, forcing them to cower and forbidding any sudden movement. The holdall with Derry's props lay on the floor at Johnny's feet, the bag seeming fuller and heavier than before. In the driver's seat sat Dunbar, wearing Sally's cowboy hat and a green camouflage jacket. Sally's rifle stood propped against the door at his thigh.

They had left the castle by a back entrance, through a courtyard surrounded by a high stone wall. The women had been hustled along, tethered together, bound wrists joined by a length of rope like a train of pack animals. And all the while, the fireworks whistled overhead from somewhere on the far side of the castle. There, in the crowd, Derry was sure Bruce would be waiting, fretful, desperate for news.

Now they were moving, the SUV nosing its way out of the courtyard and onto the unlit road. And it seemed to Derry they were leaving behind not a party of celebrating villagers, but all that was sane, human and kind.

Outside, only blackness. The bumping, lurching ride was familiar—a mountain track. On Derry's right, pressed hard against her side, Sally had her eyes shut like she believed it was all a bad dream. On her left, Jessica sat slumped, her body flaccid as a newly dead corpse. She was sobbing quietly. In Derry's heart, a dull acceptance grew like a cancer, while she writhed in an impossible attempt to find a comfortable position. Strange how terror could give way to simple animal discomfort—tingling in the hands, aching shoulders, stiff legs.

From the front seat came a faint but familiar sound. Inside Johnny's holdall a phone rang. Derry's ringtone. Unmistakable. Derry imagined she could hear the urgency in its rhythm, as if her phone were pleading to be picked up.

The caller had to be Bruce. He would know from the voicemail that her phone wasn't out of range but hadn't been answered. Derry felt a surge of hope. Bruce would know something bad had happened. But what then? If he waylaid Carson, demanding to know where she was, Carson would say, *looks like she went off with Sally on some jaunt. You know what these women are like. Impulsive. Crazy.*

What time was it now? Well after midnight, Derry thought, but she could only guess. They had been climbing the rough track for perhaps thirty minutes now. Outside, the dark was impenetrable. Jessica gave a moan, a long, low, continuous groaning. 'Shut up!' barked Johnny, twisting his body to face them and waving the orange prod. Derry nudged Jessica hard with her elbow. She sank back into her seat whimpering quietly.

∼

A brutal lurch, a change of direction, and suddenly a smoother surface under their wheels. As Derry peered into the gloom, straining to make out any hint of where they were, the moon appeared from behind cloud, illuminating the scene like someone had snapped on floodlights. And there, bathed in silver, was a house so out of place it might have been beamed down from space. *The Lodge*. Red brick, bay windows, an elegant front door with a graceful fanlight—a house so like a suburban, Victorian villa it could have been set in a prosperous suburb of Edinburgh or Glasgow. Yet no neat gardens surrounded the place. The forecourt was of levelled stone, roughly laid. Behind towered a massive mountain peak, its sheer grey face luminous in the moonlight. In front, the bleak moorland fell steeply away to a long narrow valley vanishing into blackness.

∼

How do you tell your brain to think, when all it wants to do is make you run? You can't, Derry realised. But you can breathe. As covertly as she could, Derry took deep, slow, adrenaline-reducing breaths. *Inhale. Exhale. Concentrate on the diaphragm.* And as she breathed, she sensed the fog in her head begin to clear.

As Dunbar killed the engine and Johnny jumped out to unlock the front door of the lodge, Derry forced herself to focus. Johnny was busy. Dunbar was watching his henchman not his captives. If Derry threw herself from the vehicle, dragging Sally and Jessica after her, would they be shot down? Logic said *no*. Such a crime could never be covered up. But all three women were roped together, their hands tied behind their backs. Even if they weren't caught and hauled back, where could they go without light? How far would they get in a mountain wilderness of rocks, heather and plunging ravines?

A muffled humming—an engine barely audible over a rising wind. Instantly, over the front door, a light. Derry guessed there would be no electricity supply up here. Power must be from a generator. With the thought, a small voice in her head said, *who cares? Why work it out? Soon the knowledge will drain away into the dirt along with everything else that is you.*

Johnny returned, retrieving his cattle prod to stand guard, while Dunbar strode to the open lodge door, carrying the holdall in one gloved hand, Sally's rifle in the other. Johnny signalled the women should climb out of the SUV. Roped together, hands bound and legs stiff with cramp, they shuffled across the yard like some kind of chain gang, Jessica in the lead, Derry in the middle, Sally behind.

Awkwardly negotiating a pair of steps to the front door, they stumbled into the lighted hall. Johnny was dragging Jessica, his fist clamped under her arm, roughly hustling the captives down the passage. Derry had glimpses of doors to the right and left, and a stairway with polished banisters leading to the second floor. On the walls, mounted antlers and oil paintings of Highland scenes said *hunting lodge.*

At the end of the hallway, Johnny threw open a door, pushing the captives inside to stand huddled together against a wall. They were in an old-fashioned kitchen. Once more Derry told herself to think, observe. *Hope.*

The place was spacious, fitted out with a modern fridge and oven, a gas hob, a sink and a microwave. The window was small, without blinds or curtains. Beyond, Derry saw nothing but blackness. She guessed the window must face the mountain at the back of the house. Beside the window was a door, a bolt fastening it shut from the inside. In the middle of the floor sat an oak table attended by four heavy kitchen chairs.

Dunbar lay the holdall on the floor and propped the rifle against the wall in the corner. He inspected his captives. 'Sit,' he said.

Derry could never have imagined how difficult it would be to sit on a floor with hands tied behind while roped to two people. Only by standing against the wall and sliding down was the feat possible. Jessica ended up crumpled awkwardly beside her, lying in the foetal position, sobbing. Sally seemed stunned, locked inside herself, unable to comprehend what was happening.

'This is a hoax right?' said Derry. 'A joke.' She laboured to keep her voice even, her face untroubled. She must betray no emotion, no thought, no plan. Somewhere in her head a voice said, *that's easy—you don't have a plan. What's to betray?* But another, calmer voice was louder, more insistent—*buy time. Bruce will come looking. Time is everything.*

'Can't we go home now? I mean, *ha ha*. Okay?' Derry spoke as though all anyone had to do was agree, and they'd all smile and laugh and have no hard feelings.

'You're all crazy!' The shout came from Sally, bursting out like she had suddenly woken from a coma. 'These women have nothing to do with me and Jim! Nothing!'

Dunbar leaned back against the kitchen worktop, waiting patiently until Sally lapsed into a resigned silence. He nodded to Johnny, who unzipped the holdall on the floor, rummaged inside, and pulled out Derry's props item by item. Crystal ball. Cards. Tarot. Timer. Embroidered cloth. Last came three phones. He laid out the cloth, placing each of Madam Tulip's props on the table as he imagined it might be positioned by a fortune-teller.

Dunbar opened a cupboard beneath the worktop. Inside were closely packed bottles—the golden labels of Scotch whisky, the white labels of vodka and gin. One by one he took the bottles out, ranging them on the worktop beside the hob. He closed the cupboard door, reached up and opened a wall cabinet, taking out three glasses. One he placed on the table by the crystal ball; the others opposite. Next, he positioned a small plastic container and an elaborate silver box like an antique cigarette case. Finally, matches and an ashtray.

As Derry watched, she felt as a person might watching a movie based on their life. Familiar scenes would play out in front of their eyes before drifting weirdly into fiction, the product of some scriptwriter's overactive imagination. She could guess what was in the containers. Cannabis in the cigarette case. Something stronger in the plastic box—cocaine?

Again, Dunbar threw open doors beneath the worktop, rummaging until he found a small saucepan. He stood and placed the pan on the hob. Now he was searching the wall cupboards. He took out a tin. Derry recognised the label at once. Soup. Chicken. A well-known brand. He rifled in a drawer and found a can opener.

Dunbar nodded to Johnny who again rummaged in the holdall, extracting a flashlight. Johnny strode to the back door, slid back the bolt and stepped into the darkness. Outside, it was raining. A cold wind swept into the kitchen. The door closed behind him.

Dunbar poured the contents of the soup can into the pot on the stove, and fiddled with the control knob. A click, a faint whoosh and a flame. He turned the gas high, folded his arms and waited, watching the pot. The aroma of chicken soup slowly filled the kitchen. He leaned back against the worktop, relaxed, calmly observing his captives.

Derry watched Dunbar's face but could learn nothing from his expression. *A soldier.* She remembered Bruce saying how military life was mostly about waiting, patience, sleeping if you could, or lapsing into an unthinking trance. Dunbar had that look now.

The pot boiled over with a violent sizzling and the acrid smell of burning soup. Dunbar turned sharply and hastily switched off the gas. He made no attempt to clean the mess on the hob.

A knock came on the kitchen window. Johnny's face was white in the kitchen's light. He grimaced, probably getting wet as he stood there. Dunbar nodded, and Johnny disappeared only to return at the window moments later giving a thumbs-up.

Dunbar turned back to the stove. He did something with the knob, and Derry heard a hissing sound that lasted only a moment before gradually fading and dying away. The sour smell of raw gas assaulted her nostrils.

She was strangely aware that no thoughts would come. None. Blank. Like someone had pulled the plug on her brain so whatever was the answer to the puzzle playing out, would stay hidden forever. Yet she found she was speaking. 'You can't,' she said.

Dunbar shrugged.

Sally spoke up. 'You'll never get away with this.' Her voice was level, but Derry could hear her breathing was fast and shallow. 'You're crazier than he is.'

She meant Carson. Her husband. The man who … Slowly, Derry's mind stumbled into life … the man who meant to kill her. *Us. Me. With gas.*

Dunbar turned to Johnny, signalling he should come back in. Johnny's face disappeared from the window. Seconds later, the door opened and he was back in the kitchen, wiping his hair. 'Pishing down!' he said.

Dunbar grinned. 'No hurry. We'll give it a couple of hours. Wouldn't want to ruin your hairdo.'

'Thanks boss,' said Johnny. 'Like old times, eh?'

Again, Sally spoke up. 'Like Derry said, we get the joke. Now we all laugh and go home. If you're doing this for Jim— okay, he got his kicks.'

Did she believe what she was saying? Sudden pressure on Derry's right knee said not. Sally was doing as she herself had tried to do—buy time.

'What's the worst that could happen?' said Derry. 'Even if we go to the police and say, "they kidnapped us," nobody will believe it. So okay, we went off for a crazy party with you guys. We got drunk. A stupid fortune-telling game got out of hand.'

Dunbar turned away. In a cupboard he found a roll of patterned kitchen towelling. He tore off a paper strip, twisting it until it looked like something with which you might light a fire. He went to the microwave sitting on the worktop, opened the door and placed the twist inside. He pulled open a kitchen drawer and took out a roll of cooking foil. He tore off a large sheet, crumpled it into a ball the size of a grapefruit and placed it too in the oven. He closed the door and checked his watch.

Foil. Metal. Never put metal in a microwave. Derry struggled to remember why not. *Sparks. Flame. The timer. He meant to set the timer. Flame. Gas. Explosion. Drunken, drugged women boil the soup. The gas flame goes out. Bang. The End.*

Derry's wrists hurt in their bindings. The pins and needles in her left leg were excruciating. She struggled to think—not to think as a captive, but to think like Dunbar, like he was a character in a play she was studying. *What would he want?* To escape. To leave no hint that the scenario he had created was anything other than an accident. To use the prejudices of his audience to make the accident seem plausible. Witchcraft. Weirdness. Drugs and drink. *Misbehaving women.* Derry struggled to make herself imagine the aftermath as Dunbar must have planned it. A wrecked kitchen, everything burnt and blasted. Bodies. Would the table be overturned? It didn't matter. The crystal ball would survive. The bag of bones too. Even if the cards were scattered and charred, they too would remain.

Derry forced herself to imagine the bodies. Where? Not here. Not on the ground. They would have to be around the table, drinking their booze and taking their drugs, playing sinister games with the bones of dead sheep. But not roped together with their hands tied.

Alright. At some point, Dunbar would have to release them. Then what? Somehow, he would have to make them take their seats and stay passive while gas filled the room, while he and Johnny escaped. They couldn't even lock the doors if their scheme was to be convincing. How did they mean to immobilise their victims?

'Damn the clocks,' said Dunbar. Derry remembered then that the clocks in Britain went back an hour at the end of October to cope with the seasonal change in daylight. Why would Dunbar care? For some reason he was concerned morning would come an hour later. Why? Why would he want daytime?

Johnny peered out the window into the blackness. Rain was still hammering on the pane. 'Your call, boss,' he said.

Dunbar came to a decision. 'Let's get on with it.'

35

Dunbar turned on the kitchen tap. He poured water into each of the three glasses he had set out, returning them to their places on the table. From his inside pocket he took a small container like a test tube, undid the top and sprinkled a powder into each. He uncapped a whisky bottle, adding to each glass a generous measure.

Like a glimpse into the future, Derry understood. The scene was to be a party, and the powder Dunbar had so carefully dispensed was some sort of party drug. When the time came for Dunbar and Johnny to escape, their captives would be so stupefied they would hardly know what was happening. Outside, the men would turn on the gas at the canister; the timer and microwave would do the rest. A drug-fuelled drinking session ends in a tragically careless gas explosion.

Johnny hunkered down, a knife in his hand, cutting the tape binding Jessica's wrists. 'Up,' he commanded, hauling her to her feet. Jessica could barely stand for stiffness. Johnny pushed her to the table and forced her into a chair.

'Drink,' said Dunbar. 'Quickly, please.'

Jessica sat staring in puzzlement at the glass of yellow liquid. So absorbed had she been in her misery, she seemed not to have understood what Dunbar intended.

'Drink!' Johnny picked up the glass and thrust it at Jessica's face. She shook her head dumbly. Perhaps she did, after all, comprehend.

Dunbar took the glass from Johnny. 'Persuasion,' he said, nodding towards Sally. 'Her.'

Johnny retrieved his cattle prod and in three strides was standing over Derry and Sally. Sally's eyes opened wide in terror. She shrank back against the wall, the hideous orange tip hovering barely six inches from her cheek. Somehow, the delicate bracelet of red and black beads on Johnny's wrist, cute and somehow innocent, made the threat seem all the more brutal.

Dunbar gave a heavy sigh. *Theatrical*, thought Derry. *He's enjoying the limelight.* Something about that realisation brought to the surface a new and unfamiliar emotion. Hatred. She detested this man. Until now, all she had felt was fear, disbelief, a deep incomprehension. Now, she felt a profound and visceral loathing.

'Jessica,' said Dunbar, his voice level, as a sympathetic teacher might counsel a student. 'Drink, or Sally will suffer great pain. Do it now.'

Jessica's eyes were beseeching as she stared helplessly at Sally, as though she were begging her to help, imploring her for permission, even begging forgiveness.

'Drink!' Dunbar roared in Jessica's face. Johnny waved the prod even closer to Sally's cheek. The hideous orange tip almost brushed her skin. Sally pedalled frantically with her heels against the floor as if trying to push backwards clean through the wall.

Jessica shook her head. She would not drink. Instead, she stared at the glass, mesmerised by its amber glow. Silence hung over the room like time had stopped.

Johnny let the orange tip drift upwards from Sally's cheek. Now it hovered over her right eye. Sally gasped, driving her head back against the wall, clenching her eyelids shut.

'Enough!' said Dunbar, his voice commanding. Johnny withdrew the prod and stood back, relaxed, waiting for further orders. 'So there you have it,' said Dunbar. 'Ladies, I show you Jessica. I show you a treacherous, selfish, altogether despicable creature.'

'Coward!' Sally screeched out the insult, her voice disintegrating into a rasping croak. Who she was accusing, Jessica or Dunbar, Derry couldn't tell.

Dunbar watched with evident satisfaction, as though he were conducting a psychological experiment. He nodded at Johnny who resumed his place beside Jessica. This time Jessica's was the cheek menaced by the luminous orange tip. In a sudden motion, like a dam had burst, she swept up the tumbler and drank.

The effect was instant. She swayed, then slumped head down on the table, her face cradled in her folded arms.

Derry shouldn't have been astonished. How had she persuaded herself that her turn would never come? But it *had* come. Johnny squatted beside her, so close she could smell his musky odour as he crouched, knife in hand, slicing through the tape binding her wrists. In a fluid manoeuvre, he hauled her bodily to the table, shoving her roughly into a chair.

Derry was placed opposite and to one side of Jessica, facing her cards and crystal ball, the bag of bones, her antique timer and her Tarot. She found herself thinking the array was untidy, nothing like the neat and orderly way Madam Tulip laid out her stall. Irrelevant, but thinking about her props meant she could ignore something else. On the table in front of her sat her glass. And in that glass, the end of all hope.

'Drink.' Dunbar spoke quietly. This time he needed only to glance towards Sally for Johnny to understand and obey.

Sally held herself rigid, staring straight at Derry, her jaw clenched tight, the orange prod once more inches from her cheek. On Johnny's wrist that pretty bracelet, its beads of red and black, seemed to mock her terror.

'Drink!' repeated Dunbar, standing at Derry's elbow. He lifted the glass to her face, wafting it by her nose before placing it once more in front of her. Derry smelled the unmistakable tang of whisky, like she had already taken that fateful sip.

The silence was like a heavy, slow-moving liquid, pressing down with a weight hardly to be borne. Dunbar's eyes were patient, as if he were watching an insect make some life or death decision, so full of meaning in its tiny world, so inconsequential in his. Even Johnny seemed transfixed; he was staring at Derry as though waiting for an answer to some private question.

How precious is each and every second? The question crystallised in Derry's mind like it had coalesced from the air she breathed. What price the agony of another compared to the infinitely precious prize of one more moment of life? And into Derry's head, like she was hearing a voice, came another question. *When is her pain my pain? When is she me?*

Derry lifted the glass. She sniffed its bouquet like a connoisseur at a wine tasting. She gave an exaggerated sigh. She put the glass back on the table.

'I mean, *really*,' she said. 'At least get this right.'

Dunbar frowned, then his face broke into a broad grin. 'And what might *right* be?' He glanced at Johnny, who lowered the cattle prod. He too was grinning.

Derry worked to keep her voice light. *Who was she?* A dinner guest at a party. Challenging the boys. Flirtatious. *Who were her audience?* Men. Arrogant. Pleased with themselves. Confident men with time on their hands, curious about the game being played.

Derry felt the change. For now at least, her captors were intrigued—like hunters who had set a trap for a fox only to find in the snare an unfamiliar animal not to be immediately despatched but, for a brief while, to be studied for amusement.

'Like this,' said Derry. On the table, the crystal ball sat awkwardly placed. She moved it to sit near her right elbow, beside the glass with its horrible liquid. She arranged her deck of cards and her Tarot to her left. Off to one side she placed the beautiful timer with its hollow glass spheres in their ornate wooden frame. She flipped it, so the sand filled the upper sphere and began its careless trickle. As she hoped—without understanding why, all eyes in the room save Jessica's were drawn to that tiny stream of grains, as though deep in the mind of every person present was an inborn knowledge of time's irreversible flow.

The spell couldn't last long, and Derry knew it. With an elaborate motion, she swept up the little pouch of bones, tugged open the drawstring and upended the bag. Out tumbled those chalk-white relics of a once living thing.

And now a memory came—the props man, his brow furrowed, trying sincerely to be helpful. 'Make with some mystical looks,' he had said. In Derry's head she seemed to hear her own voice reply, *just watch me.*

If there was an award for actors playing psychics badly, that statuette was hers. Derry wove her hands in abstract patterns above the scattered bones. She closed her eyes as though in communion with entities known only to her. She swept up the bones in one hand in a practiced movement, and cast. The bones tumbled, rolling haphazardly on the embroidered cloth.

No need to look to know that Dunbar and Johnny were staring, like some meaning might indeed be miraculously revealed. But Derry knew their fascination would last no more than a moment.

More! More action!

In theatre they call it *business*, the small, inconsequential behaviours actors use to keep a scene in motion—drinking tea, smoking a cigarette, polishing spectacles. Derry took up the deck of cards. She cut, and in a stylised motion, her hands fluttering like a conjurer saying *look here!* she dealt. Eight cards, but not arranged like a normal spread. Instead, she laid the cards in a square around the mute scatter of bones.

She scooped up the bones and cast once more, this time making sure all fell neatly inside the square of cards.

Now what? Time. Time bought at no one's expense.

Suddenly, without theatricality, in the most matter-of-fact way she could muster, Derry turned to Dunbar.

'You nearly died,' she said.

∼

That beaded bracelet? Or Dunbar's unmistakeable air of military command. Or was the spark the certain knowledge that somewhere deep in the history of these two men, some-where in Africa, was a world of killing.

What had Bruce said? *All sailors are superstitious. Soldiers too.* Why did death take one man and not another? Why did a few yards of distance or a few seconds of time favour one and condemn his companion? *Fate. Providence.* And the human brain, unwilling to believe in chance, reaches for magic and a lucky charm.

'You nearly died,' Derry repeated. 'In Africa.'

'Come on!' said Johnny, waving the prod at Sally. Was that a faint tremor of nervousness in his voice?

Dunbar held up his hand. 'Let her talk,' he said. He pulled up the vacant chair and sat, as a client would consulting his fortune-teller.

Sierra Leone. Derry racked her brains to remember any-thing at all about that obscure country. *Insane*, Bruce had said. Driven mad by war. A place without logic or reason, where everyone lived in fear of curses, spells and the malevolence of the witch doctor.

'The witch gun,' said Derry, her voice a hoarse whisper.

Dunbar failed to mask his surprise. *A hit.* She had touched something. But what?

He leaned towards Derry. He spoke quietly, intimately, like he really was her client. 'Tell me, what do you know about the witch gun?'

The words came unbidden, like slim threads of memory, slivers of recollection weaving themselves into the beginnings of a story. 'A grain of rice,' said Derry. 'A kernel. The bullet came. You were hurt, but you lived.'

Dunbar seemed to hold his breath. He waited.

337

'You were meant to die.'

Dunbar's gaze was almost gentle. 'You and I, we could have had … One gets bored of the ordinary. I regret this. Truly, I do.'

And now Derry understood how this man saw himself. He was the lead in his own movie, the star of some drama running in his head.

He stood briskly, like he was terminating an interview, and turned to Johnny. 'Her,' he said, nodding towards Sally. 'Over here.'

Johnny hauled Sally to her feet, his fist gripping the back of her neck, forcing her head down. 'Stay!' She stood motionless, bent double as he cut the tape binding her hands. He pushed her roughly to the table, forcing her into a chair opposite Derry.

Dunbar nodded towards Derry. Johnny understood at once. The hideous orange prod, horribly magnified, filled Derry's vision as Johnny inched the orange tip towards her cheek. She struggled to keep her breathing steady. She reached for the glass, as aware of everything in the room as if she were floating above, gazing down on the unfolding scene—Jessica, head on her arms, seeming to sleep. Sally staring intently, as though pure will could deflect the inevitable. Johnny poised with his vicious prod, his eye on Dunbar as he waited for the signal.

Derry raised the tumbler to her mouth. She felt the rim against her lips, and in her nostrils the scent of the whisky was sweet and heavy. She tilted the glass, feeling now the dreadful potion slosh lightly against lips held tightly closed. All the thoughts of a lifetime condensed instantly in her mind like the mass of a giant star collapsing into a pinprick. *One more second. Please, please, please—just one more.*

The shriek broke over them like a blast. For a fraction of a second Derry imagined she had somehow roared out her refusal while the glass was still pressed against her lips. But the banshee wail came from Sally.

The violence of her assault on Dunbar was shocking in its sheer ferocity. An explosion of rage, and before Dunbar could move, Sally's fist had clenched on his windpipe, the full weight of her body slamming into his torso, her fingernails clawing at his eyes. Like the sudden chaos had released her from a spell, Derry's right hand whipped out and up, flinging the contents of her glass over her shoulder into Johnny's face. As he reeled, half blinded by the stinging alcohol, Derry flung herself backwards, upending her chair, barrelling into Johnny and sending him staggering to trip over the holdall. With a crash, he fell, smacking the back of his head off the countertop and thudding to the kitchen floor.

'Stop! Now! Stop right there!' Dunbar was bellowing, standing behind Sally, his forearm locked around her neck, his wrist against her windpipe.

'Back off! Back off!' The shout came from Johnny. He was lying propped against the kitchen cabinets. In his right hand he held his pistol, the gun pointed at Derry.

'Sit!' Dunbar's voice was steady.

Johnny glared at Derry, a look of pure malice. He rose to his feet, the pistol never wavering. Dunbar thrust Sally onto her seat at the table. She sat, passive now, but stony faced. Her eyes met Derry's. 'I'm sorry,' she said.

Only now, as she saw the lines of defeat on Sally's face did Derry understand what she had been trying to do. Her wild gesture wasn't about escape. It was a stubborn attempt to die in a way that would destroy Dunbar and Carson's carefully contrived story. A fight not for life but for justice.

Dunbar knelt, searching in the holdall. He took something out, but Derry couldn't make out what. He stepped to the corner of the kitchen. He picked up the rifle stacked against the wall. Now Derry saw what he had retrieved from the bag. Without removing his gloves, Dunbar fumbled in the box of cartridges. One round at a time, he loaded the rifle's magazine. Each went home with a tiny but distinct click. Five rounds.

And now Derry understood. All the elaborate scene setting—the crystal ball, the gas, the microwave—was mere set-dressing. *Women get drunk and take drugs, accidentally blowing themselves up.* Was that believable? But a psychotic wife, a gun nut—raging with jealousy or just plain crazy—that story would play well enough. A drunken, drug-fuelled Halloween adventure in the wilderness. The sinister influence of a rogue fortune-teller dabbling in magic. Then the massacre, as in a frenzy of hatred, possessed by evil, Sally shoots her companions. In the final sign of her insanity, before turning the gun on herself, she contrives to obliterate the scene with a cleverly timed gas explosion. A last, fiery message of rage and despair.

The police would rake through the wreckage. The medical examiner would give their considered opinion on the bodies—death by gunshot. In the end, the authorities would congratulate themselves on piecing together the story of a woman lost to madness.

The tabloids would lap it up.

Highland tragedy. Triple murder. Occult ritual insanity.

The men dressed for the occasion. Or that's how it seemed to Derry as she watched in a kind of trance. From the holdall they extracted camouflaged waterproof trousers, overjackets with hoods, and two pairs of gumboots. As one dressed, the other kept the rifle trained on the captives.

Of course. To fit with their story, they would have to leave the SUV behind. They meant to travel somehow across the moor in the rain and dark. On an ATV? Probably. No protection from the elements but easily capable of taking them wherever they meant to go. To the Doon? Or to some other hiding place where they would wait for … what? *The helicopter.* At first light. Perhaps pretending to search for the missing women.

Derry knew now how a person must feel lying in a hospital bed, drugged to ease the pain, unable to move or speak, waiting to die but unable to quieten endlessly circling thoughts, aware only of their futility. So deep had Derry sunk into inertia, her senses slowed to a crawl, that when the light in the room brightened momentarily only to fade once more, the fact hardly registered. Then she heard it.

The sudden rasp of a wildly revving engine. Another blaze of light. Through the window, the glare of headlamps piercing the rain and dark. The sound was moving, left to right, traversing the patch of ground at the back of the house, turning, travelling back, turning again, as though taunting the occupants. Not a jeep—an ATV, its motor an angry rasp. Raising herself in her seat, craning her neck, Derry caught a fleeting glimpse as the machine careered past before vanishing into the blackness. *Bruce!*

As one, Johnny and Dunbar dropped to their haunches, pressing their backs against the kitchen cabinets. 'Don't move!' Johnny barked out the order, his pistol aimed first at Derry's chest then at Sally.

The men showed no signs of panic. No confusion. No swearing or shouted recriminations. Derry's newfound hope died in her breast. Dunbar and Johnny were soldiers, professionals, seasoned fighters. And now the pair swung into action with a precision Derry found more terrifying than anything that had gone before.

Crouching low, Dunbar scuttled to the back door, rifle in his hands. Johnny followed suit, taking up station to one side of the window, well out of sight of whoever was outside. All the while, even as he moved, Johnny's pistol stayed trained on Derry and Sally.

Dunbar knelt, inching the door open a crack and peering out. He slid the barrel of the rifle through the gap, raised the butt to his shoulder and aimed.

Crack!

The clack-clack of the bolt action. A spent cartridge rattled to the floor and rolled.

Crack!

The ATV's motor stuttered. Silence.

Derry's heart felt like it would break.

~

Dunbar ejected the cartridge, working the bolt to load another round. He waited, watching through the crack in the doorway until satisfied that no further interference would come from outside. He stood, back against the door, facing the table. He raised the rifle. Derry saw his eyes flick from herself to Jessica to Sally. He was choosing. Which should be first to die?

Jessica made a small moaning sound, like she was having a bad dream. Dunbar's rifle swung to aim at her head, then swung away to fix on Derry.

She should have felt terror. The black pinpoint of the gun's barrel should have bred in her heart an abject horror, even hysteria. Instead, deep inside her soul a profound melancholy grew, a sadness deeper than she had ever known. Time slowed and stood still. As though in a vision, she saw the countless possibilities that were a human life—her life—fluttering like butterflies, blue and red and orange, rising in a swirling cloud towards the Sun. One by one as they rose higher and higher, ever closer to the fiery orb, they burned, falling shrivelled and desiccated. Of the myriad beautiful creatures, only two now remained. As the last pair slowly circled, their colours fading, Derry knew that all her life had come down to a single question—*how to die.*

～

The lights went out.

In the silence left by the sudden absence of the generator's hum, Johnny swore. The quiet lasted only seconds. The muted roar of an engine, revving furiously, tore the night apart, as headlights blazed through the kitchen window throwing crazy beams and shadows randomly against the walls. Not an ATV, some kind of jeep. Loud, powerful.

Derry flung the heavy crystal ball. With all the strength in her arm she catapulted her missile not at the dim outlines of the crouching men, but at the window. The pane collapsed as though in slow motion—clinking, glistening shards blazing with reflected beams as they exploded and fell. A wind, cold, smelling of mountain and sodden heather, filled the room.

Almost the instant the crystal ball left her hand, Derry was on her feet, throwing herself around the table to seize Jessica's arms and drag her upright. A chair crashed into the wall where Dunbar and Johnny crouched, and Sally too was hauling Jessica from her seat. *The hallway!* No need for words as Derry and Sally together dragged Jessica's dead weight towards the door faintly visible in the near darkness.

The force that hit Derry, sweeping her aside and throwing her to the ground was like her body had been charged by a raging animal. Barged aside by Johnny and Dunbar, all three women lay tangled in a chaos of limbs and an overturned chair.

Derry struggled to her knees unable to grasp what had happened.

The door to the hallway was open. Moments went by, but the women dared not move. Of Dunbar and Johnny, the only sign was the frantic revving of an engine growing fainter with every passing second.

～

Derry felt a hand on hers. *Sally.* Neither woman spoke, as though believing if a word were said the miracle might reel backwards and be undone, and they would have nobody to blame but themselves.

Jessica groaned. 'What?' she said. 'I don't think so,' she added, her words slurred.

Derry hooked Jessica's right arm over her shoulder. Sally took her left. They staggered to their feet. Ahead, the hallway was a dark tunnel, but at its far end the front door of the lodge gaped open. Derry felt the cold, clean air on her face.

One step at a time, Jessica propped between them, they half-dragged her down the hall. 'My fault,' Jessica was repeating. 'I'm sorry.' All Derry could say was *shush* and make meaningless noises like she was comforting a miserable child.

They stood together in the open doorway. The darkness outside was so profound Derry could make out nothing, as though the vast expanse of mountain and heather was devoid of human life.

The voice, a man's, came out of the blackness.

'It's over,' said Rab. 'We have you.'

36

Of the three women, only Derry was able to speak. As Rab's Land Rover lurched down the mountain track, headlights barely penetrating the blackness, she sat in the passenger seat and talked. All the while, Bruce's hand was on her shoulder, now and again giving a gentle squeeze of encouragement as her story flagged or lost its way. In the back with Bruce, Jessica and Sally sat, mute, each lost in her thoughts.

As Rab drove, Derry told of their capture and the hideous scenario hatched by Carson and Dunbar to cover for three convenient deaths. Bruce told how he had waited at the fireworks, calling Derry's phone, getting only voicemail. He had accosted Carson, who had claimed she was with his wife, before persuading Jen to let him back inside the castle. He found the library deserted, but in the storeroom Madam Tulip's costume was hanging, unpacked, and her wig lying on a shelf. Derry's case was on the floor open, seemingly abandoned. 'No way would you have left your costume like that,' said Bruce. 'Your cool wig and all, just laying there. I knew then we had a situation.

'So I sweet talked Jen into giving me Rab's number. And what do you know, he was already on the hill with his men, staking out some poacher. I briefed him, and the rest you know. We played a few games to flush y'all out, I mean who knows you might have been havin' a whale of a time in there. But like I said to Rab—Derry has a temper, but she ain't shot at me yet.'

'I thought you were dead,' said Derry.

'Naw,' said Bruce, cheerfully. 'I got this …' He wriggled in his seat, digging in his pants pocket. He took something out, leaned over the back of Derry's seat and held it out in his open palm. A tiny carved ivory elephant.

'My lucky charm.'

$\approx$

Again they stood outside the Bunnapole Country House Hotel in the middle of the night waiting for a light to go on. But this time, nobody was throwing stones. Instead, Rab was on his phone talking urgently to Jen. In a few minutes the front door opened, and she and the laird were ushering them into the empty dining room, Jen fussing and clucking, the laird trying to look sympathetic. Unprompted he rolled two electric heaters on little castors into the room and offered whisky all round.

Rab did the explaining. Dreadful things had happened, shocking things that meant Dunbar and Carson would be wanted by the law. The women couldn't go back to the castle until the villains had fled, as they surely would. The thing now was to call the police.

Derry could hear only Rab's half of the conversation, but she had no trouble understanding. He explained first to the emergency operator then to a policewoman that he was reporting a kidnapping and attempted murder. Reluctantly, he admitted that no, nobody had been injured. But shots *had* been fired. And no, the shots hadn't actually hit anyone. And yes, the victims of the kidnapping were safe and well, but the kidnappers were still in their castle. At that, the policewoman seemed to conclude that the call was probably a hoax, but in any case no emergency.

Rab hung up, shaking his head. 'I cannae believe it,' he said. 'They'll send four policemen to throw late drinkers out of a bar, but all we get is a promise someone will take statements tomorrow. Meanwhile, the criminals can pack their bags at leisure. Unreal.'

Derry had a sudden thought. 'What if they mean to deny everything? Our word against theirs. A party game gone wrong. All a misunderstanding. Then what do we do?'

'I don't think so,' said Jessica. Her voice shook, but she gathered confidence as she spoke. 'They can say what they like about tonight. I know what I know. I … got access to Jim's files. I copied everything. And I know now what it all means. They can't explain that away.'

Derry could hardly hide her surprise. Jessica must have stolen Carson's passwords and been systematically plundering his records. For week after week, month after month, she had lived a lie, imagining herself empowered. But she was right when she said Carson and Dunbar would have a lot of explaining to do.

'Give me ten minutes to sort out rooms for you all,' said Jen. 'You'll stay until everything settles down.'

Jessica looked like she couldn't take another step. Sally was worried about Amelia, but was persuaded she was probably asleep blissfully unaware anything had happened. Staying at the hotel was the only thing to do until they knew where Carson and Dunbar had gone.

'Hey Rab,' said Bruce. 'How about we do a little sightseeing?'

Rab nodded. 'Thank you Jen. Will Bruce be able to get back in later?'

'You'll be the first guest ever to be given a key, Mr. Adams,' said Jen, addressing Bruce in formal tones, as though he were being awarded a special prize. 'My husband thinks guests should stay in their rooms and never leave.'

Derry thought about that. Maybe it wasn't such a bad idea.

37

Derry was at dinner, the sort of dinner you see in TV ads in which implausibly handsome waiters fawn, you're wearing your best diamond necklace, and sitting opposite is an Adonis with soulful eyes, gleaming white teeth and a millionaire's tan. Except that in Derry's dream the millionaire was Alex Dunbar.

She didn't wake screaming, though even in her dream she wondered why not. Instead, she told Dunbar of her hopes and ambitions. She told him of the spine-tingling highlights of plays she had been privileged to see—performances so fine the memory would stay with her forever. Dunbar sighed. Such shows were magic never to be repeated, persisting only in the mind, he said.

Derry found the man's empathy deeply attractive. He leaned across the table and took her hand in his. He kissed the tips of her fingers. And in her dream Derry knew something wonderful was beginning.

She woke confused, unable to grasp where she was. But she wasn't awake, or couldn't have been. All around, stretching to a dizzying infinity, was an impenetrable blackness—not a star, not even the glowing cloud of a distant galaxy could be seen. She was floating in space, but not freely. Attached to her body were threads like spun silk—filaments impossibly fine but unbreakable, stretching in every direction into eternity. And she knew that with the slightest tug, the gentlest of pulls, any one of those threads could yank her away. And she would spin and tumble wherever it led, on a trajectory from which there could be no return.

Sergeant Sillars seemed embarrassed. 'You can understand, we have to be economical with our time. It's an awfy big area to cover. And it *is* a Sunday.' The young constable accompanying him nodded dutifully, pleased he could agree that mountains were large and the moors equally so. And who ever heard of an investigation on a Sunday?

If Sillars expected sympathetic nods of agreement from those gathered in the castle sitting-room, he was to be disappointed. His listeners had waited all morning for Sillars, the constable and a plain-clothes detective to show up. Then the detective had spent half an hour privately interviewing Jessica before rejoining the rest.

The detective was a pale, hatchet faced man with thinning hair, greying at the sides. He looked more like a bank clerk than a policeman, Derry thought. She hadn't caught his name—had he even introduced himself?

He cleared his throat and spoke. 'I have to apologise. The delay in coming to see you wasn't the fault of the police, in fact it was my fault. I had to get here from Edinburgh.' Derry was surprised at the way he said police like he wasn't a policeman himself. Only then did it occur to her. Perhaps he wasn't. If not, what was he?

The detective addressed Rab and Bruce. 'I appreciate you gentlemen taking the trouble to observe the suspects leaving this morning. We have arrest warrants out now and a watch for the helicopter.

'I can't tell you everything,' the detective continued, 'but perhaps I can fill in some of the story. I am here because we—that is to say the department for which I work—has had an interest in Alex Dunbar for some time. He is, perhaps I can now say *was*, a big fish indeed.

351

'We knew a lot about his contacts, his network, even his sources of wealth, but we had no idea how he operated. We were lacking the key to the puzzle. That key, we now understand, was Jim Carson. The movie business, seemingly a sideline for Dunbar, was a money-laundering enterprise on the very largest scale.

'Naturally, we will be especially interested in everything Jessica can give us. She has kindly agreed to come to Edinburgh, and of course we will look after her there.' He turned to Sally. 'Mrs. Carson, we will need to talk to you in the coming days. You may stay here if you wish, but our searches will be thorough, I'm afraid. The team will get here later today. I imagine computers will have been taken away or destroyed, but when people leave in a hurry they often overlook the small things.'

'Will you catch them?' Derry found she wanted to know.

The detective considered the matter carefully. 'I believe so,' he said. 'Their financial crimes will take us many months to unravel, perhaps years. But we will pursue them wherever they go, and they will have to live in some unpleasant places to escape us and to avoid some very angry warlords and drug smugglers. Meanwhile, in Edinburgh and in London too, cages are already being rattled in high places. Soon, many of Dunbar's business associates will discover in themselves a sudden overwhelming urge to tell tales.'

'As I said, the full team will be arriving within a couple of hours,' continued the detective. 'Perhaps you could recommend a good local hotel?'

～

Derry wondered what kind of maniac she was. Did all actors lose their grip on reality or was it just her? While the detective was describing how the police meant to catch Carson and Dunbar, she had been worrying about her Madam Tulip costume. Might it be seized as some kind of evidence? The thought of her beautiful dress and that wonderful wig being roughly handled by police and lawyers made her want to weep. As the detective and the two policemen stood to go about their business, she plucked up courage. Her suitcase was, she suggested, a witness to her abduction by Johnny, but was otherwise innocent. Could she take it away? To her immense relief, the detective saw no problem. She could retrieve her belongings.

Sally led Derry through the library and into the little store-room behind. And there, on the floor where Derry had left it, was her case, lid open. Sally leaned against the wall, watching in silence as Derry lovingly folded her dress and carefully packed her wig and accessories.

'You said—*Madam Tulip* said—I'd get some peace. Crazy, but I guess that's what I've got,' said Sally. She contemplated Derry. 'Until it happens, you can't imagine what it's like to be hated, really hated by someone.' She paused. 'Does everyone in the world think they're the good guy?'

To that, Derry had no answer.

'Rab told me everything,' continued Sally. 'Hamish ran away from me. Rab tried to be kind about it. He said Hamish had other problems. Maybe he had. Either way, it don't change a thing.'

To Derry's surprise, Sally smiled. 'Imagine, I thought a man couldn't just up and leave me, he had to be dead.'

Derry closed the lid of the case, snapped the fasteners shut and stood. 'What will you do now?'

'I'll be okay. I've got savings. I've got Amelia. She's all that matters now.' She paused. 'I envy you. You've got something you love to do. Beats loving a man.'

Sally struggled to contain her emotion, but the tears came. She leaned against the doorjamb for support, folding her arms over her chest, turning her face away. Derry was hugging her, and now the two were crying, until from behind came a third pair of arms enveloping them both. And Derry saw they belonged to Amelia, and she too was weeping.

And in their tears, somehow Derry knew, was a kind of forgetting.

38

Derry lay on the bed, shoes off, trying not to think about anything and failing. A fire was blazing in the grate, set and lit by Jen. A brass scuttle of peats had been left beside the hearth. For a long time Derry stared into the flames, her mind unable to settle. Her thoughts kept returning to Sally and her daughter. As Derry left the castle, Amelia had followed her to the door, apologising. She had blamed Madam Tulip for telling her father about her boyfriend, not knowing Carson was recording everything. The distaste on her face was upsetting. Derry asked her what she was going to do now. 'I'm gonna look after Mom,' Amelia said. 'I guess.'

Bruce's knock was a relief. 'I got your phone,' he said, standing in the doorway holding up the handset like an exhibit in a court case. 'You got missed calls. I guess fifty of 'em are me.' In his other hand he held a bulging canvas bag, the green recyclable sort used by eco-conscious shoppers.

'I went up with Rab to the lodge—he wanted to fix the busted window. We took Sillars with us, though the cops don't seem much interested in what happened there at all. Sillars took some notes, a few photos, but that was it. The evidence will be your three testimonies he said. If you ask me, he didn't think there'd ever be a trial. Or not for kidnapping anyhow.'

'What about the rifle? Isn't that evidence?' Derry tried to make herself feel she cared.

'No sign of the rifle,' continued Bruce. 'Dunbar must have taken it with him. Dumped, most likely. I found your phone on the table and your other stuff.' Bruce strode to the bed, rested the bag on the coverlet and opened it for Derry to inspect. 'Rab found your crystal ball outside the busted window. You should have been a pitcher—missed ya vocation. Got your timer, and your cards—but they're all mixed up, and I don't know if some are missing. And your bones. I collected 'em up off the table. How many are there supposed to be?'

Bruce took out the little leather pouch, opened the drawstring and poured the bones onto the coverlet. Out they tumbled. *Four. No, five.* Bruce scooped them up and dropped them back into the pouch, laying it on the bed beside Derry. She watched but felt no urge to take it. The pouch sat on the bed beside her as Bruce carefully placed the bulging shopping bag on the dressing table.

'Thanks, Bruce. I appreciate it.'

'Hey, can't lose your props. The stage manager would have something to say.' He took a chair and sat facing her. 'You okay?'

Derry thought about that. Was she? She nodded anyway, unsure whether Bruce believed her or not. 'How long will they want us to stay?'

'Uh, Sillars thought maybe tomorrow. Day after at most.' He hesitated, and Derry saw he was watching her carefully. 'Come on, hon. What's buggin' you?'

Derry looked down at the little brown bag of bones lying passively on the bed beside her. How could she explain? Even if she knew what the question really was, how could she ask it out loud?

'Open the box, right?' said Bruce, gently. 'That's what we said.'

True, that's what she herself had preached. How easy to give advice to someone else. But Bruce was right. Derry looked up and nodded. 'Why do these things ... happen?'

Bruce waited. Perhaps he knew what she meant to say but couldn't—'why do these things happen *to me?*' But she said no more.

'You're are the one with the crystal ball,' said Bruce. He smiled. 'I got a question for you. What would have happened to all those folks if you hadn't come along? Down the line—where would they be?'

The words almost came to Derry's lips—*I don't care. Why should I?* But the syllables never formed. Instinctively, she knew once uttered their spell would be cast over everything she was and wanted to be. Instead she said, 'I guess.' And the memory came of a dream in which she was suspended in the void by countless threads, and she wondered at the mystery of simple luck.

'You know, I wish I could say to my old shipmates—"You guys think you got a tough job? Try acting, man."'

Bruce's grin was infectious, and Derry found herself smiling. 'I thought learning the lines was the hard part.'

'Naw. I still say auditions. I thought this gig was gonna be a breeze. I guess if a thing is too good to be true, that's what it is. Shame. You know I might check out if I've got Scottish ancestry in me. I kinda feel I have. Like when I put on that kilt, I just know I've been here before. Like in another life. Don't you get that feeling?'

But Derry's phone rang, and she never did get a chance to explain her doubts about reincarnation and how, no matter how she figured it, the sums never did add up.

❧

'Dad!'

'Light of my firmament! All is well, I trust?'

'Fine, I guess.'

'Do you know what it is?' said Jacko. *'Your father is a gen-ius!'* He paused, like a professor inviting sensible questions, but Derry was not to be drawn.

'I thought I was done for!' continued Jacko, undeterred. 'And there he was on the news! Yer man Gordon, the politician, his offices raided along with some big-wheel banker! Let me tell you, there's some publicity even your mother doesn't want.'

Derry was stunned. But what had the detective said? The authorities were rattling cages in Edinburgh and London. Who knew where Dunbar's tentacles might have led.

'But what about Mom's gallery? The building is only half finished.'

'Solved with two phone calls,' announced Jacko, triumphantly. 'The gallery opening is postponed until spring, but my Armenian friend Mikayel, says he'll invest. Your mother isn't the only one who can *wheel and deal.*

'There's only one problem,' added Jacko. 'Mikayel can't stand that fraud Edgar Booth. A terrible shame, but sacrifices have to be made.'

'Hey, that's great. Mikayel loves your work. But what about your problem with the castle? Don't you need the cash now?'

'Didn't I tell you I was a genius? Remember Paddy, the treacherous hound calling himself an architect? A friend happened to mention he bumped into him in the lobby of a Dublin hotel with a young woman on his arm who was *not his wife.* Two can play at blackmail!' He paused to allow the extent of his brilliance be fully appreciated. 'By the by, I'm thinking I may put myself up for election as clan chief of the O'Donnells.'

'Dad, I don't think the Irish have …'

'Never too late to learn from our neighbours,' replied Jacko, solemnly. 'Must go! My hosts are insisting on a bracing walk up a mountain. Thankfully, for once unarmed. Ah, the romance of the Scottish glen!'

Derry's smile refused to leave her face. Who cared about anything else if the people you loved were happy? And even if fate had other plans, what was the point of worry?

Beside her on the coverlet sat the little pouch of bones. She took up the bag and in her stockinged feet padded across the room. In the fireplace, the flames burned merrily.

In Derry's hand, the little leather bag felt heavier than she remembered. She squeezed, feeling the shapes of the bones inside. Gently, she placed the pouch on the fire, covering it with two brown sods of dry and flaking peat.

39

Crack!

As Derry made her way down the castle path to the shooting range, she had a strong sense of *déjà vu*. Beyond the wooden hut the red flag flew from its pole. Rab was standing on the decking, peering downrange through the telescope. He waved to say she should come on up, and Derry saw the person lying on the mat, rifle to his cheek, was Bruce.

She climbed onto the deck. Bruce grinned up at her. 'Just havin' ourselves a little fun.'

'Take a look,' said Rab, standing aside so Derry could look through the telescope and inspect the target. And there, magnified in her sights, was Bambi. Someone, she guessed Bruce, had drawn sunglasses on its face and adorned its head with a ten-gallon hat. But that wasn't what Rab had invited her to see. The outline of Bambi's heart was punctured by half a dozen neat holes right in the centre. Not a shot had strayed outside the bullseye.

'Wish I had some of Bruce's sailors in my old company,' said Rab. 'Amazing.' He turned to Bruce. 'Where on earth did you learn to shoot like that?'

Bruce contemplated the question. 'Um, seagulls,' he said, after a moment, his expression deadpan. 'Sailors get a lot of practice.'

Rab gave a doubtful nod, and Derry had to turn away to hide her amusement.

Bruce checked the safety of his rifle, laid it on the ground and stood. 'Uh, why don't I go see how the wildlife are gettin' along.' He jumped lightly from the decking and strolled downrange, leaving Derry and Rab standing together side by side.

'I suppose you'll be away, now it's all over?' said Rab.

Derry nodded.

'Who would believe such terrible things could happen here?' he said. Derry knew he expected no answer.

'What will happen to the estate?' she asked. 'If Dunbar is caught or disappears? Will it be sold off?'

'Aye,' said Rab. 'I'd say that's certain.'

'Sad,' said Derry. And she meant it.

Rab shook his head. 'Not really. Estates come and go. As long as the hills stay the same, and the water is clean, and the deer are still on the moor, we'll be happy enough. Aye.'

How was it that Derry found herself suddenly fascinated by the subject of the Highlands' future and the welfare of its inhabitants? But she was. She felt obliged to enquire further. 'And so, you'll carry on as before, whoever buys the place?'

'Oh aye,' said Rab.

Derry felt a familiar tingle at the back of her neck.

'You'll be leaving tomorrow?' said Rab. His brown eyes met hers.

'Yes, tomorrow. Afternoon.'

'Afternoon,' said Rab, 'Aye.' He nodded, as though she had said something profound. 'I was wondering ... if we might ... perhaps this evening?'

'This evening?'

'Being Monday, there's nowhere to go, and you mightn't want to eat in the hotel, so I … I'm a good cook, if I may say. I could make us a …'

Derry must have heard what it was Rab intended to cook, but the details somehow escaped her.

'So …?' asked Rab.

There was only one possible answer.

'Aye,' said Derry.